PRAISE FOR THE ALASTAIR S

"The magic is believable, the chara and the twists, turns and mysteries ̣.... your eyes to the page. You will never forget these characters or their world."
—*Jacqueline Lichtenberg, Hugo-nominated author of the Sime~Gen series and* Star Trek Lives!

"Alastair Stone is like Harry Potter meets Harry Dresden with a bit of Indiana Jones!"
—*Randler, Amazon reviewer*

"Somewhat reminiscent of the Dresden Files but with its own distinct style."
—*John W. Ranken, Amazon reviewer*

"I am reminded of Jim Butcher here...Darker than most Urban Fantasy, not quite horror, but with a touch of Lovecraftian."
—*Wulfstan, Amazon Top 500 reviewer*

"An absolute delight for 'urban fantasy' fans! Smart, witty and compelling!"
—*gbc, Bookbub reviewer*

"In Alastair Stone, author R.L. King has a major winner on her hands."
—*Mark Earls, Amazon reviewer*

"Once you enter the world of Alastair Stone, you won't want to leave."
—*Awesome Indies*

"Great series, awesome characters and can't wait to see where the story will go from here."
—*Amazon reviewer*

"I have read every book in this series and loved them all."
—*Soozers, Amazon reviewer*

"The writing is extremely good, and the plot and characters engaging. Closest author comparison probably Benedict Jacka and the Alex Verus series."
—*MB, Amazon reviewer*

"The Alastair Stone Chronicles is one of the best series I have read in years…"
—*Judith A. Slover, Amazon reviewer*

"A continued thrill to the urban fantasy reader…"
—*Dominic, Amazon reviewer*

"This a great series and one of the best ones I have had the pleasure to read in a long time."
—*Skywalker, Amazon reviewer*

ALSO BY R. L. KING

The Alastair Stone Chronicles

Happenstance and Bron

Shadowrun (published by Catalyst Game Labs)

BLOOD TIES

ALASTAIR STONE CHRONICLES: BOOK TWENTY-NINE

R. L. KING

MAGESPACE
PRESS

CHAPTER ONE

"RETURN HOME."

Lately, Alastair Stone had come to dread those words.

This time, the message came in the late morning, shortly after he'd settled on the sofa in his Encantada living room with a glass of wine and a good book. The call came on his mobile phone instead of his landline, and as usual the number showed as *Blocked*. He would have ignored it, except several people he actually wanted to hear from had blocked numbers these days.

Just as it had been all the other times, the words were the only message. As soon as they were delivered in the familiar monotone, the caller broke the connection.

That didn't mean anything, though. Stone knew exactly who'd been on the other end.

He appeared, as he expected, in the same familiar room. There were a few differences: the paintings on the walls weren't the same, and a different priceless rug covered the hardwood floor, but the pair of chairs with the little table between them were the same. He wondered two things as always: whether the room was an illusion, and whether Aldwyn would ever trust him enough to let him see any other parts of his home. It occurred to him that he didn't even know where on Earth his dragon ancestor had established his domain. As far as he knew, Aldwyn could have settled just up the street from his Encantada home, in Europe somewhere, or in Antarctica.

No point in wasting mental cycles on thinking about that, though. He wasn't sure he *wanted* Aldwyn to trust him that much.

"Good afternoon, Alastair. I hope you are well."

Stone didn't whirl around—there was no way he'd give the old dragon *that* satisfaction. In fact, he didn't even turn, even though the room had been unoccupied when he'd shown up. "Hello, Aldwyn. Let's skip the pleasantries, shall we? You don't give a damn whether I'm well, and you know it."

The dragon moved past him and settled in his usual chair. Today, his impeccable suit was dark blue. He didn't appear perturbed by Stone's response. "I wonder why you resist me so, scion. I am aware of your interests—you are a seeker of knowledge about the magical world, with a brilliant intellect and a voracious appetite for information. I could help you with that, more than you can possibly imagine, if only you could let go of your stubborn ideas about events that have occurred long before any of your kind were born."

"Events like murdering at least forty people to prop up your power? Not bloody likely."

Aldwyn sighed. "As I have told you before, I did not kill those people. And it is unreasonable to assume that any being—particularly one as old as I and my associates—remains static throughout their life. Can you truly tell me that even you, with your minuscule span of years compared to ours, have not changed? Obviously, I did not know you personally during your youth, but I would safely wager most of my considerable fortune that I am correct."

The last thing Stone wanted was to get drawn into this conversation again. "What do you want, Aldwyn? I assume you've got a reason for bringing me here, and it isn't because you wanted to share a pint and catch up on recent events."

Aldwyn inclined his head. "Indeed I do have a reason."

"And I'd bet most of *my* considerable fortune that I know what it is. You've got another little job for me, don't you?"

"I do. Though in this case, I would not call it a 'little' job."

"No more sending me off to some tiny, obscure town with a bizarre magical problem?" He flashed the dragon a wry smile. "Afraid I'll see through the pretense again and bollix up your byzantine plans?"

He had been surprised that nothing about the Oregon towns of Rydell and Tuttleton had appeared in the news over the past three months since the strange events had gone down there. He'd even asked Gina to flag them, but she'd come back with nothing. He'd thought about reaching out to Agent Renata Huxley about it, until he remembered she hadn't given him her contact information. He wondered if that had been on purpose, since she obviously knew how to contact *him*. In truth, he'd been a little disappointed that she hadn't turned up with any consultation work in the intervening time. Perhaps the wheels moved more slowly in the government world.

"Not at all." Aldwyn leaned back in his chair, relaxed, and crossed his ankle over his knee. "As I said at the time, despite the setback to my plans that you caused, I was impressed by both your investigative talents and your ability to adapt to dangerous conditions."

"Ah, so you want me to do something more dangerous this time."

"That depends on how careful you are."

Stone hadn't sat yet. He leaned against the wall, facing Aldwyn, and crossed his arms. "Enough dancing around. I didn't think you were the type, and I'm certainly not. What do you want me to do?"

"Something you might find distasteful, but given the subject, perhaps not." Before Stone could say anything else, Aldwyn fixed a steady stare on him. "I want you to kill James Brathwaite."

Stone had drawn breath to reply, but it caught in his throat. He stared at the dragon in shock. "*What?*"

"You heard me." Aldwyn looked satisfied, as if pleased to finally get a rise out of his scion.

"You want me to *kill* him? That's absurd. I'm not a hired assassin, Aldwyn."

"It is not absurd. It does not violate any of the strictures to which I agreed. You certainly cannot suggest that you consider this man a friend." He tilted his head in obviously feigned curiosity.

Stone snorted. "Of course I don't. Believe me, I want him dead as much as you do, and I think the world would be a better place without him in it. If he bothered me or any of my friends or family again, I wouldn't hesitate to eliminate him. But that doesn't mean I have any desire to make a special effort to kill him in cold blood."

Aldwyn shrugged one shoulder. "What you desire, Alastair, means little to me at present. You made an agreement and swore an oath. You do not consider Brathwaite a friend, he certainly isn't a member of your family, and, while you will no doubt find this assignment challenging, I do not believe it is outside your capability. Do you disagree?"

Damn it, he's right. Stone tried to figure out a way around it, but nothing presented itself. "I haven't got a clue where he is," he said, even though he knew that wouldn't deter the dragon in the slightest. "I haven't seen him for…well, *years,* now, thanks to you. For all I know, he's already dead."

"He is not dead."

Stone narrowed his eyes. "You sound fairly certain of that. Does that mean you know where he is?"

"Not precisely, no."

"You don't just want me to kill him, then. You want me to *find* him. What makes you think I can do that if you can't?"

"I did not say I cannot. Merely that I do not wish to expend the effort." Aldwyn uncrossed his leg and leaned forward. "Only two assignments remain, according to the terms of our oath. I do not plan to waste them on tasks I could easily perform myself, or retain someone who does not possess your…unique talents."

Stone didn't bother trying to turn down the assignment. It wouldn't do him any good—he couldn't break the oath, and what Aldwyn wanted him to do *didn't* violate its terms. Furthermore, if he was honest with himself, he didn't have any particular qualms or resistance about killing James Brathwaite. If Aldwyn was telling the truth and he hadn't killed the innocents who'd been buried in the catacomb beneath the Surrey house, Brathwaite had certainly had a hand in their deaths—and worse. Dragons hated necromancy, but now, thanks to the reborn Brathwaite, it was back in the modern world. Maybe getting rid of him would help stem the tide.

There was also Sharra to think about. Brathwaite had not only murdered Verity's dear friend, but reanimated her corpse into a semi-sentient undead creature Verity had been forced to kill. He'd been responsible for the deaths of all the people killed during the New York City incident, and he'd had his greasy fingers in the middle of the situation with Frank Grider and the civilized ghouls. There were a lot of reasons the world would be a better place without James Brathwaite in it.

"Okay," he said firmly. "You're right—I don't object to killing the old bastard. But I'm serious—I *don't* know where to find him these days, or what he's up to. And I can't do this one alone."

Aldwyn's expression was unreadable. "I can provide you with a few bits of information you may find helpful if you are initially unsuccessful in your search, but I will not participate directly in any way."

"Yes, I didn't expect you to." He sharpened his gaze. "But this time I want to change the terms a bit."

"In what way?"

"Last time, you told me I couldn't involve any of my friends or family because you'd agreed not to give me any tasks that affected them. But that's not part of the oath. I can't do this one on my own. I'm going to need help. So I want your permission to involve them if I need to. Naturally, I won't tell them anything about you or your involvement."

Aldwyn considered, frowning.

"Listen," Stone said quickly. "Either this is another busywork assignment you're giving me, or you genuinely want Brathwaite dead. Which one is it?"

"I want him dead. I have wanted him so ever since I learned he has managed to survive into the modern era."

"Well, then—if you want him dead, some of my friends are dab hands at the sort of investigations I'll need to do to track him down." He paced in front of the seated dragon. "Come on, Aldwyn—you know I won't tell anyone about you. I don't want them to know I'm related to a nasty old dragon who's been on ice for the last two hundred years any more than you want anyone to know you've resurfaced."

Aldwyn regarded Stone for long enough that the mage wondered if he would answer at all. Finally, he inclined his head. "Agreed. You may involve your associates if it will aid you in performing your task more quickly. But do not reveal anything about my existence or our agreement."

"Done." Another thought occurred to Stone. "What about dragons?"

"What about them?"

"Kolinsky, or Gabriel. I'm not sure I'd want to involve Stefan in this mess, but Gabriel is my son's master. He could be very helpful, even if he can't get involved directly."

The dragon frowned. "You skate very close to the edge of my patience, scion."

Stone stopped his pacing and faced him. "Believe it or not, that's not what I'm trying to do this time. Okay, I'll be honest—I don't *like* it that you're forcing me to kill Brathwaite, just because I'm stubborn like that and I don't like to be forced into *anything*. But I'd be lying if I told you I didn't want him dead, and if I've got to do it, I won't lose a lot of sleep about it. But I refuse to hamstring myself by not having access to the best resources. So, what do you say?"

He waited, his gaze still fixed on the dragon, his whole body tense as he waited for an answer. Loath as he was to admit it, Aldwyn held the cards here. If he decided he wanted his scion to go this one alone, there wasn't much he could do about it. And this would be a hell of a lot harder than the Rydell/Tuttleton situation. Even with Elias Richter most likely dead, Brathwaite wouldn't be easy to take down.

Especially with three more years to get his little necromantic empire up and running.

Finally, Aldwyn made a languid gesture, as if it were of no consequence. "Do as you will, then."

"You *do* remember Gabriel knows about you, right?"

"Yes, of course. I trust you will exercise all due discretion."

"Haven't got much of a choice, do I?" Stone muttered. He took a step back. "How long have I got? This isn't something I can do in a week, you realize. The legwork alone will take a lot longer than that, unless you want Brathwaite catching wind I'm on to him."

Aldwyn considered, then nodded. "I will give you two months to complete this assignment. If you cannot locate and neutralize him by then, I will be highly disappointed in both your abilities and your motivation." He gestured, and the swirling teleportation portal appeared in its customary place. "Otherwise, I advise you to remain both careful and vigilant. You may not believe it, but I value our association, and I would not wish to see you fall victim to Brathwaite's foul arts."

"Yes, well, you and me both. Cheers, Aldwyn." He infused the proper amount of sarcasm into the words. "I'll be in touch."

Before the dragon could reply, he stepped through the portal.

CHAPTER TWO

STONE THOUGHT FOR A LONG TIME about how he wanted to play this, and the more he thought about it, the worse he felt.

Yes, he *could* try to do the job alone. It was certainly an option. But he'd grown in a lot of ways over the years, and one of the most significant was that he now accepted that asking for help wasn't an admission of weakness. In fact, especially in cases like this, it might even indicate the opposite. Adding more sharp minds and powerful magic to a problem, especially *this* problem, could only ensure that success was more likely.

That didn't make it any easier, though. Braithwaite was smart, utterly immoral, and commanded forces Stone didn't even want to understand. Even without Elias Richter behind him, he'd be a formidable foe. The job was certain to be dangerous, and it went against Stone's every instinct to put those he loved in harm's way.

But you promised, the little voice in the back of his head reminded him. *Don't forget that.*

Promised what?

Verity lost as much as you did—maybe more—to Brathwaite and his necromancy. You promised her if you ever went after him, you wouldn't leave her out.

He'd forgotten about that. Good thing he had an overactive subconscious to remind him.

He stroked Raider, who'd jumped up on his desk and was looking at him with the clear-eyed, empathic gaze he always got when his human was troubled over something. Sometimes, Stone could swear the cat understood him when he talked.

"I don't know, mate," he said with a sigh. "I don't know how I get myself into messes like this."

Raider said nothing, but the little voice now seemed to come from the cat: *Sure you do. If you'd settle down and stop chasing Things Humans Weren't Meant to Know, you'd have a lot more sedate life.*

More boring, though.

You can't have everything. Choices must be made.

"Yes, yes," he muttered. Truth be told, he couldn't even get too angry at Aldwyn for giving him this assignment. If he had to be forced to do something for the dragon, this wasn't exactly a task he hadn't thought about a lot on his own. He *did* want Brathwaite dead, but before he couldn't justify hunting the man down and murdering him in cold blood.

This way, he didn't have a choice. He'd sealed the oath.

That's bollocks and you know it. You're looking for excuses.

He was. He couldn't deny it. But even acknowledging that, he couldn't legitimately come up with a remotely plausible reason why the world wouldn't be a better place minus one master necromancer. Brathwaite should have died two hundred years ago, and it was only a freak accident of magic that his noxious spirit stuck around to stuff itself into his descendant.

And besides, poor, mousy Miriam Padgett hadn't asked to have her own spirit destroyed, kicked out of her body by her mad old ancestor who needed a convenient place to park his own. It was possible Aldwyn hadn't been responsible—directly, anyway—for the murders of the people in the catacombs, but Brathwaite certainly had. And worse, he hadn't just killed them. He'd practiced the darkest of dark arts on them.

Yes, it was settled.

Brathwaite deserved to die, and Stone wouldn't lose any sleep about being the instrument of that demise.

He thought a moment, came to a decision, and pulled out his phone.

He didn't tell Verity and Ian why he wanted them to come to his house that evening, only that he needed to discuss something important and confidential with them.

Verity got there first, arriving in her red Toyota because none of Bron's extended family had private portals in San Francisco.

"What's this about?" she asked Stone, who had come out to meet her. "Sounds suspicious, whatever it is." She wore black slacks, a white silk blouse, and a long, sweeping coat of deep emerald green. Stone was still getting used to her updated style of dress and her new maturity.

"I wouldn't call it suspicious. Just something I want to discuss with you two, privately."

She followed him inside, looking quizzical. "Just me and Ian? Not Jason and Amber?"

"Er…no. Best not, I think." That was one of the things he'd thought hard about before making his calls. He knew Jason would be angry and hurt if he found out he'd been excluded from this job; he'd probably feel betrayed. But none of that changed the facts. Jason and Amber had two young children to care for, and despite how useful his new adrenaline-based powers and Amber's shifter abilities would be in locating and dealing with Brathwaite, Stone couldn't bring himself to risk making two children orphans if things went sideways.

"Okay," she said, still sounding dubious. "I won't ask any questions until Ian gets here. But I've got a lot of them."

"I'll do my best to answer most of them, I promise." Stone poured them each a glass of wine and led the way into the living room. As soon as Verity took a seat on the sofa, Raider leaped into her lap and settled there.

Stone chuckled. "Sorry about that—he'll shed all over your black trousers."

"Oh, don't worry about that," she said with a big grin. "When I got Luna, I learned a spell to get rid of cat hair on clothes. I call it my Magic Lint Roller."

"Bloody hell. You'll have to teach me that one."

"Teach you what?" came a voice from the doorway.

"Ah. Good evening, Ian. Thank you for coming." His son had obviously arrived via the portal downstairs, which he'd expected. "Wine?"

"Uh, sure. Curiosity, mostly, though." Ian accepted a glass of wine and took a seat at the opposite end of the sofa from Verity. Raider languidly rose from her lap and stalked down to investigate the newcomer.

Stone settled in his usual chair and regarded them. It wasn't just Verity—they both looked so much more mature, if not physically that much older, than they had before he'd taken his involuntary three-year hiatus. He hadn't had a lot of time to ask them about their adventures, but something had obviously tempered both of them. He absolutely couldn't think of them as kids anymore.

"So, what's this about?" Ian asked. "Why aren't Jason and Amber here? And why didn't you want me to tell Gabriel about whatever it is?"

Part of Stone wanted to bail on the whole thing—to tell them he'd been mistaken, or come up with some other reason for calling them here. But then he looked at Verity's serious face and pictured her sobbing over Sharra's body when she'd been forced to bring down a massive chandelier to stop her undead friend from attacking them. Brathwaite had been responsible for that. She deserved to be in on this.

"Okay," he said before he lost his nerve. "Let me start by saying that I can't tell you everything about what I want to discuss with you tonight. Please don't ask me to, because no matter what you say, that won't change. It can't."

Ian frowned. "Sounds ominous."

But Verity, as quick-witted as Ian but possessed of more information, caught on. "Wait. This has something to do with…you know what, right?"

"What you know what?" Ian glared at her.

"It does." Stone shifted uncomfortably in his chair.

"What are you talking about?"

It was Verity who answered. "If I'm right, it has to do with agreements he had to make to get you back when you were kidnapped."

Ian's glare sharpened, focusing first on Verity, then on Stone. "Wait, this is *still* going on? And you *still* won't tell us who was responsible?"

"I *can't,* Ian," Stone said, not meeting his eyes. "I'm sorry."

"Why not?"

"Because he took an oath," Verity said. She patted Ian's arm. "Come on. Let him alone. He can't tell us, and that's that. Let's listen to what he has to say, okay?"

Ian's glare smoldered for a couple more seconds, and then he nodded grudgingly. "Yeah. Okay. I'll listen. But I don't like all this secrecy—especially if it involves me."

"It only tangentially involves you." Stone settled back, relieved the tide seemed to be receding for now. "What I've asked you here tonight to discuss *does* involve you—both of you—but not for the same reason."

"You're not making a damned bit of sense, Dad," Ian grumbled. "You know that, right?"

"I'm aware. Just…hear me out. This isn't easy for me. I'll admit there was part of me that didn't even want to involve you. But when you hear what I have to say, you'll see why I felt I didn't have a choice."

Both of them remained silent, leaning forward with anticipation, ignoring their wineglasses.

The best way to do this was to get it out there, where he couldn't take it back. "You two remember James Brathwaite, right?"

Verity's expression darkened with anger. "Hell, yeah, I remember him. I'll never forget him. He killed Sharra."

"He's the necromancer, right?" Ian looked serious, but not as agitated as Verity. "The one who sent all those things after us at the Surrey house a few years ago, and messed with the ghouls?"

Stone remembered that it had likely been more than three years since either of them had thought seriously about Brathwaite. "He hasn't been up to anything while I was out, has he?"

"Not that I know of." Verity wasn't cooling off. "It's one of my biggest regrets. I wanted to track his ass down and make him pay for all the stuff he did. But I didn't have any way of finding him. As far as I know, he's disappeared. I keep hoping maybe he's dead."

"Apparently he isn't," Stone said.

"How do you know that?" Ian asked.

"Can't say. But it's reliable information."

"Okay…so why are you bringing him up now?"

"Do you know where he is?" Verity demanded.

"No."

He definitely had their attention now, but he could see they were as confused as they were angry. "Listen—before I go on, I want you both to give me your word that what I say in this room goes no further. That means no telling Jason, Amber, Gabriel, or anybody else without my express permission. Understood?"

"Why don't you want them to know?" Ian asked. "They could help."

"I get it," Verity said softly. "At least about Jason and Amber."

Stone nodded soberly. "They've got more important things to be getting on with than dealing with what I'm proposing. And as for Gabriel—involving him is certainly possible, but I wanted to share it with you two first. And if I do bring him in, I want to be the one to tell him about it. So I ask again: do I have your word that nothing I say here tonight will leave this room?"

"Yeah," Verity said instantly. "You have mine."

Ian took a little longer, but finally he nodded. "Okay. I promise. But I don't like it, given I don't know what I'm promising."

"Thank you for trusting me." Stone swirled the last of the wine in his glass, downed it in one swallow, and levitated the glass to the table. He looked first at Verity, then at Ian. "I'm planning to track Brathwaite down and kill him."

"Wow," Ian said. "That is *not* what I expected."

"I'm in," Verity said instantly. "I hope that's why you brought us here and told us about this. Because if it isn't, we're going to have some words."

Stone bowed his head. "That's exactly why I brought you here. But I want you both to know that I won't be upset in the slightest if you decide you don't want anything to do with this. I asked you because you're both powerful, smart, and have reason to hate Brathwaite. But Ian, if you'd rather not—"

"Oh, hell no. I'm in," Ian replied almost as fast as Verity had. "I don't have V's grudge against him, but he fucked up our family big-time in a lot of ways. We should have taken him out years ago."

In truth, Stone was a little surprised at how fast both of them had agreed to aid him in an assassination. There was no dancing around the morality of it: this was first-degree murder. But he supposed it shouldn't have been that odd: Verity was normally a peaceful, mellow person, but she had an intensity that rivaled—and possibly exceeded—his own when she felt she or someone she loved had been wronged. And Ian, after all, had killed his tyrannical step-father. Perhaps not in cold blood, but he hadn't shown any regrets about it.

"So, how do you want to do it?" Verity asked.

Stone was likewise surprised at how even her voice sounded—like she was discussing the weather, or what she planned to buy at the store.

"I don't know yet. The problem is, I haven't got a clue where he is nor how to find him. If I go looking and he discovers I'm after him, he could disappear—or decide to go after the people I care about. We've got to be careful."

"Are you planning to bring anyone else in?" Ian sipped his wine thoughtfully. "I know you said not Jason and Amber…though you know they're going to be pissed if they find out. Are you sure you have the right to make that decision for them?"

Stone sighed. "It's not just making that decision for them, un-fortunately. If that were all it was, I'd be more inclined to consider it. But don't forget—Jason is a private investigator. He's got a lot of friends in law enforcement, and his livelihood depends on main-taining those relationships."

"You don't think he'd turn us in, do you?" Verity looked indignant.

"Of course not. But…"

"But Jason's a Boy Scout. Even if he went along with it, he'd still be conflicted between his loyalty to you and his sense of justice," Ian finished.

"Exactly." He was glad he hadn't had to say it.

"Yeah…" Verity said with obvious reluctance. "I can see that. I guess it's not really fair to ask him to make that choice."

"What about Gabriel, though?" Ian asked. "He could be a big help. He's got contacts all over the world, and he's good at the kind of discreet hunting we'd need for this."

Stone nodded. "If you think he'd be willing to help, I'd definitely like to have him in our corner." For more reasons than one, though he couldn't tell them the main one. Dragons had a pathological hatred of necromancers, so he was certain Ian's master would welcome the chance to take down the man who'd brought necromancy back to the modern world.

"I'll ask him. To talk to you, I mean," he added hastily. "I promised I wouldn't tell him the details, and I won't. But I'd be really surprised if he didn't want to help."

"Brilliant. Thank you, Ian." Stone wondered how *much* Gabriel would be willing to help, given the dragons' non-interference pact. But Brathwaite was by no means a normal human—not even a normal *mage*—so he hoped the whole anti-necromancy thing would take precedence over the don't-interfere-in-human-affairs thing. There was also the more specific stricture about not being allowed to interfere between a sire and his scion, which might come into play here. Then again, it might not, since helping with the task might not qualify as "interfering." And Aldwyn *had* said "do as you will" when he'd asked about enlisting other dragons' assistance.

Verity poured them all another round. "Anybody else you're thinking of bringing in?"

Stone pondered. He'd been thinking a lot about it before he called these two. "I'm not sure. This is a big deal. It's murder I'm asking people to help me with. There's no way to argue around it: we're going to be planning and executing a murder."

"But is it, really?" Ian tilted his head. He was staring off into the middle distance as if deep in thought.

"What do you mean?"

"Is Brathwaite truly alive? He's a two-hundred-year-old echo who got sealed in a crypt and managed to stay alive long enough to steal the body of his descendant. What's her name again, Dad?"

"Miriam Padgett." Stone was pleased his son was thinking along the same lines as he had been earlier.

"Right. I mean, from what you said before, there's no bringing her back, right? When he took over her body, he killed her spirit."

"Far as I know. I mean, we can't be certain, of course, since we weren't there. But very few echoes hang about for long following death—or in this case, ejection from a corporeal body."

"That sounds like the sort of question mage philosophers would salivate over," Verity said. "Assuming there are any."

"I don't know about that," Ian said, "but I do know doing what he did makes Brathwaite a murderer—even if you *don't* count all the stuff he did when he was properly alive."

"And the stuff he did in New York City," Verity said grimly. "I know his helper with the portals was the one who technically brought down that building, but he was doing it on Brathwaite's orders. *And* there's no ambiguity about what he did to Sharra. That's worse than murder, in my mind."

"You won't get any argument from me about any of those points," Stone said. "Yes, it's true that I'm oath-bound to do this job, but in this case I've got no objection to it. I'd been meaning to do something about Brathwaite since before I went away." It amused him how that had become his neat little euphemism for "the time I was in a magic-induced state of suspended animation against my will for three years."

Ian narrowed his eyes. "How many of these jobs do you have to do for this guy? Can you tell us that, at least, if you refuse to tell us who he is?"

"I keep telling you—it's not that I refuse. It's that I *can't*. But he didn't say anything about the other bit, so he can't get cross with me about that. The deal was three jobs in five years, whichever comes first."

"And then he knocked you out for three of them?" Verity looked confused. "That doesn't make a lot of sense."

"Yes, well, this person is…let's just call him 'inexplicable' and be done with it. Half the time I haven't got a clue about what his motivations are, and honestly I'd rather keep it that way. But in any case, I've already completed one of the jobs, as you know. This is the second. So there's one more after that, and he's got the better part of two years to assign it. I'm hoping he'll leave me the hell alone for a while after I finish this one."

"How long have you got to do it?"

"Two months, minus a couple of days."

"You think you're going to be able to find him in that time?" Ian asked. "He's a pretty powerful mage. If he's in hiding…"

"I don't think he's in hiding, *per se.*" Stone spoke slowly, going over his thoughts before he gave them voice.

"Why not?"

"Because James Brathwaite has an ego that rivals some of the most big-headed mages I've ever encountered. Not so much about himself, but about his work. He's the one who brought necromancy back to modern times, and I'm betting he's bloody proud of that."

"What does that get us, though?" Verity tilted her head. "What do we do, follow the trail of zombies back to him?"

"Possibly. Maybe not quite so literally, but I do know there are certain darker corners of magical study that are very interested in learning the necromantic arts. Including the organization he's re-established himself with."

"Ordo Purpuratus." She leaned forward, suddenly energized. "You think *they* might know where he is?"

"I'm sure some of them do."

"But what makes you think they'll give him up?" Ian stroked Raider, who'd settled in his lap. "They're not exactly your biggest fans, are they?"

"Not mine, no, though they have tried to recruit me in the past so there's that. But both the European and American arms of the organization are always on the lookout for the same thing."

"Knowledge," Verity said. "Right? Or power?"

"Both—though they consider the two to be nearly indistinguishable. And I've got access to something that might encourage some of their members to part with a bit of information in exchange for what I can offer."

"What's that?" Ian asked.

But Verity, as usual, caught on. "The research material at Caventhorne. The stuff that's not available to the magical public."

Stone pointed at her with a "got it" gesture. He wasn't surprised she caught on faster than Ian—it wasn't that his son was any less brilliant mentally, but Verity spent a lot more time with him and was more familiar with his thought processes. Plus, Ian was more of a hands-on guy than a scholar, so he hadn't spent much time at Caventhorne. "Exactly."

"So you want to bring Eddie and Ward into this?" Ian looked dubious.

Stone *didn't* want to bring his friends into it. Eddie Monkton and Arthur Ward were world-class researchers and every bit as sharp as he was, but they avoided offensive magic unless absolutely necessary. Like Jason, their loyalty to him would no doubt make them agree instantly to be involved if he asked, so he didn't want to ask. But unless Gabriel could come through with something, he was fresh out of other ideas about how to find the elusive necromancer.

"Not...directly," he said. "But I'd be surprised if Eddie, in his capacities as London Library custodian and Caventhorne administrator, hadn't encountered some Ordo members. As long as they play nice and don't cause trouble, they've got as much right to use the research facilities as anyone else. And I doubt *all* the modern Ordo members are as horrible as the ones in the past. One thing I've managed to pound into my head over the past few years is that times change, and so do people. The Ordo might be a bit on the amoral side as a rule, and willing to go down paths most decent mages won't touch, but that doesn't make them all evil."

"So the enemy of your enemy is your friend," Ian said.

"Something like that." Stone thought about Aldwyn, and wondered which side his dragon ancestor fell on. He'd claimed he wasn't the same person he was two hundred years ago, and that dragons were nothing if not adaptable to changing times. But what did that mean? He had no idea—except that, regardless of his current moral proclivities, Aldwyn was dangerous, and not a dragon to cross lightly.

At least not without a lot of planning.

"So," he said, rising. "Let's sum things up, so I don't keep you here all night: first, you're both in? If you need time to think, please take it. I'm on a timetable, but I can set a few things in motion on my own if you need to give yourselves some time to ruminate."

"I don't need any time," Verity said instantly. "As long as you promise I can be in on the kill so I can see that bastard's eyes when he knows we're taking him down, try to keep me away."

"Yeah." Ian stood too, gently tipping Raider off his lap. "This guy's bad news for a lot of reasons, and like I said, I don't even consider this murder, since the guy shouldn't even be alive in the first place. If anything, we're cleaning up some trash that should have been cleaned up a long time ago."

"Right, then. Stay reachable, and I'll be in touch shortly. And…thank you. Both of you."

Verity nodded soberly. "You want us to do anything in the meantime?"

"Not yet. Ian, I might be contacting you to put me in touch with Gabriel soon. I'll probably need to talk to him alone, though, so I hope you're all right with that."

Ian shrugged. "Eh, not really, but I get it. I don't like that you're keeping secrets from me—especially with Gabriel—but you're not the only one who's had a few things pounded into his head. In my case, it's that not everything's my business."

Stone patted his shoulder. "Good man. Be safe, both of you, and don't say anything to anyone until I tell you to. I've got no idea how many ears Brathwaite has out in the wild. I'm probably being paranoid, but we can't afford to botch this one."

After they left, he drifted back to the living room and dropped onto the sofa, suddenly weary. As hard as he tried, he couldn't shake the low-grade feeling of dread that he'd just pulled one of his dearest friends and his only son into something that could potentially get them killed—or worse—and it wasn't sitting well.

On the other hand, though… He scratched Raider behind the ear and bowed his head. "They're adults, Raider. They're powerful, fully trained mages, and they know what they're getting into. It would be insulting for me to treat them like I need to protect them anymore. Right?"

The cat rose, putting both paws against Stone's chest, hit him with a vigorous head-butt in the nose, and purred.

"Yes. I know. You're right. But I don't have to like it, do I?"

CHAPTER THREE

STONE KNEW HE DIDN'T HAVE A LOT OF TIME to be indecisive about whom to contact next, but that didn't mean the decision was easy.

Gabriel made it easier, though. The next morning, Stone texted Ian and asked him to let the dragon know he wanted to talk. An hour later, Gabriel texted back. They arranged a meet at a high-end sushi restaurant in Toronto.

"I've heard good things about this place," the young dragon said when Stone arrived and they were seated in the elegant, minimalist space. "This is a fine excuse to try it. What can I do for you, Dr. Stone?"

Right down to business. That was good. They placed their orders, and Stone looked around. "No one can hear us talking, can they?"

"No. I'm employing a subtle magical effect that will muffle our conversation."

"Good." He could use his 'cone of silence' spell, but that one only worked reliably against mundanes. "I've got something I need to discuss with you. I need your help, but I'm not sure you're allowed to offer it."

"Intriguing." Gabriel sipped his drink and tilted his head. "Go on."

"Remember the oath I had to take to Aldwyn, to get Ian back?"

"Of course."

"And that the oath requires me to perform tasks for him? Three, to be precise."

"I wasn't aware of the number, but yes."

"Well, it's three. One's done, and now he's given me another one. This time, I'm allowed to involve my friends, as long as I don't reveal anything about who's behind them."

"And you want to enlist my help with this new task."

"Yes. I know you can't get involved directly. That's right, isn't it?"

"I am not permitted to knowingly interfere between a sire and a scion. I'm sure my father already told you that."

"He did, yes. But in this case, it doesn't constitute interference. When I asked Aldwyn if I could ask for other dragons' help—" Even with the draconic silence spell, Stone still looked around nervously and dropped his voice to a near-whisper when he uttered the name "—he said 'do as you will'. I'm not sure if that was a trick, an agreement, or if he just knew none of you lot would get involved, but there you go. I won't know the answer if I don't ask."

"What is it that you want me to do, Dr. Stone?" Gabriel's expression hadn't changed. Their plates arrived; he thanked the waiter in Japanese, deftly picked up a roll with his chopsticks, and paused to taste it. He nodded approvingly. "This *is* good."

Stone had noticed before that no matter how crowded a place was, his dragon associates always got served very quickly, but he'd never asked why. He tried one of his own rolls—Gabriel was right, they were excellent—and washed it down with a swallow of sake. "I need to find someone who won't be easy to find."

"Indeed? That is your task? I would think Aldwyn would have a much easier time locating anyone than you would. No offense, of course."

"None taken." Stone hesitated, but only for a moment. If he couldn't trust Gabriel, he'd be in a lot of trouble. "He doesn't just want me to find him. He wants me to…deal with him after I do."

"He wants you to kill him." Gabriel spoke matter-of-factly, without judgment.

"Yes."

The dragon raised an eyebrow. "And how do you feel about that, Dr. Stone? That he has asked you to become his assassin?"

Stone shrugged. "Surprisingly, I don't object. I'd been planning to do the same thing at some point, to be honest."

"Oh? Who is this man you are to kill, then?"

"James Brathwaite."

Gabriel's eyes widened, but only slightly. If Stone hadn't been looking for any change in expression, he wouldn't have spotted it. "I see."

"Ian told you about him, I assume."

"Oh, yes. The necromancer." His eyes darkened slightly, and his jaw tightened.

"I trust from your expression that you share your kind's opinion of necromancy."

"Indeed I do. Even if you didn't have a history with Mr. Brathwaite, I can see why you don't object to Aldwyn's task in this case."

Stone nodded. "I don't know how much Ian told you, but you're right. I've got several issues with him, and will be all too glad to hasten his demise. But first I've got to find him. That's where my request to you comes in."

"You want me to help you locate him."

"Yes."

"Why not ask my father?"

"Honestly? Two reasons. One, he's not easy to contact these days. He still hasn't given me a way to get in touch with him, which leads me to believe that he's either busy or he doesn't *want* me to contact him. Two, I don't want to get him involved in this."

"But you don't mind involving me." Gabriel didn't seem annoyed; in fact, his handsome face now showed faint amusement.

"Well, Ian's involved, and you're involved with Ian. I thought it would be easier."

"Ian is involved?"

"Yes. I've asked him and Verity to help me, and they've agreed. Verity has a longstanding grudge against Brathwaite, and Ian…well, it's his family too, that the man has mucked up. He deserves a shot at making it right, don't you think?"

"I'm surprised *you* do, to be frank."

"Oh?"

Gabriel paused to savor a bite of nigiri before responding. "In the past, Dr. Stone, you've been reluctant to involve your friends and family in your more dangerous adventures."

"Yes, well, that's honestly still true. I'm always going to be reluctant to involve others in things where they might get hurt. But reluctance and refusal are two different things." He sobered. "You probably don't know why Verity has such an issue with Brathwaite. Am I correct?"

"You are. Ian told me about the situation with the catacombs at your Surrey house, and about what happened with Mr. Richter and the ghouls more recently. There is something else?"

"Oh, yes. Something big." Quickly, with another glance around to make sure no one was watching him, he filled Gabriel in on the situation with Richter, Brathwaite, and what the necromancer had done to Sharra.

The dragon listened in silence, his gaze never leaving Stone's face. He said nothing at the conclusion of the story.

"So Ian never told you about any of that? I'm not sure how much Verity told him."

"I knew about part of it—the destruction of the building in New York City, obviously. But I didn't know about what happened to Verity's friend. Aside from the obvious reasons to be disturbed about that, there are others. If he has found a way to raise mages as volitional undead…"

"I don't know what he's done in the meantime. It's been quite some time since that occurred, and I didn't see any hints of it during the ghoul situation. Perhaps Sharra was an aberration, I don't know. Last time I saw him, he was trying to use something from ghouls to help Elias Richter, who was in the early stages of dementia. I think the idea was to do something with the ghouls' regenerative abilities to stave off or stop the effects. We interfered, though, and I'm fairly sure Richter is dead. Even if he's not—if he somehow managed to survive the botched ritual—without some kind of treatment, after all this time he's probably not a threat anymore."

"Probably not." Gabriel spoke as if distracted. "But we're not discussing Richter—we're discussing Brathwaite. And I fear you won't like my answer, Dr. Stone."

Stone was afraid of this. "You can't help me. Or you won't."

"No. Not directly, anyway. I cannot interfere."

"Damn. It doesn't surprise me, but I'm disappointed. I thought perhaps since you'd be helping me do what Aldwyn wants done, this would be a different situation."

"Unfortunately, that isn't the case. It is one of our strongest strictures: the activities between a sire and his or her scions are inviolate. Normally, I remain outside our society as much as I can manage, and thus I have a great deal of freedom to pursue my interests without interference from the others. If I should suddenly involve myself in something like this, all of that could—and likely would—change."

Stone noticed he didn't look happy about it. "You want to help me, don't you?"

"I do. And honestly, I would be surprised if any of my people would raise more than a token objection. There is not one among us who is pleased that necromancy has returned."

"But you're not willing to take the chance?" Stone paused to sample another roll. "I thought you were the daredevil, Gabriel.

The risk-taker." He watched the dragon closely for signs he'd pushed too far.

Instead, Gabriel smiled. "I am, by my people's standards—and by yours. But there are limits to how far even I am willing to go." He considered, staring into space for several seconds. "I do want to help you, though—especially if Ian is involved. I will give you this: if you legitimately exhaust your other means of locating Brathwaite, contact me again and I will see what I can do. Perhaps I can devise a way to aid you without breaking the letter of our agreements." His smile grew sly. "That is another thing dragons are masters at: coming up with creative ways to bend rules without truly breaking them."

Stone returned the sly smile. "I suppose I can't ask for more than that." He didn't like it, but given the circumstances it was probably better than he could have hoped for. Plus, he *did* have other options. "Fair enough, then. Thank you, Gabriel. I honestly hope we don't have to take you up on that offer."

Due to time-zone differences, it was early evening when he returned home to the Encantada house. He'd barely gone to the kitchen to prepare Raider's evening meal, his mind still on his conversation with Gabriel, when his phone rang.

He pulled it from his pocket, surprised. Was Gabriel contacting him again with something he'd forgotten? Verity or Ian with something about Brathwaite?

But it wasn't any of them, nor anyone else he would have expected. The number surprised him. "Hello, Gerry."

"Hey, Stone. Are you home, or have you gone on extended walkabout again?"

In the three months since he'd awakened, Stone had made it a point to reconnect with several people from his old life. Mackenzie

Hubbard, his fellow Occult Studies professor at the University, had finally retired to travel with his wife and pursue his modest career as a literary horror author. Brandon Greene, former graduate student, had taken a full-time position in the department along with a new hire Stone hadn't met yet. And Leo Blum, his magic-savvy detective contact at the San Francisco PD, had been promoted again and now supervised a detective division. Aside from Hubbard being a bit grumpy that Stone had disappeared with no notice, everyone had believed the reasons he'd given them for his absence. After a brief, uncomfortable period, they'd all fallen back into their old patterns without much difficulty.

Gerry Hook, drummer and founding member of The Cardinal Sin, the casual bar band composed of professors from the University, had been a bit harder to mollify. It had taken the band almost a year to find a new lead guitarist following Stone's disappearance, and he'd been annoyed that Stone hadn't given them more of a heads-up. Stone hadn't asked for his old job back, and Hook hadn't offered it. They'd ended their last conversation, two months ago, more than a bit uneasily.

Now, Stone didn't miss the sarcasm in Hook's tone, but he also didn't miss that it was of a more good-natured variety than before. "No, no more walkabouts planned for the foreseeable future. What can I do for you?"

There was a long pause. "Hey, well, this is more than a little awkward given the last time we talked…"

"I'm used to awkward with you lot. Spit it out." He set down Raider's food dish and carried the phone to the living room.

"Well, the truth is, and don't laugh too hard—I'm calling to see if you want your old gig back."

That wasn't what he'd expected to hear. "You're having me on."

"Nope. I was fully prepared to be all indignant and make you beg for it, but the truth is, your replacement never really gelled with the rest of us."

"Is that right?" Stone didn't know anything about who they'd tapped to replace him.

"Yeah, well, we tried to make it work for a long time. He's a good guy, but he's got even less charisma than Kurt Hedding."

"The accountant?" Kurt Hedding was the Accounting professor whose impending parenthood had compelled him to leave, opening the spot Stone had taken several years back.

"Yeah. Kurt had the stage presence of a wet dishrag, but at least he could play well. Dusty, the new guy…well…like I said, he's a good guy, but…" He paused, then spoke faster: "Look, the truth is, Radha wants you back."

Stone smiled. Radha Unger was the band's lead singer, a bluesy-voiced Indian professor of Electrical Engineering. "*Radha* wants me back. None of the rest of you do."

A loud sigh came through the connection. "Come on, Stone, don't make me do this. I'm still pissed at you for taking off without even telling us you were leaving. But—okay, yeah. We all want you back."

"I'm not even sure I qualify as a professor anymore." He'd met with Beatrice Martinez, head of Cultural Anthropology, Occult Studies' parent department, but so far the situation was still up in the air. Technically, Stone was considered to be on an extended leave of absence, and while Martinez had told him she'd be glad to reinstate him, he wasn't sure yet whether he *wanted* to be reinstated. They'd agreed he could extend his unpaid leave for six more months—three of which had already passed—and he could make his decision then.

"Eh, it's not like anybody checks credentials." Hook snorted, changing his voice to sound like a disgruntled fan: "*Hey, this is bogus. How can you guys be a professor band if this guitar dude isn't even a professor?* Besides, they'll probably be too busy being happy the lead guitarist actually has some stage presence for a change.

You *do* still remember how to play, right? You didn't forget while you were off communing in Africa or wherever?"

Stone had to laugh at his spot-on imitation. "Yes, Gerry, I can still play. And I haven't a clue where you got the idea I was in Africa."

"Well, none of us know where you were, so I had to make a guess. Sue me. So, what do you say? You want back in or not?"

Stone almost asked if he could think about it, but then reconsidered. He'd always enjoyed playing with the Sin—except for the time he nearly died after drinking a dosed beer, anyway—and he could use a little normalcy in his life right now. Especially given that the rest of his current life consisted of plotting the murder of a two-hundred-year-old necromancer. "Er...sure. Yes, I want back in, if you'll have me."

"Great. Glad to hear it. Of course, you're gonna be on the hook for a *lot* of rounds of drinks. You're three years behind, man. None of the rest of us are paying for drinks for the foreseeable future."

Stone laughed, genuinely feeling the stress lifting from him. "That's quite all right, mate. Happy to do it. So, when is the next gig?"

Another pause. "Well, see, that's the thing. It's Friday night."

"Bloody hell, Gerry, that's in two days."

"Yeah. We're gonna give Dusty the bad news right after I get off the phone with you. We can't take it anymore, Stone, and I think he sees it coming. I'd try to reschedule, but...well, in the interest of full disclosure, we haven't had that many gigs lately. So I'd hate to lose this one. It can be your big comeback. So...can you make it?"

Stone was hoping there wouldn't be another gig until after the Brathwaite situation was handled, but he couldn't deny his heart was beating faster at the prospect of being back on stage again. "I can. Send me the details and I'll be there."

"Fantastic. That's the Stone we all know and love."

"Or at least tolerate because I buy the drinks."

"Yeah, that too. If you still remember how to play our usual standards, we shouldn't need to practice in the meantime. It's a short show—just one set. See you then."

Stone still had a smile on his face when he broke the connection. He picked up Raider, who'd finished his dinner and was ambling in licking his chops, and looked into his green eyes. "Things are looking up, Raider. I don't expect that to last, but I'll enjoy it while it does."

CHAPTER FOUR

STONE WAITED UNTIL THE NEXT DAY to text Eddie. *Got something I need to discuss. Are you and Ward available?*

The answer came back quickly: *Always. Want to go pick up a pint or three at the Dragon?*

He considered. Most of their conversations took place in the back room of the Dancing Dragon Inn, but he wasn't sure this one was the kind of thing he wanted to be discussing with a bunch of other mages hanging about. *No, let's do it at Caventhorne. Don't worry, we can go to the Dragon after, and I'll buy the rounds.*

Sounds ominous, if you don't want to discuss it there.

Just a bit sensitive.

Eddie sent a cheeky smiley face. *You're not gonna tell me you've always had a thing for me, are you? Because I love you, mate, but you know I've only got eyes for Ward.*

You can only wish that was what it was. I see the way you look at me when you don't think I'm paying attention.

Damn, you found me out. He changed to a new line, back to business again: *When?*

As soon as possible. Stone glanced at his watch. It was eleven a.m. in California, which meant it was seven p.m. in England. *Now, if you're not busy.*

Come on over. It's a rare quiet night, work-wise. I hope this is worth it, though. I was planning to pull up a few pints and watch the Hammers trounce Millwall.

Knowing Eddie's loyalty to his favorite football team as he did, Stone was impressed that he'd forego viewing a match to talk to him. *Thanks, Eddie. Call Ward, and I'll be right over. Maybe you'll have time to catch the end.*

Stone arrived at Caventhorne before Eddie and Ward did. Because the place was on a confluence of five ley lines and he'd tweaked the wards long ago, he had a lot of destinations inside the house to choose from. He picked William Desmond's old, hidden office, which was in the wing not open to the public.

After shimmering back into existence, he paused to look around. He rarely used the office, and in fact hadn't been back to it since he'd awakened. Because of this, he hadn't made any appreciable changes to it since he'd discovered Desmond's body there years ago. He wasn't sure whether it was because he didn't have time to update it or because some part of him wanted to maintain it as a sort of shrine to his old master, but either way the familiar books and papers still covered the massive, carved wooden desk, the tomes on the shelves remained the same, and the antique chair with its cracked leather upholstery still resided behind the desk.

On a whim, Stone drifted to the floor-to-ceiling bookshelf that covered the office's north wall. He studied it, but he wasn't looking at the books. He wasn't looking at anything, in truth, except what was in his mind's eye. The old feelings of despair and grief came flowing back, along with anger. Desmond shouldn't be dead. He should have lived for dozens more years—maybe longer. Not only had he been a powerful mage, but he was also, unknown to Stone, another scion. To lose him so early had been a blow to the magical world that was still being felt to this day.

Stone knew he didn't have much time before he had to meet Eddie and Ward—it wouldn't be polite to keep them waiting after he'd asked them to come—but he took a moment to retrieve an old-fashioned key from its illusionary hiding place. He moved the books from the third shelf, then inserted the key into a likewise hidden keyhole. When a small *click* sounded, he took hold of the shelf and swung the whole section outward.

The space behind it was no larger than a large bathroom. To mundane eyes, it would appear to be nothing more than a dusty storage closet, stacked with a few boxes, odd items, and more books. But when Stone shifted to magical sight, a crisscross of bright lines erupted into being: a ward within a ward, designed to protect this small vault from discovery and incursion. Idly, he wondered if even the dragons could breach this space—or find it. He wasn't sure, and didn't want to find out, so he'd never told anyone about the space. Not even Eddie and Ward. He used it to store the most powerful and potentially dangerous of Desmond's artifacts and reference materials, the stuff he'd never make available to the magical public who came to Caventhorne to do research.

In the middle of the room was a pedestal, currently empty. Stone looked at it for only a moment, remembering the strange, unsettling wooden artifact that had been responsible for not only Desmond's death, but his father's. With conscious effort, he wrenched his gaze away, stepped back, and shoved the bookshelf closed. He didn't have time to dwell on the past right now. He had things to do.

Eddie and Ward were waiting in the main hall when he emerged, chatting with Kerrick.

The estate steward waved when he saw Stone. "Good evening, sir. It's good to see you again."

"It is indeed." Stone had included Kerrick, Desmond's oldest and most loyal friend, in his re-introduction tour, of course, so they'd already spoken since his return. Despite Kerrick's mundane heritage, he was well-versed in magical theory, mostly due to the osmosis of spending so much time around the world's premier arcane minds. He handled the day-to-day running of Caventhorne, commanding a sizeable staff of magic-aware mundanes and ensuring that everything about the place's operation not directly connected to magic remained smooth. "We won't bother you tonight, Kerrick. I need to discuss some things with these two miscreants."

"Oi," Eddie said, grinning. "That's no way to talk to the bloke who's given up valuable evenin' plans to 'ear you blather on."

Kerrick laughed. "Right, then. I'll leave you to it. I'll be around, though, so don't hesitate to call if you need anything."

Stone refused to reveal anything until they reached one of the warded rooms on the third floor, and by the time they got there, both his friends were clearly brimming with curiosity.

"This must be a big deal," Eddie said. "I 'aven't seen you this secretive in a long time. You plannin' a murder or summat?"

Stone jerked his head up in shock before he could stop himself.

Eddie frowned, raising deep furrows in his high forehead. "Bloody hell, I was kiddin'. At least I thought I was."

Ward was looking even more serious. "That can't be true... can it?"

Stone dropped into one of the conference-table chairs and spun it around so he could gaze out at the twinkling lights of the back garden. "Listen, both of you—before I say anything else, I want you to know I will absolutely understand if you don't want to get involved."

Eddie leaned forward, pressing both palms onto the table. "Let's 'ear it, mate." Unlike his usual flippant tones, he now sounded deadly serious.

"I'll tell you, don't worry. But I want to get the important bits out first. Such as the most important one: all I'm asking you two to do is help me locate someone. Nothing more."

"Someone…you plan to kill," Ward said soberly. He was looking at Stone like he didn't believe what he was hearing.

He'd intended to be a bit more circumspect with his reveal, but he should have known his friends were sharp as hell. There was no point in dancing around it at this point. "Yes." He even managed to look at them when he said it.

"Who?" Eddie was still dead calm.

"James Brathwaite."

Clearly, sharp as they were, they hadn't been expecting that answer. They exchanged glances, then faced him again.

"Brathwaite," Ward said. "The necromancer."

Stone inclined his head.

Eddie almost looked relieved. "Well, I've got to say, if I were plannin' to 'elp kill *anybody,* that bastard would be at the top of the list. But why now? Is this some new bug you've got in your pants after you've woke up from your sleepytime?"

"Not…exactly." Stone rose and paced in front of the window, focusing on the garden again. "This is the part I can't tell you much about." He wished now that he'd shared the story of what had occurred in Rydell and Tuttleton with them, but at the time it hadn't seemed a priority. "Suffice it to say it's got to do with what happened to me—and to Ian."

"You aren't making sense," Ward said, tilting his head. "What does killing Brathwaite have to do with that?"

"I…had to make certain agreements in exchange for getting Ian back." He spun. "Please don't ask me for details. I can't give them to you, and all it will do is sidetrack what I've really come here to discuss. Suffice it to say, I need to locate Brathwaite. Have you two heard anything about or from him in the last three years? Even rumors?"

"Not...really." Eddie stroked his chin thoughtfully. "Never really looked, honestly. That whole mess was more your thing than ours. As long as 'e stayed safely tucked away, I don't think either of us 'ad any desire to rattle 'is cage. That's right, Ward, innit?"

Ward nodded, looking as serious as Eddie had.

"Yes, of course you didn't." Stone didn't blame them for that. As brilliant as they were with research, his two friends had never possessed his adventurous spirit. They were content to remain in their libraries and research halls, providing their help in a more indirect way. The few times they'd been drawn into the front lines, they'd performed bravely, but with obvious reluctance. "And that's fine. I wouldn't want to see you two go up against his lot on your own anyway. But things are different for me. Brathwaite has caused a lot of trouble for my family and my friends, and it's time he paid for it."

Eddie's gaze sharpened. "But wait...this is something *you* want to do, all of a sudden? Or something someone *else* wants you to do? You said it 'ad summat to do with what you 'ad to do to get Ian back."

"Both, honestly. Yes, someone's asked me to do this. But that doesn't mean it's something I haven't wanted to do on my own for a long time. This is just...a catalyst." He met first Eddie's gaze, then Ward's. "So—that's why I'm asking for your help."

"To find 'im? But you already know 'ow to do that, don't you? Except I'm sorry, Stone, but there's no way in 'Ell we're gonna 'elp you with that ritual where you use yourself as a tether again. Don't even ask."

Stone shook his head. "I thought about that, but I don't think it will work this time, even if I wanted to do it. I think the other tethers we had at the time were necessary, and we don't have them anymore. No, I'm thinking of another way: Brathwaite was working with Elias Richter, who was strongly connected with the Ordo

Purpuratus. I'd be very surprised if some of that lot didn't pop by Caventhorne on occasion to do research. Am I wrong?"

Eddie shrugged. "That's a relief that you're not completely daft. But we don't ask a lot of questions about who uses the facilities. That was part of Desmond's bequest—as long as everybody minds their manners and doesn't go wanderin' about lookin' for things that aren't available to the public, our doors are open to anyone."

"Of course. I understand that, given that I helped set up the rules. But…I know you two, and the others you've employed to help you run the place. You do pay attention, don't you? Particularly when it involves the special collection."

"Of course," Ward said. "For those resources there are records, but mostly to ensure they don't—"

"—wander out the door," Eddie finished. "Not that they could. That place is warded to the 'ilt. If anyone tried takin' anything off the premises without permission, it would set up alarm bells you'd 'ear down in Surrey."

"Okay." Stone resumed his pacing. "Good. That's what I was hoping to hear. And that's all I'm asking you for: to do a bit of snooping about and see if you can identify any Ordo members who might know anything about Brathwaite's current whereabouts. But the difficult part is that it's got to be with utmost discretion. I'm not sure if Brathwaite even knew I was out of commission for three years—or if he did, if he knows I'm back now. He might even think I believe he's dead. I can use that to my advantage, since he's got no idea I'm looking for him. But only if we can keep it quiet."

Eddie looked at Ward again, then turned back. "I'll do what I can. I don't know 'ow much 'elp I'll be, since this sort o' thing isn't really in my wheelhouse, but you know you can count on me."

"And me as well," Ward said instantly. "Although I'm afraid I'll likely be even less helpful than Eddie. You don't need a researcher—you need a detective."

Stone thought about Jason, and wondered again if he was doing the right thing by keeping him and Amber out of the loop. "I'm afraid I'm fresh out of magical detectives, so you lot will have to do for now. If you can find me an Ordo member or two, maybe I can tempt them with something juicy from Desmond's private collection to tell me what they know. You know as well as I do that they're not a monolith these days, and the possibility of getting their grabby little hands on some hidden knowledge might be enough to loosen their tongues."

"You're right, though," Eddie said. "We'll 'ave to be bloody careful. If it gets back to Brathwaite that somebody's lookin' for 'im…"

Stone jerked his head up as his friend's words flipped a switch in his mind. "Wait a moment. That might be the answer, Eddie. You're brilliant."

He mock-preened. "I know that. And *you* know that. But what'd I do this time?"

"You're right—if he catches on that someone's trying to track him down, he could either retaliate or go so far underground we'll never find him. *Unless* they're tracking him for the right reason."

Eddie looked momentarily confused, but Ward thrust a finger up. "I get it. If they're trying to find a necromancer."

"Of course!" Eddie slapped his head. "That bloke's always 'ad a giant ego about bein' a master necromancer. We can play to that."

Stone nodded, picking up his pace as the ideas piled on top of each other, energizing him. "He's no doubt trained more necromancers in the last few years, but he's never going to concede the top spot. If we can appeal to his ego or his desire to advance the study of necromancy by presenting a problem that needs solving or some newly unearthed bit of knowledge, maybe we can lure him in—or someone closely connected with him—without making them suspicious."

"But how will we do that?" Ward looked dubious. "I wouldn't know the first thing about appealing to a necromancer."

"Yes, well, that's a good thing about you. But I think I do."

"Care to share?" Eddie wasn't looking any more excited about this plan than Ward was.

Stone paced some more, letting his mind go. His friends, who knew him and his ways well, didn't say anything until he whirled around. "What if we let it get out that Caventhorne's acquired an interesting new collection of reference material—something that's strictly controlled and only available to those who can demonstrate serious scholarly intent?"

Eddie narrowed his eyes. "You're talkin' about necromancy references."

"I am."

"But we don't 'ave any necromancy reference material. The only stuff I was ever aware of were those books you destroyed." His gaze sharpened. "You *did* destroy them, didn't you?"

"Yes, unfortunately." He wished now that he'd snapped photos of the pages before he burned them, but that ship had sailed years ago. And he didn't have Eddie's photographic memory, so reconstructing them wouldn't be an option either.

"So, what are you proposing?" Ward asked. "That we fake the material? That could be dangerous, if someone bites and they catch on."

"You didn't find anything in Desmond's secret stash, did you?" Eddie looked interested in spite of himself.

"No." He let a slow smile spread across his face. "But once again, Eddie, you've given me an idea. You're two for two tonight. I hope you've got some money on the Hammers."

"I do." He glanced at his watch. "Which is why I'd love to wrap up this little soirée with enough time to get back to London before it's over. What's this new idea?"

"Can you spare fifteen minutes? I know you've got something electronic on you, so you can check in on the match while I'm gone."

"What are you going to do?" Ward asked.

"Just wait—you'll see." Without giving them a chance to reply, he dashed off.

He found what he was looking for faster than he'd expected, so it was only ten minutes before he arrived back at the conference room. Eddie had propped up a tablet and was staring intently at something, while Ward was perusing an old-fashioned newspaper and looking bored.

"Yes!" Eddie yelled, pumping his fist and pounding on the table so hard he startled Ward. "That's the way to do it, boys!"

Stone dumped two books on the table with a loud *thump.*

Reluctantly, Eddie dragged his gaze from the match. He tapped the mute button but didn't close the tablet. "What'cha got there?"

He slid them over. "Take a look."

Eddie and Ward each grabbed a tome and began paging through them. After a moment they both looked up, confused. "What's this, then?"

"Haven't got a clue. Well—not much of one, anyway."

"You're not makin' sense, Stone. Where did these come from?" Eddie peered closer. "Wait a mo—I've seen these before, 'aven't I?"

"You both have. They're from Desmond's private collection. You looked at them shortly after you took over here, but didn't recognize the language. I've been keeping them in the vault because I didn't want anyone *else* looking at them who might work out what they are before we do." He'd been meaning to ask Kolinsky to take a look at them, but life got in the way and he'd forgotten.

Ward tilted his head. "Isn't that dangerous, though? Letting would-be necromancers peruse these books if we don't know their subjects? For all we know, they could *be* about necromancy."

"They're not," Eddie said. "That much I do remember. It's comin' back to me now. The closest we got with the translations had somethin' to do with herbalism, if I recall correctly."

Stone nodded. He took back the one from Ward and opened to the flyleaf, which contained a slip of paper. "I took down some notes at the time." He shrugged. "And remember—this is a long-dead magical language. The likelihood that anyone else is going to be able to make any sense of it is fairly low. At least not quickly. They might try to surreptitiously snap a few photos of the pages, but that's all right. If we catch them at it, it'll be an excuse to ask them a few questions."

Eddie appeared to be warming to the idea. "And besides, herbalism and necromancy are related. From what I remember from Brathwaite's notes, there's a lot of mixin' up of various potions and concoctions involved."

"Yes, exactly. We don't need to fool them for a long time—just long enough to work out who they are. I'm willing to bet a lot of money that anyone currently practicing necromancy has a connection to Brathwaite. It's not an easy art, and three years isn't *that* long when we're talking this level of magical study."

"It's unfortunate we can't associate it with another known necromancer," Ward said. "That might be more effective at luring him in."

"Yes, that's a good point. We—" Stone stopped, an electric tingle jolting up his back as another idea hit him. "Wait!"

"What?" They both looked at him quizzically.

"You two are both on fire tonight!" Stone knew how manic he must look, but he suddenly felt like a five-year-old trying to tell an exciting story—the words were in his head, but he was having trouble getting them out in a coherent order. "A known necro-mancer is a brilliant idea!"

"But we don't *know* any other necromancers," Eddie said. "At least I don't. You're probably right that 'e's trained some, but they keep their 'eads way down. I've never even 'eard rumors of such a thing."

"Yes, but that's because you're thinking in the present!" Stone grabbed one of the tomes and slammed it down on the table. "What about Burgess Crowther?"

"What?" Eddie looked at him like he'd gone mad. "Brathwaite's old rival from two hundred years ago?"

Ward didn't, though. A slow smile spread across his face. "You want to convince the magical community that more of Crowther's references have turned up."

"Exactly!" Stone flung himself back into his chair, pointing at the book. "It doesn't even *have* to be about necromancy! You're right—herbalism and necromancy are often in bed together, so it wouldn't even look suspicious. And anyway, since I'll wager my house that there isn't another mage out there who can translate more than a tenth of either of these tomes, all we have to do is con-vince them that they turned up in a collection associated with Crowther. That shouldn't be too hard, right?"

"You want to lure these necromancers in with the promise of more of Crowther's research? You don't honestly think Brathwaite himself would show up, do you?"

"Almost certainly not. He'd be a fool to do it. But he might ei-ther send someone else, or one of his necromancy students might pop in on their own, hoping to impress him—or gain an advantage over him—with this new knowledge."

"So then we identify them and either track them back to Brathwaite or…what?" Eddie started his question with confidence, but by the time he reached the end he was looking perplexed again.

"You don't want to grab 'em and question 'em, do you? That sounds way too dangerous."

"No, no, nothing of the sort." He pushed the book back across. "Just set it up, through whatever normal channels you use to tell people about new acquisitions."

"That's called an email list, mate." Eddie grinned. "Sometimes mundane methods are the easiest. What, you think we use owls or summat?"

Stone didn't favor that with an answer. "*Any*way, make some subtle reference to necromancy without coming right out and saying it. If you can work out how to do it while sounding a bit thick, like you don't realize what you've got, all the better. And make sure anyone who wants to look at the books needs to make an appointment and can only get a limited time with them."

"Don't worry your pretty 'ead, Stone. This kind of thing is what we're good at." Eddie patted the nearest book. "You leave that bit to us. But I gotta warn you, it might not be quick. It'll take us at least a few days to set this up, maybe longer, if you don't want it to look suspicious."

"That's fine. I've got two months to do the job, and I think once we find him, the actual deed won't be the long part." He sobered, looking at his friends again. "Before I go, though, I just want to remind you what you're signing on to. Even if you aren't actually going to be assisting with the final act, you're still complicit by helping me. If you're not comfortable with that—"

Eddie waved him off. "Don't worry, mate. You're right—I'm *not* completely comfortable with it. If it was anybody else but Brathwaite, I'd probably try to talk you out of it. But that bastard needs to die, right and proper this time. Far's I'm concerned, you're doin' the world a favor."

Stone could see he wasn't lying. Eddie and Ward were loyal as they came, but both of them were as stubborn as he was and true to their own consciences. "Ward? Is that how you feel, too?"

"It is." He took a deep breath, looking troubled, but then his expression settled into hard resolve. "And if you need help with the actual deed…please don't hesitate to ask."

That had to have been difficult for him to say. Stone swallowed hard. "It's okay, Ward. I appreciate it, but I don't think it's going to come to that. Your help—*both* your help—will be more valuable than you know. I couldn't do this without you. You know that, right? So…thank you."

"Yeah, yeah." Eddie was watching the screen again with the corner of his eye. "Glad to help. We'll ring you when we've got somethin'. Meantime, off you go so I can see the rest of this match. It looks like it's gonna be a real blinder."

CHAPTER FIVE

EDDIE AND WARD hadn't got back to Stone before Friday night, which didn't surprise him. This effort would require subtlety and care, so it couldn't be rushed.

Verity and Ian checked in with him to make sure he wasn't moving on without them, and he assured them both that he wasn't. He didn't tell them about the Caventhorne plan, since they could do nothing to help with it, but he did let them know he hoped to have something actionable in the next few days.

Great, Ian texted back. *I'll be in Paris with Gabriel until the end of the week, but we'll be near a portal.*

Stone thought about inviting Verity to his comeback gig with the Cardinal Sin, but before he could, she told him she had plans to go down to Los Angeles and hang out with Bron for the weekend. *You can come along if you want.* She said she and Nick would love to see you again.

He smiled. Verity and Bron must really have become good friends over the last three years, because Bron's extended family didn't have one of their many private portals in Los Angeles, so she'd have to fly there to visit. *That's all right,* he sent back. *You enjoy yourself. But stay reachable. If you want in on this, we'll likely need to move fast when things start happening.*

Don't worry. And I definitely want in.

The club the Sin was playing was a lot smaller than the venues they'd been getting toward the end of Stone's stint in the band. He didn't spend much time speculating about how much his absence might have contributed to that—his ego was massive when it came to magic, but not so much when it came to music—but he did notice how…cozy the place was when he nearly ran into three different tipsy patrons while trying to work his way toward the tiny stage in the rear.

"Hey, Stone!" Gerry Hook called from behind his drum kit, which he was trying to set up in a space barely large enough to contain it. He shifted from his crouch and nearly knocked his floor tom off the edge. "Long time no see, man!"

Radha Unger, the lead singer, broke into a big grin and hurried over to engulf Stone in a hug. "We've missed you. It's really good to have you back! And *damn,* dude, you look good. Do you even age?"

The third band member, bass player Jake Cohen, hung back, taking a swallow from his beer bottle. He waved to Stone, but it was clear he still hadn't quite forgiven him for deserting the group.

Stone wasn't worried about it. Jake was an easygoing guy and would come around once they started playing. Besides, he deserved what he got, considering he *had* left them in the lurch. "It's good to be back. I wouldn't have been surprised if you lot didn't want me back after what I did, but I'm glad you asked."

Radha leaned in and whispered conspiratorially, "I wouldn't take no for an answer. Dusty's a nice guy, but he had the stage presence of a slug in a salt pile."

Stone chuckled. "Gerry said as much—though not quite as colorfully. How have you been?"

"Eh, same old, mostly. Prisha is in college now, so we've just got the one kid at home. That's the other reason I'm glad you're back—maybe we'll get more gigs now, so I can occasionally do something that's not teaching, research, or picking up after a teenager." She eyed him curiously as he pulled his Strat from its case, plugged in, and began to tune it. "Any chance you might tell us where you were for three years? I know they said you were off doing research, but that's not very specific."

"That was part of it. The rest was…personal." He offered a rueful smile. "You'll see the research part in the papers I publish, if you want to bore yourself reading them."

"I guess I'll have to stay in the dark, then. I've got enough papers in my *own* field I have to read…and write." She patted his arm. "Anyway, hopefully you still remembered how to play, or this is going to be a short night. Good luck!"

Stone, of course, *did* remember how to play, since it had only been a few months—not three years and a few months—since he'd last performed with the Sin. He fell immediately into his onstage rapport with Radha, and before the first song ended, the two of them had the small audience cheering wildly.

The show was only one long set that night, so they didn't have a chance to rest or compare notes until the closing strains of their second encore rang out. Stone got the impression the others didn't expect to have even *one* encore, so they had to scramble a bit to identify a song for the second one. As the crowd's enthusiastic applause died out, they all reconvened in front of Hook's drum kit.

"That was amazing!" Radha said, puffing. She shoved her long, black hair off her sweaty forehead and grinned like an idiot. "I haven't felt that energized in a long time."

"Yeah, I gotta say, Stone, it's good to have you back," Jake said. "Radha's awesome, but even she couldn't pull in that kind of response on her own."

Or, more likely, with Dusty, Stone thought but didn't say. He'd never met the other guitarist, so he couldn't speculate on how much of tonight's success was due to his own return. It might have been that any competent musician could have done the job. Still, his body thrummed with adrenaline, his heart beating fast and his black T-shirt sticking to his back. "Come on—let's have a round or two. I'm buying, of course."

They adjourned to the bar after securing their instruments, and Stone instructed the bartender to keep the drinks coming.

Radha laughed. "You'll get off cheap—I'm only going to have one. Still have to get home and help my son with his homework."

"Yeah," Hook added. "Maybe you have a portrait moldering in some attic, Stone, but I'm not as young as I used to be. These shows always take a lot out of me. In a good way, but I still need a good night's sleep or I'm shit in the classroom the next day."

"So, you're saying nothing will have changed, then."

Hook punched him playfully in the arm. "Hey, at least I'm *in* the classroom, smartass. You planning to come back?"

"Haven't decided yet. I—" Stone trailed off as he glanced over Hook's shoulder into the crowd. Most of them were ignoring the band at this point—the Sin wasn't big enough that anyone cared to come hang out with them after shows—but one figure was watching him from a table at the far side of the room, near the front.

He tensed as he caught the figure's eye and recognition dawned.

He swung back around toward the band. "Er—would you lot mind if I stepped away for a few minutes? I think I see someone I know."

Hook waved him off. "Gonna take off soon anyway. Thanks for coming back, Stone. I'll be in touch about the next show."

Radha leaned over and gave him a casual kiss on the forehead, and Jake waved.

Stone half-expected the shadowy figure to be gone by the time he reached the table, but that didn't prove to be the case. He stopped next to the other chair. "Well. Agent Huxley. I didn't expect to see *you* tonight. Or at all, honestly."

Agent Renata "Ren" Huxley gave him a controlled, but nonetheless sincere, smile. "Hello, Dr. Stone. Nice set. I'd heard you were quite the axman, but none of us ever saw you in action."

"Ah, is that in my file too?"

"It is, actually. We even know you used to be in a band called *Fever Dream* when you were in college in the UK. Maybe you missed your calling."

Stone didn't answer. Once again, he wasn't happy to find out that some obscure government agency had stockpiled that much data on him, but at this point it wasn't as if he could do anything about it. "What can I do for you, Agent? I'd have expected if you needed to contact me about something, you'd use…more clandestine means."

"Eh, nobody around here knows what I look like, and even if they did, my cover is that I'm a marketing specialist for an obscure San Francisco tech company nobody gives a damn about. Have a seat if you want."

Stone did, looking her over as he set his beer glass down. She wore a buttoned shirt of deep maroon that complemented her dark skin, jeans, and a leather jacket of a slightly darker red. She definitely fit in with the crowd of thirty- and fortysomething Sin fans. He indicated her half-empty glass. "Want a refill?"

"No, thanks. Can't stay long."

"Is this a…professional visit, then?" He tensed a little. Last time he'd spoken with Huxley, he'd found out she represented the organization that had been keeping tabs on him, and other powerful mages, from the shadows. Together, they'd dealt with the situation in Rydell and Tuttleton, Oregon, but her partner had been killed in a bogus ritual sacrifice at the same time. She'd asked him if he might be willing to help out occasionally with jobs requiring a high level of magical expertise, since they did employ mages but not top-tier ones like him. He'd told her he'd consider it on a case-by-case basis. But right now, with the whole Brathwaite thing hanging over his head, wasn't a good time.

"It might be, if you're willing. I could use a little help with something."

"Oh? What sort of help? I'm a bit busy at present, but if it's only information you're looking for—"

"Information would definitely be appreciated, but there's a little more to it than that." She gestured, encompassing the bar. "You know that spell that prevents people from hearing us, right?"

He smiled. She *had* done her homework. She'd known about tracking rituals before, but everybody who knew anything about magic had heard of those. The 'cone of silence' spell was a bit more obscure, and definitely not universal among mages. "I do. Or we could, you know, just go somewhere a bit more private."

"Nah, this is fine. I trust your magic to keep any curious ears from listening in."

Intrigued in spite of himself, Stone figured it couldn't hurt to hear what she had to say. Under cover of reaching for his beer glass, he wove the simple spell around their table. Now, anyone who might try to eavesdrop would hear something that sounded like speech, but too muffled and unintelligible to make out. "There. Talk away."

She glanced around, almost as if trying to verify that no one was watching him, then leaned in closer like they were sharing a romantic conversation. "This is something Rick and I had been working on for a while." She dropped her gaze when she spoke her partner's name, and her fingers tightened around her glass.

"Did you get that situation all sorted?" he asked gently.

"Yeah. He wasn't married—wasn't even seeing anybody. A lot of us are like that—married to the job. Makes it easier when…things like this happen."

"But it's never easy. I get it. You have my condolences."

"Thanks." Her voice was rough. "Really. But this job never stops, and just because he's gone doesn't mean the case went away."

"Okay. As I said, I'll do what I can. Tell me what you need."

She took a healthy swallow and visibly returned to her no-nonsense demeanor. "I'm assuming you've heard of the Changelings."

Ah, so *that* was what this was about. "Of course. I'd be surprised if anyone familiar with the magical community hasn't, at this point. What about them?"

"Not *them*. A particular subset of them."

"Okay…" Stone leaned back and made a "go on" gesture. "What subset are we talking about?"

"Have you ever heard of Freakshow?"

"The movie?"

She glared. "No, not the movie. The group."

"Er…no. Don't think so. I assume by your context that they've got something to do with Changelings." Verity had told him a while back that some of the Changeling community, particularly the younger members, had taken on the identifier of "freaks" as a way to reclaim their power.

"Yeah. They've only popped up in the last couple of years. They're a…" She considered her words. "Some would call them a militant Changeling-advocacy organization. Others would call them domestic terrorists."

"I see." Stone kept his voice even. "And what would you call them?"

She sighed. "As usual when dealing with anything in the supernatural realm, it's…complicated."

"How so?"

"Well…for one thing, they're a scattered group, with cells in several major cities. They don't seem to have a lot of centralized organization. And they do a lot of good, given the difficulties they experience."

"Difficulties." Stone thought he knew what she meant, but he wanted to hear her side of the story.

"Come on, Stone, don't play dumb with me. You know exactly what I'm talking about."

Busted. "Okay, I suppose I do. It's hard to be an advocacy organization when nobody but other members of your group even believe you exist."

"Exactly. Every similar organization has something that's obvious to the world—or that they can *make* obvious. Ethnic or national groups, LGBT groups…hell, even sports fans and furries. But what are the Changelings supposed to do? They don't even have a lot in common with each other in a lot of cases, and they haven't got any way to reveal their true selves to anyone outside their groups even if they want to."

Stone nodded. "You believe they exist, then, even though you can't see them?"

"Yeah. Like I told you before, we've got a few mage agents in our organization, and they've given us enough information that it's hard not to believe, even though it sounds crazy." She shook her head. "But none of our mages are anywhere near your level. They're low Bs at best. You're familiar with the classification system, right?"

"I'm surprised *you* are."

She gave a bitter chuckle. "We hear things. A lot of things. The problem is, a lot of times we can't do much about them, other than gather information. We've had to let a surprising number of bad situations go by because we haven't got the firepower to handle them."

"So why not hire more A-level mages?" The classification nomenclature the magical community begun using while he was away still amused him. He pictured rows of mages in a classroom, diligently scribbling away at exam papers under the watchful eye of a dour old proctor.

Huxley snorted. "It's not that easy. In the first place, there *aren't* that many of them out there. Most of the ones we suspect are at the top level haven't even been assessed."

"Not surprising. We don't like to be classified. *I* haven't been assessed, and I don't plan to. I think the whole system is a bit rubbish, to be honest, but I suppose it's valuable for…" He let that trail off, not wanting to sound more pretentious than he already did.

"…for keeping track of the more garden-variety mages," she finished. "Yeah. But in any case, we take what we can get, and what we can get is a small group of fair-to-middling mages, most of whom were either self-taught or apprenticed to other mages not much higher up the pole than they were. They're good agents," she added hastily. "No knock on them. They're smart and capable. But they don't have the magical horsepower to deal with the most challenging cases."

"Hence why you're tapping me."

"Yeah."

Stone wasn't sure he liked that, either. "How many higher-ups at your little group know about what you're doing tonight? Did you have to get official sanction to go outside your normal procedure?"

She gave him a dirty look. "Listen, Stone—you might be a badass mage with a head as big as the Goodyear blimp, but you don't have to act like an asshole."

She had a point. "Okay, okay. I'm sorry. We *did* work together well on that last case, and I *did* tell you I was willing to help out if the case is interesting enough. But I was serious about being busy right now. I've got something else going on that's got to take higher priority."

"So you're saying you can't help?"

"I didn't say that. I'm waiting for some feelers to come back on the other thing, so I might have a bit of time to help you if it doesn't take too long. Just telling you, in the interest of full disclosure, that if there's a conflict between the two, mine will have to take precedence."

"I guess I can't argue with that."

"What do you want me to do about these Freakshow people? What have they done that's got you lot so worked up?"

"We think they're kidnapping children."

Stone snapped his head up. That was *not* what he'd expected to hear.

"We're not sure why yet. Needless to say, we haven't been able to infiltrate them."

"You haven't got any Changeling agents?"

"No."

"That's a bit of a surprise, given what we know about what brings on the Change. It's much more common in magical families. You knew that, right?"

"Yeah. Mundanes with magical heritage, but no arcane abilities. The kidnappings have only started happening recently, mostly in and around California."

"How do you know it's this group that's doing it?"

"We've managed to identify a few of their members. And one of them got caught on a security camera breaking into one of the houses where a kid was taken. They were careful, though—no prints, no identifying characteristics, except for an odd and unique way of moving."

Stone was intrigued, but he maintained his calm. "How old are these children?"

"The oldest is three. The youngest is six months. Needless to say, the parents are frantic."

"And the mundane police aren't able to get anywhere? I assume they were contacted first."

"They were, but they've got nothing. It's as if the kids have disappeared off the face of the Earth. No ransom demands, no bodies…" She spread her hands. "I don't know how much you've kept up on things when you disappeared, but a lot of Changelings are organizing in big cities—taking over areas, driving others out to create their own neighborhoods. Mostly they try to stay away from mundane society as much as they can, and most mundanes avoid them even though they haven't got any idea why. If Freakshow is trying to make some kind of statement, or get some concessions for their group, it doesn't make sense that they wouldn't provide demands."

"Could they have some issue with the children's families?"

"Not that any of us can dig up, but we haven't been able to put many people on the case. Remember back in Tuttleton, I told you we're a small organization? We've got a couple other bigger cases going right now, taking a good chunk of our manpower. We're working with local law enforcement, of course, but there's only so much they can help with since they don't know the whole story. That's part of why I came to you." She looked down. "I have kids of my own, Stone. I can't imagine how these parents must feel, with their kids gone and no information."

Stone nodded. "Have you tried tracking rituals? That would be the easiest way to find them, if they're still in the area. Your mages can do those, right? Changelings can't guard against them, unless they've got mages of their own."

"Oh, yeah, of course our mages can do that, and they have. Their ranges aren't large, but as far as they can tell, the kids aren't still in the cities where they were taken."

"So they're moving them. Interesting." Stone had the beginnings of a hypothesis forming, but he didn't want to share it with Huxley until he had better data. He also didn't want to split his concentration when he was already so focused on the Brathwaite business, but he couldn't deny he was intrigued by Huxley's problem. "All right, I'll help you. Give me what you have on the missing children, including things I can use as tether objects if you've got them, and a number where I can reach you."

She frowned. "I said I wanted *help*. Not for you to take over the case."

"I'm not taking over. But there are things I can do, and people I can talk to, that I don't care to divulge. You lot have enough dirt on me already, and I don't like that. If you want more, at least you'll have to work for it."

He met her gaze with a steady one of his own. "Do you want those kids found, Agent Huxley? If you've come to me for help, let me do what I'm good at." He looked around, coming up for air for the first time since he'd sat across from her. The rest of the Cardinal Sin were gone now, and the crowd had thinned out. "I've got to go now, but I promise I'll keep you updated with what I find." He stood. "Send me that information as soon as you can. It was good to see you again."

She looked at him as if she wasn't sure whether to growl at him or thank him. Finally, she settled for sighing. She took a card from her pocket and scribbled a phone number on it. "Good to see you too. I'll send the rest of the stuff over tomorrow. I hope you can figure this one out. I hate to admit we're stumped, but those kids are counting on us."

CHAPTER SIX

S TONE THOUGHT ABOUT CONTACTING VERITY to ask her if she'd ever heard of Freakshow, since she had a lot of Changeling friends. He'd pulled out his phone and was preparing to send the text when he remembered why she hadn't been at the Cardinal Sin show: she was down in Los Angeles with Bron. This probably wasn't a big enough deal to ask her to cut her weekend short—especially since he had a potentially better source closer at hand. One that stayed up late, even.

He tapped out another text and put together a late-night snack for Raider while he waited for a reply. As he expected, it came quickly.

Hey, Doc. You don't usually text this late. Something wrong?

Not wrong, but I'd like to chat if you have time.

Now? You want to call?

Honestly, I'd rather do it in person. It could be tomorrow if you've already settled in for the night.

LOL. If I go to bed before three a.m. on a weekend, something's wrong with me. I know what—I've got a burrito jones, and La Victoria on San Carlos is open late. Want to meet there?

Stone almost declined, but realized he *was* hungry. Playing gigs always did that, and his conversation with Huxley meant he hadn't shared his usual after-show bar nibbles with the band. *Sounds good.*

Half hour? Traffic's not bad this time of night.

See you there.

He drove down to San Jose instead of ley-line teleporting. On his way, he thought about Gina Rodriguez and how much her relationship with the team had changed over the years.

When Jason had first hired her as a receptionist for Thayer Investigations, Stone hadn't focused much on her. He'd considered her competent but flaky, her interests too far removed from his to consider her more than a casual work associate.

As she'd settled in to her job, though, both he and Jason had discovered she had other talents, which where potentially far more useful to the agency than answering phones and filing case data. Her computer and internet expertise, both legal and less so, had proven invaluable on several occasions to solving some of the cases the agency didn't include in its normal records. But she was a mundane, and neither Stone nor Jason had felt comfortable about revealing the supernatural world to her.

All that had changed (or rather, *Changed*) three years ago when Gina's astral form had transformed overnight from a couch-potato anime fan to a furry, pointy-eared cat. At that point, Stone no longer maintained his reservations about letting her in on the existence of magic. Her research during the early days of the Change had been instrumental to locating the source of the rift that had initiated the process.

In the three years Stone had been asleep, Gina had continued working for Jason, switching roles from receptionist to IT and records specialist. She'd also done something else, though, expanding on the time when she'd reached out to connect Changelings soon after the phenomenon had begun. Now, she was one of the premier Changeling activists and advocates in northern California, using the same skills she used to help the agency to assist Changelings in need and aid in dealing with flare-ups between them and the mundanes who had no idea what they were but sensed somehow that they were different—and potentially a threat.

In short, Gina knew lots of Changelings—a lot more than Verity did—and more importantly, she knew many of them at the fringes of society. As a whole, Changelings didn't trust mundanes, and they *definitely* didn't trust mages, so working with another of their own kind might be the only way Stone could locate more information about Freakshow.

He reached San Jose and cruised around until he spotted La Victoria Taqueria on San Carlos. Most of the other businesses around the area were already closed, but the restaurant's vivid red sign still glowed brightly against the yellow-and-green Victorian house.

Gina was waiting for him inside, munching on a burrito as big as her forearm, slathered with the restaurant's signature nuclear-orange sauce. She waved. "Hey, Doc. You must have lead-footed it pretty hard to get down here this fast."

Stone didn't deny it. He ordered a smaller burrito and a drink at the counter, then carried them over and took the seat across from her. "Thank you for seeing me tonight."

"Eh, don't worry about it. I always like to talk to you. You usually have interesting things to say."

"I think I might tonight. I need your help."

"Juicy computer problem? Need me to straighten out your taxes?"

"Er…no. Thank you." He took an experimental bite of the burrito, which turned out to be quite tasty. "Give me a moment—let me make sure no one overhears us."

The place was surprisingly crowded at this hour, probably attracting SJSU students and the throngs from theater productions, concerts, or sporting events that let out late. Stone made a small gesture, summoning the "cone of silence" spell around their table. "There. Now we can speak freely."

"Cool." She grinned. "Magic must be awesome."

"It…can be." He shifted briefly to magical sight, watching her shimmer from her normal human form to the black-furred cat. The grin looked a bit menacing on her fanged face, but her eyes still sparkled. He shifted back before speaking.

"I…need some information about Changelings," he said carefully, watching her for any reaction. Gina was quite passionate about Changeling causes, and had been known to get prickly if she thought anyone was trying to take advantage of her people.

"What kind of information?" She spoke as cautiously as he did.

"Have you ever heard of an organization that calls itself 'Freakshow'?"

She tensed. "Why?"

For a moment, Stone hesitated. He hadn't considered the possibility that Gina might not just *know* about Freakshow, but actually be a member. "Just curious."

She shook her head, looking serious. "No, you're not. Don't lie, Doc—your nose will grow. Nobody is 'just curious' about Freakshow. If you even know who they are, you've got a reason."

Her Change obviously hadn't done anything to lessen her intellect, and her cat senses probably helped her tune in even more deeply to subtle changes in a conversation. He sighed. "Yes, I've got a reason. Can you tell me anything about them?"

There was a long pause. She took another big bite of her burrito and chewed deliberately, watching him the whole time. She swallowed, washed the bite down with a slug from her oversized soda, and regarded him seriously. "They're an activist organization for Changelings."

"I knew that much. Gina, I need to ask you a question, and I'd like you to answer me honestly. It's very important."

She snorted. "Why do you need me to cooperate? You can tell, I know you can. With that sight thing you mages do."

"I can tell, but I won't. We're friends. I trust you. I've trusted you with a lot of secrets about me, and you haven't betrayed me. I promise, I won't use my Sight to check up on you. So…will you give me an honest answer?"

"Maybe. Depends on the question. I'm not going to put any of my friends in danger."

"I wouldn't ask you to do that." He set his burrito down and leaned forward, meeting her gaze. "Gina—are you a member of Freakshow?"

Her shoulders relaxed, as if that hadn't been the question she'd been expecting. "No."

He watched her a moment, then nodded. "Okay. Thank you."

"I do know some of them, though. Casually. We don't hang out at each other's houses or anything, but I've met them at parties and meetups. What about them?"

"Can you tell me anything about them? The organization, I mean, not your friends?"

"And I ask again: why?"

"I'd like you to believe me, that I've got a good reason. I'll tell you what it is, or at least part of it, after you've answered my question."

She tilted her head. "You're trying to feel me out on this, aren't you? They've done something, and you want to find out my opinion on them before you let anything slip."

There was no point in denying it. "That's exactly right. This is sensitive information, and depending on your answer, I'll have to decide how much I want to tell you—just as you'll have to decide how much you want to tell me."

She paused again, dipping the end of the burrito in the orange sauce and taking another leisurely bite. Finally, she set it down and didn't look at him. "I don't know that much, really. Honestly, they scare me a little."

"Why is that?"

"They take things too far. I mean, I'm an activist. I fight for Changeling rights, which is hard to do since we can't even prove we exist. I help folks in trouble—you know, making sure they can get food, find housing, that kind of thing. A lot of us do that."

"But Freakshow don't?"

"Well, yeah, they do. But they do other things, too."

"What sort of other things?"

She still didn't look at him. "Hassling mundanes…sometimes even low-powered mages. Busting up mundane businesses to drive them out of Changeling areas. Threatening people to get them to do what they want."

"Sounds like a terrorist organization," Stone said with care.

Her eyes came up flashing. "Don't use the T word, Doc. That's not what they're about. They just want to get what they feel they deserve. But maybe some of them go too far with it, you know?" She looked back down at her basket. "There's another thing about Freakshow, that kind of makes me understand them a little more. You know, why they do what they do, and why they think they're justified in doing it."

"What's that?"

"They aren't just Changelings in general. How much do you know about our society, Doc? When you were away for three years, did you keep up with it at all?"

"Not…really. Where I was, there weren't any Changelings."

"I wonder where *that* could be. We're all over the world now. But anyway, don't jump on me if I'm telling you something you already know. Have you heard about how we've…split up, I guess, even among our own people?"

Stone remembered something Verity had told him the night they'd encountered the Changeling-based riot in San Francisco. "You mean how the so-called 'prettier' Changelings tend to feel they're better than the so-called 'ugly' ones?"

She looked miserable. "Yeah. It sucks, by me. I mean, I'm considered one of the good-looking ones, since everybody likes cats. I've got Changeling privilege, which is why I can do what I do…mostly. But I certainly don't think that makes me better than anybody else."

"But some Changelings do," Stone said soberly.

"Yeah. Quite a few of them do, actually. Which would you rather be, a cat person or an elf or a sexy satyr, or a frog-looking guy, somebody covered with chunks of rock, or a goblin?"

Stone honestly would have preferred none of the above, but he didn't say so. He waited for her to continue.

She didn't appear to notice his lack of response. "We've actually got it going from both sides, which makes it worse. The pretty ones lord it over the ugly ones, and the ugly ones have sort of banded together for a kind of 'ugly pride' thing. Nobody wants to feel like an outcast."

"Of course not." He'd forgotten about his food now. "I think I see where you're going with this. The so-called 'ugly ones' have formed their own organization within the Changelings, and they feel they're justified in causing mayhem because no one treats them with any respect."

"Not even most of their own people, yeah." Gina definitely didn't look happy about it. "Freakshow's only been around for the last year and a half or so, but they're growing. Mostly, they still just want to be left alone, but you know how it can be. Somebody charismatic shows up and starts putting ideas in their heads, and then things can go wrong in a hurry."

"Is that what's happened? They've got someone leading them to do these things?"

Her gaze sharpened. "What things? Remember, you said you'd tell me why you wanted to know if I told you about them. Now's the time for you to trust *me,* Doc."

"Okay. Fair enough. You're right." He hoped he wasn't doing the wrong thing. He hadn't interacted much with Gina since he'd returned, but Jason and Verity still trusted her, so that had to amount to something. And more importantly, *he* still trusted her.

"I can't tell you where I've got this information from," he said. "But I promise you, it's a reliable source. I've been asked to help look into allegations that Freakshow has been…kidnapping children."

Her eyes got big. "No way."

"I'm afraid so. Young children, I'm told. The oldest is three, the youngest six months."

"How many are we talking about here?"

"Don't know yet. I'll be getting more details tomorrow. But it's happening mostly around California."

"And whoever told you about this thinks Freakshow is behind it?"

Stone inclined his head. "They're fairly sure it's Changelings, and apparently one of their known members was caught on a security camera entering one of the children's houses."

She let her breath out, staring into the remains of her burrito. "Wow. That's…bad. Does whoever this is know what they're doing with the kids? Are they asking for ransoms? Or…" She let it trail off, her meaning obvious.

"—or killing them? No. At least not as far as my source is aware. There've definitely been no ransom demands, and if Freakshow is hurting the children, none of them have been found yet."

"But it doesn't make any sense. What would they *gain* from it?" She stared off into space, thinking hard. "I told you—Freakshow is an activist organization. Their whole purpose is to get justice for Changelings, especially the ugly ones. I mean, yeah, they'll hurt people if they think it will advance their cause. But they're not evil,

Doc. They feel like they're justified in what they're doing, even if I don't agree with their methods. But hurting *kids?*"

"We don't know they've hurt anyone yet," he pointed out. "As I said, we've got no evidence beyond that the children have been taken, and one video image of the person who did it."

Her gaze sharpened. "Who are these people who told you this? Who are you working with? Some kind of law-enforcement organization?"

"I can't say—not specifically, at least. Yes, they are law enforcement, but not the normal type."

"Not police."

"No."

She pondered, still picking at the remains of her burrito. "So…some kind of underground organization, then. Are they related to your world?"

There she was, being quick-witted again. "Yes. *Our* world."

"What do they want?" Her voice picked up a faint growl. "What's their stance on Changelings?"

"I honestly don't know." He realized it was true—he had no idea where Renata Huxley and the rest of her groups stood on Changelings. "I need to ask more questions."

"It sounds like you do. I can't—*won't* help you until I know what their plans are. If they want to round up Freakshow people and throw them in jail, I won't help with that. I told you before—I don't know that many of them, but the few I've talked to didn't seem like the type who'd snatch kids. And even though we disagree on methods, they do a lot of good work."

Stone privately wondered what that "type" was. Maybe he was getting even more cynical as he got older, but he'd seen too many horrific acts committed by people he'd never suspect to believe anyone was immune. Everybody had their breaking point. But that line of thinking wouldn't get him anywhere with Gina—especially since he didn't have all the facts yet.

"No, I don't expect you to help me with that. I don't think these people are after Freakshow as a group—only the ones who've been kidnapping the children. They want to find out what's happened, why they're doing it, and above all return the children safe and well to their parents."

Her intensity notched down a bit. "Yeah," she said with a sigh. "That sounds like what we'd all want. So, what do you want me to do?"

He thought about it, realizing he didn't have a plan. "I'm not sure I can answer that yet. I don't know enough about Freakshow, Changelings in general, or this situation to offer a viable plan."

Surprisingly, she smiled. "That's what I like about you, Doc. You have an enormous ego, but you're not afraid to admit when you're in over your head. You'd be surprised at how many people a lot less smart than you are would never do that."

"No, actually I wouldn't. But I can't learn anything if I don't keep my mind open to new data."

"Exactly." She finished her burrito and wadded the wrapper into a tight ball. "Tell you what I'll do for now, while I wait for you to get back to me with more information. I'm tied in to a lot of the Changelings' online presence, including a couple of places where Freakshow hangs out. I'll send out a few queries and see if I can come up with anything. But I'm not telling you anything about what I find until I know what these people's plans are."

Stone, as usual, hadn't thought about the online aspect. He was competent with technology and hardly a Luddite, but every time he talked with Gina he was reminded of how much of the online world he had no clue about—sort of like mundanes and magic. Apparently, the Changelings had taken to the online world more than mages had. It made sense, especially for the "ugly" ones who preferred to interact with the world without being seen. "That's all I can ask for. In the meantime, I'll try to prod my source for more data I can pass along." He stood. "Thank you, Gina. You've given me a lot to think about."

"I'm glad to hear it. I know most of us don't like mages, and with good reason. But you're okay. Hell, you and Verity and Eddie and Ward are all okay. Maybe there's hope yet."

CHAPTER SEVEN

LATE THE FOLLOWING MORNING, Stone called the number Renata Huxley had given him. It reached voicemail, which responded with an impersonal, electronic-sounding "Leave a message."

"It's me," he told it. "We chatted last night. Call me."

While he waited for her to get back to him, he popped over to Caventhorne to find Eddie. His friend had told him before that he wouldn't recognize the place; he'd been so focused on his business before that he hadn't noticed, but now he saw what Eddie was talking about. At a little after seven p.m., the house's halls were crowded with magical scholars from all over the globe. He walked past several of them seated at tables in some of the larger halls, and nodded to a few he recognized who were going from one smaller room to another. With a twinge of grief, he wondered what William Desmond would have thought about this new use his home had been put to. He'd had a vision of Caventhorne as a world-class magical resource center, and Eddie and Ward, along with Kerrick, had made it happen. He hoped Desmond would be pleased, and proud.

He found Eddie in one of the private chambers, surrounded by drifts of papers, three different laptops, and a whiteboard scribbled with magical sigils.

"You look busy," he said. "Tell me you've got something for me about Brathwaite."

Eddie jerked his head up, looking frazzled. "Evenin', Stone. You should've texted—I could've saved you a trip. Nothin' yet, but we've got a few irons in the fire. The bait's out there, so we're just waitin' for somebody to bite."

"Where's Ward?"

"I sent 'im 'ome to rest for a bit. Don't worry, though, 'e'll be back at it by tomorrow."

"I'm not worried. I'm hoping *you're* resting as well. Seriously, Eddie, don't wear yourself out over this."

"It's a good challenge, and we're on a timetable. B'sides, you know me—I thrive on this sorta thing, even more than Ward does."

Stone couldn't argue with that. He'd seen it in action too many times before in the past. "So, what did you end up using as the bait?"

Eddie grinned. "I put out a call on a few of our special channels—the ones the serious scholars frequent—sayin' we've acquired these new reference books we can't translate. I mentioned we think they've got summat to do with herbalism, and also that we found a 'alf-readable name: first initial *B* or *R* or *F*, last name Crowley, or Crowder, or somethin' similar. I figure since we never publicized that we're even aware of Burgess Crowther's existence, it might be enough to tweak somebody's curiosity without lookin' too suspicious." His expression grew serious. "Only thing is, it'd probably be best if you stayed well away from this one, Stone. At least until we've hooked a fish."

"Why is that?"

"Brathwaite knows *you* know about Crowther, right?"

"Damn. Yes. Verity, too. But it's reasonable to assume he knows I'm connected with Caventhorne, as well. Do you think he'll catch on?"

Eddie shrugged. "Eh, I dunno. 'E's bright, yeah, but it's also been three years since you've been seen, and you've been keepin' a low profile since you got back. 'E might not even know you've surfaced again. I'd say 'e's probably got more pressing concerns by now, as long as you don't turn up in the middle o' things."

"Good point. Well, keep me up to date—especially if someone bites."

"I will. We've already got a special room prepared for anyone who wants some time with the books."

"Special?" Stone frowned. "If you've set up anything magical, they might catch on. I'm sure Brathwaite won't risk showing up himself, but he'll probably send some strong magical talents."

"Oh, ye of little faith." Eddie's grin grew even wider than before. He patted Stone's shoulder. "What are most strong mages—especially old-style ones like Brathwaite's lot—sorely lacking in?"

Stone thought about it and almost said he didn't know, but then nodded. "Technological knowledge."

"Bingo. Even you, mate—you're better than most, but there's still a lotta stuff you 'aven't got a clue about. I'm countin' on that bein' true for that lot as well."

"You've got the place wired."

"Indeed we do. We've got 'idden cameras—over'ead view of the table, all four sides so we can get good views of their faces, concealed microphones, the whole nine yards. Plus, we'll be ready to grab any potential ritual samples they leave behind: stray hairs, sweat, anythin' like that. *And,*" he added with a flourish, "Ward's also got a law-enforcement contact who might be able to run prints for us, if they leave any. Though there's not much 'ope of that, honestly. Any scholar worth 'is salt will expect us to make 'em wear gloves while 'andlin' old tomes like that. They'll get suspicious if we don't."

"Still, it sounds like you've got this well in hand. I'm impressed, Eddie. I can see I put the right men on this job."

Eddie preened. "Thank you, thank you. But don't 'eap on too much praise until we've actually got you somethin' you can use."

When Stone returned home an hour later and checked his email, he found one from an unknown sender. At the top was a single link. The only other text was "Enjoyed the show last night. Thought you might enjoy these photos, and be sure to pass the word on to the others. Especially your lead singer. She's amazing."

Stone clicked the link, which took him to a page containing a single folder. When he clicked on that, a box popped up: *Password?*

He frowned a moment. Huxley hadn't given him a password.

Or had she?

Smiling, he tapped in *RadhaUnger.*

The box disappeared, and the folder downloaded to his laptop.

Feeling like an extra in a spy movie, he clicked the folder. Files popped up, including several photos, a video clip, a couple documents, and one text file labeled READMEFIRST. He clicked on that one.

> *Here's what we have. This is information about the missing kids including photos, the video clip I told you about of the suspected FS member, somebody who goes by Squeak, and some other data you might find useful. If you get anything, contact me. R.*

He started with the video clip. It had been taken at night, and although it included a fairly clear shot of the kidnapper as they passed across the camera's field of view, it was obvious the person had been careful about being identified. It wasn't even possible to tell if it was a man or a woman. Tall and gangly, they wore an over-sized hoodie, baggy jeans, and gloves. When they turned slightly so part of their face was visible, Stone saw they were wearing a mask.

He'd have agreed with Huxley that there was nothing identifiable in the video, except he immediately saw what she meant about an "odd and unique way of moving." He ran the clip again, watching more closely. Though tall, the person seemed to be trying to minimize their height. They crept across the screen hunched over, with a lurching, almost rat-like gait. He was certain he could identify it if he saw it again—but that still didn't help much. Maybe Gina had a better idea.

He put the video aside and looked at the other files. There were six photos, each one with a matching file containing data about a kidnapped child. As Huxley had said, the children ranged from six months to three years old. Four were girls and two boys. They didn't seem to have much in common: two were white, one black, one South Asian, and two Latino. Socioeconomically, they were all over the map, too: the two-year old black child was the son of a successful attorney and a corporate finance manager; one of the white children and one Latino came from poverty, while the remaining three kids were middle-class. They were *literally* all over the map geographically: two from the Los Angeles area, one from the Central Valley, two from the Bay Area, and one from the suburbs of San Diego.

Stone scanned the files several times, growing more frustrated. He'd picked up a few investigation skills from Jason, and one of them was to look for commonalities among victims. These had none, beyond living in California and being very young children. He wasn't even sure all of them had been kidnapped by the same person.

"Let's think about this from a different angle," he told Raider, who'd jumped onto his desk and was sitting primly next to the laptop. "Given what we know about Freakshow from Gina, *why* would they want to kidnap these children?"

The best answer he could come up with was that Freakshow, or some member of it, had an issue with the children's parents. He looked at the files again, but nothing stood out there either. Perhaps the organization had run afoul of the attorney, but it appeared she was in fashion-industry law—hardly the kind of thing your average person would encounter. The other parents' occupations were equally uninspiring: mail carrier, unemployed bartender, shop worker, stay-at-home mother, seamstress.

Was there any chance, assuming all the kidnappings were even related, that some of them were diversions? That the unknown kidnapper's target had been one of the kids, but they'd taken the others to hide their tracks? It seemed odd to him that the kidnapper would range out as far as they had, too. If the kidnappings were all intended, that implied there was something rare or unusual about the children or their parents. Something that didn't occur very often.

Something that doesn't occur very often…

A sudden idea struck, jerking him back in his chair. He snatched up his phone and hit Huxley's number again. When the robotic voicemail message answered, he said, "Call me. I've had an idea, and I want to run it by you."

This time, she called back in a few minutes. "You got the files, I take it?"

"Yes, and I had a thought."

"Let's hear it. This case is frustrating—especially because we can't afford to assign many resources to it until we get a couple other ones put to bed."

"First, let me ask *you* a question. How do you know these kidnappings are related? I saw nothing in common between them, other than approximate age. Different locations, different races, different life circumstances. And you've only got the one video clip, right?"

She sighed. "Yeah. I know. The truth is, we *aren't* sure they're related. But call it a strong hunch. Most of the time when a child that young is kidnapped, it's a relative or family friend. You know, non-custodial parents, creepy uncles, someone jealous of the baby—that kind of thing. They usually get caught fairly quickly, because that kind of person doesn't have the skills to pull off a crime like that. Or else…"

"…or else the child is found dead," Stone finished.

"Yeah. And if that's not the case, the other situations are usually either ransom demands or somebody trying to coerce the parents into doing something. But as I told you, we've had nothing like that. The kids and the kidnappers are in the wind, with no traces of how they got in or out, no fingerprints, nothing. Which in and of itself might suggest supernatural involvement. Anyway, what's your idea?"

"I was getting quite frustrated, because I didn't see any potential similarities between the victims or their families. But am I wrong in thinking that, if the kidnappings *are* related, it's odd that they're spread out over such a large geographical area?"

"Maybe so. I mean, if Freakshow is behind them, they're all over the place. They're not a big organization, but they have cells all around the country."

"Which brings us back to *why* Freakshow is interested in these children. If they're spread out that much, I though perhaps it might mean whatever it is they're looking for is rare or unusual."

There was a long pause. Then, Huxley whispered, "Fuck."

"You see where I'm going, don't you?"

"I think I might. You're thinking the kids might be Changelings."

"Exactly. The oldest is three, which suggests they're targeting children too young to talk—or at least too young for anyone to believe them when they say they're really wolves or lizards or whatever."

"Fuck…" she said again. "I'm kicking myself because I didn't think of that."

"Don't beat yourself up over it too much. You've had a lot on your mind, and Changelings are still relatively new. You said you don't have any Changeling agents—has anyone with magical talent talked to the parents? Are any of *them* Changelings?"

"I'll have to check, but I'm thinking not. We were mostly focused on the angle of Freakshow having something against one or more of the parents." She paused. "But it still doesn't make sense. Why would they target Changeling kids?"

"Don't know yet. Don't even know if that's what's going on. We're still looking at quite a lot of speculation. But it's another lead to pursue."

"Yeah." Her voice suddenly sounded odd, as if an uncomfortable thought had occurred to her.

"Something wrong?"

"No, nothing wrong. I'm just frustrated that I can't do more on this. If you're right and they *are* kidnapping Changelings, we can't even expect much help from local law enforcement. They'll do what they can, but they don't even know what they're looking for, and we can't tell them. And as far as our agency goes…this case is pretty much me and a couple of others." She gave a bitter chuckle. "You might think we're some big monolithic agency, Stone, but that's our secret: we're tiny, not very well funded, and even some of the people funding us don't entirely believe what we're doing. We're great at research, but field work can sometimes be a challenge."

"So you're saying you don't think your people can move fast enough on this."

"Yeah. But that's not your problem. I know you said you had some other stuff going on. I appreciate your help, and even the suggestion we might be looking for Changeling kids is more than we had. So, thanks for that."

Stone wasn't sure he wanted to say what he had in mind, but that didn't mean he wasn't going to. Huxley's case had intrigued him now, which meant there was no way he wouldn't see it through—at least as long as it didn't interfere with his search for Brathwaite. "Agent Huxley…"

"I keep telling you—call me Ren."

"Ren. I wonder if I might be able to help you a bit more."

"How? I thought you didn't want to be involved."

"Yes, well, I assume my file includes notes on my pathological curiosity."

"You could say that, yeah," she said, amused.

"How would you feel about my bringing in a few more resources?"

"What kind of resources?" The amusement turned to suspicion.

"Some friends who are uniquely suited to this sort of thing. I assume you've got dossiers on all my associates as well."

"Are you talking about Jason Thayer, the PI?"

"Him, yes. And my former apprentice, Verity Thayer…and one other person I won't name, but who has connections to the Changeling community. Full disclosure, I've already contacted this person to ask about Freakshow, and they've given me some valuable information."

Long pause. "You sure you trust this person? I'm assuming they're a Changeling, since not too many people who aren't have ties to that bunch."

"They are, yes. And I trust them implicitly. I've worked with them before."

Even longer pause. "I'm not sure I like it…but I'm not sure I have a choice, either, if we want to get this solved and these kids back where they belong. Just don't say anything about us and our involvement. You haven't already, have you?"

"Not…in specific terms. Some of them know about the existence of your agency, though. They have since the auction in San Francisco a few years back."

"Auction…oh, yeah, right. I heard about that. That pyramid thing never did turn up, did it?"

"No comment."

"Damn it, Stone, you're irritating sometimes."

"I am. But I can also help you, if you're willing to put up with a bit of irritation."

She sighed. "Fine. You can bring your people in, as long as they're discreet. And we're not payin' them."

"Wait…you're paying *me?*"

"Depends on how official you want to be in your consulting work."

"Yes, well…let's keep it off the books, then, shall we? I'm not exactly worried about where my next meal is coming from."

CHAPTER EIGHT

STONE WAS RELIEVED he could get Jason involved in the kid-napping case. It helped assuage a bit of his guilt about keeping him in the dark about the Brathwaite situation. He texted his friend after he got off the phone with Huxley: *I've got an investigation I could use your help with. Are you free?*

Jason answered after a few minutes: *What kind of investigation? How urgent?*

Are you busy?

The dots cycled. *We're at Gilroy Gardens with Amber and the kids. If you need me, though…*

Ah. It wasn't the first time he'd forgotten that Jason's newfound parenthood came with a lot more demands on his free time, especially on weekends. *No, it's fine. We can discuss it later.*

Want to come by for dinner tonight? We can talk then if you want.

He wasn't sure he was ready for the chaos that was evening dinner with two small children, but Jason and Amber's help would be too valuable to miss out on and he didn't want to wait until Monday. *Sure. What time?*

Depends. We eat earlier now with the kids, but if you want to come by later and don't mind eating leftover spaghetti, you can come at seven and they'll be in bed.

He sighed. Funny how big changes, like the emergence of the Changelings, had less effect on his day-to-day life than one of his best friends becoming a father. *I'll come at seven. And never mind the leftovers. I'll pick up some takeaway on the way home after.*

You sure?

Quite sure. Do you mind if I invite Gina?

This has to do with Gina?

Yes, very much so.

Sure, go ahead. You've got us curious now. Gotta go, though. Jaden's trying to climb a tree. See you tonight!

"I've never been out here," Gina said as Stone pulled the black BMW up the long driveway toward Jason and Amber's house in the Santa Cruz mountains. "They invited me a couple times, but my car's a little wonky and I don't trust it out here in the sticks."

She'd eagerly agreed to come along when he'd called earlier that day to invite her, especially after he'd told her he had more information about the Freakshow case and was willing to give her a ride.

"I don't know how much I want to get involved in this," she'd said dubiously, "but I'll help out as long as I don't have to put anybody at risk. Except the kidnappers, anyway."

"That's all I'm asking," he'd assured her. He hadn't updated her on any of the new information, figuring it would be easier to tell everyone at once.

Jason appeared in the doorway when they pulled up. "Hey, you two." He wore jeans and an untucked blue T-shirt. "Glad you could make it. Amber will be along in a minute—she's giving Jaden his bath and putting him to bed."

"Unca Alicer!" shrieked a voice from behind him. A small, pajama-clad form rocketed past Jason and slammed into Stone, flinging her arms around his legs.

"Er—" Stone looked down, alarmed. She wasn't heavy enough to knock him off balance, but he was afraid if he moved, he might knock *her* off balance.

Gina burst out laughing, reaching into her pocket. "Oh, this I gotta get a pic of!"

"No photos!" Stone snapped. Then he turned his attention back to the little girl and softened his tone. "Hello, Alice. It's good to see you. Perhaps your father could—"

"Sorry." Jason didn't seem terribly sorry, though, as he stifled a grin. "Come on, kiddo. Uncle Alastair's not a hugger."

The little girl showed no signs of letting go. Instead, she tipped her head to look up at Stone with wide-eyed excitement. "We went to Gilly Garden today! We went on rides and ate corn dogs and saw big trees and Jaden tried to climb one! Do you like corn dogs? Can you climb trees? Do you want to see my new dolly?"

"Er…" Stone had no idea what to say. Which was all right, because Alice was talking so fast he wouldn't have gotten a word in anyway.

Gina was laughing uproariously, wiping tears from her eyes. "Oh, man, this was worth the drive out here, all by itself!"

Jason grabbed Alice under her arms and gently but firmly pulled her free from Stone. "Alice, we talked about this, remember? It's bedtime."

"Don't *wanna* go to bed! Wanna play with Unca Alicer!" She began to wail, reaching her little arms out toward Stone.

Jason slung her over his shoulder, bouncing her playfully. "It's not playtime right now. You had a big day today. You've had your bath, and now it's time for bed." His voice was firm but kind. With an apologetic glance over his shoulder at Stone, he carried Alice out of the room. Her wails faded away as he disappeared down the hallway.

Gina grinned at Stone. "Wow. You *really* don't know what to do around kids, do you? It's not just a big curmudgeon act."

"It's not an act. I haven't been around small children since I was one myself—and even then, I wasn't terribly comfortable around other ones. I didn't even meet any other children until I got to boarding school. Before that, I had nannies and tutors at home."

She waved her hand airily. "Oh, I *see*. Little Lord Fauntleroy at the manor house. Why does that not surprise me? Though I can't quite picture you in one of those little velvet suits with short pants and a lace collar."

Stone sighed.

She patted him on the arm. "Come on, I'm just messin' with you. And anyway, you just have to roll with kids. They're fun, but you can't be all grown-up and pretentious around them. They see through that right away."

"I am not pretentious." He glanced down the hall, hoping Jason would return soon. "And it's not that I don't like them—those two, anyway. Not liking someone and not being comfortable around them are two different things."

She was still grinning. "Yeah, sure, Doc. Keep believing that."

Jason returned a few minutes later, looking frazzled but resolute. "Sorry about that. She got really wound up today—both of them did—and having you come over was a big deal. She's in bed now, and Amber should be out in a minute." He took a deep breath, let it out, and squared his shoulders. "Anyway. Good to see you two. Finally made it out here, huh, Gina?"

"Yeah, well, I'm curious about what this is about, and Doc drove so I don't have to worry about breaking down halfway over the mountain."

"C'mon out to the living room where we can be comfortable. You want anything? We do have leftover spaghetti if you're hungry. With meatballs, even."

"Thank you, no," Stone said. "But a glass of wine or a beer would be nice."

Gina, however, perked up. "I will never turn down free food. I'll take you up on that."

By the time Amber showed up, her shirt damp and her hair in disarray, Gina was chowing down on a big plate of spaghetti and Stone had settled back in his chair with a glass of red wine.

"Hey, you two," Amber said. "Thanks for coming over. It's a little harder for us to get out these days, as you might be aware." She took a seat next to Jason. "What do you need our help with, Alastair?"

"And what's it got to do with Gina?" Jason asked. "Is this a Changeling thing?"

"It is." He'd already thought about how much he wanted to tell them, so he launched immediately into his story. "Remember the people we saw at the auction three years ago? The ones Verity called 'Dad Bod' and 'Redhead'?"

Jason frowned. "Yeah, of course. They were some kind of agents with a secret organization. Are they botherin' you again?"

"No. I haven't seen them since around that same time. But I *have* encountered another one, working for the same agency."

"No shit? Where?"

"I can't give you the details, but it was recent."

"Since you…got back?"

"Yes, just after. You were busy at the time with a case, so I didn't involve you. I worked with her to deal with a…dangerous situation. In exchange, she told me a bit more about her organization." He gave them a brief overview of what Renata Huxley had shared with him.

"Makes sense," Amber said, nodding. "There's a lot of crazy magical stuff going on out there—it only stands to reason that some of the mundanes would catch on and want in on the party."

"So you *helped* her?" Jason asked. "With some problem having to do with Changelings?"

"No, not last time. But their organization is small and perpetually thinly spread, so she asked me if I might be willing to consult on an occasional case that eluded them. They apparently have a few mages in their employ, but not…"

"Not any badass ones like you," Gina finished.

"Well…yes, if you want to put it that way."

"So, she took you up on the consulting thing, and this time it *does* have to do with Changelings?" Amber asked.

"Yes. Exactly. And I've secured her permission to bring in some knowledgeable friends—that would be you—to assist me if you'd be willing."

Jason flicked his gaze to Gina. "You already know about this, don't you?"

"Some. He's asked me a few questions, but I still don't have the whole story. I assume that's why I'm here tonight."

"Exactly."

"What are the Changelings doing?" Jason put his arm around Amber, pulling her close.

"Kidnapping young children."

Amber's eyes widened, and she exchanged a quick glance with Jason. Both of them immediately looked toward the hallway, down which their own two children were asleep. "Why would they do that? Do you know?"

"Not yet." He gave them most of the details he'd learned from Huxley, and the discussion he'd had with Gina the previous night, with Gina herself filling in spots he missed.

"That's…scary," Jason said, looking grim. "So they're taking these kids and disappearing. No ransom demands or extortion or anything, and nobody's found any of the kids?"

"Yes. And I've got some new potential information since we last spoke, Gina." He swept his gaze around the three of them. "A current working theory is that the children who were taken might be Changelings too."

"*What*?" Amber clenched her fists, and a bit of her bearish heritage showed on her face. "How do you know that? Are their parents Changelings?"

"No. But I was trying to work out why the kidnappers would be interested in six children with nothing else in common—geography, socioeconomic status, no common friends or relatives. I thought perhaps the thing they had in common might be rare, which is what led me to that thought."

"It makes sense," Gina mused. "I mean, if they're too young to talk, they can't exactly tell Mom and Dad they look like cats or lizards or goblins."

"Or they can," Stone added, thinking of Alice's nonstop jabbering, "but no one would believe them because children that age are always making up fanciful stories."

"But what do they *want* with them?" Jason asked, addressing Gina more than Stone. "Why would Changelings kidnap other Changelings?"

"And what about these Freakshow people?" Amber said. "Alastair, you make them sound like they're some kind of Changeling terrorists."

Stone glanced at Gina, who was already looking angry. "Not terrorists, necessarily," he said hastily. "They're activists at the more extreme end of the spectrum, but Gina says she hasn't heard of them doing anything as serious as kidnapping."

"Yeah," Gina growled. "I've been doing a bit more research since Doc and I talked last night. I checked in with a couple of people I know are connected with them and asked a few careful questions."

"Did you tell them about the kidnappings?" Stone asked.

"Not in so many words, but I did prod a little about what kinds of stuff they might be willing to do. I can get away with that, since I kind of straddle the line between the Changelings who just want to be left alone in peace and the ones who want to agitate the masses."

She popped another meatball in her mouth. "The thing is, the worst these guys have heard of is a few skirmishes at the edges of Changeling and mundane territory, a couple of bricks tossed through windows, and two or three strongarm extortion attempts. Not great, sure, but the people I talked to seemed pretty adamant that they wouldn't do anything really extreme unless there was a good reason."

"Kinda makes you wonder what they'd consider a good reason," Jason muttered.

"Let's put that aside for a moment," Stone said. "Gina, I forgot about something you said the other night—we got off track and I didn't pursue it. But you mentioned that most of the so-called 'ugly' Changelings—"

"Just call them ugly, Doc. It's okay. They're not here, and anyway most of them have kind of taken the word on as a pride thing, sort of like calling themselves 'freaks.'"

"All right, then—you said most of the ugly Changelings, even the ones affiliated with Freakshow, just want to be left alone, but in some cases a charismatic leader might come along and put ideas in their minds. Is that happening? *Has* this type of charismatic leader shown up in the past few months? Someone who might be willing to take things a bit farther than before?"

Gina looked at her plate, suddenly uncomfortable.

"Come on, Gina," Amber said. "If you know something, please tell us." She pointed toward the hallway. "Don't forget—Jaden's a Changeling, and he's in the age range these guys are taking."

Gina looked up and snorted. "Don't worry, Amber—between the wards around this place and your nose, nobody's gonna get within a mile of Jaden." She looked away again and swallowed. "But…now that you mention it, there might be someone like you mentioned."

"Is that right?" Stone sat up straighter. This was something new. "Who are they? *Where* are they? Can we talk to them?"

She held up both hands. "Hold on, Doc. It's not that easy. I said I heard rumors, but it's not like I know the guy personally. And like I told you before—I'm not putting anybody in danger until I know they're really the one."

"What's that mean?" Jason demanded. "You won't tell us who it is?"

She didn't back down. "Not yet. And definitely not Doc's secret agency. I'm not naïve—if they find out about this, they'll take things into their own hands and the whole situation could get nasty."

"What, then?" Stone regarded her with care. Based on his past association with her, he knew she wouldn't be intimidated—and that was before she'd Changed. If he wanted her help, he'd need to play this smart, and diplomatic.

"I'll do a little digging into the guy's history," she said. "And I'll see if maybe we can work out a way to talk to him. No promises, though. He's not around this area."

"Where is he?"

"He's based down in L. A."

Stone nodded. "All right, then—it sounds like that's a good lead to follow. Thank you, Gina."

"What about us?" Jason asked. "You said you wanted our help, but so far I haven't heard anything we can do."

Stone took a thumb drive from his pocket and tossed it to Jason. "This is the information I have about the missing children. Photos of each, along with files about them. I was hoping you could check into their histories, and perhaps even contact the parents and ask them a few questions. Be discreet, though, and don't let any-thing slip about the agency's involvement. Can you do that?"

"Sure we can. It'll have to be outside normal agency business, but yeah."

Stone took out his wallet and put a twenty-dollar bill on the table. "If anyone asks, just tell them you were hired by an 'interested party' to investigate the kidnappings."

Jason didn't touch the money. "Yeah, that's gonna work. Let's hope nobody asks."

Stone didn't miss that Amber kept snatching glances toward the hallway. "Everything all right?"

"Just mother-bear instinct kicking in. Are you sure those wards you put up are still strong? It *was* three years ago…"

"Verity and Ian have been keeping them refreshed," Jason said. "And they made some changes to them after the kids were born, to make them more potent."

Stone finished his wine and stood. "I'm sure they're fine. My original structure was meant to last for years, and those two do good work. But I'll double-check them to make sure. Trust me, you two—nobody's going to get in here and take your children. I might be a bit uncomfortable relating to them on a personal level until they get a bit older, but anyone who tries to mess with them will be in for some very nasty surprises before they even *get* to their parents."

"Thanks, Alastair," Amber said. "Just the thought of somebody snatching kids makes me want to catch them and rip their heads off."

"Wow." Gina's expression was half-awe, half-fear. "In your case, I'm betting that's not hyperbole."

"Let's just say I hope you'll do whatever you can to help get these people caught."

"I will. I want them caught too. But I also know how much crap Changelings have to put up with, and I'm not gonna let anybody go off on some wild rumor and grab the wrong people."

"Okay," Stone said. "That about does it, then. Give me a few moments to check your wards, and we'll leave you to your peaceful evening. Thank you for your help, both of you. All of you."

Jason followed him outside while Amber stayed inside with Gina. "What do these wards do? I don't think I ever asked about specifics."

"I'm a bit curious myself, to see what they've added. Give me a moment." He shifted to magical sight, walking slowly around the house's perimeter. It was considerably larger than it had been before he'd gone to sleep, which meant Verity and Ian would not only have needed to augment the structure, but add to it. He was a bit surprised to find that the boundary between his original wards and the new additions was nearly seamless. They had both grown even more in their magical abilities since he'd been away.

"What are you smiling about?"

He'd almost forgotten about Jason. "Oh, nothing much. My son and your sister are amazing."

"Yeah, I know that, but what did they do now?"

"Just—" He gestured around. "The wardwork here is top-notch, where they've added bits to cover the new parts of the house since I've been gone."

"They worked for days on those, I remember. But what will they do if somebody tries to break in?"

Stone didn't answer right away. He kept walking, paying particular attention to the doors and windows. "Oh, this is nice."

"What?"

"They've set it up so if anyone other than you and Amber tries to enter through the windows, they'll be immobilized indefinitely—probably until one of them shows up to release them." He smiled again, remembering the same wards around the portals at Caventhorne and the London house. Verity had been caught in the same type when Desmond had died, until Stone could tweak them to let her loose. She'd probably remembered that and suggested they duplicate it.

"Nice. What about the doors? I'm guessing those are tougher, since we do need to let other people in occasionally."

"Yes." He rounded the back of the house and levitated over the deck railing to examine the rear sliding-glass door. "Bloody hell. This is even *more* impressive."

Jason didn't climb over the railing, but watched from below. "Yeah?"

"These are set the same way, to immobilize—but they're keyed to your aura. Yours and Amber's—and one other's that I don't recognize. Alice's?"

"Nah, Alice knows she's not supposed to open the doors without us around. Probably Sarah, our part-time nanny, who looks after the kids when Amber's working on something."

"That makes sense."

"How does it work, though?"

"If any of the doors open to anyone other than you three without at least one of you being inside the house and awake, it will activate the immobilization."

Jason leaned on the rail and looked amazed. "Come to think of it, I think they did ask at the time whether we ever let anybody else in the house when we're not home. Except for the nanny, we don't. We do all our own repairs, so there's no need. That *is* pretty impressive. I didn't know Verity and Ian were that good with wards."

Neither did Stone. But if Verity had been learning from Bron's family, and Ian from Gabriel, he wasn't surprised. "Well, the bottom line is, it would take a mage of my caliber to even think of getting through these wards quickly—and even breaking them down over time would require some fair skill. So I don't think your children have anything to worry about. You can reassure Amber of that, too."

Jason gripped his arm. "Thanks, Al. Really." He looked away. "I never had any idea how many feelings having kids can bring out. I want to let them explore and learn and take risks, but I'm scared to death of something hurting them and us not being able to do anything about it."

"I get it." They came back around the front, where Amber was saying her goodbyes to Gina. "Don't worry. We'll find these people and sort out what's going on. Hopefully, you'll turn up something with your more in-depth search of the children's backgrounds."

"I hope so. Because if anybody comes after Jaden, never mind me. Amber wasn't kidding about ripping their heads off."

CHAPTER NINE

THREE DAYS PASSED without any information about either the Changeling case or the Brathwaite situation. Stone forced himself not to contact any of his friends, accepting that they were moving as fast as they could, and bothering them would only slow them down. He wished there was something he could do to be useful on either case, but had to acknowledge that he *had* done the best thing he could do: given skilled people the information they needed and let them do what they did best.

He did leave a message with Renata Huxley on Monday night, asking her to let him know if she had any new information and if any new children had been taken. Her reply by email the following morning was a terse *Working on it, but another case is heating up. No new kids. Stand by and keep doing what you're doing.*

He couldn't hold that against her; in fact, he had no trouble reading the frustration between the email's two short lines. She wanted to be focused on this case, but she couldn't argue with her superiors. It sounded as if she was depending on him more than ever to make something happen.

Gina texted him Tuesday afternoon. *Still working on setting up a meeting. Might have something in a day or two.*

What does that mean?

Dunno yet. Sit tight and I'll see what I can do.

Stone hated 'sitting tight.' He wanted to *act*—especially since he continued to subliminally feel the time ticking away on Aldwyn's deadline. Eight days had already passed, and he wasn't any closer to finding Brathwaite than he'd been when he'd started. In fact, he only had Aldwyn's assurance that the necromancer was even still alive.

Jason, at least, came through with some useful information—sort of, anyway—the following day. He invited Stone down to the agency for lunch, where they shared sandwiches from Togo's in the conference room with Gina. They used the cone of silence spell so Derik the receptionist wouldn't overhear them.

"Okay," Jason said, tossing several folders on the table before unwrapping a sandwich. "I did a little digging into these families. Obviously, I found no connection with Changelings, but then I wouldn't."

"I didn't either," Gina spoke up. "I did a different kind of digging that Jason couldn't do. The parents definitely aren't Changelings, and as far as I can tell none of the relatives are either. There's no way to tell if the kids are since they're missing, but in cases where there are siblings, all the siblings are mundane."

"That's not unusual, though." Stone used magic to drag one of the folders to him and opened it. "The Changeling expression is rare, occurring only in a fairly small subset of people who have magical heritage but no overt magical power. So it's not at all unexpected that only one child in a family would present with it." Without anything else useful to do with the case, he'd spent the last couple days reading some of the scholarly papers the magical researchers had written about the phenomenon in the last three years. There had even been a few papers written by Changeling scientists. He had a much better understanding of the current state of the situation than he had before—not that it helped much.

Jason grabbed the file back from Stone and lined all six of them up across the middle of the table, then opened another one, revealing the photo of a dark-skinned boy around two years old. "This is Montrel LaRue, age two. He's the most high-profile of the cases, since his parents are well-off. His dad is a high-level manager for a securities company, and his mother is an entertainment attorney focused on the fashion industry. Montrel has been missing for three weeks, and the cops assigned to the case are starting to fear that he's dead and will never be found. They're still looking hard, though. The parents have been keeping the kidnapping under wraps, cooperating with law enforcement, because they don't want the whole thing becoming a media circus and spooking the kidnappers if Montrel's still alive."

"They're wealthy," Stone said, gazing at the little boy's smiling face. "But no demands. No ransom, no extortion attempts, no blackmail."

"Nothing. And according to the information I got from a couple law-enforcement contacts in the L.A. area, the family doesn't have any enemies they're aware of."

"No sign of any problems with the marriage?"

"Not that I could tell by checking court and police records. I didn't talk to the LaRues because out of the six missing kids, Montrel's getting the lion's share of the attention. I figured having some random PI from the Bay Area suddenly calling without provocation might raise the wrong kind of suspicions."

Stone nodded. "That's reasonable. What about this one, then?" He pointed at the one he'd opened. This time, the photo showed a three-year-old girl with dark hair and brown eyes.

"That's Gurpreet Singh. She's from Milpitas. Her parents are both in high tech—the dad's a QA engineer at a software company, and the mom took a leave from her job as a program manager at a different one when Gurpreet was born. She's been back at work for about a year."

"Okay, why is this one different?"

"She's not—but this time, I actually did talk to her mom. Their daughter has been missing for a little shorter time than Montrel. The Singhs aren't wealthy, especially since Mom hasn't been back at work long and they have to pay for daycare for Gurpreet and her younger brother Deepinder. She couldn't think of anybody who might want to kidnap their daughter."

Stone sighed, shifting his gaze between the two photos. "This isn't helping much, is it?"

"Well, just wait a sec. I did find out one thing from Mrs. Singh that supports your theory."

"Which theory is that?"

"That the commonality among the kids is that they're Changelings."

Stone leaned forward. "How so?"

"I took Amber with me when I did the questioning, figuring the mom would be more comfortable talking to another woman with a girl the same age. Turns out that was a better idea than I figured. Amber did most of the talking, and pretty soon they were sharing stories. She brought up the way kids can make up all kinds of crazy stories, like how they say they're cats, or fairies, or whatever…and Mrs. Singh said something really strange."

"What's that?" Both Stone and Gina were fully focused on him now.

"Get this—she said she and her husband had been a little worried, because Gurpreet had started telling them she was some kind of alligator, with green skin and big teeth…and she kept trying to eat the neighbor's cat's food."

Stone and Gina exchanged glances. "Bloody hell."

"Yeah. She said that was really disturbing to them, since they're Sikhs and strict vegetarians. Their kids have never had meat. They don't even have any pets that eat meat."

"You're right," Gina said. "That *does* sound like maybe she's a Changeling. Sometimes they'll even change their dietary habits to match their new form."

"And it's not necessarily a voluntary thing," Stone added. "I've been reading some of the research, and it appears that Changelings with carnivorous forms develop a spontaneous psychological dependency on eating meat, even if they didn't before. Same with people who were fine with meat before, but changed into something that isn't."

"So it's not a biological thing?" Jason asked. "The kid isn't going to die because her parents don't feed her meat?"

"No," Gina said. "I mean, look at me. I'm a cat. Obligate carnivore. Ever since I Changed, I've noticed I eat a lot more meat than before, but I still eat other stuff too. Not sure what would have happened if I'd been a vegetarian, though."

"If she's anything like the other cases I've read about," Stone said, "she'll be quite unhappy."

"Damn. That fits too. Mrs. Singh said their daughter has always been a bit of a problem child…crying a lot, not gaining weight, acting out. They've taken her to a bunch of doctors, but physically they found nothing wrong."

Stone pondered. "Unfortunately, I don't think we're going to be able to get even this close with the other children, since they're all two years old or younger. I don't know—do children speak coherently at two?"

"Not…really. I mean, Alice was using simple sentences at two, but she's pretty high on the verbal scale. Even then, I'm not sure she could have conveyed enough to let us know if she was a cat or something."

Stone opened the other folders one at a time and scanned the files. "It looks like the only time the kidnapper got caught on camera was during the abduction of Aidan Lewis, age one year, in the San Diego suburb."

"Yeah. Their house had been robbed before, so they'd added some cameras a while back. Not much help, though. I've been over the footage and so has Amber, but so far all we can tell is that the person moves oddly. Can't even tell if it's a guy or a woman."

"And as far as the police can tell, none of these people have enemies who'd want to hurt them or their children."

"Nope. Like I said, Montrel's family is the most likely one to have them, since they have money and Mom's job is a bit more high-profile. But they swear there isn't anybody. The rest of these people are…no offense…nobodies. No criminal records, no major enemies, no recent disagreements that might have caused somebody to—"

Gina's phone buzzed on the table. She picked it up, scanned it, and looked startled. "Hey, that's a surprise."

"What?" Stone and Jason spoke at the same time.

"I just heard back from my source in Freakshow. She says she talked to the guy I was telling you about, and he's willing to talk to us."

That *was* a surprise. "Where is he?" Stone demanded. "We can leave right away."

"Now, hang on. She says he won't talk in person."

"Why not?"

"He trusts her, and she trusts me—but they don't trust anybody else I might bring in. So he wants to do it online, so he can't be identified."

"Damn." Stone didn't like online communication, because it hamstrung his most valuable skills: reading facial and body language, with or without magical sight and auras. "Are you sure you can't convince them? They can name the place, and I'll go along with whatever demands they make to keep them safe."

Gina shook her head. "No can do, unfortunately. They're pretty adamant about it. Maybe if you talk to him and gain his trust, he might let us set something up later. You want to go for it?"

"If that's all we've got, then I suppose we don't have a choice."

She tapped on the screen and waited for a reply. Stone and Jason had gone back to examining the files by the time it arrived a few minutes later. "Okay, we're in." She looked apologetic.

"Unfortunately, though, she says he'll only talk to me and one other person. Sorry, Jason…"

Jason did look disappointed, but he waved it off. "This is Al's show, so he should be the one. Is there any way you can record the exchange without him catching on?"

"Maybe, but I won't do it. He's trusting me, and I'm not gonna betray that unless we have a lot more suspicion that he's behind this."

"It's all right," Stone said. "We can rely on notes. Go ahead and set it up, Gina, and let me know the details. Hopefully he can tell us something—intentionally or not."

CHAPTER TEN

GINA TEXTED BACK THE NEXT MORNING. *Got the meeting set up, but not until early next week. They're gonna need time to get things ready on their end. He's really nervous about getting identified.*

That looks a bit suspicious, doesn't it?

Maybe. But it could also be because he's somebody high-profile in mundane life. Let's just let them run the show. We don't want to spook him.

Stone didn't like waiting that long, but he couldn't argue. *Where will we do it?*

Probably my place. I'll send you the details soon.

Stone put his phone away and absently stroked Raider, frustrated again. He was actually starting to miss working at the university—at least it gave him something to do while he waited for things to happen. He couldn't even work on his portal anymore, since Ian and Gabriel had already finished it for him. Finally, he decided to go out for a run. At least if his mind was stagnating, he could give his body a workout.

He'd made it through three-quarters of a five-mile loop around Encantada when his phone buzzed. Thinking Gina was calling with an update, he slowed his pace and pulled it out.

It wasn't Gina. "Eddie? Please tell me this isn't a social call."

"Bit short o' breath, there, are you, mate?" Eddie's voice was amused. "Catch you in the middle o' somethin'? Little mornin' quickie? Should I ring back later?"

"Oh, sod off. I'm out on a run. Have you got something?"

"I do. We got a bite this mornin'."

"A bite? You mean somebody wants to look at the books?"

"Yep. We actually got three bites, but two o' them are folks we're familiar with. Reputable researchers, no known connections to mad necromancers. More like older witches, focused on the herbalism end."

"But the third one *does* have a connection?"

"Not to Brathwaite, but definitely to the Ordo. 'E's come in 'ere a few other times in the past to look at some o' the darker stuff in the collection."

"What makes you think he's interesting?"

"Because the way we positioned these books, they're *not* dark. We went out of our way to make 'em sound dead boring, to be honest. The only thing that might interest Brathwaite's lot is the implication that they might be from Crowther's stash."

Stone hadn't realized he'd picked up his pace. "Brilliant, Eddie. Have you replied to him yet?"

"Not yet. Wanted to check with you first, since I'm sure you'll want to be 'ere. Let me know when you're available, and I'll set it up. We've already got the study room wired and tested, so we're good to go."

"Okay. How soon can we do it?"

"'E sounds pretty eager to get 'is mitts on the books. 'E's based in Germany, and says 'e can come through the Berlin portal and be 'ere whenever 'e can get an appointment." He chuckled. "We sort of implied that there are a few more folks interested than there really are."

"That devious streak of yours is working to our advantage, it sounds like."

"Oh, that was Ward's idea. The bloke might look mild-mannered, but I've got nothin' on 'im for sneakiness when 'e gets motivated."

"Okay. Good. I'll get in touch with Verity and Ian, since they want to be involved. Does your secret observation room have space for all of us?"

"Oh, yeah. It's quite comfy. Even got tea and a full range of libations to enjoy during your viewing pleasure."

"Brilliant. I'll get back to you soon. Thanks, Eddie."

"Just doin' my part to rid the world of mad necromancers."

Verity and Ian were both eager to participate in the spy mission.

"I was starting to think you weren't going to call," Verity admitted when Stone contacted her to ask when she was free. "It's been several days."

"Well, these things take time, and I've got another unrelated situation I've been dealing with. Are you available?"

"Name the time. Wouldn't miss it."

Ian's schedule was open as well, so Stone texted Eddie to go ahead and set up the meet.

The reply came an hour later: *Our fish is hooked. He's coming tomorrow at two p.m. We've allowed him an hour with the tome. Hope you can get something you can use.*

Stone had a couple ideas about that—ones he'd gotten from previous conversations with Jason. In this case, mundane technology definitely had its uses.

Verity and Ian came through the portal at the Encantada house at five a.m. the next morning. Verity grinned when she got a look at Stone's expression.

"Haven't had your coffee yet, have you?"

"I have not. I'm hoping Eddie has something strong, or I'll be nodding off during the viewing. Human beings were not intended to be awake this early."

Ian's grin was even bigger than Verity's. "The trick is to just stay up all night, Dad."

"Oh, bugger off. You probably came from Prague, so you're rested and ready."

He sobered. "You think this is the guy who can lead us to Brathwaite?"

"No idea. I hope so."

"What are you planning to do?" Verity asked. "Grab a hair or something after he leaves and do a tracking ritual?"

"That's one option, but not the best one." He pulled a small device from his pocket. "I'm hoping there'll be an opportunity to slip this into his bag at some point."

She plucked it from his hand and studied it. "Is this a tracker?"

"It is. Got the idea from Jason. Its range isn't stellar, but we can follow him when he leaves. If he goes back to Berlin, we can pop through the portal to follow and then track him from there."

"Nice. Did you get the tracker from Jason, too? I thought you weren't going to tell him about this."

"No, just found a local place that sells them." He took it back and returned it to his pocket. "The Ordo doesn't like technology, so they'll be much more on the lookout for any magical tracking. I'm hoping we can get to him before he discovers this little thing."

"Let's go, then," Ian said. "The faster we figure out if this guy is the one we want, the faster we can get Brathwaite."

Eddie and Ward were waiting for them when they arrived. They obviously knew their friend well, because Eddie showed up at the portal bearing a tray of steaming cups of coffee. "You look like death, mate," he told Stone, chuckling. "Better get yerself together before old Vogel arrives."

Stone didn't even bother with a smart remark. He grabbed a cup, muttered thanks, and downed a healthy swallow. "Okay—that should help a bit. Where are we going?"

"Right this way. I'm pretty proud o' this, actually. Our folks did some good work."

He led them upstairs to the vast house's west wing. Stone looked around. "Odd that nobody's here. This is prime research time, isn't it?"

"That's why we're up here," Ward said. "This part of the building is closed for cleaning for a couple of hours."

"We didn't want anybody spottin' you," Eddie added. "Since most o' the magical world still thinks you're missin'."

Stone exchanged approving glances with Verity and Ian. It was definitely nice, having people like Eddie and Ward on their side. Not having to think of everything himself was nice, too.

"'Ere we are." Eddie opened a door and waved them in ahead of him.

The room had obviously started life as one of Caventhorne's many studies or workrooms, but it bore little resemblance to that now. Eddie and Ward's experts had repurposed it for surveillance, with large monitors on the walls, blinking computer equipment, and several comfortable chairs lined up with good views of the monitors. One of the chairs was in front of a console with a keyboard, mouse, and several smaller monitors. Currently, all the monitors, large and small, were focused on different views of a simple room with a table and chair in the center. As Eddie had mentioned, the back part of their observation room included a table with a coffee maker, several cups, and a collection of liquor bottles with glasses. A squat refrigerator sat next to the table.

Stone examined the views. It appeared there were cameras somewhere along all four walls, as well as one in the ceiling that looked down on the table. Someone had placed a sheet of paper with several lines of text on the table in front of the chair, but Stone couldn't make out the contents.

"Check it out," Eddie said proudly. He tapped a key, and the ceiling-camera view zoomed in on the sheet. The scribbled text snapped into focus, revealing it to be a list of the latest West Ham football scores.

"Wow," Verity said. "Very nice!"

"But you're sure he won't catch on?" Ian narrowed his eyes, leaning in for a better view.

"It's possible he could get suspicious," Ward said, "but there's no reason why he should. On the surface, this isn't any different from all the rooms we use for researchers to study the rarer texts."

"And even if he does suspect anything," Eddie added, "those cameras are *well* 'idden. The wall ones are tiny and buried in the scrollwork, and the ceiling one is hidden in the light fixture, which is fairly bright. 'E'd basically 'ave to stand on the table and take the fixture off to find it, and we'd catch 'im before 'e did that."

"Okay," Stone said. "This is all very impressive, but there's part of this plan I'm not clear on."

"What's that?"

"Well…*why* do we need all this high-tech surveillance? I was thinking about that after we talked last. What do we expect him to do? You don't think he'll try to steal the tome, do you?"

"No," Ward said. "There isn't any real way he could do that. The only possibility is to try switching it with an identical copy, but he doesn't know what the original looks like. Or he could use an illusion, I suppose, but I doubt he'd risk that. I'm sure he suspects we'll be using strong magic to keep the collection safe."

"What, then?"

Eddie shrugged. "We'll get some good images of 'is face and any notes 'e takes, and also a good look at what 'e focuses 'is attention on. 'E's only got an hour, remember, so 'e's got to prioritize. All the cameras are recording, so if we miss anything the first time 'round, we can go back and take a closer look later."

"And," Ward said, "the room is fully wired for sound. So if he makes any calls while he's in there, we'll be recording his side of those as well."

"Or if 'e talks to 'imself," Eddie added.

"Bloody hell," Stone said. "When did you two give up research to become master spies?"

Eddie grinned. "Mostly not us, I've got to admit. But we do have some mundane mates who are quite good at this sort of thing. You're not the only one with useful contacts." He stood, glancing at his watch and clapping his hands once. "Okay! That's it for 'ere. Our guest should be 'ere soon. Kerrick will welcome 'im and then 'and 'im off to me. I'll bring 'im to the room, set 'im up with the book, and clear out so 'e can 'ave some privacy. Meanwhile, Ward will man the setup 'ere 'til I get back. You lot can just sit back and enjoy the show."

Stone, Ian, and Verity all refreshed their coffee, then settled into chairs facing the screens. Stone watched the empty room with dubious interest. "I do hope this gets us somewhere. It will be a shame to do all this work for nothing."

"Well, we do know he's affiliated with the Ordo," Ward said, swinging his chair around to face them. "Whether he's connected to Brathwaite is another matter, but the way we positioned that tome, anyone with an interest in necromancy will definitely want to see it."

"I wonder if all the necromancers are still connected with Brathwaite," Stone said. "I mean, it's been three years since I've been keeping up with this sort of thing. Is that enough time to train others and have them go off on their own? I've got no idea."

"I don't think it is." Ward looked sober. "Remember, Eddie and I got a good look at Brathwaite's notes before you destroyed them. We've been discussing that while we set this up."

"And Eddie remembers everything he reads," Verity said. "So he should know."

"Exactly. He doesn't remember *everything,* but he did say the information was highly complicated—and there wasn't enough in the journals to learn from without a teacher to fill in the gaps. Brathwaite undoubtedly *is* training more necromancers, but we don't think three years is enough time for them to go off fully on their own. That's not even a full apprenticeship."

"You've got a point," Stone said. "I don't have Eddie's eidetic memory, but I *did* spend a fair bit of time studying that stuff before I torched it. It's a whole different system of magic. It *would* be like an apprenticeship, for someone to learn enough of it to be getting on with on their own."

"I hope you're right," Ian said. "If you are, that means if this guy *is* interested in this book for necromancy tips, either Brathwaite sent him or he's trying to make points with the master. Either way, all roads lead back to the big boss."

"Settle in," Ward said. "Mr. Vogel should be arriving just about now, since I can't imagine he wouldn't be prompt. They'll be entering the room in the next few minutes."

Stone leaned back and watched the monitors, switching between the different views, heart beating faster with anticipation. He'd never heard of this Vogel before. Was he one of Brathwaite's necromancer apprentices? Would he lead them to the man himself? It seemed as if there were a lot of ways this plan could go awry, but right now it was the best one they had.

A few more minutes passed before movement registered on one of the monitors. Everyone turned to face it as the door opened to admit Eddie and another man. Eddie carried a wooden box.

"Here we go…" Ian murmured.

Ward clicked something on the computer screen, and voices flooded the room over speakers on each end of the table.

"'Ere we are," Eddie was saying. "This is one of our private study rooms where you'll have an hour with the tome. It's been preserved with the standard spells, of course, so you should use normal care, but don't worry about extraordinary measures. Feel free to make any notes you wish, and you're welcome to take photos of any pages you like as long as you don't use a flash. We don't allow eating or drinking in the study rooms—standard procedure, I'm sure you're well acquainted with it. If you need to step out to use the loo or get refreshments, use the intercom by the door and someone will show you the way. 'Ave you got any questions before I leave you to it?"

Vogel shook his head. "I don't think so. Thank you for this opportunity, Herr Monkton." He was a slightly stooped man of around forty-five, with thinning brown hair, a narrow face, and protruding eyes. He wore slacks and a dark-brown sweater over a buttoned shirt, and spoke with a faint Austrian accent.

"That's what we're 'ere for," Eddie said cheerfully. He set the box on the table, opened its magical lock, and levitated the book to the space in front of the chair. "I'll be back in an hour to collect you. Good luck. I 'ope you find what you're lookin' for." He left the room, taking the box with him.

As soon as the door closed, Stone shifted his attention to the other camera views. Vogel, obviously mindful of his limited time, hurried to the chair and sat. He opened his slim leather briefcase and withdrew a legal pad, several pens, and his phone, all of which he placed to the right of the tome. Then he took a pair of white gloves from his pocket and donned them.

"Damn," Stone muttered. "No prints, then." He wished he could see Vogel's aura, but obviously that wasn't possible from his remote vantage point. "Is there somewhere I can get a look at him before he leaves?" he asked Ward. "You know—in person?"

"Possibly. Ask Eddie when he returns. You'll have to be careful, though. If he spots you and recognizes you—"

Stone certainly didn't recognize *him.* He'd been half-hoping Vogel would be one of the mages they'd fought in the Tennessee mall during Richter's ritual. He'd been fairly sure they'd been killed, but never found out for sure. That would have made things a lot easier, that was certain. But Vogel was older and looked a lot more scholarly. He could easily have been one of Stone's fellow professors at the University. "I get it. But I'll pit my illusions, or my invisibility, against him. Let's see what happens."

He returned his attention to the monitors. Vogel worked quickly but carefully, starting by opening the book's cover and examining the inscription. Stone knew from his own examination of the book that it was illegible, but after Eddie and Ward had told him their plan, he'd taken a second look and agreed it was possible someone given the proper preparation might interpret the last name, which was probably "Crowley" or "Carruthers," as "Crowther." The mind was a very suggestible thing, especially when dealing with people as obsessed as Brathwaite and his crew.

"You think he'll bite?" Verity whispered, almost as if afraid Vogel would hear her.

"No idea. But he certainly seems interested. And so far, he doesn't seem to be at all suspicious that he might be under observation."

"Or else he doesn't care," Ian said.

Vogel snapped a photo of the inscription with his phone (Stone noticed he followed Eddie's rules and didn't use a flash) and then began flipping slowly through the pages. Occasionally he would pause to snap another photo, or to check his watch.

Ten minutes into his study, the door to the surveillance room opened and Eddie entered. "Anything yet?"

"He's still interested," Stone said, pointing at the screens. "He's been taking a few photos, but hasn't written any notes yet."

Eddie dropped into an empty chair. "As soon as 'e clapped eyes on that book, that was all 'e gave a damn about. I coulda stripped off and done a Morris dance right there on the table."

Stone shuddered. "There's *my* brain corrupted."

"*Anyway,* I took the opportunity to get a shufty at 'is aura while he was otherwise occupied."

Stone was still trying to get that image out of his head. "Yes, and?"

"'E seemed excited, maybe a little nervous, but nothin' out o' the ordinary. I mean, I 'aven't got your sensitivity, but I sure didn't see any malevolent intentions."

"But then, he wouldn't have any, would he?" Verity asked. "If he's doing this for Brathwaite, he's probably excited about maybe finding something his master can use. As long as he doesn't suspect anybody's on to him, he probably does this kind of thing all the time."

"I hope he does more than just page through the whole thing." Stone slumped back in his chair. "If we can't connect him to Brathwaite, I'm not even sure it's worth it to follow him."

"Keep watchin'," Eddie said. "There's a bit a little further in that might interest a necromancer more than your standard herbalist. It's the other reason Ward and I though o' this idea. I remembered from Brathwaite's own notes that a concoction of mullein, yew, and mugwort was used in part o' the necromantic ritual, and those three 'appen to be mentioned on the same page about 'alfway through this tome. At least I think so—so far, we've 'ad a 'ell of a time translating this mess."

Everyone remained quiet, watching Vogel as he continued paging through the tome. He stopped every few pages to snap a photo, but still didn't write any notes. He also didn't look around, maintaining full focus on the pages. He either didn't suspect he was being watched, or he didn't care.

As he drew closer to the middle of the book, everyone in the observation room leaned slightly forward in anticipation. Ward clicked something on his screen and the ceiling camera zoomed in tighter.

"Should be any minute," Eddie whispered. "There'll be an illustration of mullein leaves on the page."

Vogel flipped a few more pages and stopped.

"There it is," Ward said.

The Ordo man's shoulders visibly tensed. He bent closer, peering at the unfamiliar text and the intricate, hand-drawn illustration for almost two minutes. Then he snapped photos of the two facing pages and dashed off his first note on his legal pad.

"What's it say?" Verity asked, squinting. "Looks like some kind of shorthand."

"Yeah, I don't know either," Eddie said. "We can examine it later."

Vogel turned another page, but whatever was on the next one didn't seem to interest him so he returned to the previous one. The camera on the wall opposite him showed his gaze fuzzing out as he continued to stare down at the book.

"Magical sight," Stone said. "He's trying to see if the pages have any inherent magic."

"None of 'em do," Eddie said. "We went over it thoroughly."

"Wait." Ian pointed at the monitor. "He's picking up his phone again. Is he going to take another photo of the same page?"

But this time, Vogel didn't snap a photo. Instead, he called up his text app and started tapping out a message.

"Get closer, Ward," Stone urged. "I want to see what he's sending."

The overhead view zoomed in even tighter, went blurry, and then locked into focus.

Stone peered at the tiny screen. No name showed at the top for the recipient, but only initials: *HMB.*

"The message is in German," Verity said. "Can you guys read it?"

Eddie, Ward, and Ian were all watching closely. When Vogel finished the message and hit *Send,* they all spoke at the same time, with minor variations in phrasing. "*I have found useful information. Advise attempting to determine where this volume was acquired. Good chance it was part of BC's collection.*"

They all continued to watch as the message was delivered. Vogel stared at the screen for another minute, then set the phone aside, tore off a bit of his legal pad and bookmarked the page of interest, then continued flipping. He'd made it three-quarters of the way through, snapping a few more photos but taking no further notes, when a faint buzz sounded. He jerked his head up and snatched the phone.

"Bloody good microphones, if we could hear that," Stone muttered.

The returning message was also in German. Eddie translated it as, "*Well done. Finish examining the volume but take no further action. We will meet to discuss options when you return.*"

Vogel, appearing satisfied, returned to flipping pages and snapping photos.

"*HMB,*" Verity said. "Is that Brathwaite? I thought his first name was James, and that he's going by something else now. Could it be somebody else?"

"Could be," Eddie said. "Or it could be an honorific: Herr Meister Brathwaite. Those Ordo blokes are an old-fashioned bunch, especially regardin' anybody 'igher in rank."

"Okay, so what do we do now?" Ian asked. "If that *is* Brathwaite he's talking to, it sounds like they're planning to get together. Do we follow him?"

Stone pulled the tracker from his pocket. "We'll need to work out a way to slip this into his briefcase."

"I have an idea," Ian said. "Didn't you say you had another similar book?"

"Yes," Eddie said. "It's not as interestin', though, and it doesn't have the inscription."

"That's okay. Show it to Vogel when he's leaving, maybe to see if he's interested in scheduling some more time to look at it later. Talk it up like it's a big deal, and show him a few pages as a teaser. While he's distracted, I'll slip up invisibly and use magic to put the tracker in his bag."

"Risky," Stone said, shaking his head. "If he catches you—"

"He won't catch me. You know I'm a lot better at invisibility than you are, and Gabriel's taught me more tricks in the last three years."

Stone still didn't like it, but his son spoke truth. "Okay. That's a good idea. Once the tracker's in place, as long as he doesn't find it before we find him, we should be able to pop through the portal to Berlin and follow him from there."

"And with any luck, he *will* meet up with Brathwaite," Verity said in triumph. Her eyes narrowed. "I can't wait to get my hands on that bastard. I can almost taste it."

"Don't get ahead of yourself," Stone said. "It's a good plan, but it still won't be easy. Do *not* take anything for granted. I don't want to lose either of you over this."

Ward pointed at the screen. "The hour is almost up. If you're going to do anything, best if you prepare now."

By the time Ian and Eddie returned to the sitting room where everyone else was waiting, Stone was grinding his teeth in frustration. He knew it would be a bad idea for him to be anywhere near the tracker-planting operation, but that didn't mean he had to like it. This time, he didn't even have any cameras to watch, so he was forced to wait without any information, spinning out increasingly dire scenarios if Vogel caught Ian trying to slip the little thing into his briefcase.

Fortunately for him, however, the process didn't take long. The pair returned fifteen minutes later, looking pleased.

Stone hurried over. "Did everything go all right?"

Eddie grinned. "Calm down, mate. It went off without a 'itch. Your son here is bloody brilliant at invisibility. Best I've ever seen, and that's no lie."

Ian looked smug. "It was easy. I just hid in one of the rooms off the main hall while Eddie showed him the book. Of course, it made it even easier that the guy was practically salivating over it. He even disobeyed his boss a little."

"How so?" Verity asked.

"'E was probin' me a bit about where the two books came from," Eddie said. "I told 'im they were from a collection we acquired, but I couldn't reveal the source without authorization. I promised to talk to the donors for 'im and ask if they 'ad anything else."

"Meanwhile," Ian said, "I opened the flap of his briefcase and dropped the tracker in. I watched his aura while I did it—didn't even budge."

It sounded like a simple statement, but Stone was impressed. Ian had just casually admitted to keeping three spells—magical sight, invisibility, and telekinesis—going at the same time. Even Verity couldn't easily do that.

"We'd better get going," Ian said. "If he's already through the portal and back to Berlin, we need to find him before he heads off somewhere else."

"Good luck with that," Eddie said. "We've done our bit, but followin' fugitives is a bit outside our skill set."

Stone clapped him on the shoulder. "Thanks, Eddie. You too, Ward. We couldn't have done this without you."

"Keep us updated. And be sure to let us know when you get the bastard."

CHAPTER ELEVEN

THE BERLIN PORTAL was located in the basement of a combination pub-bookstore that had been in continuous operation (as the pub part, at least) since shortly after World War II. When Stone, Ian, and Verity popped through, half-expecting Vogel to be waiting for them on the other end, they found the room empty.

Stone looked around, taking in the weathered brick walls, stone floor, stacked wooden boxes, and faded, framed travel posters depicting other locations with public portals. Faint strains of bouncy classical music wafted down from somewhere above them. He hadn't been to Berlin in years, but this place, at least, hadn't changed.

"Is he around?" Ian wasn't acting as if this place was new to him, which didn't surprise Stone. Given his globetrotting with Gabriel, Stone suspected his son had seen more of the world's portals than he had.

Stone took out his phone. He'd synced the tracker with the app earlier that day and tested it. It was a GPS-type device, which meant it would only last for one to three days before its battery gave out, but if they hadn't found Vogel by then something was wrong anyway. It was also a little larger than he was comfortable with, meaning it might be more likely Vogel would discover it if he searched thoroughly, but if the Ordo man was anything like Stone, he didn't make a habit of rummaging around in the bottom of bags without a reason. He'd chosen the larger one because its accuracy was better, at least according to the enthusiastic saleswoman at the electronics shop.

Now, he examined the map that popped up in the tracker app. After a moment, a little blue dot appeared. "Good. He's still in Berlin."

"Is he moving?" Verity leaned in to look over his shoulder.

"Looks like it—and quicker than walking speed. Somebody must have picked him up when he arrived."

"Do you think he'll head straight to Brathwaite? Could he be right here in Berlin?"

"I don't know." Stone headed for the sliding bookshelf that separated the public part of the building's basement from the part containing the portal. "We'd best get a move on, though. I don't want to give him too much of a head start."

They exited the pub, which was sparsely populated at four p.m. Stone took a surreptitious glance around as they left, but nobody seemed to be paying them any attention. Once they were outside, he scanned the street for a cab.

Ian spotted one first, and waved to hail it. They piled into the cream-colored sedan with Verity reluctantly stuck in the middle. As it pulled back into the flow of traffic, Stone regretted once more than he'd never learned German. He glanced at his phone again, watching the little blue dot creeping along the Bundesstraße 1 heading southwest. From the speed it was progressing, it seemed the road was congested.

"Do you speak English?" he asked, hoping he wouldn't have to depend on Ian's serviceable but non-fluent German to get them by.

The cabdriver, a portly middle-aged man in a workman's jacket, glanced at the rearview mirror. "*Ja.* Yes, sir."

"Thank the gods," Stone muttered. He looked at the phone again. "Head southwest on the B1. I'll let you know you if that changes."

The strange directions didn't even seem to faze the man. He merely nodded and continued driving.

Stone had been right—the Bundesstraße 1 *was* fairly congested, with traffic moving along at a slow but steady pace. Watching the dot stay a relatively constant distance ahead of them was maddening. He half-expected it to exit the highway at any moment, but it didn't. It appeared it might be leaving Berlin.

Verity leaned over for a look. "Any idea where he's going?" she whispered.

"None." He didn't want to say much within the cabdriver's earshot, but he wondered if Brathwaite had access to a private portal in the area—perhaps one peons like Vogel wouldn't be privy to. If that were true, he might have set up the meet in a place that would be easy for him to reach.

"Doesn't seem like he's trying to lose us, though," Ian said, also speaking quietly so he wouldn't be overheard.

"No—but I doubt he's had time to look through his briefcase in depth yet. We should be more concerned when he stops."

They subsided into silence as the taxi continued driving, all three of them leaning in to watch the blue dot on Stone's phone screen. The driver still didn't seem to care what they were doing; in fact, appeared to be focused on listening to some German-language podcast.

The sky was overcast as they left Berlin, still heading southwest on the B1. The driver glanced over his shoulder. "How far do you plan to go?"

"Not sure yet." This could be a problem. If Vogel continued too far outside the city, the local cabbie might not be willing to pursue their chase forever. "Please, just go a bit further. Hopefully it won't be too much longer."

"I'll give you a hundred euros on top of the fare if you'll keep going," Ian said. "It's important."

Stone shot him a sharp look. "You have a hundred euros in cash?"

"Sure. I spend a lot of time in sketchy parts of Prague, remember? Cash can be useful sometimes."

"You're not doing anything illegal, are you?" the driver asked. "I obey the law. I don't want to get in trouble."

"Nothing illegal," Stone said. "I promise you." Okay, maybe he was stretching the truth a bit, since he was fairly sure tailing someone without their knowledge after planting a tracking device in their bag wasn't strictly lawful, but the lie didn't bother him.

"Wait," Verity whispered furiously, pointing at Stone's phone. "He's leaving the highway."

She was right. The map app showed the blue dot in the Potsdam area now, exiting the main highway and heading north. "Here we go," Stone said. "Looks like it won't be much longer now. Will you keep going?"

The cabbie shrugged philosophically. "For a hundred extra euros, sure. For a while, anyway."

Stone passed the phone to Ian, who was clearly more familiar with the area, so he could take up the directions. They crossed a bridge, passing out of Berlin and into Brandenberg, then drove for a few more minutes before Ian directed the driver to turn north at the same place Vogel had.

They all sat tensely, watching the screen, as the cab continued north on city streets. It continued for another five minutes, then turned right at Ian's direction.

"It's just up here," he said, watching even more closely. The dot had stopped moving by now. "Slow down—we're almost to the spot."

When the cab finally rolled to a stop, Stone, Verity, and Ian exchanged glances.

"This is…weird," Verity said.

They were in what looked like a lower-class residential district, its streets lined with three-story rowhouses. Some had lights in the windows now that the sun was going down, but most were dark. A few appeared abandoned, with plywood covering their lower-story windows. Vehicles cruised by, but the streets were largely free of pedestrians except for a small group of figures slouching near a shop, and a couple more walking away from them on the opposite side of the street.

"Are you sure this is where you want to be?" the cabbie asked. He looked nervous.

Stone checked his phone again. According to the tracker app, Vogel was inside the building two doors up, on the other side of the street. It was one of the dark ones, but its windows were still intact.

"Maybe he's meeting you-know-who there," Verity whispered. "Sometimes people hide you-know-whats in obscure places. Bron's family has a few in places like this."

"Well, whatever's going on, that's apparently our destination. Thank you for being so understanding," Stone said louder to the cabbie, slotting his credit card to pay for the ride.

"Eh. Tourists. Not even the oddest thing I've done this week." He looked expectantly over his shoulder at Ian, who'd already pulled the promised pair of fifty-euro notes from his wallet.

The three of them exited the cab and quickly cast disregarding spells on themselves, melting into the shadows between two buildings where they could keep an eye on the one across the street. A faint drizzle hung in the air, but so far it didn't seem as if it might rain any time soon.

"No lights," Verity said. "That's strange, isn't it?"

"Maybe not," Ian said. "The sun's not fully down yet. And anyway, if they don't want anybody to know they're meeting, they might be in a basement or something."

"You don't think he could have figured out we were following him, do you?"

"I don't see how," Stone said. "It's possible he found the tracker, of course, but he's got no way to know who put it there. It could have happened at any point. I used one of my fake IDs to set up the account, so there's no way to trace it back to me. And even if he did find it, why wouldn't he just destroy it, or toss it somewhere? The fact that it's inside a building suggests he hasn't discovered it yet. We should definitely be careful, though."

With their disregarding spells still up, they crossed the street but didn't approach the house yet.

"Should we split up?" Ian asked, looking around. The figures outside the shop had gone inside, and no one else on the street was paying any attention to them. Along the road, the streetlights were beginning to wink on, casting weak pools of illumination across the sidewalks at regular intervals. "One of us can go around the back, one look in the upper windows, and one to the front?"

Stone didn't like that idea, reluctant to put his accomplices at risk, but he couldn't deny its value. He shifted to magical sight, hoping to catch a glimpse of an aura through one of the windows, but nothing appeared. "Yes, but recon only, though," he said firmly. He consulted his phone again; the tracker's blue dot was still inside the house, though it wasn't precise enough to give him an elevation. "Look through the windows and see if you can spot anything, but stay sharp. Do *not* go inside yet."

Ian shot him a narrow-eyed glance, but nodded. "Okay. Text if you see anything. Meet up in ten minutes to compare notes?"

"Yes, let's meet back in the alley across the street where we started."

"Great. I'll take the upper floors."

"Why?"

"I'm best at invisibility."

Again, Stone couldn't argue with him. "Fine. I'll take the back. Verity, you take the front. But be careful. Make sure nobody on the street spots you poking around."

She gave him a *duh* look, then her expression hardened. "I hope he's in there. Brathwaite, I mean." Before Stone could reply, she headed off toward the house.

"Good luck," Ian said. He waited for Verity to get a head start, then faded to invisibility.

Stone, alone on the street now, looked around to make sure no one had noticed their odd actions. He couldn't be certain someone wasn't spying from one of the many windows along the street, of course, but the pair who'd been walking had disappeared around a corner, and the others hadn't emerged from the shop yet. He augmented his disregarding spell and slipped down the narrow passageway between two of the buildings.

The space behind the line of rowhouses consisted of a one-lane alley with small, fenced-off yards lining both sides. Each yard had a gate, with garbage receptacles placed in the alley just outside most of them. The place Stone's group was interested in had no receptacles outside, but the gate was locked. Several houses down, a homeless man in a shapeless coat was rummaging in one of the containers, but he seemed fully intent on his activity and didn't even glance in Stone's direction.

Moving quickly before the man *did* notice him, Stone levitated over the fence and crouched in the yard. The thing barely qualified for the name, overgrown with scrubby weeds that almost covered an overturned, dented trash can and a broken bicycle missing a wheel. The place smelled of neglect, old garbage, and a hint of decay, but nothing fresh. If anybody lived here, they clearly didn't spend much time in their backyard.

Conscious of the ticking clock, he crept forward and ducked below the level of one of the ground-floor windows, rising only high enough to take a look inside.

No curtains or blinds covered the window, but the space beyond was too dark to make out anything other than a few indistinct shapes of furniture or boxes. Stone shifted once again to magical sight, pressing his face against the lower window and scanning the area inside.

Nothing.

Even from here, the place felt deserted.

Had they been wrong? Was the tracker glitching, registering its location incorrectly? He thought of Gina, and wondered if somebody could have hacked it, hijacking its signal to report it somewhere different.

Don't be absurd. He shook his head, banishing the thought. That kind of high-tech stuff existed, sure, but old-school mages like the Ordo likely wouldn't use it. And Brathwaite, while he certainly appeared to have adjusted nicely to both Miriam Padgett's body and living in the twenty-first century, still had a lot of catching up to do, even after more than three years.

He crept to the window on the opposite side and peered in there. This time, it was obvious the room was a kitchen: the counters, refrigerator, and a small table with four chairs confirmed it. He couldn't see anything *on* the counters, though—no small appliances, food, or other signs anyone lived here.

He pulled out his phone again and texted Ian and Verity. *Anything?*

Nothing in front, Verity sent back. *Seems empty.*

I'm above you, Ian responded. *Nothing up here either. Should we go in?*

Stone glanced upward, but saw no sign of his son until his shifted back to magical sight. Even then, he was hard to spot. *Come around the back,* he sent to Verity. *We'll go in there.*

She arrived less than a minute later, levitating over the back fence and shimmering into visibility. Ian appeared after a few more seconds, crouching near the rear door.

"I don't think anybody's inside," Verity whispered. "I looked in all the lower front windows, and just saw furniture covered with sheets."

"Well, let's verify that," Stone said. It was getting too dark to see much now, but he raised a faint light spell to examine the door, looking for signs of an alarm system. When he saw none, he used magic to open the lock.

"I'll go first," he whispered. "I've got the best shield." Again using magic so he wouldn't leave fingerprints, he swung the door open before Ian could protest and closed it behind them when they'd all entered.

Inside, Stone's light spell illuminated a long hallway with a threadbare runner rug extending most of its length. On their left was a closed door, on the right a wider opening leading to the kitchen he'd spotted from outside. Further up the hallway, a stairway led up on the left side, and another large arch opened to the right. With the door closed, the garbage smell from the backyard faded, but the faint odor of decay now combined with dust and disuse. Perhaps the former occupants had left something to rot in the refrigerator, or a small animal had found its way inside and died in the walls.

Verity pointed at a light switch next to the kitchen archway. "*Should we check for power?*" she mouthed.

Stone shook his head. "Let's keep looking."

They spread out to check the lower floor, which didn't take long. When they reconvened in the hallway, all of them had nothing to report.

"They might be upstairs," Ian said. "But there's definitely nothing on this level."

"The fridge isn't running," Verity, who'd checked the kitchen, said. "Nothing inside, just that musty smell when you leave it closed without power."

Stone was starting to think something was wrong. *Had* Vogel discovered the tracker, and perhaps passed it off to someone else to stash here and lead them on a wild-goose chase? If so, he could be anywhere by now. Hell, if he'd handed it off as soon as he got through the Berlin portal, he could have hopped back through and be halfway around the world, while Stone, Ian, and Verity poked around an abandoned house like a trio of idiots.

He sighed. They were here now, and if someone had left the tracker in the house, maybe they could get some impressions if they found it. If Vogel had taken off his gloves, there might even be a print Eddie's friend could process. "Let's check the upstairs rooms, including the attic if there is one. I don't see a basement door, do you?"

"Nope," Verity said.

"I think there is one, though," Stone said. "I saw some of those half-windows along the ground line at the back."

"I'll stay here at the stairway," Verity said. "I'll try to find the door down, and make sure nobody makes a run for it while you two are checking upstairs."

Stone didn't like that idea either, but once again he didn't have a better one. They didn't have time to put up alarm wards on the doors. "All right—but call me and keep the line open."

She did as requested, and headed back down the hall as Stone and Ian crept upstairs to check the second and third floors.

A few minutes later they were back, discouraged.

"Nothing up there," Ian told Verity, who'd returned to the stairs to meet them. "The rooms are empty except for a few pieces of old furniture, and the attic isn't even big enough to stand up in."

Stone looked at the tracker app again. "It still says it's here, though. Unless the location isn't as precise as the saleswoman promised it would be, in which case we might need to check the houses on either side."

"I don't think so," Verity said, looking pleased with herself.

"Did you find something?" Ian demanded.

She dropped her voice to a whisper. "Right before you got back." Making a 'follow me' gesture, she led them back down the hall toward the back door. When Stone pointed silently toward the closed door they'd noticed when they came in, she shook her head and pointed down toward the runner rug.

Light dawned with both Stone and Ian at the same time. Using magic, Stone lifted the rug's corner and folded it back, revealing a trap door with a fingerhole.

"You think he's hiding down there?" Ian whispered. "Seems like a weird place to have a meeting."

"Maybe they heard us coming," Verity said.

"How are we going to get down there without them seeing us, though? Even with invisibility, I don't see how that's possible."

"It's not," Stone said firmly. "So we're not even going to try. Put your shields up and let me go first. If we can't surprise them, let's take the offensive."

Both Verity and Ian nodded, obviously liking that idea. "Don't forget," Verity said, "if Brathwaite's there, I get at least one good shot at him before you take him down."

"You'll have it. Let's go."

They all raised their shimmering shields. Verity and Ian stood with their backs against opposite sides of the wall, and Stone used magic to grab the fingerhole and pull the long trap door open. It swung on silent hinges and made no sound when he lowered it gently down on top of the folded rug.

Everyone leaned forward for a look at the wooden stairway leading down into darkness. There was no light switch.

Stone shot admonitory looks at Ian and Verity, then raised a light spell and crept down the stairs. The stairs, though clearly old and weathered, did not creak. Stone's bobbing light revealed a closed door at the bottom of the stairway.

Ian raised a finger and slipped forward, pressing his ear to the door. After several seconds, he shook his head. "*No sound,*" he mouthed.

Once again, Stone was beginning to think they'd been led on a wild-goose chase, and nobody was here after all. If they checked this room and found it empty, or even if they only found the tracker, he wasn't sure what his next steps should be. He fought to quell the growing stress around what Aldwyn might do if he failed to fulfill this part of the oath.

He waved them both back. If anybody *was* in there, he planned to give them a surprise. He gathered magical energy, focused it, and let it loose as a battering ram of force.

The door blew free, clattering into the room as if a real, solid ram had hit it, revealing a dark room beyond.

"Go, go!" Stone urged, hurrying into the room and raising his intensified light spell.

The basement consisted of a single room, somewhat smaller than the footprint of the house above it. A series of wooden columns held it up, and most of its floorspace was bare concrete. Along the walls, numerous boxes were stacked, blocking the small windows Stone had noticed at ground level.

All of this occupied their attention for only a moment, though, because the dead body lying in the middle of the floor was much more compelling.

CHAPTER TWELVE

"THAT'S VOGEL!" Ian whispered furiously.

He hadn't needed to say it, though—it was obvious to all three of them. The middle-aged Ordo man still wore the same brown sweater and slacks he'd worn at Caventhorne, and his leather briefcase lay on the stained concrete floor next to him. His eyes were open and milky, his skin chalk-white. A pool of blood spread beneath his head.

"I don't think he's been dead very long," Verity said. "Look—the blood's still wet."

Stone and Ian both looked around as if expecting the killer to leap out from behind the stacked boxes. "Looks like somebody clubbed him in the back of the head," Ian said.

Shield still up, Stone used magic to levitate the briefcase to him. "Keep watch," he ordered, and opened it.

The case was empty—with a single exception. "The tracker's still here, but all his other papers and whatnot are gone."

"Something's not right about this," Ian murmured. "But I can't put my finger on what it is."

"I'm getting the same feeling," Verity said.

"Well, we obviously aren't going to question Vogel," Stone said. "Let's take a quick look around and get out of here before someone else discovers us. We'll take the briefcase and the tracker back with us, and perhaps Eddie and Ward's people can find something on it."

Without waiting for a reply, he edged toward the body. "I wonder if he's got any identification on him."

"I'm not sure we should move him," Ian said.

Stone crouched next to Vogel. The man's wide, staring eyes were creepy, fixed on some point on the ceiling. Almost unconsciously, Stone directed his own gaze upward, but nothing about the rough ceiling looked unusual.

Ian, meanwhile, was patrolling the room. "I don't think we should stay here very long," he said. "Brathwaite's not here, so either they already had their meet or he was never here at all and somebody ambushed Vogel. We're wasting time."

Verity approached Stone, peering over his shoulder at Vogel. "I wish I could figure out what's bothering me…" she muttered. "It's something I feel like I should know."

Stone was still examining Vogel, only halfway listening to her. He wanted to check the man's back pocket for a wallet, but, mindful of Ian's admonition, wasn't sure he should do it.

"It's something about Vogel's body…something that isn't right…" Verity continued. And then, suddenly, she gripped Stone's shoulder. "Oh, gods, I know what it is. Come on—we've got to get out of here!"

"Why?" Stone leaped back to his feet, and Ian spun. "What is it, Verity?"

She grabbed his arm and tugged. "Come on. This is a trap. This isn't Vogel."

"What do you mean, it's not Vogel?" Ian demanded, but he was already hurrying toward them.

"Whoever this is, he's been dead too long! Eyes take two hours to go cloudy, and there's no way he was that far ahead of us!"

Stone mentally kicked himself. He'd been so caught up in the chase—all of them had—that he'd failed to check the basement with magical sight. Now, as Verity urged him toward the door, he shifted.

The body still looked like the body, but swirling magical energy hung in the air.

Something had happened here—and recently. "Get out!" he ordered, spinning toward the door.

Behind him, Ian yelped in pain, followed by a crash. Vogel's body—which no longer looked like Vogel—sat up, and all around them the walls and boxes were melting away to reveal more shambling undead figures.

Stone spun back, hot dread slicing through him when he saw Ian on his knees, clutching his head, with a pair of the gray-faced undead clawing at his sputtering shield. One of the things held a baseball bat, and had apparently clocked his son—not hard enough to completely blow the shield away, but hard enough to compromise it and send psychic feedback spiking into Ian's brain.

Without conscious thought, Stone pointed his hands and loosed a solid wall of concussive force at the creatures above the kneeling Ian's head. It slammed them back into the wall with a loud *boom,* cracking the plaster and raining dust down on their heads, but aside from that didn't seem to affect them appreciably. They staggered back to their feet and shambled forward again.

Meanwhile, three more were approaching them, one to the right and two to the left. Now that the illusion concealing them had faded, the faint smell of decay they'd written off to a dead animal in the walls had grown much stronger, sending off waves of nauseating funk as the creatures moved.

"Get out!" Stone yelled to Verity. "Go! Up the stairs!"

"I'm not leaving without you!" She focused her attention on the two to their left, taking them down with a concussion wave of her own. It didn't hit as hard as Stone's had, but it did the job, knocking the two creatures off their feet.

Stone augmented his shield as the right-side creature slammed into him. This one didn't have a weapon, but its balled fists hit like sledgehammers, raining down blow after blow. His shield flickered from clear to pink.

He barely paid that any attention, though. His entire focus was on Ian, who was now on his hands and knees, still stunned from the sucker punch he'd taken. One of the zombies behind him, a beefy male with gray skin and patchy blond hair, raised its club, preparing to bring it down on Ian's head once more before he could strengthen his shield.

"No!" Stone barked. Fighting feedback from the creatures pummeling his own shield, he reached out with a telekinetic spell and grabbed the club, wrenching it from the zombie's hands. It roared and stumbled away, trying to retrieve its weapon, but that still left two more on Ian. Stone wished he hadn't blown the door off the basement room—perhaps if they could have retreated to the stairway, they might have used it to hold the creatures off for a respite. But it lay on the floor now, its hinges twisted and useless.

I can still use it as a shield, though.

That was the thing about necromantically-created undead: they were almost immune to direct magic. You could throw fireballs or lightning at them all day and they'd shrug it off like it was nothing. But they *weren't* immune to mundane damage, or its magical equivalent like concussion or telekinetic spells. Crushing their heads or pulverizing their bodies was as deadly to them as it would be to a normal human—the unfortunate situation with Sharra had proven that.

Heart pounding, adrenaline coursing, he used magic to snatch up the heavy door. "Get Ian and get behind me!" he yelled to Verity. "I'll hold them off with this!"

"Yeah." Her voice sounded tight and already strained from the magic she'd been throwing around, but she acted quickly and without question. Using her own telekinetic spell, she grabbed the stunned Ian and yanked him back. He did his best to help, scrabbling awkwardly across the floor.

The zombies, apparently even their low-watt brains catching on that their easy prey was being snatched from them, surged forward with guttural, mumbling growls.

"Haven't got any *brighter* in the last three years, I see," Stone muttered. As Verity dragged Ian behind him, he raised the door like a riot shield and pummeled the first line of zombies back.

Apparently, however, some of them *had* gotten brighter. Driven by the force of Stone's magic, the heavy door bowled three of them over—but the other three flanked it and resumed pounding on the mages' shields.

"We have to get out!" Verity yelled. "It's too tight in here! If we can get outside, we can levitate!"

Stone darted a quick glance at Ian. He still looked stunned, and wasn't moving at anything like his normal quick speed. "Ian—can you move?"

"Yeah," he rasped through gritted teeth.

Stone made a quick decision. "Okay. I'll hold this door on the exit. Verity, get Ian upstairs."

Her eyes flashed. "I won't—"

"You *will*. It's the only way." He backed up a couple steps, pushing the two of them behind him, and pulled the door back until it fit into the opening. From there, he used magic to hold it in place. "Go! I'll follow when you're upstairs!"

Verity's glare would have battered down the door all on its own, but she growled and grabbed Ian's arm. "Hurry *up*. I'll yell when we're at the top."

Stone's focus was fully on the door now. He felt Verity and Ian's weight drop away as they backed up the stairs, but didn't look over his shoulder. It was taking all his magical strength to hold the door in place, and he knew either it or the door itself wouldn't last longer than a few more seconds—a minute at the most.

A terrifying thought struck him then: what if there were *more* of the things upstairs? This was clearly a trap; had whoever laid it assumed the ambush in the basement would be sufficient, or had they left reinforcements concealed behind more illusions in the main house? "Verity!" he boomed. "Are you upstairs?"

"Just reaching," her strained voice replied.

"Watch out for more of them up there!"

"Could've gone all day without saying that. Come *on!*"

In front of Stone, the door cracked, its thick wood splintering as the zombies continued raining blows on it. He poured more Calanarian energy into his barrier, risking a quick glance over his shoulder. The shadowy figures of Verity and the still-staggering Ian had reached the top.

"Come *on,* Alastair!" Verity screamed. "No more up here! Go!"

Stone had no idea how long the door would last. "Get outside!" he yelled back. "I'm coming up!"

Slowly, mindful of how easy it would be to trip as he backed up the steep flight of stairs, he began taking the steps one at a time. He kept up his spell, holding the door in the frame as he moved. Once he reached the top, they could close that door as well. It wasn't as strong as the basement one, but it might hold them for the few seconds they needed to get away.

He'd made it halfway up when he thought he heard something from upstairs.

Was that glass breaking?

An instant later, Verity screamed, her single word unmistakable.

"Fire!"

Oh dear gods, no—

Wait—was that smoke coming through the cracks in the door he was holding?

Was there fire there too?

A loud *whump* sounded from down below, blowing the door up the stairs with enough force to knock Stone over backward. He locked his hand around the railing, barely managing to avoid tumbling back down to the basement, and used his other hand to fling away what was left of the splintered door.

Beyond it was a pretty good vision of Hell—in microcosm, anyway. An inferno of flames lit the basement, while pieces of the zombies littered the room and the stairs. Stone clawed at something cold and wet that had hit his neck, jerking back in horror when it proved to be a gray, severed zombie hand.

Why had their ambusher destroyed his own creations?

Because they're just the first line.

"Alastair! Are you all right?" Verity's cough-laced voice came from the smoke-choked doorway at the top of the stairs. It sounded oddly muddy; the heavy door had muffled most of the downstairs explosion, but not all of it, and now Stone's ears were ringing.

"Coming!" He was coughing too, caught between the smoke from the downstairs blaze and from the one upstairs.

A strong hand gripped his arm as he reached the top. At first, he thought Ian was dragging him back, but then he was looking into Verity's wide, scared eyes. Her sweat-stained face was smeared with soot.

"Come on!" she urged, still coughing.

"Where's Ian?"

"Here." He rose up behind her, still clearly unsteady on his feet. At least he was conscious, though.

"Where are the zombies?" Verity asked, shooting a glance toward the doorway. "Is there more fire down there?"

"Explosion," Stone coughed out. Around them, more fire blazed in the hall. He thought he heard the far-off sound of sirens, but it might just be the ringing in his ears. "Come on—we have to get out of here before they find us."

"Who?"

"Anybody." He grabbed Ian's arm. "Ian—are you with us?"

"Y-yeah. I think so."

"Can you make us invisible until we get away from here?"

His face was dead pale, and he was sweating as hard as Verity. "Don't—know. Head's splitting. Not sure I can—"

There wasn't time to stand around and debate it. The emergency personnel would be here any moment—they might have two or three minutes to get away if they were lucky. "Okay—everybody do their own spell, then. I'll blow out the kitchen window so it looks like the fire did it. Verity, levitate to the roof of the house across the street. I'll get myself and Ian over there."

"Got it." She was already snapping into action, grabbing Ian's arm and dragging him toward the rear of the house. There were definitely sirens approaching now, their strident two-tone wails still not close but getting closer.

Stone's mind spun and his head pounded, but he couldn't waste time thinking things through now. He acted on pure instinct, following Verity to the kitchen, where the fire hadn't reached yet. "Ready?" he rasped.

"Yeah."

Ian nodded.

Stone was concerned about him. He was still dead pale, and didn't seem as if he was coming back as fast as he should. *Can't worry about that now. Verity can tend him when we get away.*

He pointed his hands at the window and let go with a punishing wave of Calanarian energy, blowing it into shards as if another explosion had gone off. "*Go! Go! Go!*"

Verity and Ian were already fading to invisibility. Using magical sight, Stone watched Verity launch herself through the window and upward. As soon as she was free of the opening, he summoned his own invisibility spell and grabbed Ian in a telekinetic grip. He pushed his son out first, then climbed out himself, lifting away. His breath came fast and hard, his heard pounding with the exertion of maintaining two spells, one of them difficult for him, while struggling not to cough.

You've got to do it, he told himself. *No other options.*

It seemed for a moment as if he wouldn't, though. As they drifted across the street and approached the other building's roof, Stone's strength faltered. He bobbled himself and Ian in the air, and might have lost control if a last-second burst of power from Ian didn't grip them and push them over the edge. The two of them landed hard and collapsed, panting.

"Alastair?" Verity's harsh whisper broke through the increasingly-louder sirens, now accompanied by flashing red lights. "Are you all right?"

"I'll be fine. Check Ian."

"We need to get away from here. When the police find those bodies—"

"Don't...think they will." He could barely get the words out around more coughs. "Explosion...in basement. I think...the zombies will be ash before they find them."

"What about Vogel?" She crawled over next to Ian, who wasn't moving.

Stone rolled over onto his back and stared up into the night sky, now choked with smoke from the fire. "Wasn't Vogel… Illusion."

"The body was an illusion?"

"No. Vogel was an illusion. Body was a zombie. Definitely not Vogel." He rolled to his side so he could see them. Was Ian unconscious—or worse? "How is he?"

"Shh. If you can, use illusions to hide us while I check him over. Are you hurt?"

"Nothing major. Worry about him, not me."

Now that he was back in fresh air, Stone's head began to clear. It still hurt, and the exhaustion from all the spellcasting and feedback wasn't going away, but he'd functioned in far worse shape. Fortunately, illusions were easy for him. He wove one of an empty roof, devoted a corner of his mind to maintaining it, and then watched Verity as she worked over the prone Ian. A quick glance with magical sight revealed his son's aura still burned strong, though it flickered with red patches indicating all was not well.

"Is he—"

"Let me work." She sounded distracted, kind but brisk, as she hunched over Ian.

Stone hated being useless, but healing was Verity's strongest magic and there wasn't any way he could help her. If anything could be done, she could do it. His best bet, hard as it was, was to shut up and let her concentrate. He rolled back over and thought about the events of the last few minutes.

Somebody had been on to them—that much was clear. They'd somehow known that Vogel was being tracked. But had they known by whom? Had it been Brathwaite, or were his associates sufficiently advanced now that they could create those mindless zombies and conceal them in the basement on their own? How could Brathwaite or his people possibly have known anyone was after him?

His head hurt too much to dwell on the answers to those questions now—if indeed he would come up with any answers normally. Instead, he focused on the actual rather than the hypothetical. Someone *had* known Vogel was being tracked. They *had* left the zombies in the house, along with the illusions. They *had* used powerful explosives and firebombs to destroy the house—but was that to kill him and his friends, or to eliminate the zombie evidence so the authorities didn't find it?

Stop it, he thought, frustrated. *All you're doing is giving yourself a headache.*

A whole squad of emergency vehicles had now arrived on the scene, spread out along the street below with their red lights whirling. Stone crept to the edge of the roof and peered over, picking out two fire trucks, an ambulance, and a police car. Personnel swarmed around the area, doing their jobs and holding back the growing crowd of concerned onlookers trying to figure out what was going on. So far, at least, the fire didn't appear to have spread to the neighboring structures. That was a relief, at least. It would have been a tragedy if innocents had been injured or died because of this.

Behind him, Verity let out a loud, shuddering sigh.

Stone spun back around. "Is he all right?"

She nodded wearily, brushing sweat and soot off her forehead. "Yeah, he'll be fine. He got smacked pretty hard in the back of the head, but I got to it fast. He might be unconscious for a while, though. His body needs to rest." She coughed a couple times, turning her head away. "What's going on down there?"

So the zombie *had* managed to get through Ian's powerful shield and do enough damage to cause injury. That was impressive—and terrifying. They were getting stronger. "They're dealing with the fire. I don't think anybody's hurt."

She settled back against the roof's edge. "What happened down there, Alastair? How did they know we were following? You said there was an *explosion* in the basement?"

Stone's attention was focused on Ian. He checked with magical sight again, relieved to see most of the red patches in his son's aura had faded. "Yes. Probably to eliminate the evidence. Can't have the mundane authorities finding a flock of zombies." He remembered something Verity had said earlier. "Did you say something about a firebomb?"

"A couple of them, yeah. Somebody tossed them through the windows."

"I thought I heard glass breaking." Damn. If they'd been fast, they might have caught whoever had tossed them, but they'd be long gone now. As the pounding in his head began to subside a bit, he considered. "I think they figured the zombies would kill us, and then the fire would destroy the evidence that they were there. I don't think the fire was meant for us."

"That's not very comforting, you know."

Ian stirred, and Stone immediately crawled over to him. "Ian? Are you back with us?"

His eyes fluttered open. He raised a hand to the back of his head and groaned. "Ow."

"Yeah, it's going to hurt for a while," Verity said. "But I healed the worst of it. You'll be fine."

Ian gingerly sat up and looked around. "How did we get up here?"

"You don't remember?" Stone gripped his shoulder. "You saved us. It was that last burst from you that got us over the roof, or I'd have dropped us."

"Oh. I don't remember that at all. Yay me, I guess." He sighed, then perked up as he noticed the sirens. "We'd better get out of here before the cops start checking the neighborhood."

"My thoughts exactly," Stone said. "Fortunately, illusions are easy. Let's go—we've got a lot to talk about."

CHAPTER THIRTEEN

"They *knew* you were coming?" Eddie couldn't keep the astonishment out of his voice. "I don't get it. We were so careful—"

Two hours had passed since Stone, Verity, and Ian had returned to Caventhorne through the Berlin portal. They, Eddie, and Ward sat around a table in one of the private conference rooms, picking at delivered Indian food and beers Kerrick had brought up.

"I don't get it either." Stone hadn't thought he was hungry, his lungs still aching from all the coughing he'd done, but when the food arrived he'd discovered he was wrong. "But they had to know we were after Vogel."

"Do you think it was Brathwaite?" Ward asked. "Obviously the undead ambush points to him, but it could have been his associates."

"No way to tell for sure," Verity said. "We sure as hell didn't see him around the area."

"We didn't really look, though." Ian picked at his food. He still looked pale, and Stone had tried to get him to lie down for a while. He was having none of that, however, and had insisted on joining the meeting. "We were a little busy at the time."

Eddie turned to face Stone. "But you don't think the fire was meant for you lot?"

"I don't. I haven't got anything to base that on, of course, but I'm guessing they assumed six zombies would be enough to take us out—especially if they got the drop on us." He flashed Verity a smile. "Good job catching on about the milky eyes, by the way. That might have saved us."

She shrugged, looking pleased. "I'm surprised they'd mess up a detail like that, with their knowledge of dead bodies. They probably did it for shock effect."

"Well, it worked on me, at least, but you had your wits about you. Ward, anything about the situation showing up on the news yet?"

Ward had been tapping away on a laptop in front of him. "A couple of stories are hitting now—they describe a firebomb at a Potsdam residence, but no mention of bodies found on the scene. The police and forensics people are sifting through the house, but they say it will be days at minimum before they have anything."

Stone nodded. It was what he'd expected. Something about the process of creating undead caused them to decompose much faster when they were destroyed, with even fresh reanimated bodies turning rapidly to amorphous goo. A fire that hot would have obliterated any vestiges of them, probably including DNA evidence. Zombies made efficient grunt troops, if you were certain you could get rid of them before they were discovered.

"What's our next step?" Ian asked. "If Brathwaite knows we're looking for him, that's going to make him harder to find, I'm guessing."

"Yes." Stone took a moment to quell his growing dread. Brathwaite had been hard enough to locate before—if he went underground, Aldwyn's two-month timetable was beginning to look a lot less generous.

"We still don't know Brathwaite knows you were after him specifically, though," Verity said. "We don't even know if Vogel is working with him."

"No, but I'll bet my house Vogel is, and Brathwaite somehow knew or at least suspected," Stone said. "He's smart, that one, and paranoid. I just didn't think he'd be *that* paranoid."

"Or that technologically aware," Ian said. "This guy comes from two hundred years ago, and the Ordo are magic snobs. What are the odds they'd figure out we'd planted an electronic tracker on Vogel—at least that soon?"

"He comes from two hundred years ago, yeah," Verity said. "But he's had several years to get up to speed. Depending on how open-minded he is, he could be all caught up with modern times by now."

Stone had only been half-listening, as another thought scratched at the corner of his mind. He jerked his head up as it came to him. "Wait. The tracker!"

"What about it?" Eddie looked confused.

Stone leaped from his chair and hurried to his black overcoat, which he'd tossed over another chair near the door. Using magic, he carefully extracted the tracker he'd taken from Vogel's briefcase and tossed it on the table.

Eddie's eyes lit up. "You brought it back with you?"

"I remembered what you said before about having people who can trace fingerprints. I've got no idea if it has any on it, but I didn't touch it."

The librarian grinned. "You're brilliant, mate." He used his own magic to levitate the little thing into an envelope. "'Ang on a tick, and I'll get this sent out right away. Probably won't get anythin' back until tomorrow, though, it bein' this late. Keep yer fingers crossed." He stood. "And after that, I think you three should get some rest. You all look like 'ell, no offense intended. Nothin' more's gonna 'appen tonight."

Stone wanted to object—there was so much more he wanted to discuss—but Eddie was right. The evening's activities had been ex-hausting, and in any case, as long as he insisted they keep going,

Ian would insist on remaining part of the discussion. Even if he and Verity could get by without rest, Ian needed to finish recovering. "Yes, I suppose you're right. Please contact me if you get anything from the tracker."

"You'll be the first one to 'ear," Eddie promised. His expression clouded. "Be careful, though, all of you. If Brathwaite *does* know you're after 'im, 'e might go on the offensive."

Stone honestly didn't think so—in the past, the necromancer hadn't shown himself to be particularly brave or proactive about looking for trouble—but it was good advice.

"We'll be careful," Verity said firmly. "Come on, Ian—time to go. Doctor's orders. You suck at trying to pretend you don't feel like shit."

Stone's phone rang on his nightstand shortly after six a.m. the following morning, startling Raider into darting away, digging his claws into Stone's chest in the process.

He snatched it up, rubbing his chest with his other hand and preparing to give the caller a colorful greeting, but stopped when he saw Eddie's name.

"Really? This early?" he grumbled.

"Mornin', mate," the librarian said brightly. "Did I wake you?"

"You woke me and nearly got me killed by my own cat. I hope you've got something good to make up for it."

"Aww, poor baby. You want me to pop over there and sort out your boo-boo for you?"

"Sod off, Eddie." Stone's heart wasn't in it, though, because he knew his friend well enough to know that if he was taking the piss, he had something to report. "What have you got?"

"My mate got back to me about the tracker."

"Yes, and—?" Stone sat up as Raider tentatively hopped back on the bed looking for forgiveness.

"Let's just say it's a good thing 'e works where 'e does, owes me a favor, and is willin' to work on Saturdays. There *was* a partial print on the tracker, and guess who it came back as?"

"Eddie, it might be lunchtime for you, but it's six in the morning here. If it weren't for bleeding out from cat scratches, I'd barely be conscious. Just spill it, will you?"

"Aww, you're no fun at all." Before Stone could protest, though, he added, "It's from a lovely not-so-young lady by the name of Miriam Padgett."

A thrill went up Stone's spine. "Bloody hell. It *is* Brathwaite."

"Yup, or at least he touched the thing at some point. Why else would 'e do that if 'e didn't know we were trackin' Vogel?"

"And now we know he *does* know." Stone stroked Raider in his lap and pondered. "Why did you say I should be glad your friend works where he does?"

"Because otherwise, we probably wouldn't've got this. You don't think dear old Miriam had any normal reason for her prints to be in the system, do you? It's not like an old bird like that ever got herself arrested."

"So, then, who *does* have her prints, and why?"

"Best if I don't say, because I don't want to compromise this source. But trust me, it's legit. They've got access to all sorts of prints they're not technically supposed to 'ave."

Stone wanted more information, but he'd be a hypocrite if he asked Eddie to divulge confidential sources after all the secrets he was keeping to himself. "Okay, Eddie. Thanks. I'm not sure what we'll do with the information at this point, but it's nice to have it confirmed." *At least now I know Aldwyn was right and Brathwaite's not already dead,* he thought.

"You want us to keep lookin'? I doubt the book ruse will work a second time."

He sighed. "No, I know you've got other things to do. Let me work on this a bit. I'll let you know if I think of anything else." He was about to say goodbye and hang up, when another thought struck him. "Oh—one thing you *can* do, if you're willing."

"I'm always willin' for you, mate." Eddie injected exaggerated salaciousness into his tone. "Just name the time and place and I'm there with bells on."

"I hope you'll have trousers on too. I don't need that kind of image before I've had my coffee. But anyway, if your special clandestine friend can get us anything about what the Potsdam police find, that might be useful. They won't find the zombies, but they might find usable information from the firebomb fragments."

"Good thought. I'll pass that along. Talk soon."

Stone tossed the phone on the nightstand and lay back against the pillows. Eddie's news was useful—at least they now had confirmation of their theory that Brathwaite had been personally involved—but it didn't get him any closer to finding the man. In fact, the contrary was probably true.

He stared into Raider's big green eyes. "Oh, bugger, Raider, what am I going to do? If I can't find the bastard, I don't want to think about what Aldwyn might get up to." He wasn't worried about what Aldwyn might do to *him*—at this point, he was fairly sure he was too valuable to kill, even if it was possible. But his friends and family were another matter. He wondered, if the dragon genuinely did want Brathwaite dead, if he'd be willing to either extend the deadline if Stone could show he was making reasonable progress, or perhaps assist in some way in locating the necromancer.

Somehow, though, he doubted either of those would be good bets. He was on his own with this one, and right now, he was low on options.

CHAPTER FOURTEEN

GINA GOT BACK TO STONE with a text on Monday afternoon, while he was working on a paper to get his mind off the Brathwaite situation. *You still up for talking to you-know-who?*

At least *something* was moving. *You arranged a meeting?*

Yeah, they just got back to me. Tonight, my place?

I'll be there. Even though he felt faintly guilty for spending any time on a side project at this point, he was glad for something to distract him. It was probably best to give Brathwaite some space—if he felt like someone was trying hard to find him, he'd go even deeper underground. It was still difficult to do, though. Stone wasn't deluding himself: the necromancer wouldn't be easy to kill even if he did manage to find him, and the time was ticking away.

Today marked two weeks—a full quarter of his two-month allotment.

Gina had moved sometime in the three years since Stone had been away, but not far. Instead of the small, cramped apartment on the top floor of a building on Delmas Street near downtown San Jose, she now lived in a larger place two streets over.

"Hey, Doc. Come on in. You haven't seen my new place yet, so welcome."

The interior hadn't changed much from her previous apartment. Computer equipment, electronic gear, and geeky toys still covered every flat surface and several square feet of floorspace. She just had more space to spread it out here. Stone carefully picked his way over the drifts.

"Sorry it's a mess—I've been working on a few projects here, and been busy at work. But c'mon—I've got a setup in the guest room. I use it for making YouTube videos, but it should work great for our meeting."

He followed her without comment through the living room and down the hall into a tiny bedroom. She'd set up a table with two chairs in the middle, with a green screen attached to the wall behind it. A camera on a tripod mount faced the table, with a large ring light behind it. A laptop and a microphone on a stand sat in the middle of the table, along with the familiar pink stuffed "tentacle cat" Stone remembered from his only other visit to her previous apartment.

"The light's dimmable," Gina said, puttering around adjusting the camera and something on the laptop. "He doesn't want us to see much of him, so it's only fair he doesn't get to see much of us."

Stone wasn't crazy about this idea, now that he was here. "What's to stop him from recording our conversation and posting it to the internet?"

"Nothing, really. But he won't. I trust the person who set this up, and she trusts him—and besides, it would be as bad for him as for us if he did that. A lot of people are looking for him, and the cops have some pretty good ways of tracking people down through stuff they post. Best not to take chances, especially since he hasn't done anything wrong."

In this case, we hope, Stone thought, but he kept his mouth shut. This wasn't the time. He glanced at his watch. "What time is the meeting?"

"Seven-thirty. I'm just putting the finishing touches on the set-up here." She pointed at the green screen. "Where do you want to be?"

"What?"

She grinned. "It's cute sometimes, how technologically behind the times you are. The green screen makes it easier for me to put up any background you like. Newsroom? Underwater? Mars? Say the word and I'll make it happen."

"Does it matter?"

"You are *no* fun," she muttered. "Okay, *I'll* pick then. Don't say I didn't give you a chance. Go ahead and take a seat, so I can make sure the camera's picking us up properly."

Stone sat in one of the chairs behind the table while she puttered some more. Then she took the seat next to him and clicked something on the laptop. "There we go. See?"

A window appeared on the screen, showing them as their guest would see them. They showed up as shadowy figures in front of what looked like the interior of an ancient gothic castle.

"Like it? I thought it would make you feel right at home. You ready?"

He wasn't, but it was too late to back out now. "Let's do this."

She clicked something else on the laptop. A tone sounded, and a few seconds later a shadowy, full-screen image of a slim male figure appeared. It was difficult to make out any detail, but apparently the man wasn't trusting entirely to electronic means of obscuring his appearance because he also wore an obvious rubber mask—most likely of a clown, given the wild hair and large nose. The background behind him was black.

"Hey," Gina said. "Thanks so much for helping us out. I'm Gina—your friend told you about me, right?"

"Yes." He'd done something to obscure his voice too; it came out as a robotic near-monotone. "Good work you're doing up there."

"Thanks."

"Who's that?" He nodded toward Stone.

"Oh—this is…Doc. He's the one who needs the help."

The clown face turned slightly. "Are you a cop, Mr. Doc?"

"Er…no. I'm not."

"Then why are you interested in what Freakshow is up to?"

Stone glanced at Gina. He'd assumed she would carry most of the conversation, but she merely made a 'go on' gesture below the level of the camera.

"I'm…investigating a rash of kidnappings, which we have reason to believe were committed by at least one Changeling."

"Investigating. Reason to believe. You sure do *sound* like a cop."

"He's not a cop," Gina said. "I promise. He's kind of a…freelancer. You know I work for a P.I., right? He works with him too."

Several seconds of silence passed as the clown-faced man remained still. Stone had almost thought the image had frozen when he spoke again. "What else are you, Mr. Doc?"

"What…do you mean?"

"Come on—don't make me come out and say it. We both know what I'm talking about."

And then Stone did know. "Yes. We do. And yes, I'm a mage." He spoke evenly, with no hesitation. "Does that matter?"

"I don't know. Does it?"

"Look," he said, frustrated with this annoying man and his annoying ways. "I haven't got a clue what you're talking about, and I don't really want to. All I want to do is find out who's been taking these kids, and why. I'd think you'd care too, since it looks like at least one of them might be a Changeling."

The silence this time was different. When the man spoke again, his robotic tone sounded contemplative. "One of the children might be a Changeling?"

"We suspect so, yes. In fact, I suspect *all* the kidnapped children are Changelings. That's the other reason I wanted to talk to you about this. From what I understand, you've got your finger on the pulse of what the Changeling underground is up to. Have you heard anything about this?"

"No," he said immediately. "I haven't."

"You don't have any idea who might be responsible?" Gina asked.

"Why do you think I would know such a thing?"

"Listen," Stone said, keeping his voice calm. "Nobody's suspecting you." That wasn't true, of course, and he was sure the guy knew it, but the longer they could keep things polite, the more information he was likely to get—and the more likely the Freakshow leader would let something slip if he *did* know something. It was a lot harder to do this with no auras and no facial cues, but even in shadow, his body was visible. "The reason Gina suggested I speak with you is *because* you're familiar with…certain subcultures within the Changeling community."

"The freaks," the man said. "Go ahead and say it. It's not a slur."

"I was under the impression it was—at least if *I* were to say it. I'm trying to be polite here, Mr.—"

"You can call me Quasi."

"—Mr. Quasi. I'm referring to the…less conventionally attractive members of your community."

"Ah, yes. The undesirables, who've banded together to form their own bonds when rejected by the rest of our society. What makes you think they—we—are responsible for this terrible crime, Mr. Doc?"

"Look—you can stop calling me 'Mr. Doc.' I'd be surprised if you didn't already know who I am."

"I do—but we don't use names when speaking by electronic means. Safer that way for all involved."

"Fair enough. But the answer to your question is that in one case, the kidnapper appeared briefly on a doorbell camera at the home of one of the victims. Based on analysis of this person's gait, my source has identified them as a Changeling who goes by the name of 'Squeak.' Do you know this person? Have you heard of them?"

Another longer-than-expected pause. "Not personally. I've heard the name, though. You're certain of your identification?"

"I can send you the video if it will help you. My sources seemed fairly sure."

"Yes, please do."

Stone looked at Gina. He'd already forwarded the video on to her.

"Hang on," she said, fiddling with the laptop. To Quasi, she said, "give me a place to send it."

Quasi did something offscreen, and an email address popped up on Gina's screen.

"There," she said.

"Give me a moment."

Stone sat still, closely watching Quasi as he turned away, while Gina toyed with her pink stuffed cat. Five minutes later, the Freakshow leader focused back on the screen. "That isn't Squeak."

"It isn't? How do you know that?"

"Is the timestamp on the video correct?"

"As far as I'm aware, yes. The person I got it from wouldn't gain anything from trying to fake it."

"I checked it against the metadata," Gina said. "Nobody's messed with it. So why do you say that isn't Squeak?"

"Because I didn't tell you the truth before. I *do* know Squeak, and I was with him that night, at a party. Big blowout out in West-wood. We were there most of the night. No way he could've been snatching kids in San Diego at the same time."

Stone exchanged glances with Gina and let out a slow breath. "So you're saying someone is trying to *frame* this Squeak person? Why would they do that?"

"No idea," Quasi said. "This is bad news, though. If somebody's trying to frame Changelings for crimes…especially ones as bad as kidnapping…"

"That's not a good look for any of us," Gina agreed soberly.

"And if they're grabbing Changeling kids…" Quasi's electronic voice took on a low growl. "I need to investigate this further, Mr. Doc."

"Perhaps we can work together, if we're on the same side."

"No, I don't think so. We both want to catch whoever this is, yeah, but don't think that puts us on the same side."

Before Stone could say anything he might later regret, Gina spoke up quickly. "Can you at least tell us if you get any leads? We can't put these kids at risk, whether we're right or not about them being Changelings. We have to be careful."

"Let me see what I can find out," he said. "No promises. This sounds like something we need to handle on our own. Because I'm not sure I believe you, Mr. Doc, that normie law enforcement doesn't have their noses stuck into this, and I don't give a damn about what they want."

"They're not," Stone said. "I promise. There *are* others involved, but they're…a specialized group, not affiliated with mainstream law enforcement."

"Ah. Mage stuff."

"Sort of."

"That might make it worse. But like I said, I'll think about it. Best I can do. Gina, keep up the good work."

The clown-headed figure winked out, and the screen went to black.

Stone stared at the screen. "Well. That didn't go as planned."

"No. And now it sounds like your friends' best lead is a dud."

"Do you believe him when he says it wasn't this Squeak person? He could be trying to protect him, if they're friends."

Gina shook her head, looking sober. "I don't know Quasi, but I do know my friend who helped me set up this meet, and she knows him. He's passionate about the Changeling cause. He would never cooperate with anybody who's hurting Changeling kids."

"We don't know they're hurting them. But I'll take your word for it. I'm still fairly ignorant about Changeling culture." He sighed, getting up. "I'll report that back to my friend, but it *does* leave us without a lead."

"Maybe not." Gina closed the laptop and stood. "There are other ways to approach this."

"How?"

"How good are your friends? What kind of tech do they have access to?"

"Not…certain. Fairly good, I suspect. Why?"

"Well…I can probably do part of this. If there really *was* a party in Westwood on the night the kid in San Diego was taken, it'll be all over social media. Changelings don't show up on camera, remember, so it would just look like a normal party to anybody who isn't one of us or a mage. If somebody really did frame Squeak, including mimicking his mannerisms, their human form will have to look a lot like his. We can scan the photos and videos and see if we can find somebody who looks similar."

Stone frowned. "What's that going to do, though? If Squeak didn't do it and you trust Quasi, that won't get us any closer to our kidnapper."

"No, but it will give Squeak an alibi. If Quasi thinks we're genuinely trying to help clear his friend, he'll probably be more willing to help with other stuff."

"Like what?" Stone was definitely out of his element as Gina warmed to her idea.

She spoke fast and enthusiastically. "Like trying to figure out who'd *want* to frame Squeak. Somebody obviously doesn't like him a lot, if they're trying to get him arrested for kidnapping. So there's got to be a reason for it, and somebody else might know what it is."

"That's a good point," he admitted. "But where do my friends and their technology come in?"

"If we can figure out who the person might be, they might have more information about them." She shook her head. "Something weird is going on here, Doc."

"I'm beginning to concur. This sounds like there might be more to it than simple kidnappings. But it still leaves us with the main question: whoever did this, *why* did they do it? We can't get ahead of ourselves—we still don't know for sure that all the children *are* Changelings. But going on the assumption that they are, what's the kidnapper to gain from taking them, if they're not looking for a ransom?"

"No idea. But I'm sure, whatever it is, it's the key to solving this." She waved for him to precede her out of the room. "Let me give that some more thought, and talk to a couple more people. I'll update Jason too, unless there's some reason you don't want me to."

"No, of course not. I'm hoping he and Amber will have some other insights. Just remind them to be discreet."

"Don't worry." Her normally cheerful expression was still grim. "I sure hope whoever's doing this hasn't killed those kids. Not just because that would be horrible, but because if somebody's trying to frame Changelings for something like that, it could end up causing a lot more trouble. And getting a lot more people hurt."

Stone hadn't even thought about that. His little side job was getting worse by the day—just when he couldn't afford to let it take up much of his time.

CHAPTER FIFTEEN

A FEW MORE DAYS PASSED without any useful updates on either of Stone's two cases. Eddie got in touch on Thursday morning, and he popped over to London to have a pint with him and Ward at the Dancing Dragon.

"Wish we could give you better info," Eddie said. "Tracing the firebombs was a good idea, but I'm afraid it turned out to be a dud."

"How so?"

"Turns out both the firebombs tossed through the window and the ones planted in the basement were put there by a local gang called 'die Teufel,' which means 'the Devils.' They're a small-time gang in the area, and they're known for 'avin' a thing for explosives."

"Did the authorities catch them?"

"They found enough bits and bobs in the wreckage to identify their 'andiwork, and picked up a few of 'em. They claim they were 'ired by an anonymous source and paid with a cash drop."

"Damn. Do the police believe them?"

"Yeah, unfortunately. The blokes 'ave done this kind of free-lance work before. The authorities are still tryin' to track down the source of the payment, of course, but between you and me I doubt they will since magic was involved."

Stone sighed. Another lead lost, and time was still ticking away.

"'Ey, Stone?"

Stone looked up to see both Eddie and Ward watching him with concern. "What?"

"You said before that whoever's got you doin' this job gave you two months to do it. If I'm countin' right, a good chunk of that's already passed."

Leave it to his perceptive friends to get right to the heart of things. "Yes. Seventeen days, to be exact. Not like I'm counting."

Ward looked uncomfortable, as if he didn't want to say his next words. "What…happens if you can't do it? Brathwaite is smart, and clearly he's very interested in remaining underground. Do you know what this person will do if you fail to locate him in the allotted time?"

"Not a bloody clue." Suddenly, Stone was tired. He drained his pint and stood. "Whatever it is, though, I suspect it won't be pleasant—and it likely won't affect me directly. So failing isn't an option, even if I end up having to get much more proactive than I'm comfortable with."

"What's that mean?" Eddie asked.

Stone waved him off. "Don't worry—it won't involve you. I know you two don't want to put yourselves directly in the path of danger, and I respect that."

The two exchanged glances. "We'll keep lookin'," Eddie said at last, resolutely. "We'll make this work, mate."

Stone wasn't so sure of that. He wasn't sure of much of anything at the moment.

Back home in California, Stone invited Verity and Ian over to give them the latest information, since he didn't want to send it in texts. They met at the Encantada house, and he told them what Eddie and Ward had found out.

"Great," Ian said. "So we're out of ideas." He'd recovered fully from his knock on the head, thanks to Verity's prompt healing and possibly some additional ministrations from Gabriel.

"*Are* you out of ideas?" Verity asked Stone.

"At the moment, yes." He considered. "Ian…"

"Yeah?"

He hesitated, reluctant to open this door but seeing no other option. "I met with Gabriel a while ago, and asked if he'd be willing to help. At the time, he told me he couldn't, but that if we legitimately exhausted all our other means to find Brathwaite, he might be willing to see what he could do."

"And you think this might be that time."

He spread his hands. "I don't see any other avenues, do you? At this point, we know Brathwaite knows someone is looking for him. I'm not sure whether he knows *who* that is—and specifically whether it's me. I'm almost certain he doesn't know *why.* Why would I want to kill him after all these years, if I haven't bothered to try before? As far as he knows, he hasn't done anything to get back on my radar. But if we push this too hard, he might grow even more suspicious and either go deeper underground where we'll never find him, or go on the offensive—and I do *not* want either of those things to happen. If he hurts someone I care about, I'll never forgive myself. So, reluctant as I am to involve Gabriel, I'm not seeing a choice."

Ian nodded soberly. "I'll ask him."

"Thank you. I have a feeling he's got sources we can't begin to match. He's also based in Europe, which means he's certainly got a better handle on magical goings-on over there." Once again, Stone wished he could let Ian in on his master's true nature. It seemed wrong not to, given Ian's status as a fellow scion. It would also make a lot of things a lot easier. But as much as he ached to do it, it wasn't his place to reveal that particular truth. Perhaps someday

Gabriel would reveal it himself, but until then, he'd have to pay close attention to his mental scorecard and make the best of it.

Stone didn't hear back from Gina until the next evening. She texted him at seven-thirty, as he was returning to the Encantada house after picking up some takeaway.

Squeak has turned up.

He remained in the car as he answered. *Where?*

Call me if you can—too much to text.

He immediately did, and she answered on the first ring. "You found him?" he demanded. "Where?"

"The way I mentioned—checking photos and videos of the party in Westwood. It's pretty obvious from watching the videos. He doesn't make any effort to hide the way he moves. He's probably proud of it."

"How does that help us, though?"

"Well, for one thing, it'll make him easier to spot if I see him again."

"If you'll forgive me for saying so, that still doesn't sound like a lot of help. What kind of party was it?"

"I dunno, typical Hollywood party, I guess. Edgy, lots of B-list actors, hangers-on, cool kids, fashion people…you know. It was held in a warehouse which I'm pretty sure isn't really a warehouse. And before you ask, I didn't see anybody I could identify as Quasi. I didn't actually try. It's a trust thing again."

Stone was reasonably convinced the Freakshow leader had been telling the truth about not being involved, so that didn't bother him. "Okay, so now we know how to identify Squeak. But I still don't see how that's going to help us."

"You wanted to talk to him, right?"

"Yes, but without a name—"

"I don't have a name yet, but I know where he is. Unfortunately, that's not going to help us much either, though."

"Why not?"

"When I say I know where he is, I mean right now. He's at a restaurant with some friends. I've been monitoring social media for some of the other people who were tagged at the party, and a couple of them were just tagged at a place called The Green Room in West Hollywood fifteen minutes ago. It's a trendy vegetarian restaurant. I checked the photos, and he's definitely with them."

"Bloody hell, that's amazing."

She laughed. "It *is* pretty amazing what you can do with tech these days, but that's bush-league stuff. No hacker skills required, just a lot of patience. But anyway, I guess I'll have to keep looking, since nobody tagged him specifically. That's actually kind of odd, since the way he's dressed, he looks like he wants attention."

"Maybe he's lying low because Quasi told him someone is trying frame him."

"Yeah, good point. But that means we don't know his real name. Once we track that down, maybe I can figure out where he hangs out more often."

"But wait—you said he's at this restaurant now?"

"Yeah—looks like they just got there. But—"

"Can you send me a good photo of him from whatever you saw?"

"Sure, but—"

"Brilliant. Thank you, Gina. Please send it right away. I'll take it from here."

"But—"

"You mentioned how amazing technology can be—magic can be fairly amazing too. I'll talk to you soon."

He ended the call before she could respond, grabbed his bag of takeaway, and hurried into the house. Raider eyed the bag longingly as he strode by, but he stopped only long enough to stash it in the refrigerator.

"Sorry, mate—this curry would play hell with your digestion. You'll have to settle for kibble right now. I'll get you something better when I get back, I promise."

Occasionally, luck favored Stone, and this was one of those times. When he located The Green Room on an online map and compared it against his network of ley lines, he discovered one that passed only a block away.

He studied the photos Gina sent him, used his disguise amulet to make himself appear as an early-twenties club kid dressed in the same style as the others, and formed the pattern in his mind that would take him to Los Angeles. Once again, he silently thanked Stefan Kolinsky for teaching him to travel this way, since there were no public portals in the area and the only private one he knew of would take longer to get permission to use than he probably had before Squeak moved on.

He used an invisibility spell to avoid being seen when he rematerialized, and found himself on a sidewalk in front of a closed clothing store. After checking his map again, he set off at a brisk walk toward his destination.

The Green Room was easy to spot. A low-slung building with a retro-style neon sign, it sat back from the street behind a parking lot studded with tall palm trees strung with twinkling lights. Every spot in the parking lot was full, and several groups of young people lounged outside talking and smoking.

Based on the photos of Squeak, Stone didn't think he'd have much trouble spotting the tall, gangly young man even if he hadn't been wearing a red velvet sport jacket. Still, he had to enter the restaurant itself and bribe the hostess to let him pass without putting his name on the list for a table.

The inside was even more crowded than the outside. Most of the tables were packed full of more people than they were designed to hold, sometimes with small young women sitting on their boyfriends' laps. Stone didn't recognize the music, which pounded so loudly it was hard for him to hear himself think. Between his students at the University and the gym where he worked out, he used to at least be able to identify current popular songs, but after his three-year hiatus he was thoroughly out of the loop.

He spotted Squeak on his first trip through, holding court with five other early-twenties club kids at a horseshoe-shaped booth barely big enough to hold them all. They were all laughing and drinking; it appeared they had already finished their meals but didn't plan to leave any time soon.

Using a disregarding spell so nobody would notice him watching, he studied the group with mundane sight, starting with Squeak himself. The young man's jacket was ironically garish, with satin lapels, a brocade pattern, and an acid-green silk pocket square poking untidily from the breast pocket. Under the jacket, he wore a gray T-shirt with the logo of a band called the "Sewer Rats," complete with cartoon image of a leering rat giving the viewer the finger. Topping off his ensemble, he'd teased his white-blond hair until it stood up straight from the top of his head. Stone wondered why whoever had tried to frame Squeak had worn a hat—that hair alone would have easily given him away. Perhaps they'd been attempting to be subtle.

The others at the table, four men and two women, all had the same look—young, energetic, noisy. The kind of people who took up space and set trends—or more likely didn't care about them at all—rather than following them. They weren't exactly the Beautiful People, but all of them had the excess of confidence that made them seem more attractive than they were.

All of that changed when Stone shifted to magical sight. Instantly, the glitzy, trendy clubgoers melted away, leaving in their place what looked like a collection of monsters out for a night on the town.

All six of them were Changelings, and all six were unsettling in different ways. One of the women's dark skin changed to chunks of gray rock, while the other had green scales, a long, pointed nose, and prominent fangs. The men on either side of Squeak looked like a muscular, hairy ape and something that resembled a misshapen possum with beady black eyes and a prehensile tail holding his drink, while the one on the far end defied description. The best Stone could come up with was some kind of fish-creature from far below where divers normally ventured.

Mindful that if he didn't move soon, someone might notice him despite the disregarding spell, he shifted position and studied Squeak. The young man's T-shirt, it turned out, was a sly nod to his true form—assuming his name hadn't already given it away. Squeak was a scruffy-looking rat, with a pointy nose, black oil-drop eyes, patchy gray fur, and prominent rounded ears. The thin, bony pink hand gripping his beer had tiny claws at the end of the fingers. Far from resembling the cute rodents children purchased from pet stores, he looked like he'd just crawled up from the same sewer featured in his shirt's band logo.

Stone looked away before he got caught staring, wondering how many of the six were members of Freakshow. He hadn't seen that many Changelings before his hiatus, and now that he saw six of the so-called "ugly" ones together, he understood a little better why they'd want to spend time with their own kind. Since Changelings only saw their, and each other's, true forms, Stone could see why associating with the "attractive" Changelings—the cats, foxes, wolves, and other forms society found aesthetically pleasing—could be hard on them, both physically and emotionally. Especially if the "pretty" ones developed superiority complexes due to their genetic privilege.

Hell, he'd seen it enough among mundanes, and even mages. He knew with no particular conceit that society considered him attractive, and he was certain he'd received many advantages, both professionally and socially, because of it. It was difficult sometimes for him to watch his less attractive and socially adept students struggle to find acceptance. It was a hard thing to get around, even for him. He occasionally felt guilty that his dating preferences leaned strongly toward beautiful women, whom he usually had no trouble convincing to go out with him (although maintaining a relationship with them was another story that had nothing to do with physical characteristics). And his students weren't, for the most part, actively ugly, but merely plain. These Changelings were frightening in their conventional ugliness—but they'd found each other, and now they looked like they were having as much fun as everyone else in the restaurant.

Stone faded into the shadows, debating his next move. He glanced around the other parts of the restaurant, noticing for the first time that Squeak's group weren't the only Changelings here. On the other side near the front window, another group of six included four of them, all male—a handsome red fox with a plumy tail, an intense-looking, shaggy gray wolf, a satyr with a red beard and flowing, curly hair, and what looked like a sleek, black seal. They sat with two mundane women, and as Stone continued to watch, a couple of them shot contemptuous looks toward Squeak's table. One said something, and all four of them laughed while the two women looked confused.

That group wasn't Stone's concern, though. He needed to talk to Squeak, but not while the Changeling was surrounded by his crew. He didn't have a vehicle, so if they all got up and left, he'd have no way to follow them. It would be best if he did it here.

He was debating how to get Squeak away from his friends when the group suddenly shuffled around. The fish-man and the possum exited the booth and stood aside, making room for Squeak to slide out. He said something to them and headed for the back of the restaurant.

Aha. Nature calls, even for humanoid rats.

Stone gave him a few seconds' head start, then augmented the disregarding spell and followed him. As expected, he pushed open the door to the men's room and strode inside.

Stone pondered his next move. It wasn't likely Squeak would be alone in there, but at least he was away from his friends. Sure, it would be awkward to try initiating a conversation in the loo, but given the choice between awkwardness and losing sight of his quarry, the option was obvious. He followed the Changeling inside.

Surprisingly, based on most club restrooms Stone had been in, this one didn't hit him with a wall of stench when he opened the door—unless you counted pot smoke, anyway. The music from out front seemed even louder in here. The place had two stalls, a row of four urinals, and some sinks along the side wall with scratched, graffiti-scrawled mirrors. Squeak stood at the urinal farthest from the door. The other three were unoccupied, but a quick surreptitious glance revealed the feet of someone inside one of the stalls.

Stone went to a sink and began washing his hands, hoping the stall guy would leave before anybody else came in. Once again, fortune favored him. The toilet flushed and a beefy man exited the stall, sweeping out without looking at either Stone or Squeak—and without washing his hands.

Squeak, who had finished his business and was now washing his own hands, muttered, "Gross, dude…"

Stone figured that was the best opening he was going to get, so he drew breath to say something.

The door opened again—this time to admit two of the Change-lings from the other table. The red fox and the wolf stopped just inside the door, slow smiles spreading across their faces.

"Hey, wouldya look at what we got here," the fox said. Without magical sight, he was an unremarkable-looking Latino man with brush-cut hair and a bright white tank top. The wolf was white and pasty, his prominent nose dominating an equally plain face. They both ignored Stone.

"Whoa, man, you go out in public lookin' like that?" the wolf added. "'Course, compared to that butt-ugly crew out there at the table, you the pretty one, aren't you, Ratso?"

Squeak glared at them. "Fuck you, asshole."

Fox snorted, his face wreathed in contempt. "Yeah, like any-body'd ever wanna fuck *you*." He took a step closer.

Stone had no idea why they were all acting like he wasn't there—perhaps he'd turned up the volume a bit too much on the disregarding spell—but he remained silent for now. If this was only posturing, it would be over soon. Hopefully before anybody else came in. He remained at the sink and watched the exchange via the mirror.

Squeak finished washing his hands and approached. "Get outta my way, pretty boy."

Fox and Wolf stood shoulder to shoulder, blocking the door. "We ain't stoppin' ya."

The rat Changeling was no coward—or at least he'd downed enough liquid courage to be a good substitute. "I said, get outta my way." He stalked forward and tried to shove Fox aside.

Fox's face twisted in disgust. "Fuck you, man—who said you could touch me with your ratty hand?" He gave his shoulder an ex-aggerated swipe. "Shit, man, I prob'ly got the boo-monic plague or some shit now!"

Wolf, apparently, was a man of fewer words. He glared at Squeak, then, moving faster than a guy his size should be able to, he buried his fist-paw in the other Changeling's gut.

Or tried to, anyway. Squeak moved fast, ducking to the side so Wolf's fist swished air. Squeak grabbed his collar and used his own momentum to send him sliding across the floor, where he stopped just short of the urinals.

"That was a big mistake, ugly," Fox growled, wading in.

"Oh, yeah? You wanna mess up your pretty little tail, himbo? Bring it."

Stone, still watching with magical sight, saw that Squeak's aura was now on high alert. He was trying not to show it, but he was scared. He might be strong and scrappy enough to take one of these guys, but not both of them.

Wolf scrambled back to his feet, putting Squeak between him and Fox. "We gonna fuck you up, Ratso."

Fox snatched a glance at Stone, appearing to notice him for the first time. "You better clear outta here, man. This ain't your problem."

Stone turned around so he was facing them. "I don't think so. I was just about to talk to my friend, here." He indicated Squeak, who looked at him like he was crazy.

"This ugly dude your friend? I'm sorry, man. But I ain't gonna say it again. Get the fuck out."

"And *I* say again—I'm not going anywhere."

Fox glared. "You *wanna* get hurt?"

Squeak took his opportunity as soon as Fox's attention was off him. He rushed forward, threw his arms around the other Changeling, and bulled him hard into the door.

Unfortunately for Squeak, it didn't do much beyond knocking the wind out of the guy. Fox *oof*ed and slid partway down the door before catching his balance, but by that point Wolf was moving in.

"Bloody hell, *enough!*" Stone barked. He raised both hands, picked up both Fox and Wolf in telekinetic grips, and raised them two feet off the ground.

"Fuck! He's a *mage!*" Fox yelled.

Stone held them there, letting them pump their legs and thrash around like a pair of cartoon characters trying to run in midair. "You were just leaving, weren't you? I'll let you down if you leave here and exit through the back door. What do you say?"

"*Fuck* you, mage scum!"

But Wolf, apparently, had gotten the message. "C'mon, dude," he said to Fox. "Let's get outta here. We don't want no trouble with no magic man."

"Listen to your friend, Mr. Fox," Stone said calmly. "There's no reason for this to escalate. What do you say? If I let you go, will you leave peacefully?"

"Yeah," Wolf said. "We're outta here."

Fox glared, but finally snorted and nodded. "Whatever. Ugly ain't worth gettin' no plague over."

Stone watched their auras, setting the odds at about fifty-fifty that they'd actually leave without trying to take another swipe at Squeak. "Okay, I'm going to let you down now. Off you go, and don't let me see you around here anymore tonight."

They'd stopped pumping their legs by now, settling for glaring at him. He lowered them to the floor, held them there a moment longer to show them he could, and then let go.

For a second, they hovered at the decision point. Stone could almost see the gears turning in their heads, and hoped Squeak wouldn't do anything stupid. He preferred to end this confrontation with no bloodshed if possible.

Finally, wisdom prevailed. With a last glare first at Stone, then at Squeak, the two Changelings sloped out of the bathroom. They tried to slam the door behind them, but the hydraulic closer robbed them of even that satisfaction.

"I coulda taken 'em," Squeak muttered.

"I'm sure you could have. But I'm guessing you came here to enjoy some time with your friends, not get into a fight in a bathroom that smells like piss and marijuana."

The Changeling's eyes narrowed. "What do you want, anyway? You said you wanted to talk to me. Were you lyin' to get rid of those guys?"

"No, I actually *do* want to talk to you. But could we do it somewhere else, before anyone else comes in here?" When Squeak seemed about to hesitate, he added, "I won't take much of your time. Perhaps a few minutes in exchange for helping you avoid that confrontation?"

"What do you *want,* man? I don't know any mages." He moved in jerky jolts, darting his gaze around as if expecting to get jumped again. Even his voice was a little ratty.

"I want to talk about your friend Quasi." He lowered his voice. "I'm sure he told you by now that someone's trying to frame you for a series of kidnappings."

"Shit…" He looked nervous.

"Come on—let's get out of here. I promise, I mean you no harm. I just have a few questions."

He considered. "Okay. But I'm not goin' far. Lemme go tell my friends I'll be back."

"I'll go with you. Don't worry, no one will notice me."

After re-applying the disregarding spell, Stone followed Squeak back out into the restaurant. He noticed immediately that Wolf and Fox's party had left, and spotted no other Changelings in the area aside from Squeak's friends. He watched the rat Changeling carefully, more than halfway expecting him to try to run, but surprisingly he didn't. He spoke to his group for a few moments, leaned into kiss the lizard-scaled woman, and then came back over.

"Okay, what? Let's go out front. Nobody will bother us out there, and I need a smoke anyway."

They found an unoccupied corner of the parking lot, and Squeak immediately pulled out a pack of cigarettes. "Want one?"

"No, thank you."

The Changeling lit up and studied Stone. "Okay, what about Quasi?"

"I assume he told you about the kidnappings?"

"Yeah. That's some scary shit. Are you the guy he talked to? He said the dude had a British accent. You don't look like the guy he described, but I'm guessin' that's a magic thing."

"I am, yes. I talked to him earlier this week, along with a Changeling friend of mine."

"Oh, right, Gina. I've heard of her. She does good work."

Stone couldn't continue looking directly at Squeak; the man's twitchy movements were setting his nerves on edge. Instead, he stared out over the parking lot. "What I want to know is, do you have any enemies? Like perhaps those two blokes in the bathroom?"

Squeak snorted. "Those assholes? I never saw them before tonight."

"Really?"

"Yeah, man. Happens a lot—you know, the pretty boys fuck with us freaks 'cause they think they can get away with it. Mostly we just avoid each other, y'know?"

"Okay, then—do you have any *other* enemies? Anyone you think might want to frame you for kidnapping children?"

Squeak considered, then shook his head several times. "Nah. No way."

"Are you sure? No one you've got on the wrong side of for whatever reason?"

He considered longer this time, but once more shook his head. "I can't think of anybody. I mean, come on, dude—I like every-body. I'm a friendly guy." He gave a sly laugh. "Except my exes, you know. Some o' them don't like me very much. But everybody's got those, and they don't frame you for kidnapping."

"So you don't have any animosity going between your fellow…"

"Go ahead and say freaks. It's okay. I'm proud of who I am."

"…your fellow freaks and the so-called 'pretty boys'?" He leaned in closer. "I know you're affiliated with Freakshow, so…"

Squeak glanced around as if afraid someone might overhear. "Don't say that too loud, okay?"

"Sorry. But you are, then?"

"Yeah, sure. Us freaks get the short end of things, so we gotta take steps to even the playing field a little, y'know? But shit, man, that doesn't mean I'd mess with *kids*. Especially not *our* kids."

"Even if they were pretty?" He thought of Gurpreet Singh, who sounded like some kind of lizard or alligator. Were there attractive alligators? It was all a matter of perspective, he supposed.

Squeak looked genuinely shocked. "Dude, I'm tellin' you— there's no *way* I'd hurt a kid. Pretty, ugly, normie…doesn't matter. Whoever's doin' that is messed up." He sighed. "But I wish I could tell why they'd want to frame *me*. Like I said, I haven't done any- thing to anybody to make 'em that pissed at me."

"Okay. Well, if you think of anyone later, I'll leave you my number. I'm on your side, Squeak. I want to figure this out as much as you want to clear your name."

The Changeling aimed a suspicious glare at him. "Why do you even care? Magic man like you, I'd think you got better things to be worried about then some freak he doesn't even know gettin' framed."

"I was asked to look into this. Quasi didn't tell you that?"

"Not really. He didn't tell me much, except somebody who looked like me got caught on camera snatchin' some kid."

"Do you mind if I show you something?" He pulled his phone from his pocket. "It's the video those people took. Perhaps if you see it, you'll recognize something. I assume Quasi didn't show you that, either?"

"Nope. But sure, whatever. I'd like to see it."

Stone looked around again to make sure nobody was watching them, then cued up the video and held out the phone so they could both watch it.

Squeak studied it in silence, but shook his head. "Sorry, man. I see where folks might think that was me, though. Whoever it is, they really got the way I move down. But I don't know who it is."

Damn. Well, it was a faint hope anyway. "All right. Well, thank you for speaking with me. If you do think of anything else, or hear anything else, please contact me." He tore a page from his notebook and scrawled his mobile number on it.

"I will. I hope you catch the dude. Quasi said one o' the kids they took might be a Changeling. That pisses me off, even if it *wasn't* somebody tryin' to mess with me. And hey, thanks to you too. I coulda taken those two assholes, but the help was appreciated."

Stone returned to the Encantada house and texted Gina while picking at his warmed-over curry. *Do you have time to talk?*

Yeah, sure. Got something?

He hit her contact number and put it on speaker. "I talked to Squeak."

"What?" She sounded surprised. "How? We don't know who he is, so you couldn't have called him."

"Don't ask."

"MFM?"

"Precisely." He glanced at Raider, who was enjoying a plate of aromatic cat food at the other end of the counter. "I went to Los Angeles. He was still at the Green Room."

"Oh. Right. You went through a portal."

Stone hadn't been aware that Gina knew about portals, but it made sense. "Er…yes."

"And he actually talked to you? What did he say?"

"He's as upset as we are that someone's trying to frame him, but unfortunately he couldn't come up with anybody who hates him enough to do something like that. He claims he's a friendly bloke and the only people who don't like him are his exes, who wouldn't do something like that."

"Hmm…" Several seconds passed as she pondered. "Well, while you were gone, I managed to dig back into his social-media history and find a name for him. It's Justin Chan. He's a graphic designer who works in advertising and fashion, mostly. I'll keep digging to see if anything turns up. You'd be surprised at what people post online and then forget about. Maybe a connection will turn up. I'll update Jason too. A couple of paying cases heated up right now, but maybe he can find time to help out some."

"Sounds good. I'm not sure there's much more I can do at this point, unless you do manage to find more information."

"You should talk to your shadowy contact. If they have access to better tech than I do, they might get something faster."

"You know, that's a good idea. It's been a while since I updated them anyway. Thank you, Gina."

"No problem. I live for this kind of thing, even if it *wasn't* pissing me off that somebody's framing Changelings."

Agent Huxley didn't answer when he called the number he had for her, so he left a message that he had something to report. She got back to him in fifteen minutes.

"That was fast." He'd finished the curry and was rinsing the dishes so Raider didn't try to lick them. He hadn't been kidding about what spicy Indian food did to cats' litterbox output. "Don't you have anything else to do on a Friday night?"

"I've actually got my kids this week, so we were watching a movie. What have you got?"

"Quite a bit since we last spoke." He quickly brought her up to speed on what he'd discovered, starting with their suspicions about the kidnapped children being Changelings and the talk with Quasi (whom he didn't name) and ending with the conversation with Squeak. "My associate is checking into Squeak's social media presence, hoping to identify someone who might have an issue with him, but she suggests things might go faster if you bring your own resources to bear."

"Yeah. I'll see what I can do." She lowered her voice. "I'm frustrated, to be honest. This is a huge case—I was going to call you because another kid went missing the day before yesterday. I don't know if it's connected to the others, but I'm gonna assume if any kids three or younger get snatched in California and we can't explain why, they're connected."

"Probably a reasonable assumption. So this new one fits the demographic?"

"Yeah. One and a half years old, grabbed without a trace, no ransom demands or body found."

"Bloody hell. Okay, well, send me the details on that one, too. We'll do the best we can, but I hope you're prioritizing this too."

"As much as I can. Like I said, I'm frustrated, because it's pretty much just me on the case, from our agency. The mundane cops are all over it, of course—even the FBI is getting interested, even though we have no evidence the kids have been taken across state lines. There's a lot of pressure to solve this one."

"Okay. We'll keep working. You get back to your movie."

She snorted. "Don't think I'm not working. I've answered four emails and taken two calls, and the movie's only half over. My kids are used to it by now. And thanks, Stone. That's good info you've given me. It'll help. You sure you don't want a job?"

"Trust me—you don't want me working for you."

CHAPTER SIXTEEN

STONE SLEPT BADLY, haunted by unsettling dreams that combined hideous-looking, menacing Changelings devouring screaming babies, and James Brathwaite at the head of an army of undead soldiers ripping his friends to pieces one by one while he reanimated each of the pieces and added it to the army. Above the whole thing, Aldwyn loomed larger than life, his arms spread to encompass the vision and his thin lips twisted into a macabre smile. The dragon radiated an overpowering sense of impending doom, with the sound of a ticking clock growing increasingly louder and faster until it boomed like a bass drum during a heavy-metal solo.

Stone jerked awake, heart pounding, to discover himself wound up in his sheets and Raider looking at him with concern.

"It's all right, mate," he murmured, stroking the cat's head until he settled in and began purring again. His phone's clock on the nightstand read 5:42. He never got up that early unless he had a good reason, and nightmares weren't a good reason.

Still, the dream did give him one solid bit of motivation.

He needed to talk to Aldwyn.

Part of what had been bothering him subliminally all this time was that the dragon had never come out and told him what would happen if he failed in one of his oathbound jobs, and as usual his mind was very good at suggesting possibilities.

Would Aldwyn kill him? Good luck trying that. As far as he was aware, none of the dragons had any idea of his strange immortality, so Aldwyn probably still thought killing him was a viable threat.

Still, there were a lot of things worse than death. Even if the dragon did suspect his scion would be tougher to kill than he thought, that still left him with many options, some of which sent core-deep chills of dread running up and down Stone's spine.

What if he imprisoned him again, this time augmenting the mental chains to the point where Stone couldn't break free of them? He could spend decades, even centuries locked inside his own brain, as around him his friends died and the world went on without him.

What if he imprisoned *Ian* again?

What if he hurt one or more of Stone's friends—or worse?

Stone barely realized his breath was picking up and his heart had begun to beat faster as he stepped out of the shower and dried off. There were so many things the dragon could do—probably including a bunch he couldn't even conceive of. Being several hundred years old or more and having a history of cruelty gave one a lot of options.

By the time he'd dressed and gone downstairs to feed Raider, who was delighted that breakfast was arriving much earlier than usual, he'd firmed up the idea he'd begun considering before.

He *had* to talk to Aldwyn.

He hadn't heard anything from his contacts—including Gabriel, if Ian had indeed enlisted his help in locating Brathwaite—and two more days had already passed. He had to know what the dragon had in mind. It probably wouldn't change anything, but it would give him at least some idea of what lay in wait for him if he failed. Depending on what it was, it would either take the pressure off him or light a fire under him to take more desperate chances.

He hadn't consciously noticed it until now, but the ticking, thundering clock hadn't just been in his nightmare. It had been lurking in the back of his head ever since Aldwyn had given him this assignment. If he couldn't do something to quiet it, he'd start making mistakes.

And when dealing with James Brathwaite and his necromantic horde, that was a very dangerous thing to do.

For lack of a better idea, he travelled to the Surrey house. That was the Stone ancestral manor, inhabited by generations of Stones at least back to Aldwyn, so it was probably his best bet at contacting the dragon.

He wondered if Aldwyn would ever tell him where he'd settled. It had surprised him, when he'd discovered the dragon's true connection to him, that Aldwyn hadn't tried to claim the Surrey house as his own. He supposed it wouldn't have been as easy in modern times, especially considering all the legal snarls Aldwyn would have to unravel to make it happen, but the place *was* a symbol. Maybe dragons didn't care about those kinds of symbols—or maybe he'd found a more modern place that didn't require the Surrey house's upkeep. Either way, he had to be somewhere, and so far Stone had no idea where that was. He hadn't even bothered to ask Kolinsky, since dragons didn't reveal those sorts of things about each other even if they couldn't stand each other.

But the house was indeed a symbol of the Stone family, and it was highly magical due to the three ley lines that ran through it and the generations of powerful mages—scions—who had inhabited it. Maybe that would be worth something.

He looked around for Aubrey and Selby when he arrived, but neither they nor anyone else was around. Aubrey had cut back on his work hours since Stone had disappeared, focusing more on his beloved garden and grounds (as well as spending time with his wife) and letting Selby handle the interior. The younger man, in his position as estate steward, had hired a few part-time staff from the village to handle the basic household tasks, though aside from Selby himself and Aubrey, none of the other staff lived at the house. Stone was glad of this. As someone who preferred his alone time, he'd never liked housefuls of staff members.

In any case, the place appeared to be empty, which was just the way he'd hoped it would be.

But what should he do? He couldn't do a ritual to call Aldwyn, since he didn't have anything belonging to the dragon. Other than their shared blood, he supposed, but he didn't think that would work. Dragons were stronger mages than any human, so they certainly had protections against that sort of thing.

Aldwyn had once given him a card as a contact method, instructing him to press his thumb to it and mentally call for him, but that had been a one-use item. He had no idea where it even was anymore, after three years. So that was out.

This was annoying. How the hell was he supposed to contact the dragon once he'd completed his assignment? Would Aldwyn just *know,* like he had last time?

In frustration, he pressed his palms against the massive stone fireplace, threw his head back, and called into the shadowed rafters high above: "Aldwyn, you bastard, I need to talk to you! How the hell am I supposed to do that if you don't give me a way to contact you?"

His voice rang out loud and clear, echoing around the vast room before an eerie silence settled once more over it. He remained where he was, hands still pressed against the cold rock, breathing hard.

Come on, you didn't really expect that to work, did you?

In his pocket, his phone buzzed.

He stiffened.

No. It's just a coincidence. It's Gina, or Ian, or a bloody telemarketer trying to reach you about your auto warranty.

With a shaking hand, he pulled it out and tapped the button.

"Return home," a deep voice he didn't recognize intoned.

"I *am* home," he protested, waving the phone around as if trying to show it where he was.

The line clicked and went dead.

Stone let out a loud, ragged sigh. "Aldwyn, you are *the* most irritating person I have ever met in my life. And if you know some of the people I've met, you'd know that's saying something."

Return home. In the past, the command had always been given when he was somewhere else. It was a way to get him to use a portal—or later, a ley line—to travel so Aldwyn could hijack it. But how could he go here if he was already here? Did the dragon want him to go somewhere else and then come back?

No. Because "home" could mean different things. It was possible to have more than one place where one felt like home.

You did ask for it, he reminded himself. *Don't whinge because he's giving you exactly what you wanted.*

Without giving himself too much time to dwell on the matter, he formed the pattern in his mind, pictured the route to his Encantada house, and released the energy.

"Well. I honestly didn't think that was going to work. I guess I underestimated you, Aldwyn."

Stone stood in the familiar room with its two chairs, priceless rug, and paneled walls. As usual, the artwork on the walls had changed, and the room had no windows or door.

Aldwyn sat in his usual spot, looking as calm as ever in a suit of dark blue. "What can I do for you, Alastair? You have not yet completed your assignment."

"What was your first clue?" Stone wondered once again just how much the dragon was keeping tabs on him.

Aldwyn didn't reply, but merely waited, hands in his lap.

Stone didn't sit, but rather paced. He stopped in front of one of the room's two paintings; it could have been painted by one of the old masters—Botticelli, perhaps, though Stone had never been much of an art-history buff—but he didn't recognize the specific piece. When it became clear Aldwyn wasn't going to speak, Stone spun back around to face him.

"It occurred to me that there's one part of our little arrangement that was never specified. I'd like to ask you about it."

Aldwyn made a barely perceptible "go on" gesture.

Stone's heartbeat quickened again. This was one of those questions he had to know, even if he wondered if it might not be better for it to remain unstated. "When we made this little bargain, I agreed to do as you asked, because I didn't have much of a choice. You had Ian, and I would have done anything to get him back."

Aldwyn inclined his head as if this were obvious.

"But when you asked me to swear an oath to complete your three tasks, the one thing you didn't tell me was what would happen if I didn't—or rather, if I couldn't."

"So far, my tasks have not proven difficult for you."

"Task. Singular. It's true that the whole business with the tapestry didn't end up being terribly difficult—even if I *did* complete it in a way you weren't entirely pleased with. But what happens if I can't find Brathwaite?"

"Are you having difficulty locating him?"

Stone pondered whether to reveal the truth, and finally decided the dragon probably already knew anyway. "Yes, to be honest. I am. We tried to lure him out with a tome that we represented as belonging to his old rival Burgess Crowther, but somehow he managed to suss out our little plan and turned it back on us. I don't know if you heard about the house fire in Potsdam a few days ago, but that was us trying to escape that trap."

Aldwyn nodded gravely. "It sounds like a good plan. But Brathwaite is wily, and he has ears in many unexpected places. He has made good use of his few years in the modern time."

"That's all well and good. I don't disagree with you. But he's also a hermit. He doesn't seem to go out in public." He spread his hands. "I'm not making excuses, Aldwyn. Believe me, as I said before, as much as I don't like dancing on your strings, I *do* want Brathwaite dead. But I've got to be realistic, too. What if it takes longer than the two months you've given me? More than a quarter of that time is already gone, and I'm no closer to finding him than I was before."

"Then perhaps you should consider augmenting your efforts." Aldwyn's tone was mild, but his eyes were two chips of steel.

Another chill fluttered up Stone's back. "What's that mean? What happens if I don't kill him within the two months?" He glared at the dragon. "What are you going to do, Aldwyn? Kill me?"

"No. You are far too valuable to me to kill. Not to mention, you owe me another task after this one, so killing you would be against my own interests."

"What, then? I've got a right to know the stakes here."

Aldwyn held his gaze for a few more seconds, then leaned back in his chair. "I will not kill you, Alastair. Nor will I punish you in any other way—directly."

The chill intensified. "Directly. What's that mean?"

No answer.

"Are you saying you'll punish me *in*directly? Cause harm to my friends, or my son?"

Aldwyn shrugged one shoulder. "Let us not talk of specifics, scion, nor of failure. I have utmost confidence that you will satisfactorily complete your assignment in the time allotted."

Stone clenched his fists. Damned bloody dragons, anyway. They never said anything directly if they could get away with it, but

Aldwyn's message had nonetheless been clear: *finish the job on time or somebody you love will suffer.*

"Someday," he said softly, "you're going to pay for what you're doing to me."

"And as I have said before, I welcome you to try. If nothing else, your efforts might provide some amusement. But now, you have a job to do, and your presence here contributes nothing toward your efforts to complete it."

Stone muttered an obscenity under his breath, without caring if the dragon heard it. "Fine. Message received." He waved around the room. "Let's have the portal, then, so I can get on with it."

Aldwyn didn't summon the portal yet. "Do not contact me again until your task is complete. I will not respond."

"Don't worry—you're the last person I want to talk to." He turned, pointedly putting his back to the dragon. "Come on—let's have it."

"One more thing before you go." Aldwyn's voice was soft, even, and inflectionless. If Stone was angering him, he did nothing to show it.

"*What?*"

"I know that, despite your desire to destroy Brathwaite for what he has done to you and your family and friends, you seethe against me for putting you in this position."

"Like I said before, what was your first clue?" Stone did nothing to keep the snarl from his voice. He still didn't turn to face Aldwyn.

"A word to the wise, from someone who shares your blood, and perhaps does not bear you the ill will you might suspect: this assignment is one you yourself will wish to complete, and quickly. My timeframe is not arbitrary, nor is it punitive. Things are in motion that it would be in your best interests not to allow to come to fruition."

Another chill ran through Stone—a different kind, this time. Was Brathwaite up to something specific? "What does that mean?"

When Aldwyn didn't answer, he turned back around.

The chairs were empty. The dragon was gone.

"Well," Stone muttered. "Way to make an exit, I guess."

He knew without looking that the swirling portal had appeared behind him. He stepped through it, his mind churning more than ever.

He'd come here to get answers, but instead, all he'd got was more questions.

And an even greater sense of urgency.

CHAPTER SEVENTEEN

S TONE PLANNED TO GO TO LONDON the next morning to talk to Eddie at the library. He didn't see much point in it—he was sure Eddie and Ward would update him the instant they found anything—but his meeting with Aldwyn the previous night had lit an even stronger fire under him to do *something*. He'd already forced himself to go for a run and feed Raider, but the run had been anything but relaxing.

As he was preparing the mental map to take him to England, the futility of the whole thing bled into his thoughts. Why was he even wasting time with this? Eddie and Ward might not know the full urgency of the matter, but they knew Stone was anxious to track Brathwaite before the two-month window ran out. They wouldn't hold anything back.

If you go bother them, all you'll do is distract them. You know that.

But he had to do *something*.

With a frustrated obscenity, he let the pattern slip and ebb away. Raider, perched on top of the sofa, looked at him curiously.

"Yes, I know I'm acting mental lately," Stone muttered to him.

"Meow."

"Yes, more than usual. No need to rub it in."

He needed a new plan. So far, Gabriel hadn't come back with anything, either. Ian had texted late last night to let him know the dragon was working on it, but he had to be careful. Careful meant slow, and slow wasn't something Stone wanted right now.

He paced the living room, mindful of Raider's gaze following him. There had to be someone else he could consult—someone with the resources and extensive network of contacts that might turn up a connection.

Kolinsky and Madame Huan were out—partly because he knew they'd both refuse to interfere in the business of a scion and his sire, even if it meant taking down the world's leading necromancer—but mostly because he had no idea how to contact them. Both had disappeared on their own business, and ever since Kolinsky had vacated his shop in East Palo Alto, Stone couldn't simply pop by and call his name. Gabriel could probably contact him, but the younger dragon had already said he no longer wanted to play go-between with his father.

The Ordo was out, too, unless he wanted to take dangerous chances. He had a few tenuous contacts in the organization, and Eddie and Ward had more due to their stewardship of Caventhorne, but tapping them was dangerous—especially since it appeared Brathwaite now knew of the connection between Caventhorne and whoever was trying to find him. Talking wouldn't work anymore, so the next step, if he wanted to get information from the Ordo, was to kidnap someone who possessed such information and lean on them until they talked. As much as he wanted to take down Brathwaite, Stone wasn't at that stage yet.

He didn't delude himself, though. He still had almost a month and a half left, but if too much of that time slipped away, his morals might slip along with them. Given a choice between threatening an Ordo mage and allowing Aldwyn to hurt one of his friends or family members, there was no question about which one he'd choose.

He wasn't there yet, though.

Unfortunately, he wasn't anywhere else, either. If those options were off the table, that didn't leave him with much else to go on.

For perhaps the first time, he cursed himself for not being more social with his fellow mages, especially in Europe. He's lost touch with most of those he'd known when he lived in England, and the few he still kept contact with weren't the type who'd even know about the existence of necromancy, let alone where to find its practitioners.

Stone threw himself back to the couch. "I'm stuck, Raider," he said with a ragged sigh. Even as he knew this was doing him no good—letting his brain spin in neutral never got him anywhere, and he'd probably be better off doing something else for a while to give it a chance to rest—he couldn't break out of the cycle. In the past, this would be his cue to get good and drunk, but he couldn't even allow himself to do *that* right now.

His phone buzzed on the table. Without much interest, he leaned forward.

It was a text from Verity. *Are you there?*

He snatched it up. *I'm here. Have you got something?*

No. Just haven't heard from you for a while. Wanted to see if you were okay.

Not really. I'm at a dead end, and I haven't got any other viable options. I

He stopped in mid-text, his whole body growing tense.

Wait.

Maybe he *did* have another viable option.

And maybe it had been right under his nose this whole time.

Are you still typing? Verity sent.

He cancelled the text and hit her contact button.

She picked up immediately. "What's going on? Is something wrong?"

Heart pounding with anticipation, he smiled for the first time in a while. "Maybe not. I was just going to say I was out of options, but I might not be."

"What are you talking about?"

"Can I come up there? I want to talk to you in person."

"Er—sure. Of course. Now?"

"Yes. I'll bring Raider, so he and Luna can have some alone time."

Raider was happy to see his friend. As soon as Stone opened the carrier, he darted out and ran to the gray cat. They rubbed against each other and then disappeared out onto the balcony.

Verity was dressed for hanging around the house, in a black-and-green peasant skirt, loose-fitting white blouse, and slippers. "So, what's up? I just made some coffee—want some?"

Stone still thought a shot of scotch sounded better, but it was a bit early. He could barely keep his mind on social niceties. "Yes, thank you."

They took their seats in the living room, watching the cats playing on the balcony. Verity sipped her coffee, watching Stone patiently until he spoke.

"I was getting a bit wound up about the whole Brathwaite thing this morning," he admitted. "I was beginning to think we were at a dead end, since none of the avenues I've tried to pursue have come up with anything. I was thinking about going to London again to talk to Eddie."

"Why didn't you?" She pulled her legs up and tucked them under, a gesture he remembered from ever since she'd been a teenager. Some things never changed, he supposed.

"Because I realized I was being a self-indulgent arse. He and Ward are bloody good at what they do, and they don't need me hovering about asking questions. If they've got something, they'll tell me."

She nodded sagely, as if she'd known it all along. "Yeah, that's true. But you said you had something."

"Well…that's not quite accurate. I think *you* have something."

"Huh?"

"I started thinking about the other options I could pursue, and why they won't work. Kolinsky and Madame Huan are out of communication. So is Harrison. If I go to the Ordo again, I'll have to get a lot more forceful than I'm willing to be just yet. I can't exactly hire a mundane detective to find him."

"Okay…" She looked confused, but willing to remain on this train until it reached its station.

"But then you texted me, and I realized I—or we—*do* have another option."

"We do?"

"You've mentioned it a few times. Someone you know with far-reaching contacts and a lot of influence."

She continued to look confused for a couple more seconds, but then light dawned. "You're talking about Bron's family. Her Nana."

"I am," he said triumphantly. "Do you think they'd be willing to help? You said before that they have contacts all over the place."

Verity pondered. "They do. Mostly here in the US, but I do get the impression Nana has her fingers in quite a few pies around the world."

"So…what do you think? Could you contact her and see what she says?"

"I could, yes…but I think it might be better if we talked to her together."

"Why? You're the one who has the history with her."

"Yes, but you're the one who knows the details of the problem."

She had a point. And he *did* prefer to be directly involved when possible. "Right, then. Can you ask her if she has time to meet with us, and if she's willing?"

"I'll talk to Bron. Even after all this time, I don't feel comfortable contacting Nana directly."

"Brilliant." He finished his coffee and leaned forward, watching Raider and Luna threading their way around Verity's collection of potted herbs. "I hate to be pushy, but could you do it now? I'm feeling quite a lot of urgency."

Her eye narrowed. "Did something happen? Did whoever's making you do this change the timetable?"

Still perceptive. Some things never changed, indeed. "He…didn't change the timetable. But I got a bit more of an impression of what might happen if I fail to complete the job in the allotted time, and I'd prefer not to let it happen."

She held his gaze for a few more seconds, then stood. "Okay. I'll text Bron and see what we can do. Why don't you go hang out with the cats for a few minutes? Help yourself to anything in the kitchen if you want it."

He took her advice, drifting out onto the balcony as she headed toward her downstairs bedroom-slash-alchemy lab. His brain still felt like it was in a blender, but at least now that they were taking some definitive action, the blender was on *mix* instead of *puree*. He leaned on the railing, watching the traffic crawling by on the street below. Luna jumped onto the shelf next to him, rubbing her slim, quicksilver body against his arm.

He stroked her soft fur. "I hope your mum can get somewhere," he murmured.

She tilted her head, fixed a deep green stare on him, and then leaped down to rejoin Raider.

Verity returned ten minutes later. "Okay," she said. "Got us a meeting with Nana, but she can't talk to us for long. We'll have to leave in a couple of hours. Does that work for you?"

"Whatever needs to be done, I'll make it happen." He pushed off the shelf, feeling a new energy now that they had a plan. "Come on, Raider. Or I suppose you could stay here until we get back, if Auntie Verity doesn't mind."

In answer, both he and Luna streaked back inside and disappeared up the stairs.

Verity laughed. "Guess that's settled."

They left through the portal in Stone's basement. Verity had secured temporary permission for them to arrive through the private portal at the family compound in New York, but only if she did the calibration and gave her word she wouldn't reveal the coordinates to Stone. When they stepped through, one of the family witches, a dark-skinned young woman with cornrowed, blue-dyed hair and a colorful dress, was standing by to clear the calibration.

"Welcome," she said when she finished, pausing to give Verity a warm hug. Then she smiled at Stone. "And to you too, Dr. Stone. We're glad to have you here. My name's Chloe."

"Thank you, Chloe. I appreciate your kindness."

"If you'll come with me, Nana's ready to see you. She's looking forward to meeting you, Dr. Stone."

"And I, her."

He and Verity followed Chloe from the room and out of the house. A graveled walkway led through a garden full of flowers and herbs, and out to a tree-lined street.

"It's not far," Chloe said. There were no vehicles parked along either side of the street.

"This is beautiful," Stone said, looking around as they walked. The air smelled fresh and clean, the sky above them was a bright, cloudless blue, and the only sounds he could hear were natural ones: the babble of an unseen river, the calls of birds, and the rustle of small animals moving among the trees. No engines, no planes overhead, not even any generators. "You're in New York?"

"Upstate," Chloe said. "Our compound is...a bit hard to find for anyone who doesn't know what they're looking for."

"Magical protections?"

She grinned, but didn't answer.

Less than half a mile up the street, she turned onto another gravel pathway, which meandered up a gentle grade. "Here we are," she said as they rounded a corner.

Nana's home, a low-slung structure made of wood and glass, seemed to blend in with the trees around it to the point where it was difficult to tell where the house ended and the forest began. Stone wasn't sure whether magic was involved or simply a skilled architect familiar with the area, but either way it presented a beautiful scene. The walkway bisected another colorful garden and ended in a pair of wooden steps in front of a whimsically carved wooden door. As they approached, Stone thought he caught movement from the corner of his eye. He glanced that way, spotting a cheeky garden gnome in a bright-red hat watching them pass. When he looked again, it was gone.

Chloe knocked on the door, and a moment later it opened to reveal a boy of around sixteen with a riot of dark curls and smiling brown eyes. "Welcome," he said. "Nana's expecting you."

"Thank you, Evan. I'll leave our guests with you, then." To Stone, she said, "It was nice meeting you, Dr. Stone." Then she waved to Verity and headed off.

"If you'll just follow me," Evan said, standing aside so they could enter.

The interior of the house was every bit as beautiful as the outside. Everywhere Stone looked, he saw signs of nature: open wood beams, hanging plants, earth-toned furniture with splashes of color. The windows let in plenty of natural light, bathing the open, airy space in a comforting glow.

Evan led them through an open living room and into a smaller room at the end of a hallway. "Nana? Your guests are here."

"Thank you, Evan," said a warm voice from inside. "Please, come in."

The new room was the larger house in microcosm, with the same slanted wood beams and large windows looking out over another part of the garden and the trees beyond. On the far wall, a massive stone fireplace contained a cheery blaze. The air smelled faintly of flowers and baking, and the sturdy, overstuffed furniture was obviously both top quality and well-loved. The barest hint of a gray-haired head poked above the back of a chair facing the window.

Verity moved into the room, motioning for Stone to follow her. "Hello, Nana. It's so good to see you."

"It's good to see you too, dear. It's been too long."

As they came around the side of the chair, Stone got a better look at the woman he'd been hearing so much about. Physically, she wasn't an impressive specimen: tiny, stout, wearing a simple housedress. Her hair was pulled back into a tight bun, and her black, crowlike eyes twinkled in a brown, wrinkled face. Her smile, wide and genuine, brought feelings of home and family and security.

But the physical wasn't everything. Even without magical sight, which he didn't use because he didn't want to be impolite, Stone had no trouble picking up the sheer power radiating from this small woman.

He began to entertain the faint hope that perhaps she could help him.

"Please, sit down, both of you." Nana waved them to two more comfortable-looking chairs. "Would you like any refreshments? I believe Evan baked some cookies today, didn't you, dear?"

"I did, Nana. Chocolate chip." The boy had remained in the doorway, obviously waiting to see if he could be of more service.

"I'd love some," Verity said. "Thank you." She shot Stone a look as if to say, *don't turn down her hospitality.*

"As would I, thanks," he said quickly.

"Oh, good. Evan, could you bring them along with some Keemun tea?"

"Yes, Nana." He hurried off.

Nana turned a bit in her chair to face Stone. "Well, well. So, you're the famous Dr. Alastair Stone. It's lovely to finally meet you. I've heard a lot about you."

"Good things, I hope," he murmured. "I'm so pleased to meet you as well."

She smiled. "You've trained Verity well. She's a lovely person and talented at the Art."

"I only helped her along. The talent and the drive were with her all along."

"Hey," Verity said, chuckling, "Stop talking about me like I'm not here."

Nana laughed. "I'm sorry, dear. Forgive an old woman her little foibles."

Evan returned, bearing a tray with a plate of cookies, three steaming cups of tea, and a brightly-painted teapot. He set it on the table between them and made his silent exit.

"He's such a good boy," Nana said, using magic to levitate one of the cups. "No magical talent, but he's shaping up to be masterful with the plants. He's helping out here while he apprentices with Natalia at the greenhouses."

Stone emulated her, levitating another cup and taking a sip of the amber-colored tea. It had a malty, almost chocolaty flavor, obviously a good pairing with the cookies. "This is delicious, Ms.—" He paused, realizing Verity had never told him Nana's name.

"Just call me Nana, dear. Everybody does." She took another sip, munched a cookie, then leaned back into her cushions. Her expression, still kindly, grew more serious. "I sense you're the kind of person who likes to get down to business, Dr. Stone, so what can I do for you today?"

Stone exchanged glances with Verity, unsure of how to proceed. Nana didn't exactly intimidate him—in fact, she reminded him a bit of Madame Huan—but he had no history with her and didn't want to make a conversational misstep.

Verity came to his rescue. "We're…looking for someone, Nana. We were hoping, since you know so many people in the magical community around the world, you might be able to give us a lead on how to find him."

Nana's placid face stilled as she gazed out into the garden. Another gnome, this one in a blue hat, had appeared between the trees where Stone was certain it hadn't been before. "I assume," she said mildly after a few seconds' contemplation, "that this person is also a member of the magical community."

"Yes," Stone said. "He is." He deliberately flicked his gaze sideways, away from the gnome, for only an instant. When he looked back, it had disappeared.

"May I ask *why* you are looking for him?"

This time Verity didn't answer, and it was clear she was leaving it up to Stone how much he wanted to reveal. She did flash him a warning look, though.

Stone considered what he wanted to tell her. He couldn't tell her the truth, of course. "I want to kill him" hardly seemed the kind of information this tranquil, pleasant woman would want to hear. "He…has committed a great wrong against my family and friends," he said with care.

"I see." She folded her hands in her lap and continued looking out the window. When she spoke again, her voice, which had been soft and gentle, took on a firmer edge. "Dr. Stone, please forgive me for being blunt, but I sense you appreciate straightforwardness."

"I do indeed."

"Verity is correct—I do have many friends and contacts around the world, and I am happy to assist with…difficulties. I *have* heard a lot about you, and I know of some of the good you have done in this world. I want to help you. But in order to do that, you must be honest with me. Such an arrangement cannot be based on half-truths and misdirection." She levitated a cookie to her hand and took a bite, her black-eyed gaze settling now on Stone.

Stone looked at Verity again, who shrugged. This was all him now, and how he replied would determine what type of help—if any—this powerful and influential woman would provide.

She might be your last hope.

"Okay," he said at last. "I'll be honest with you, if you give me your word that you won't share anything I tell you with anyone outside this room."

"Of course you have it," she agreed immediately, as if that went without saying.

Stone drew a deep breath. "The person I'm looking for is named James Brathwaite. He's...a necromancer."

Nana's gaze sharpened, and she seemed to tense. "A necromancer."

"Yes."

"I have heard tell of such people returning to the world, after the magical community thought the knowledge eradicated."

"Brathwaite has returned. I've met him." He took another sip of tea. It was difficult to speak of his history with the man, but if he wanted Nana's help, he'd have to. "It's a long story and one I'd rather not go into in detail, but Brathwaite lived originally in England nearly two hundred years ago. He was murdered, but his echo somehow managed to survive, trapped inside a crypt. When the echo was released, he located a descendant and we believe he tricked her into allowing him to take over her body, destroying her own echo."

Nana's hands tightened in her lap. "Dark magic indeed."

"Yes. Very much so. Ever since his return a few years ago, he has continued his necromantic activities, always remaining deeply underground so he wouldn't be discovered. He has also taught others his foul arts."

"I see. You mentioned that he has wronged your family and friends, specifically?"

Verity spoke now, her voice shaking. "He...killed a dear friend of mine—a mage—and reanimated her body with some volition remaining. We had to..." Her throat caught "...We had to destroy her to free her from what she'd become."

"Oh, my." Nana managed to look both stricken and angry at the same time.

"That's not all," Stone said. "He turned up again later, experimenting with civilized ghouls, trying to combine their regeneration properties with the necromantic arts to assist another powerful mage. We disrupted his efforts, and we believe that mage is dead now." He paused, sampling one of the cookies for the first time. It was delicious, but he barely noticed. "Are you aware that I...disappeared for three years?"

"Verity mentioned it, yes." Nana was still looking troubled.

"I can't tell you where I was, or why, but I believe Brathwaite has been growing in his abilities during that time. I don't think he knows I've returned, nor that I specifically am looking for him. But we've already made one attempt to track him, which failed. So he knows *someone* is looking for him."

"And now you fear if you don't tread carefully, he will discover the truth."

Stone inclined his head. "He is powerful and vindictive, and he has his own network of influential contacts. Are you familiar with an organization called the Ordo Purpuratus?"

"I am." The two words were delivered with even calm, but revealed everything Stone needed to know about her feelings toward the Ordo.

"Then you know their tendrils reach a long way. If any of them get wind of my interest in finding Brathwaite, he could go even deeper underground and make it impossible."

The old woman's steady gaze settled once again on Stone. "What, may I ask, is your sudden urgency to find this man? From what you have told me, your history with him goes back several years. Did he do something recently that makes it more imperative that you find him soon?"

Stone was impressed. She might look like someone's kindly old grandmother, but her mind was sharp as hell. She was asking all the right questions, even though he wished she wouldn't. "That's…part of what I can't tell you—at least not all of it. But yes, the situation has recently become more urgent, requiring me to locate him more quickly."

Nana nodded slowly. "But you can't tell me *why* it's become more urgent."

Perhaps coming here hadn't been a good idea after all. But he was here now, and Verity trusted this woman. Was it time for him to widen his circle of trust a bit? "Someone else—please don't ask me to tell you who, because I can't—has become involved."

"And this person is…somehow compelling you to locate Mr. Brathwaite?"

Stone didn't answer.

"I see," she said as if he had.

"It's not just that," he said quickly. "Believe me, I *want* to find Brathwaite. I've wanted to find him for a long time. It's just that this new situation has…moved it up considerably in my priority list."

Again, Nana gave her slow nod, returning her attention to the garden as she sipped her tea. "What do you plan to do when you locate him?"

Stone looked at Verity. This was the big question, and he had no idea how Nana would react to his answer. If he told her the truth, what would her response be? Would she kick him out of her house for asking her to be an accessory to murder? It was a risk.

He thought about Aldwyn, and the dragon's veiled threats that dire consequences might await those closest to him if he failed to complete the assignment on time. Those threats were real. Nana, as yet, was an unknown quantity.

Damn it, I have to trust somebody.

"I want to kill him," he blurted, before his filters could slam into place.

Surprisingly, Nana didn't seem disturbed by his words. She remained as calm as ever, her steady gaze moving from the garden to Stone, and didn't reply.

Stone's heart beat faster. He leaned forward. "Well? You asked, and I've told you. How do you feel about that?"

"Necromancy is a foul art," she said softly, but her voice held a harder edge than it had since he and Verity had arrived. "It does not belong in this world."

"I agree with you. I can't honestly say that killing Brathwaite will remove it, since he's no doubt taught it to others by now. But he *is* a master at it. I doubt his students have caught up to him in a few years' time. I genuinely believe getting rid of him will be good for the world."

She inclined her head. "As do I."

"So…you don't have a problem with me telling you I plan to commit premeditated murder?" Stone remained in his position, his whole body on edge.

"No."

"That…surprises me, I must admit."

"It shouldn't. Because what you would be doing would not be murder."

Stone blinked. "Why not? Or are you speaking metaphorically—that necromancers are no longer worthy of being considered human because of what they get up to?"

"Nothing of the sort." Nana gave him a brittle smile. "If the story you have told me is true, then Mr. Brathwaite died long ago. Magical philosophers have debated whether the echo—some call it the soul—is sufficient to confer humanity, or whether a body is needed as well. But if Mr. Brathwaite has driven someone else's soul from her body in order to claim it for himself, then one could argue that both that unfortunate woman—without her soul—and Mr. Brathwaite—without his body—*are* no longer human."

Stone smiled. Maybe they'd get somewhere yet. This old lady was cagier than he thought. "I suppose you could look at it that way. But, full disclosure: even if Brathwaite *is* still considered human, I don't care. I want him dead, and if I've got to do it myself, then so be it. But first I have to find him, and that's where you come in—I hope. Will you help me find him?"

"Not directly."

He almost didn't catch her words at first. When he replayed them, he stared at her in shock. "No? But you said—"

"I said it would be a boon to the world to be rid of him. But even so, I cannot help you directly, for reasons of my own." Before Stone could protest, she raised a hand. "But I *can* help you *in*directly, and that I will do."

"I don't follow."

She finished her tea and levitated the cup back to the tray. "As you mentioned before, I do have many contacts in unexpected places, all over the world—both members of my extended family, blood and not, and their own friends and associates. You are correct—subtlety will be of utmost importance, which means our efforts will take time and require careful tending. I will put out the word to certain trusted individuals, without mentioning your involvement, and we will see what grows in our garden."

Stone considered. It wasn't as much as he'd hoped, but better than he'd feared. "My timetable is short. The deadline I have been given to complete this task is less than a month and a half away."

She smiled. "I think that will allow us plenty of time." The smile faded. "But you must understand explicitly, Dr. Stone—that will be the extent of my assistance. I will not involve myself or any of my family members in anything beyond discovering Mr. Brathwaite's location."

"Of course not. I wouldn't ever expect anything else." He exchanged glances with Verity, and knew she followed his unspoken words: *And besides, we want to kill the bastard ourselves.*

"Well, then, I believe we have come to an understanding." Nana appeared satisfied. She nodded toward the plate. "Please—take another cookie. Evan will be pleased you enjoyed them."

Both Stone and Verity, who'd been uncharacteristically quiet, plucked a cookie from the plate. "Thank you, Nana," Verity said, reaching out to clasp the old lady's hand in hers.

"Of course, dear. Always happy to help if I can. We'll be seeing you soon, won't we?"

"Next month, yes. Hezzie and I will be doing some alchemy study with Bron and Phaedra."

"That's wonderful. Be well, both of you. I'll call Evan to show you out."

As Stone waited for the boy to return, he went over their conversation in his mind. He drifted to the window, trying to spot another of the whimsical gnomes, but his thoughts were far away. Something Nana had said had caught his attention, but then she'd moved on to something else. Something about her help…

Bloody hell. Could it be?

No. That's absurd.

But…was it?

He turned back to Verity, as Evan appeared in the doorway. "Nana…could I speak to you for a moment, in private?"

Verity shot him a sharp glance, but he deliberately didn't meet it.

"Of course, Dr. Stone. Evan, please show Verity out and then return in five minutes to take her and Dr. Stone to the portal."

Verity clearly didn't want to go, but just as clearly wouldn't make a scene in front of Nana and Evan. "I'll meet you outside," she said, in a clear *this isn't over* tone.

When the door closed behind them, Nana turned back to face Stone. "What is it, dear?"

Stone didn't know how to say it. It wasn't the sort of thing you could just come out and say—especially if he was wrong. "You…said something before that caught my attention."

"Yes?"

"You said you couldn't help me directly, 'for reasons of your own.'"

"Yes."

Suddenly his tongue wouldn't respond to his brain. He felt like a shy teenage boy asking the most popular girl in class for a date. "I—" He glanced toward the closed door, mindful that Evan would be returning to collect him any moment. Finally, he blurted the first thing that popped into his head: "Do you by chance know Stefan Kolinsky?"

Her smile was strange and sweet, and her eyes glittered. "Oh, yes. We have known each other for a long time." She put a subtle, almost imperceptible emphasis on *long*.

Evan knocked softly on the door.

Nana held Stone's gaze for another beat, then settled back in her chair. "I will be in touch soon," she said. "And I hope you have a lovely day."

Outside, on the way back to the portal, Verity dropped back to let Evan get a few steps ahead of them. "What was that all about?" she whispered.

He smiled. "Nothing. I just had a question to ask Nana. But now I'm a bit more confident she and her people can help us."

He wouldn't say anything else, no matter how much she glared at him. By the time they reached the portal, she'd given up asking.

CHAPTER EIGHTEEN

NOBODY GOT BACK TO STONE about the Brathwaite situation in the next couple of days, but he didn't get as stressed about it as before. He was confident that even if Eddie and Ward didn't turn up anything, Nana would. Or possibly Gabriel. Patience wasn't his strongest suit, but he worked hard not to obsess about the situation.

Gina texted him early Tuesday afternoon, as he was idly flipping through a new book he was using for research on the paper he was working on. *I think I might have something.*

For a second, he almost thought she was talking about Brathwaite, but of course she didn't know anything about that. *About Squeak?* he sent back.

Yeah. Can you come down? I'm at the office.

Sure. Be there soon.

He drove down since traffic was light. Derik at the reception desk gave him a breezy wave. "Hi, Dr. Stone. Jason's not here right now. He's off on an investigation for the rest of the afternoon."

"He's not here to see Jason," Gina called from her office doorway.

"Well, never mind then. Carry on."

Gina closed her door behind Stone and cleared off one of her guest chairs for him. "You want anything? Soda, water, energy drink? I think we have some leftover donuts from this morning, but I don't think you want those."

"Thank you, no. What did you find out about Squeak?"

She indicated her screen, which was currently facing away from Stone. "I've been doing a lot of thinking about what you said when you got back." With a significant glance at the office door, she looked at Stone and made a finger-wiggling "magic" gesture.

"Ah." He cast the 'cone of silence' spell around them. "You can speak freely now."

"Cool. Derik's a good guy, but he's a bit nosy about people's personal stuff. Better to keep this between us." She returned her focus to the screen. "Anyway, like I said, I've been thinking about what you told me."

"What, specifically?"

"That Squeak claims nobody doesn't like him except his exes."

"Well, yes, but he also said he didn't think they would do something like this."

She snorted. "With all due respect, Doc, a lot of guys don't have any *idea* what their girlfriends might do to them if they feel like they're being jerked around. Not to mention the other part of what he said: that whoever tried to frame him did a really good job mimicking his way of moving. That told me it had to be somebody who knew him really well. Even intimately, maybe."

"That's a damned good point," Stone said, impressed.

She smiled. "That's why you keep me around. Well, that and Jason pays me pretty well. Anyway, so I put aside the assumption that it couldn't be one of his exes, and did some more digging in his social media."

"I'm guessing you found something, or you wouldn't have called me down here."

"Maybe." She gestured at the screen again. "It turns out I was already Facebook friends with several of his mutuals—I'm friends with a lot of Changelings—so I spent my free time over the last couple of days going through his Facebook and Instagram history, looking for ex-girlfriends. I found quite a few. The guy gets around."

"How many are we talking about?"

"Well, I limited the search to the time after he became a Changeling, since we're pretty sure this is a Changeling-related situation. I found four."

"Okay…is there anything interesting about any of them?"

"A couple. The other two I think we can write off. One's been happily married for the last couple years—seriously, I needed a shot of insulin from looking at their photos—and the other one moved to Japan almost a year ago. There are large Changeling populations in Tokyo and Kyoto, by the way, so that makes sense. Also, I didn't see any hint of animosity in her interactions with Squeak. In fact, there were photos of him at parties with both of them after they broke up."

"And the other two?"

"Potentially more interesting. Both of them are still in the Los Angeles area. One's a woman named Inez Velasquez. They had a pretty bad breakup a couple years ago, and she said some nasty things about him at the time. Nothing recent, though."

"That has possibility. You say she's still down there?"

"Yeah. She's a wannabe actor, currently waiting tables at a restaurant in Burbank."

"Is she a Changeling?"

"Not sure."

"Is there a way to find out?"

"Not sure of that, either. I don't know her, and obviously the photos don't show it. I can ask around a little if you want."

Stone nodded. "That's all right—I can ask my contact to look into her. What about the other one?"

"She's a little more interesting. Her name is Charlotte—just the single name, like Madonna or Cher. Her real name's Charlotte Mulroney." She spun the monitor around to reveal a video clip of a tall, slim woman clad in a sparkling gown, striding up a catwalk at a fashion show. Her perfectly-made-up face possessed an almost unearthly beauty, and it was clear she knew it. Her ice-blue eyes scanned the crowd as if she owned it. "Apparently, she was a seriously up-and-coming supermodel on the fashion circuit down there, but she dropped out of the public eye three years ago. The rumor was she had a drug problem."

There was a knock on the door. "Gina?" Derik called. "Sorry to bother you, but I need you to sign off on something so I can send it on."

"Come on in."

The receptionist entered the office. He held a folder, but when he spotted Gina's screen he stopped and his eyes widened. "Oh, wow, that's Charlotte."

Both Stone and Gina stared at him. "You know her?" Stone asked.

He made a dismissive gesture. "Oh, I don't *know* her. I wish. But I remember her from when I lived in L.A. I used to follow the fashion scene." He leaned in and dropped his voice conspiratorially. "The buzz was that she was a real bitch on wheels unless you had something she wanted, but that's to be expected when you're that drop-dead gorgeous. Too bad about what happened to her."

"You mean the drug problem?" Stone glanced at the screen again, then back at Derik. He shifted to magical sight, taking in the Changeling receptionist's brilliant, peacock-like plumage.

Suddenly, Derik seemed to remember where he was. "Oh. Uh—yeah. The drug problem. Terrible thing." He shot a significant look at Gina, then offered the folder. "If you could just sign these…"

"Derik, I think you're hiding something," Stone said.

The receptionist looked like a baby bunny caught in a semi truck's headlights. "I'm not hiding anything. What makes you think that?"

Gina rolled her eyes. "He knows, dude."

"About what?"

"About us. If that's what this is about, anyway."

Derik's panicked look turned to shocked surprise. He looked Stone up and down as if expecting him to sprout fur or feathers. "But—"

"It's all right," Stone said. "Is whatever this is Changeling-related?"

"Shit…" he whispered. "You really do know?"

"Come on, D," Gina said. "Of course he knows. He's Jason's best friend, and Jason's kid's a Changeling. What you have to say might be important. It's about a case. If you know something, spill it. Doc won't out you."

"I promise," Stone confirmed. "I'm very good at keeping secrets."

Derik was having a hard time recovering from this new shock, but he did his best to shake it off. "I—uh—yeah. The rumor was that she had a bad drug problem, but what really happened is she Changed."

"Is that right?" Gina seemed surprised. "I never heard that. Makes sense, though—the timeframe's right."

"Yeah, she kept it under wraps." He leaned in closer. "Again, this is just rumor, but apparently she turned into a real uggo. All warty and toad-looking. She couldn't handle it, so she had some kind of breakdown. I don't know if she ever showed up in public again. I stopped following her after that."

Stone exchanged glances with Gina.

"She *did* turn up again," she said, annoyed. "Not as a model, but, you know, living her life as a person. This is not a good look for you, Derik. I'm kinda disappointed, to be honest."

"Oh!" He raised his hands in protest. "That's not what I meant! I—"

She took the folder from him, opened it, and dashed off her signature. "Maybe you'd better go watch the front desk, okay?"

"Yeah, okay." His feathers seemed to deflate as he slunk out. "I'm really sorry."

Stone used magic to close the door behind him, and re-cast the cone of silence spell. "Don't be too hard on him. He might have given us useful information."

"How so?"

"Perhaps whatever falling-out she had with Squeak was related to their both being Changelings."

"Maybe. We should talk to her, huh?"

"We should. Is there a way you could make contact? I can go back to Los Angeles if she's willing to talk."

"I'll see what I can do." She turned the screen back around and sighed. "Sorry, but I really am disappointed with Derik. I thought he was better than that."

"Like I said, give him a chance. I was watching his aura, and he genuinely *did* feel bad about what he said. He's young—maybe this could be a teachable moment."

"Maybe." She didn't sound convinced. "Anyway, I'll see if I can locate Charlotte and see if she's willing to talk. I'll get back to you if I get anywhere."

Stone didn't hear back from Gina until later that evening, when she texted him: *You there?*

Yes. Any news?

Yeah, maybe. It's…weird, though. Call me.

She answered without greeting. "Okay, so here's the deal. Jason got back, so I let him in on what we'd found so far. He helped me work on tracking Charlotte. But we couldn't find her."

"What do you mean, you couldn't find her?"

"She's disappeared."

"Since when?"

"The last time anybody saw her was at a party around five weeks ago, in West Hollywood."

"What kind of party?"

"I dunno—some informal thing for fashion industry people and their supporters. Is that important?"

"I've got no idea. And now you're saying she's just—what—dropped off the face of the earth?"

"Looks like it."

"Did you find out where she lived, at least? Perhaps I can sneak in and grab something to use in a tracking ritual."

"Way ahead of you. She had a nice apartment down in Westwood, but I had somebody look into it and she's moved out. The whole place has been deep-cleaned and they've already lined up another tenant."

Stone pondered. "That's odd, and definitely looks suspicious."

"Yeah, especially when you consider that the first missing kid disappeared around the same time."

He did a quick mental calculation. "Bloody hell, you're right."

"What do you want to do from here?"

"Did you turn up any connection between her and Freakshow?"

"Didn't check that yet. Good thought. I'll see if I can contact Quasi again and ask him." She was silent for a moment. "I don't get it, though—why would a Changeling kidnap Changeling kids?"

"That's a damned good question. See if you can reach Quasi. Oh, and if you can, track down Squeak for me again. It should be easier this time, now that you know his real name. I gave him my contact information, but he didn't give me his. Perhaps if we can find him, he can give us a lead."

"On it. I'll get back to you."

CHAPTER NINETEEN

STONE HAD HANDED OFF THE INFORMATION about Squeak's ex-girlfriends to Huxley, but she'd warned him it would be a few days before she could spend any serious time on tracking them down. "We got something crazy going down in the Central Valley," she told him. "Nothing we can't handle, but as usual we're strapped."

"That's all right," he told her, beginning to think he was doing more than consulting on this case. "I'll see what I can find and get back to you."

"Thanks, Stone. I appreciate it. I really do."

Two more days passed before Squeak got back to him.

Sorry, man, he texted. *Been out of town for a couple days. What's up?*

I need to talk to you again. Can we meet?

I don't know—I'm working, and then I've got some stuff going on tonight.

His nervousness came though even in the text. *Look,* Stone sent back, *this is about the situation we discussed the last time I saw you. It's important. If you won't talk to me, I can only assume you're involved somehow, and respond accordingly.*

There was a long pause where the text sat at *Read.* Then the dots cycled, stopped, cycled again, and finally Squeak's reply appeared: *I'm not involved. I told you that before. Okay, I'll talk to you. But it has to be tonight. I really am working now.*

Done. He'd already compared the area map with his ley-line map, and identified several potential locations. *How about the Short End bar on Melrose?*

Okay. Nobody knows me there. I'll meet you at 8.

Stone smiled. Apparently, whatever "stuff" he had going on tonight could wait.

He wouldn't have been surprised if Squeak didn't show up, but he did.

It did surprise him that the Changeling wasn't alone, though.

Stone found him in a booth in the back part of the bar. After a moment, he recognized the woman with him as the lizard-scaled woman he'd kissed during their previous meeting. To normal sight, she appeared as a dark-haired Latina woman of average height, attractive but not in a stand-out way. She wore dramatic makeup and clothes appropriate for clubbing. Both she and Squeak had drinks in front of them, and watched Stone with a mixture of interest and suspicion.

"Er—good evening," Stone said. "I didn't know you'd be bringing a friend."

"This is my girlfriend, Quinn," he said. "I trust her, and maybe she can help."

"He already told me about what you guys talked about," she said. "That's terrible—kids getting snatched. I'll help if I can."

Stone wasn't sure he liked this—especially if Squeak had revealed his own true nature as a mage—but nothing could be done about it now. At least he'd used the same illusionary disguise as before, so the two Changelings couldn't know his true appearance. "May I sit down?"

Squeak waved him to the seat opposite them. "Can't stay long—there's a hot party we want to hit in a little bit."

"This shouldn't take long." He glanced at Quinn. "This might be a bit uncomfortable, though—I wanted to ask you a few questions about your ex-girlfriends."

Squeak and Quinn exchanged glances, and both smiled. Quinn put her head on Squeak's shoulder.

"No big deal," Squeak said. "Those days are over. We all have pasts." He narrowed his eyes. "What about them, though?"

"I'm interested in a couple specific ones, actually: Inez Velasquez, and a woman who goes by Charlotte."

Squeak nodded as if he wasn't surprised. "I can tell you about Inez right away. She's in…Burbank now, I think? Haven't seen her for a while. We hooked up right after I Changed."

"Was she a Changeling too?"

"No. That's actually why we ended up splitting up. I was feeling…pretty insecure about my looks at the time, and of course she didn't get it since as far as she knew I looked like a normal human. I couldn't even talk about it with her."

Quinn leaned over to kiss him. "I think you look great."

Stone wondered what the kiss would have looked like if he'd been watching with magical sight—he'd never seen a scruffy, human-sized rat and a scaly alligator locking lips before (did alligators even *have* lips?)—but quickly banished the thought. "My research said the breakup was…acrimonious."

"Your research?" Squeak glared at him. "You're checkin' up on my past? I thought I told you before that there's no way any of my exes would have done anything like that."

"Yes, well, I've been assured that we blokes sometimes underestimate women's responses to breakups."

Quinn chuckled. "Ain't that the truth?"

Squeak looked between the two of them, then shrugged. "Whatever. I'm tellin' you, though, Inez and I aren't exactly best friends these days, and we don't run in the same circles anymore, but we've talked a few times since we split. She's had a couple new boyfriends after me, and I'm with Quinn now. So it's all good."

"Okay." He settled back against the bench, contemplating whether he wanted to order a drink before heading out. He decided not to; if all went well, he wouldn't be here long. "So, moving on to Charlotte."

Squeak looked uncomfortable. "We weren't together very long."

"Did you break up with her, or she with you?"

"She broke up with me. She claimed I was cheating on her."

"Were you?"

He glared. "No, man. I like the ladies, but when I'm in a relationship, I'm strictly a one-woman dude."

"So what made her think you'd cheat on her?"

"Who knows?" He shrugged. "I don't stick around when I'm not wanted, you know? She accused me, I told her that was bullshit, and she showed me the door. That was the end of that."

"How long ago was this?"

"Couple years. She was my rebound chick after Inez and I called it quits."

"I see." Stone stared into the middle distance, recalling what Gina had told him. "If I understand correctly, Charlotte is…" Even though he'd given permission to use the word, he still felt uncomfortable saying it.

"A freak? Oh, yeah." Squeak didn't seem at all concerned or disgusted by it. "Come on, I'm not an idiot. She wouldn't've looked twice at me if we were vanilla humans."

"Was that…difficult for her? Considering how beautiful she is as a human, I mean. I heard she was on track for a successful modeling career, but then dropped out of the public eye shortly after she Changed."

The rat-man nodded soberly. "Yeah, that was hard on her for a while. I didn't know her before she Changed, but from what I heard, she was pretty high on herself back then. Got all kinds of stuff and opportunities because she was so gorgeous. Men fell all over her, you know?"

"I'm not surprised. I saw a video clip of her."

"But after she Changed into a freak, she had a breakdown. She told me about it. Couldn't eat, couldn't sleep, refused to be seen in public, wouldn't look in a mirror…the whole thing. She really let herself go for a few months."

"Remember, when we Change, our true form is what we see when we look in a mirror," Quinn added. "We kind of forget about what our vanilla form looks like, which means sometimes we forget that most of the people in the world don't see what we see."

"Yeah," Squeak said. "Charlotte started thinking she was being punished for something, and that's why she ended up ugly. She looks like a toad—but kinda like me, she's not a cute toad. She's all brown and green and warty." Once again, his voice held no disgust; on the contrary, he almost sounded admiring.

"So she quit modeling because she didn't want anyone to see she'd turned ugly," Stone said.

"Yeah, even though the norms wouldn't see anything but her vanilla form. She knew that in her mind, but she still couldn't deal with it. It's pretty common with freaks, but most of us get over it after not too long. She was still kinda like that when we were together, even though she tried to hide it. Honestly, I think she resented me for bein' comfortable with what I look like, and that caused a lot of friction."

"That makes sense," Stone said. "But you're speaking as if all of this is in the past tense. Did she get over her discomfort with her Changeling appearance?"

"Far as I know, yeah. Like I said, I haven't heard much from her. I don't like bein' called a liar, you know? So I avoid her. I know she hasn't got back into modeling—when she let herself go, she hit the booze and food pretty hard. But I heard she came to terms with what she is, and now she's mostly okay with it. She even goes out sometimes to functions, but only when she's sure there won't be any other Changelings there."

"Do you know if she's a member of…" He glanced at Quinn. "…your organization?"

"Freakshow? Don't worry, Quinn knows all about that. And…I dunno. The way we're organized, there's not a lot of overlap between the groups. That's on purpose, so we can't give each other up if somebody leans on us."

Stone nodded. "Okay. Thank you for talking with me. I only have one other question, and then I'll clear out and let you get on to your party."

"Shoot."

"Apparently, Charlotte has disappeared recently. Do you have any idea where she might be?"

He looked startled. "Disappeared? You mean kidnapped, like those kids?"

"I don't know. I don't think so, because apparently she's moved completely out of her Westwood apartment, with no forwarding address."

"Wait…" His eyes narrowed. "Do you suspect *her* of being the kidnapper? Because that's crazy. She could be pretty full of herself, but she'd never do something like that. She loves kids. In fact, she told me she wanted to have a couple of her own after she got too old to model. I can say a lot of bad things about her, but I'm certain she'd never hurt a kid."

"You're probably right, but if you should happen to hear anything about where she is, I'd appreciate it if you'd contact me. I'd like to have a chat with her."

"Sure thing, man. But I'm tellin' you the truth—I have no idea where she is. I haven't seen her in months."

As Stone prepared to rise, he noticed Quinn was watching him with perhaps more intensity than expected. "Quinn? Do you have anything to add? You don't know where Charlotte is, do you?"

She shook her head. "No idea. I've never even met her." She gave an arch smile. "Just because I'm cool with Squeak's exes doesn't mean I want to be best buds with them."

CHAPTER TWENTY

THE NEXT DAY, Stone had lunch with Gina, Jason, and Amber to update them on what he'd found out from Squeak. They met at a sandwich shop near Jason's agency and ate while keeping an eye on Alice and Jaden. The little girl sat on a booster seat and picked at her small sandwich while trying hard not to chatter away, and Jaden played on the floor at Amber's feet. To magical sight, he looked like a large, two-legged puppy.

"Huh," Jason said. "Doesn't sound like you're getting anywhere, does it? Inez sounds like a complete dead end, but what about Charlotte? Do you think she might be behind the kidnappings?"

Stone shrugged. "I don't know, but I don't think Squeak was lying. He doesn't seem to think she'd do anything to harm children, despite the coincidental timing of her disappearance."

"*Is* it possible she could be another victim?" Gina asked. "Maybe the kidnappers are branching out."

"That's a pretty big stretch," Amber said. "People who kidnap kids aren't usually interested in adults—especially adults that have no connection to them."

"She *is* a Changeling," Jason pointed out. "And it sounds like at least one of the kids is too."

"There are a lot of Changelings." Gina pulled a slice of roast beef out of her sandwich and stuffed it in her mouth. "That's like saying two random Japanese guys are related."

"There aren't nearly as many Changelings as Japanese people," Stone said. "I wish there was a way to find out if the other kidnapped children were Changelings too."

"Yeah, and whether they were pretties or freaks," Gina said. "The only one we suspect so far sounds like a freak, which kinda leads me to think it couldn't have been Charlotte."

"Why not?" Stone asked.

"Because *she's* a freak. I could almost make a case for her snatching pretty kids out of spite, if she still resents losing her smoking-hot looks to go full toad-mode. But why would she hurt freak kids? I mean, even if whoever took them didn't *hurt* them hurt them, it's still pretty hard on a little kid to be snatched away from their parents."

Nobody had an answer for that.

"Okay," Stone said. "Well, that's all I've got for now. Gina, if you could continue leveraging your Changeling contacts to see if anyone knows where Charlotte is, I'd still like to talk with her. Even if she isn't connected, she might have thoughts on the matter. Until then…I guess we wait."

He hoped he was keeping his stress to himself. Given that he'd had no updates on the Brathwaite situation either, he was getting very tired of waiting. The ticking clock in the back of his mind, which had quieted for a while after his talk with Nana, had grown louder again, to the point where he couldn't ignore it.

He texted Ian and Verity about Brathwaite when he got back home. *Any updates? Ian, have you heard anything from Gabriel?*

Nothing. The reply came back quickly. *He's looking, but for whatever reason he seems not to be making this a priority. Can't really say why I'm getting that impression, because I'm not sure. He just seems evasive when I ask him about it.*

Stone knew exactly why: because the dragon was taking care not to get involved too much and attract the attention of his older brethren. *Well, hopefully he'll come up with something. Verity, have you heard from Nana?*

No. I thought she'd get back to you, since this is your show. You haven't either?

Not a word.

You want me to nudge her again? I'm not sure I feel comfortable doing that, but maybe I can ask Bron to do it.

No, it's all right. She did say it might take some time, and we've still got more than a month. I'm just impatient, I suppose.

I'll let you know the second I hear anything, she sent back.

Me too, Ian sent. *And you do the same, Dad.*

Message text couldn't convey an ominous tone and Ian wasn't much for emojis, but Stone picked it up nonetheless. He supposed he couldn't blame his son for a little lack of trust, given what had occurred in the past.

I will, he sent them both. *Hopefully something will come back to one of us soon.*

Stone was having an increasingly harder time keeping his growing impatience in check. He'd never been good at waiting for things to come to him, but in this case, there wasn't much else he could do.

He'd already done everything he could think of, without any satisfying results. He'd checked in with Renata Huxley, but got her voicemail. Without much enthusiasm, he'd updated her on the latest information from Squeak about Charlotte; however, based on their previous conversation, he didn't expect her to do much about it until her current hot case settled down. *That's why she trusted you with this one.* He did wonder in passing, though, what her current case must be if her superiors considered it higher priority than several kidnapped children.

He'd popped over to England to share a pint with Eddie and Ward, and to find out if they'd made any progress on finding Brathwaite. He didn't think so, for two reasons: first, they would have contacted him immediately to proudly share the fruits of their investigations, and second, with two dragons on the case not coming up with anything either—even with their constraints—he doubted his two friends would locate anything they'd missed.

He'd even dropped by Madame Huan's shop on the off chance she might be there, but the place was closed. Now that the dragon didn't spend much time in residence, the other staff maintained more normal human business hours.

Finally, tired of feeling like a racing engine with its gears stuck in neutral, he decided to revive an old pastime he used to enjoy back before he took his three-year hiatus. He consulted a couple of entertainment websites for San Francisco, found a few bands that sounded interesting, and checked the venues against his ley-line map. To his delight, a ley line ran less than a block past his first choice. If nothing else was going to happen, he might as well try distracting himself with music to take his mind off his obsessions.

He didn't ask any of his friends to accompany him, since he enjoyed doing this alone. Besides, Verity had already told him she'd be out with other friends tonight, and with two small children, Jason and Amber were out of the club-hopping business for the foreseeable future.

He thought a bit about that as he drifted down the block after reappearing in San Francisco, and about how much his life had begun to change, even before Aldwyn had imprisoned him. He wasn't sure how he felt about it, since it wasn't the kind of introspection he was normally comfortable with unless he'd had a few—or more than a few—drinks.

But the truth was, his life *was* changing, and there was no getting around that. It wasn't even the three-year sleep or the emergence of the Changelings that affected him as much, even though those two events had definitely been major influences on him.

No, it was more that his friends were changing. Verity used to accuse him of moving away from them, of going places she and the others couldn't follow. That was certainly true—even now, after all this time, none of his human associates even suspected the existence of the dragons, and none of them had any real clue about the true nature of Calanar and Trevor Harrison.

But it was also true, he realized with a bittersweet sense of regret, that *they* were going places *he* couldn't follow.

Like mortality.

He was already beginning to see it, and his three years away from them only cast it in a harsher light. Verity was getting older, evolving from the prickly, insecure teenager it seemed he'd only met last week into a confident, sophisticated woman who no longer looked to him for approval. That last part was a positive thing, of course, since she wasn't his apprentice anymore, and the break had probably been good for helping to cement that. And he didn't even truly miss the girl and young woman she'd been, since she was obviously so successful in her life now, and so happy. But still…

And then there was Jason. He might have changed even more than Verity had, in some ways. Stone let his thoughts travel back to their first meeting, when Jason had been a confused young slacker who'd had no idea what kind of dangerous rabbit hole the mentally-ill sister he'd emotionally neglected would lead him down. Stone wondered if he'd even recognize that young man anymore, now that Jason had matured into a strong, responsible family man who owned a successful business with his equally strong and responsible wife.

And finally, there was Ian. Stone regretted a lot of things about his son: that he hadn't had the chance to watch him grow up, that there were so many things he couldn't tell him, that he couldn't have prevented what had happened when Trin and the demon Razakal had got their hooks into him. Everything had turned out for the best; Ian had grown into a whip-smart young man and an exceptional mage, but Stone often wondered how much higher his son could fly if he knew everything about his heritage. Even so, he couldn't be prouder of Ian, and needed to tell him that more often.

But always hovering around, like a dark specter patiently waiting in the wings for its time to strike, was the inevitable fact that none of them were going to be around forever.

Verity, Jason, Amber—even Ian, though it would be slower— would eventually grow old and die. Stone had never given that much thought in the past, because he'd always thought he'd do the same thing alongside them. As mages, he, Verity, and Ian would age more slowly than mundane humans, so likely they would all live longer than Jason, but the difference wasn't that large, and it wasn't assured. Normal mages could get ill. They could die in accidents. They could be murdered.

Nobody got a guarantee.

Except that wasn't true, was it?

People were already complimenting Stone on how he didn't seem to age. He didn't even know how old he was chronologically anymore. Did the time in suspended animation count? If it did, he was almost forty-six. If it didn't, he was still forty-three—but he knew without any particular conceit that he looked more like he was in his early thirties. Would he continue to do that as he aged? Would he look thirty-two when he was fifty? Sixty? Seventy? He had no idea how old Trevor Harrison—the only other human immortal he knew—was, but Harrison only appeared to be in his middle thirties as well. And Harrison lived on another dimension, so he didn't have to worry about hiding his lack of aging.

Stone chuckled bitterly, startling a homeless man sitting against the building he was passing. These were the sorts of things one had to think about when one was immortal.

That, and his friends' inevitable deaths.

That morose thought led him back to James Brathwaite as he approached the club that was his destination, paid his cover, and headed inside.

Brathwaite had died nearly two hundred years ago—except he hadn't. His echo, the thing that made him *him,* had somehow persisted over all this time, and he'd managed to find a way to claim another body and keep going. Would it be possible, when the time came, for Verity, or Jason, or Ian to—

Stone shuddered, earning him a suspicious glance from the bartender where he was picking up a drink. That thought was chilling, and his level of abhorrence to it surprised him. It might not be the same sort of necromancy—raising soulless dead bodies to do one's bidding—but it was still against nature. Death was death, and when it was your time to go, you went on to whatever awaited you beyond the veil.

Except, apparently, for me, he thought. And Harrison. And maybe the dragons, though Kolinsky had once told him that even they died eventually.

Were there more immortals in the world? It made sense there had to be. He and Harrison couldn't be the only ones.

Could he find them?

Would he even want to?

Bloody hell, you muppet, you came here to watch the band, not to lose yourself in maudlin ruminations about mortality.

Disgusted with himself and his brain that wouldn't shut off, he dropped into a chair with his pint and tried to settle back. The band would take the stage soon. He hoped they would be good enough to distract him for a while.

His phone buzzed.

He pulled it out, not sure whether he hoped it would be something important or wished it would be a telemarketer so he could ignore it.

The number was unfamiliar, but not blocked.

He almost let it go to voicemail, but some impulse compelled him to hit the button. "Yes, hello?" He had to press the speaker close to his ear to hear the caller over the ambient club noise. The band would start any minute now, making listening impossible.

"Hello." The voice was female, and sounded tentative, as if the caller wasn't sure she wanted to be speaking.

"Who is this?"

"You don't know me, but I'm a friend of Quinn's. You talked to her and her boyfriend recently, right?"

Stone tensed. He glanced at the stage as the announcer strode up and took the mic to announce the band. "I…did, yes." He was already rising. Apparently, the universe didn't want him to hear them tonight. "Is there something I can do for you? How did you get my number?" He threaded his way through the crowd and exited the club, not even bothering to get a hand stamp. He knew he wasn't going to be back.

There was a pause. "It's…kind of a long story. I'd really like to talk to you in person if I can. Are you still in the L.A. area?"

"Er—I might be. What's this about, though?"

Another pause. "It's…about Charlotte. Quinn told me what you guys talked about."

Stone looked around. The street was busy, choked with evening traffic, pedestrians, and a row of homeless people in tents and makeshift lean-tos pressed against the buildings. "What about her?"

"I'm worried about her."

"Why do you say that?" He kept walking, slipping down a narrow alley to find a place where he could leave without being seen.

"Can you come? Like I said, I'd really rather not do this on the phone."

"I can. But you haven't even told me your name yet."

This time, the pause was even longer. "My name's Holly. I'm…Charlotte's sister."

Stone suggested meeting her at the same place he'd talked to Squeak and Quinn, since it was easy for him to get to. He arrived before she did, and was sitting in a rear booth sipping a Guinness when she arrived. She was easy to spot, peering around as if trying to recognize someone. When he leaned out of the booth and met her gaze, she hurried over. "Are you Doc?"

"I am. Sit down, please. Would you like something to drink?" He'd used the same illusionary disguise as last time, but once again made no effort to hide his distinctive accent.

"No—no, that's okay. I don't want to stay long. I'm not even sure I should be here." She slid in across from him.

He looked her over. She was in her middle twenties, with a round, plain face, medium-length red-brown hair, tortoiseshell glasses, and no makeup. She wore a Pikachu T-shirt under a denim jacket studded with buttons and patches. "You said you're Charlotte's sister."

"Yeah. Her younger sister, by a year."

"Okay. Suppose you tell me why you called me. You said you were worried about her. Is it connected to why she's disappeared?"

Holly looked unhappy. "I think it might be. Quinn told me about what you guys were talking about—that a Changeling has been kidnapping children, and that one of the kids might be a Changeling too."

"Ah, so you know about Changelings, then."

She nodded and gave him an odd look. "I heard you're a mage, so I'm surprised you didn't look already."

At that point, he realized he hadn't examined her with magical sight yet. He'd been planning to, but mostly to check her aura. He shifted now, and stared.

The mousy nerd sitting across from him had transformed. In her place sat a stunningly beautiful fox-person with glittering eyes, silvery-white fur, a pointy black nose, and a feathery, black-tipped tail.

Bloody hell, she looks like a furry's wet dream was the first thing that popped into Stone's mind, but he quickly shoved the thought aside.

Holly smiled faintly, almost as if she'd correctly read his expression. "I get that a lot from Changelings. Never met a mage before, though."

"Yes. Well." Stone shifted back to mundane sight. He scratched the back of his neck and debated where to go next. Finally, he settled on, "So, tell me why you're worried about your sister. Do you know where she is?"

"No. We've…never really been all that close, even before we both Changed. I haven't seen her in quite a while." She looked down again, appearing to gather her thoughts, and swallowed hard. "I'm…not even sure I want to say this. I feel like I'm betraying her somehow. But if it's true, I couldn't live with myself if I didn't say something."

"Say something…about what?" Stone already suspected he might know, but he didn't want to lead her. She had to say it herself.

"I…I think she might have something to do with the kidnappings," she said quickly, still without looking at him.

Stone kept his tone even and nonjudgmental—the kind he'd use on a student admitting to a misdeed. "Why do you think so? You said you hadn't seen her for quite some time."

Holly looked around, then back down at her hands. "I need to start with a little history. Is that okay? Do you have time?"

"Please—tell me your story whatever way you like. I've got no-where I need to be tonight."

After a couple false starts, she spoke toward the table. "Okay. So. Charlotte and I used to be close when we were little kids. We used to play together all the time, had all the same friends, the whole thing. But then, when we got a little older…hit puberty…that changed. She…I guess you could say she blossomed, while I…didn't." She waved vaguely at herself. "You've seen Charlotte's photos, right? Her videos?"

"I have."

"She's always been pretty, but things really went off the rails when she turned thirteen. Almost overnight it was like God opened the heavens and dumped several gorgeous people's worth of beauty on her. You wouldn't even know we'd come from the same parents."

"And how did you feel about that?" Stone shifted briefly to magical sight, looking for any signs of jealousy in Holly's aura, but he saw only sadness.

She shrugged. "I was okay with it. No, I really was. I'd always been more into reading, comics, anime, that kind of stuff than boys and clothes and parties. I was a nerd. Sure, I didn't look like her, but I was smart and had some close friends. My life was happy. I was proud of Char when she started getting local modeling jobs, and all the boys flocked around her. That was her thing."

Stone gave her an encouraging *go on* nod.

"But she…changed. She dropped out of high school so she could take more and more modeling jobs. She went to fancy par-ties, hung out with rich guys—all of which would have been fine, except then she started believing people when they told her how great she was. She turned…nasty. Stuck up. The ultimate mean girl. I tried to reach out to her, but she didn't want anything to do with me. One time when she was drunk, she said she was embarrassed if anybody knew we were sisters." Holly bowed her head again, and

Stone didn't miss the slight quaver in her voice. "It was hard to hear that, because I still loved her."

"I can imagine," he murmured.

"Eventually, I gave up trying to connect with her. She had her new fancy life, and she didn't want anything to do with me or our family. She didn't even come to our grandma's funeral, because she had a fashion show in Milan the same weekend." She swallowed hard again, pulled a tissue from her bag, and dabbed her eyes under her glasses. "Sorry. That was years ago, but it's still hard to think about."

"Please, take your time."

"Yeah." She stowed the tissue. "So anyway, she kept getting more and more famous, to the point where she'd almost made it to supermodel status. I still kept up with her news on the internet, so I saw she was about to sign a multi-million-dollar contract to do TV commercials for one of the big fashion houses. Even after how she treated me, I was still happy for her. It was what she'd always wanted."

Stone could see where this was going, based on the little information Squeak and Quinn had given him. "Let me guess—this was around three years ago."

She nodded miserably. "Yeah. She was literally a few days away from signing the contract when the Change hit her. Overnight, she went from being one of the most beautiful women around to looking at herself in the mirror and seeing…"

"Yes. I've…heard."

"At first, I didn't know what had happened, since I hadn't Changed yet. I had no idea why she suddenly gave up modeling, dropped out of public life, and spent all her time holed up in her fancy house out in Hollywood Hills. I tried to reach out to her again, thinking she had a drug problem or something, but she refused to see me. And of course, normals—her agent, her friends—

had no idea what was going on, since as far as they could tell nothing had changed."

"That must have been difficult for her."

She nodded again. "I got a lot of this secondhand, of course, because she still wasn't talking to me. But from what I understand, she couldn't stand looking at herself. She thought God was punishing her for being a horrible person. And then *I* changed, about six months later. Into—" She gestured at herself. "—this. And that made it worse."

Stone was beginning to see where this was going. "Because of…what you turned into."

"Yeah. It was like our whole dynamic flipped. Suddenly, *I* was the one getting the attention, in the Changeling community at least, while she was the hideous ugly monster. But the thing was, I didn't care what I looked like. I learned about the whole pretty-freak deal, but I didn't care. I judge people by what they act like, not by what they look like. Before long, I had friends from all parts of the community—and it got back to Char about me. I heard she didn't take it well."

"I…see. So you two have remained estranged?"

"I guess. Not because of me, though." She looked up now. "But that's all just background. The important part is that a year or so ago, Char finally came to terms with what she was. She decided if she was going to be ugly now and there was nothing she could do about it, she was going to own it. She talked to some people from Freakshow who reached out to her, and…she pretty much embraced the whole movement, from what I heard. I've talked to several people who've told me she's gone full radical now, getting into all kinds of borderline-legal things to enhance Changeling rights, and especially the less-attractive ones."

Stone wasn't completely sure he followed where she was going. "I…see what you're saying, but how does this lead you to believe she's involved with the kidnappings?"

Holly sighed. "Maybe it's just a hunch, but after I heard she disappeared right around the time the first kid was taken, and that at least one of them was a Changeling—I can't help thinking she's involved. I hope to God it's not true, but…like I said, I couldn't live with myself if I could have helped and those kids get…hurt." She met his gaze again. "I want to help. I don't know how, but if there's anything you can do—"

He hadn't expected that offer. "There may be a way you *can* help. Do you have any way to contact Charlotte?"

"Maybe. I still have one of her old email addresses. I'm not sure she checks it anymore, but she's had it since we were teenagers. I could try it…"

"It's worth a shot. Reach out to her and tell her you'd like to talk. But you've got to be careful. Don't even hint that you know about the kidnappings. Just tell her you miss her and you'd like it if you could reconnect with her."

"Okay. I'll do it. But…I don't want her to get hurt. Even after all this, she's still my sister and I love her. So…do you promise you won't hurt her?"

Stone couldn't make that promise—not if Charlotte was connected with the kidnappings and the children's lives were at risk. "I promise to do the best I can. It might be that she isn't even involved, but she might be able to help us discover who is."

"I hope so." She sniffed and dabbed at her nose with the wadded-up tissue. "Char always loved kids—babies especially. I can't believe she'd ever hurt them. If she has, it's because she's gotten herself mixed up with bad people. I have to keep believing that."

Stone wrote his email address on a notebook page and gave it to her. "You already have my phone number. Please—contact me immediately if she responds. Will you do that?"

"Yeah. I will." She stood. "I'll be honest—I kind of wish I hadn't come. I'm scared for Char. But I want to do the right thing."

CHAPTER TWENTY-ONE

THE WEEKEND and the beginning of the next week passed without any more information about Charlotte. Stone texted Holly to ask if she'd made contact, but she said there had been no response to her email.

I even contacted a couple of our old mutual friends, she sent back, *but they haven't seen her in a long time either. I wish I could be more help.*

I appreciate what you've done, he told her. *These things take time. Let me know if you hear anything, though. Anything at all.*

At least there hadn't been any other kidnappings. Ren Huxley contacted Stone on Monday to tell him she was still wrapping up her case, but she should be more help later in the week. She also told him none of the children had been found yet, and neither her agency nor any of the mundane law-enforcement organizations had any leads. Stone was beginning to fear the children were dead, and if Charlotte was involved, she'd gone into hiding.

He still wasn't completely convinced she *was* involved, though. It didn't make any sense. As far as the evidence pointed, the only tenuous connection he had between her and the kidnappings was that someone had framed Squeak—but that could have been any-body. It could have been another of the "pretty" Changelings who was trying to mess with him, or some other enemy he'd forgotten about. Easygoing people like Squeak tended not to remember slights—either against them or committed by them.

He'd just about given up hoping to hear from anyone when Ian texted him. The message came at mid-day on Wednesday: *G got a tip that someone's spotted B in Vienna. Can you come? I'm at the portal here.*

Stone had to read it twice to make sure he wasn't indulging in wishful thinking. Finally, after all this time, a lead? *I'll meet you there,* he sent back quickly, thankful for autocorrect because his shaking fingers kept hitting the wrong letters. *Let V. know.* Heart pounding with excitement and anticipation, he barely took the time to grab his coat before he ran down to his basement and strode through the portal to Vienna.

Ian was waiting for him. "Verity said she'll get here as soon as she can, but she's got to get to the portal. She said not to wait and she'll catch up."

That was good, because despite his promise to Verity, he had no intention of waiting if it meant potentially missing his chance to nab the necromancer. "Where's Gabriel?"

"He's not coming. He says he can't get involved with this part." He shook his head. "There's something about him, Dad. I don't know what it is, but it's like he's got this secret side he won't let me see."

Stone didn't reply, since there was nothing he could say to help. He followed Ian up the stairs and through the quaint, centuries-old brewpub to the street. "Tell me what's happened. What did the contact say, and where did they spot Brathwaite?"

"They didn't say much. Gabriel said he put out a lot of discreet feelers with trusted people, offering a lot of money for solid tips. One came back an hour ago, saying they spotted a woman matching the description at the bar at the Hotel Bristol. She's sitting with several other people, and they said she doesn't look like she's leaving any time soon."

"Brilliant. Is it far from here?"

"A couple miles." He waved to hail a cab, and a moment later they were crawling through the nighttime traffic toward the hotel.

Stone could barely sit still. He felt like a young boy impatient for an upcoming treat, but forced himself to calm down. *If you find him,* he reminded himself, *you're going to kill him. This isn't something to be excited about.*

But he *was* excited. The fact that killing Brathwaite would get Aldwyn off his back for a while notwithstanding, he had to admit to himself that his conscience was giving him no trouble about what he planned to do. At this point, he just wanted to get it over with.

His own phone buzzed, with a text from Verity. *Anything? I'm stuck in traffic.*

We're heading to where he was seen. I'm sorry, Verity, but we can't wait.

There was a long pause, and then: *I know. It sucks, but you can't miss the chance. Good luck. Be careful.*

He showed the exchange to Ian, who looked somber. Both of them knew how disappointed Verity was to miss the chance to take down Sharra's killer.

They were a half-block from the hotel when Ian's phone buzzed again. He glanced at it, then frowned. "That was the contact again. Brathwaite's left the bar and exited the hotel. Our guy followed him outside. Says he just got into a green Mercedes the valet brought around."

Stone leaned forward, craning his neck. The cab had crawled forward a bit more, and under the lights of the hotel's front entrance, he spotted the green Mercedes sedan just pulling away and entering the flow of traffic. "There he is!" he whispered furiously to Ian.

Ian pointed. "See that Mercedes?" he told the driver in German. "Follow it, please."

The cabbie shrugged and changed direction, re-entering the road three cars behind the Mercedes.

"Here," Stone said. "I think I can make it easier for us to keep him in sight." He'd almost forgotten about a little spell he'd created years ago, to help him keep track of people he was following. The last time he'd used it was in San Francisco with Verity, when they'd been chasing a pothead with information about the ancient game pieces they were tracking. He focused on the Mercedes, gathered energy, and sent the spell on its way. An instant later, a shimmering golden star appeared above the car's roof.

"Nice trick," Ian said, grinning. "You'll have to teach me that one."

Stone didn't answer. He hadn't done it a moment too soon, as the Mercedes turned right onto a side street. "Make the next right," he told the cabbie, hoping the man spoke English.

Apparently he did. By the time they reached the street, though, the Mercedes had disappeared into the darkness. Only the golden star remained to keep them on track. "The driver can't see it," Stone whispered to Ian. "So we'll have to point the way."

"What's the range?"

"Haven't tested it past about half a mile, so if he gets farther away we might lose him. Let's not do that, shall we?"

Fortunately, the side street was less choked with traffic than the one in front of the hotel. Unfortunately, Brathwaite seemed to be taking the scenic route. The Mercedes turned right again, then left, then right.

"Do you think he's trying to lose us?" Ian hissed, leaning in close to Stone so the driver couldn't hear. "Does he know we're following him?"

"I've got no idea what he's doing. But he's got to deal with the same traffic we do. We've still got him in our sights." The golden star continued to shimmer ahead of them as they rounded the last right.

"I wish we could just throw a spell to disable the car." Ian sounded frustrated, every bit as tense as Stone.

"That wouldn't work anyway." Stone didn't say why—not where the driver might overhear—but Ian nodded grimly. Stopping the car in the middle of a public street would draw too much attention, and do nothing to help them kill Brathwaite. That would need to be done somewhere private.

The Mercedes made another left, turning onto a ramp descending below a two-story building. "What is that?" Stone asked, gripping the seat. "Apartment building?"

"Looks like an underground parking garage." Ian pointed and whispered, "See how the star is going down?"

"Okay." Stone spoke louder to the driver. "Pull over, please. We'll get out here."

Ian paid the fare. They didn't even wait for the cab to trundle off before they were both hurrying across the dark street. The area here didn't have much traffic at all; it appeared to be a staid, middle-class residential neighborhood full of old apartment buildings similar to the one their quarry had entered.

"Why would he go *here?*" Stone whispered. "Hardly seems the sort of place he'd be living."

"Might be a trap, like the last place. We'd better be careful."

That was a good point. Stone was so eager to take out Brathwaite that he'd almost forgotten about the zombie ambush in Potsdam. "Let's stay invisible until we get inside, and hide before mine fades. We can look for illusions then."

Ian nodded. They both shimmered to invisibility, and Stone immediately took off at a fast jog down the ramp into the shadowy garage so he could gain cover before he had to drop the spell. He could still see the golden star up ahead, but it was no longer moving. That made sense, if Brathwaite had parked. They needed to catch him before he disappeared into the building.

It didn't seem as if they'd have any trouble with that, though. As they crept along behind other parked cars to get closer and Stone dropped his invisibility spell, they both spotted a figure getting out of the car. They couldn't make out much detail from where they were, but it appeared to be a thin woman dressed in a long, sweeping coat. She paused a moment, then moved to the rear of the car, opened the trunk, and leaned in to pull out a bag.

This might be the best chance they were going to get. The garage was deserted; if that was Brathwaite, no one would see them confront him. Stone motioned Ian forward, then started to move himself.

Ian touched his arm.

"*What?*" he mouthed, impatient.

"*Let's check the aura.*"

Damn, but Ian was once again making a good point. *You're getting sloppy,* Stone told himself in disgust. He shifted to magical sight, peering out from behind a parked car. The figure had pulled out a carryon-sized bag and was now lowering the trunk lid, her back still pointed at Stone and Ian. Around her body, the aura blazed a strong, unsettled dark purple.

Stone nodded to Ian. "*Let me go first,*" he mouthed. "*Cover me.*"

Ian returned the nod, remaining where he was.

Stone crept forward, edging around another car. Even with the aura for confirmation, he still needed to see Brathwaite's face before he took action. There weren't that many aura colors, and there were a lot of thin women. He couldn't take the chance of attacking the wrong person. But once he had confirmation, he planned to strike without warning. This was an assassination, not a duel of honor.

The woman finished closing the trunk lid and bent to lift the bag. Stone waited, tense, heart thudding hard, his full attention fixed on her as she turned.

Just a moment longer…

And there it was. She was facing him now, though she hadn't appeared to notice him hiding behind the car.

Positive identification. James Brathwaite, in the guise of Miriam Padgett, standing right there not twenty feet away from him.

He gathered Calanarian energy, preparing to release it in a solid, unstoppable column straight at the woman's center mass. There would be a body when he was done so he could have something to show Verity, but it wouldn't necessarily be in one piece.

"Hello, Dr. Stone," Brathwaite said. "It's so good to see you." As before, he spoke with Padgett's pleasant, lilting Estuary accent.

Stone hesitated.

"Oh, come on out. I know you've been following me. Only, are you sure it's *me* you've been following? It would be *such* a shame if you ended up following the wrong person."

The woman's features morphed, reforming into another figure Stone didn't recognize. Still a woman, but with a heavy face and straw-colored hair that poked from beneath a scarf she had wrapped around her head and covering her nose and mouth.

No, no, no…

"Come out," the woman called again. "I have a message for you from the one you seek. You'll want to hear this, I think." Her voice sounded oddly muffled from behind the scarf. Something was off about it, but Stone couldn't put his finger on what it was.

He rose slowly, forming a protective magical shield around himself. He shot a quick glance to the side toward Ian, and made a "stay put" gesture below the line of the car he was standing behind.

Ian gave a grim nod and remained crouched, raising his shield as well.

"What's the message?" Stone called.

"You don't trust me."

Stone looked around, scanning the area with magical sight. He didn't see anyone else moving. No sign of either zombies or any residents entering the garage. "Of course I don't trust you. And I'm not hanging about waiting for your associates to ambush us. If you've got a message, let's have it." He tried hard not to let his rising sense of dread reach his voice. If Brathwaite knew he'd been looking for him, that meant he'd likely become even more difficult to find in the future.

"Oh, fine. He told me you'd be like this." She reached into her coat pocket, withdrew a sealed envelope, and waved it at Stone. "Here it is. I'll just leave it here for you, then, and wait to see if you have an answer." She bent and placed the envelope on the concrete floor.

"Take the bag with you. And back up behind those other cars."

"My, you *are* a nervous one, aren't you? Fine. I'll move well away from you." She hefted the bag and backed up, never taking her eyes from Stone. When she reached the row of cars, she scooted sideways and then dropped back to stand behind a blue BMW SUV.

Stone crept forward, approaching the envelope. He looked away from her for only a second, long enough to shoot a quick magical-sight scan at it to make sure it wasn't radiating arcane energy. It wasn't, so he kept his eyes on the woman as he crouched and picked it up.

Still keeping his eyes fixed on her, he opened the envelope, withdrew the paper inside, and flicked his gaze down toward it.

It contained only a single line of text, printed on a laser printer rather than handwritten:

You'll never find me, Stone. But one day perhaps you'll thank me.

He'd barely had time to digest the message when, with sudden clarity, it came to him what had sounded odd about the woman's voice.

Even after she'd dropped the illusion, she was still speaking with Brathwaite's Miriam Padgett voice.

Was it a double illusion? Had he been speaking to Brathwaite all the time?

He jerked his head up. "Ian! It's—"

Next to him, the green Mercedes exploded.

CHAPTER TWENTY-TWO

"**D**AD?"

The words sounded muddy, as if someone was calling to him through several feet of water.

Something shook him. "Dad?" Clearer that time.

He shook his head several times and opened his eyes. He was on his back, with a worried Ian staring down at him. "Uh—?"

"Are you okay? We have to go. Now."

Stone's brain seemed to be moving at half speed, if that. "What…?"

"The car blew up, Dad. If you hadn't had your shield up, it would have killed you. Or, you know, at least put you out of action for a long time." He tugged on Stone's arm, trying to drag him up. "We have to get out of here, before people show up."

Slowly, reality trickled back in. He let Ian pull him to a sitting position and looked down at himself. No blood, and he didn't hurt enough for any bad injuries. He wasn't in the middle of the garage anymore, but lying against the side of a different Mercedes. Had the explosion tossed him there, or had Ian dragged him away? "B-Brathwaite? Did he—"

"It wasn't Brathwaite." Ian sounded grim, and continued to pull on Stone's arm until he got him to a tottery standing position. Then he flung his father's arm over his shoulder and hustled him away. "It was one of his undead things. The explosion blew it apart, and then it turned into that goo stuff they decompose into."

Stone's hearing was coming back now, too. Sirens were approaching, and several of the parked cars' alarms were going off in a strident cacophony. Something still wasn't making sense. He looked around. "Why…isn't the whole garage—"

"It wasn't a big explosion. That's the other reason it probably didn't hurt you worse. I don't think Brathwaite was trying to take out the building—just the car. And you," he added soberly. He tightened his hold on Stone's arm and increased speed. "You can rest when we get away. We don't want the cops to catch us here."

Stone gave up trying to ask questions and concentrated on moving under his own power to help Ian. His son wasn't heading for the way they'd come in, but rather toward a rear exit door. When he reached it, he stopped.

"Can you do anything? Levitate, like before? We can rest if we can get to the roof across the street."

"I think so." He'd been doing a better inventory while they moved, and it seemed as if the worse of his injury was from the psychic feedback of the explosion nearly taking his shield down. He felt moisture on his upper lip, indicating the familiar feedback nosebleed, but it didn't seem too bad. He'd been very lucky—again.

"Okay. I'll make us invisible and keep hold of you, but it would be a big help if you can levitate yourself."

"I've got this," Stone growled. The sirens were getting louder, and when he snatched a glance over his shoulders, he saw whirling red lights on the other side of the garage. "Let's go."

It was a little dicey at a couple of points, but they did make it to the roof of the building across the street. Stone dropped down below the roofline and collapsed onto his back, watching his heavy breaths making little puffs in the cold air. "Bloody hell…" he muttered. "It was just like last time. An ambush."

"Not quite." Ian was puffing a little too, but not nearly as bad as Stone. He sat with his back pressed against the chimney and watched the commotion across the street. "This tip came from one of Gabriel's people."

Stone had a sudden, terrifying thought—*what if Gabriel's working with Brathwaite?*—but immediately dismissed it as absurd. The dragons didn't have much in common with each other personality-wise, but every one he'd met or heard of shared the visceral hatred of necromancy and its practitioners.

"I need to contact him," Ian was saying. "Tell him he needs to vet his informants better. The wrong person must have gotten wind that we're looking for Brathwaite and told him about it." He turned to look at his father. "How did you know it was a trap?"

Stone's brain was coming back online now. His head still pounded like someone was hitting it with a sledgehammer, but that he could deal with. A good night's sleep would take care of it. "I wanted to see if he was really Brathwaite before I killed him, so I moved around behind the cars to get a good view."

"And it was?"

"At first, yes. But then he changed."

"Yeah, I saw. A woman with a scarf pulled up around her face."

"Right. You heard what she said—that Brathwaite had sent her with a message for me." A sudden thought hit him hard, and he spun to stare hard at Ian. "The envelope!"

"Yeah. It got blown up too, but it looked like you read it before the bomb went off. What did it say? Did it have some kind of magic or trigger on it that set off the bomb?"

"No magic," Stone said. "No tracker. Good thought, though. You did a brilliant job tonight."

Even with his cool, sophisticated façade, Ian couldn't hide his pride in his father's words. "Thanks. But you were telling me how you knew it was a trap. What happened?"

"It was her voice. When she looked like Brathwaite, she had Miriam Padgett's voice, as I expected. But then when she changed to that other woman, the voice was still the same."

"Shit…" Ian whispered. "So he can talk through the zombies he creates?"

"Apparently. And see through them, too."

"He's upped his game."

"Indeed he has." Stone watched the red lights moving around on the street below. "We should get out of here."

"What did the message say?"

Stone struggled to remember the exact wording. "Something like…'*you'll never find me, but one day you might thank me.*'"

"What the hell does *that* mean?"

"I've got no idea."

"Why would you thank him?"

"I don't know. But I'm not going to waste time thinking about it now. Come on. We've got some walking to do before we can get another cab. I want to get the hell out of here in case any more of those creatures are lurking about."

They floated down behind the back side of the house so none of the emergency personnel would see them and started walking, disregarding spells at full strength. When they'd made it halfway down the block, Ian said softly, "Dad?"

"Yes?"

"Brathwaite knows you're looking for him now."

"Yes."

"And you've only got less than a month to find him."

"Yes."

"Do you know what you're going to do?"

"I haven't got a clue." Stone forced himself to pay attention to their surroundings as they trudged along, but his mind was far away. He couldn't help thinking that tonight's encounter might have marked the beginning of his failure to complete Aldwyn's assignment.

CHAPTER TWENTY-THREE

STONE SLEPT LATE THE NEXT DAY, waking only when Raider began insistently poking him in the face because it was time for breakfast. Most of his headache was gone by then, leaving only a dull pain a couple ibuprofen took care of.

He called Verity to update her on the latest after he fed the cat.

"Yikes," she said, wincing. "That sounds like it was a mess. I'm sorry it didn't work out—though I'd be lying if I said I wasn't glad I'll get another shot at him. I know this has to be done, but I was still disappointed at not getting to be part of it because of bad traffic."

"I understand. And I hope you do. *If* we ever find him at this point."

He'd told her about the message, too. "Do you have any idea why he thinks you might thank him?"

Stone had been thinking about that a lot ever since he woke—in fact, Brathwaite's image had haunted his dreams last night. "Nothing. He's probably just being his usual unpleasant self. I wouldn't put it past him to add that message for the sole purpose of giving me something to grind my mental gears over."

"Maybe." She didn't sound convinced, though. "I assume Ian's going to talk to Gabriel about the miscommunication."

"Oh, yes. He wasn't pleased at all. But I suppose there's nothing that can be done about it. No matter how powerful you are, once you let a bit of information out, you lose control over where it goes from there." He knew that all too well, unfortunately.

"Yeah." Her sigh came through over the line. "Anyway, I'm really glad you had your shield up so you didn't get hurt. And we've still got Nana's people looking too. Hopefully somebody will come up with something. Even Brathwaite can't hide forever."

Stone hoped she was right.

Jason called Friday afternoon. "Hey, Al. You want to come down here? I think we've got something for you."

Stone had been in the middle of a rare bout of early-spring cleaning, using magic to mop the kitchen floor while Raider chased the mop around and tried to pounce on it. "Something about what? The Changeling case?"

"Yeah. Surprisingly, it was me who found it this time instead of Gina, but she's right here and pretty excited too. Can you come?"

He looked at the mop. "Yes, I think you can drag me away from the thrilling things I'm doing right now. Be right there."

Stone was glad Jason had moved his agency during his three-year hiatus, not only because he was proud of his friend for his success, but also because it was closer to a ley line. He arrived at the door fifteen minutes later.

Derik waved at him from the reception desk. "Hey, Dr. S. They're all in the back. I've got no idea what they're so excited about, but they've been back there for an hour."

"Thank you, Derik." Stone wondered if Gina had forgiven him yet for his comments about unattractive Changelings.

He found not only Jason and Gina in Jason's office, but also Amber. They were all standing behind Jason's desk, watching something on the computer screen.

"What are you lot all wound up about?"

Gina grinned. "Hey, Doc. Can you—uh—?" She made "magic fingers."

Stone cast the cone of silence spell. "You must have something good."

"Depends on how you define 'good,'" Jason said. "But I think I found a connection between Charlotte and the kidnappings. It's tenuous, but it's more than we had before." He turned the monitor sideways so they could all see it.

It was a YouTube video. Jason restarted it and leaned back. "I found this while I was looking for anything I could dig up on Charlotte. It was taken at a party held only a couple of days before she disappeared. A big, glitzy meet-and-be-seen kind of thing for people connected with the fashion industry and their families."

Stone watched the video unfold. It was narrated by some hyperactive, pink-haired woman whose sole purpose seemed to be tracking down as many models and fashion-industry bigwigs as she could find and trying to get interviews—or at least selfies—with them. Stone immediately found her chirpy voice and her flighty mannerisms highly annoying. He glanced at the timeline. "Bloody hell, this thing goes on for twenty minutes. I don't think I can listen to that woman wittering on for twenty minutes."

Jason laughed. "Okay, fair enough. I'll run it forward." He scrubbed the timeline to the nine-minute mark. A few random people appeared, and then the narrator aimed the camera at a familiar face a few feet away.

"Oh, wow," she gushed. "That's Charlotte! She's been out of the modeling business for a while now and hasn't been seen in public much lately, but she still looks awesome to me. Let's see if I can get her to talk to me. I'd never be brave enough if she was still modeling."

The camera bobbed through the crowd, and then Charlotte appeared closer up. "Charlotte!" the narrator called. "I'm Norrie Barton, and this is *Fashion Fantastic*. It's so good to see you, and you look amazing! Could I get a few words for your fans?"

Charlotte *did* still look amazing. She'd put on a few pounds, moving her from the rail-thin frame of a working model to simply slim like a normal person, but her hair and face were perfectly done up. She wore a slinky, sequined black cocktail dress, with a glittering diamond necklace accentuating her plunging neckline. "Hello!" she said, waving. "I'm so happy to be here tonight."

"Any plans to get back into modeling?" Norrie asked. "We all miss you!"

"Eh, we'll see." She was already turning away. "Who knows what the future will bring. Must go now! Byee!" She strode away into the crowd.

"Well, there you have it," Norrie Barton said, following her with the camera for several seconds as she receded. "And—oh, look! There's Byron MacRae. I *must* try to find out when his next show will be." She jerked the camera around and hurried off in the other direction.

Jason paused the video and shot Stone a significant look.

Stone had no idea what he was on about. He shook his head. "Was there something I was supposed to see there, other than that she was at the party?"

"Yeah. It was hard to spot, though. Let me run it back. Watch closely in the background, after Norrie stops talking to Charlotte and films her walking away. I'll turn off the sound to make it easier."

Stone leaned in. Norrie Barton finished her interview with Charlotte and kept the camera aimed at her retreating back before going after her next conquest.

Charlotte started by sashaying along, obviously enjoying the attention. But then she stopped suddenly, her body language radiating shock or startlement. She paused a moment, appearing to look at something, and then hastily changed direction and moved away.

"Did you see it that time?"

But Stone still shook his head. "I'm sorry, but no. She looked like she saw something that startled her, but—"

"Here," Gina said. "Let me zoom in a little. It *is* hard to see if you don't know what you're looking for." She took the mouse from Jason and hovered the cursor over the video, doing something to zoom in tighter.

She didn't focus on Charlotte, though, but rather at what she was looking at: a well-dressed black man and woman in their middle thirties. It was difficult to make out at first in the party's dim, flashing lights, but the man was holding a toddler boy dressed in a tiny tuxedo. The boy had twisted around in his father's arms and was waving enthusiastically at Charlotte.

"Bloody hell…" Stone murmured. "Is that—"

In answer, Gina minimized the window with the video and pulled up another. This one showed a local-news interview. The distraught couple being interviewed were obviously the same ones from the party, dressed more casually. "Shawn and Zahra LaRue, the parents of Montrel, the first child we know of who was abducted as part of this group." She unmuted the window so they could listen.

"—please, I beg you," Zahra LaRue was imploring with a shaking voice and tears running down her cheeks, "if you've taken our baby boy, please don't hurt him. He needs his mother and father. He's the sweetest little boy in the world, and we'll do anything to get him back. Just please contact us and let us know he's all right."

The scene cut to the reporter, and Gina muted it again. "So yeah," she said. "It's not a great lead, but it definitely establishes a connection between Charlotte and the LaRues. At least that they were in the same place at that party."

"I just noticed something that time through that I didn't see before," Amber said. "Did you see how Montrel got all excited? At first I thought he was just happy to be around all the lights and stuff. But looking again, does it seem to you like he's actually waving at Charlotte as she approaches?"

"Why's that important?" Jason asked. "I mean, she's really pretty, but a lot of people there are. Maybe he liked how sparkly her dress was."

Gina pulled up the other video and ran it again. "Oh man, good catch. My first thought was that Charlotte recognized Shawn or Zahra—like maybe she'd had dealings with them before or something. But what if it wasn't them who startled her?"

Stone caught on to her line of reasoning. "You think little Montrel is a Changeling too."

"Yeah." She froze the video on the scene with the little boy waving. "It makes sense. Jason said this party is for fashion people and their families—that's not that common. Usually they don't bring the kiddies to this kind of thing, so even if Charlotte knew Zahra—and it made sense she might, since Zahra's a big-deal fashion-industry lawyer—she probably never saw her kid before that night."

"So what's it mean?" Jason asked. "She sees Montrel's a Changeling, and—what—decides to kidnap him? It doesn't make sense. What would make her go from a supermodel to a kidnapper?"

"I dunno," Gina said. "Spite, maybe? I mean, Zahra's pretty successful, and so is her husband. If Montrel was a pretty Changeling, maybe she felt jealous of them because she went toad-mode and couldn't live with looking at herself in the mirror anymore? People have snapped over less."

"True…" Stone paced the room, pondering. "But why would she attend that party, if she couldn't stand looking at herself, or being seen?"

"I think I might have an answer for that." Gina leaned back in her chair and looked sober. "Those kinds of parties are all about photos and videos—neither of which show a Changeling's true form. I don't know if any of the other folks there were Changelings, but I'd bet a lot of money—you know, if I *had* a lot of money—that they weren't. If she checked the guest list in advance, she could feel safe going there and getting some of her old glory back, without worrying about seeing herself in the mirror or any other Changelings spotting her."

"That makes sense," Jason said. "But if Montrel's a Changeling too, and he could see her toad form, why would he look so happy? If she's really that ugly, wouldn't she scare a little kid?"

"Not if he's ugly too!" Amber said triumphantly. "Remember the other girl, Gurpreet? We think she's an alligator or a lizard or something."

"So she's snatching *ugly* Changeling kids?" Jason looked confused. "Why would she want to do that? I don't get it."

"I don't either," Stone said. "It does seem odd that she'd want to hurt what she sees as her own kind."

Gina nodded. "Yeah. But like I said before, people do strange things when they crack, and I've heard more than one story of Changelings who turned really ugly having breakdowns over it."

"We need to find her," Stone said. "I'm more convinced than ever that she's responsible, but we've got to find out why."

"We'll keep looking," Jason said. "I've got to go out of town on a case over the weekend, but Amber will be here with the kids. She can do some work from home."

"And I'll definitely keep looking," Gina said. "I'll check in with Quasi and a couple more Freakshow contacts. Somebody's got to know where she is." She looked down. "Squeak said she came to terms with the way she was. I hope something didn't unravel that, and now she's taking it out on these poor kids."

CHAPTER TWENTY-FOUR

STONE'S GROWING SENSE OF URGENCY about both cases was starting to make it hard for him to function. He spent most of Saturday pinballing between the two—obsessively searching online for other videos of Charlotte that might connect her with any of the other kidnapped children, reaching out to Huxley to see if she had any updates, contacting Eddie and Ward to ask if they'd come up with anything else, even texting Gabriel, who didn't respond. As the sun set on the day without any further positive momentum, he fed Raider and threw himself down on his sofa with a bottle of Guinness.

He was out of options. Brathwaite was toying with him, mocking him from wherever he'd hidden himself. They had solid evidence now—maybe not rock-solid evidence, but better than anything else they'd found so far—that Charlotte had kidnapped the children, but they were no closer to finding her. He strongly suspected she had left the state, but had no idea whether she'd done it with or without the children. If she'd killed them, it was possible they'd never be found.

It was a great way to end his first real consulting gig with Agent Huxley.

It might not matter, though, he thought bitterly. *If you don't find Brathwaite, who knows what Aldwyn will do to you? You might not even be around for Huxley to be disappointed in.*

He stroked Raider, who had curled up in his lap and was doing his best to play emotional support cat. "I'm stuck, mate. I can't help feeling this is all starting to come to an end, but I also can't help thinking the end isn't going to be a good one—for either case."

Raider looked up at him and purred, but had no further advice.

Purring is relaxing, regardless of the recipient's mental state. Stone must have dropped off into a light doze, because the buzz of his phone startled him.

He fumbled it out of his pocket, noting once again that he didn't recognize the number. "Yes, hello, this is Stone."

"Doc?"

A female voice, vaguely familiar. "Yes? Who is this?"

"It's Quinn—Squeak's girlfriend. Remember me? You've been talking to me and Holly about Charlotte."

He sat up straight, all traces of drowsiness ebbing instantly away. "Ah—yes, of course. Did something happen? Is something wrong, or do you have more information about Charlotte?"

There was a pause. "I…do, yeah. I remembered something I'd forgotten—a conversation I had with another friend of mine, about something Charlotte said to her."

"Is this friend…like you and Charlotte?" He changed his tone, speaking more carefully.

"Do you mean is she a Changeling? Yeah."

"What about this conversation?" Stone got up and began pacing around the living room. Raider perched on the back of the sofa and followed him with his green gaze.

"I'd forgotten about it until now—it didn't seem important at the time, but after what's happened, maybe it might be. My friend—her name's Kim—told me about it a couple days after it happened. She thought it was a little weird, but I didn't. Not at the time, anyway. But now I'm worried about Charlotte."

Stone stopped in front of the window, looking out into the dark front yard. "What did she say? If there's anything you think might help, please tell me."

"Yeah." She sighed. "I thought it was just an offhand comment at the time. But Kim and Charlotte were at the Galleria, doing some shopping. They spotted a little Changeling kid with his parents. Kim said he was maybe seven or eight—she said he looked like a mouse or something. Cute kid. She didn't see him for long, since the place was crowded. They kept going, and Charlotte seemed quieter than usual. When they stopped for coffee afterward, they got to talking about Changeling kids. Kim said Charlotte looked at her oddly and said something like, 'I feel so sorry for the freak kids who get born to normies. It must be hard when they look at themselves in the mirror and don't know how to deal with why they look so different than their parents. They should be with their own kind, who understand them.'"

Stone tightened his hand on the phone. "Did she say anything else?"

"Not about that. Kim said she changed the subject, but she seemed out of it after that, like she had a lot on her mind. Kind of sad. Neither of us heard from her again from that point on. Kim said she tried to reach her, but she blocked her number. She could be touchy sometimes, so Kim figured she must have said something to offend her. Now I'm not so sure, though."

"Bloody hell…" Stone murmured, mostly to himself. "Okay, Quinn. Thank you very much for telling me that."

"Do you think she took those kids, Dr. Stone?"

"I've got no idea, but the evidence is starting to point that way."

"Should I tell the cops?" The reluctance came through loud and clear in her voice. Most Changelings didn't like dealing with mundane law enforcement, and apparently she was no exception.

"Not…yet. I'm working with a special law-enforcement group who might have a better chance of locating her."

"So, what I told you was helpful?"

"Almost certainly. Thank you, Quinn. If you happen to re-member anything else, or hear from her, please contact me, day or night."

"I will. I hope you find her—and I hope the kids are okay."

"So do I."

Stone called Huxley and left a voicemail message describing what Kim had given him. Then he texted Gina. *Can I call you? I have information.*

Sure. I was just playing CoD.

He had no idea what that was, but he also didn't care. He tapped her number.

"What's up, Doc?" She giggled. "Sorry, that's never gonna get old."

Stone wasn't in the mood for joking. "I think I might know Charlotte's motive for snatching those kids."

She got serious in a hurry. "No shit?"

He quickly updated her on the latest.

"Daaamn," she muttered. "It makes sense. She's not snatching them because she wants to hurt them. She's doing it because she thinks she's *helping* them." She paused. "That means they're probably still alive…but it still doesn't help us figure out where she's keeping them. And…" She trailed off, sounding troubled.

"What?"

"Well…I was just thinking that doesn't seem like a really ra-tional thing to do. So if she's not in her right mind and she's grabbing kids thinking she's helping them, she…"

"…might not be," Stone finished, catching on. "She might *think* she's helping, but if she isn't taking proper care of them…"

"Yeah." She let her breath out in a loud *whoosh.* "Is there anything else you can do? Another one of those tracking rituals? I know you said it didn't work before, but—"

"I don't know, Gina. The problem is, the children weren't all taken from the same area, which doesn't give us too many good places to start. The people I'm working with already did them. My range is a lot better, but there are seven missing children now, and they all came from different places. That suggests she's got them somewhere well away from where they originated."

"Yeah…" Gina was quiet for a few seconds, then said grimly, "…and it suggests to me that she's not doing this alone. She probably has help."

"Help? You mean, she's enlisted *more* delusional people to her mad plan?"

"They don't have to be delusional, if she convinced them she's right. Freakshow is pretty out-there philosophically to start with, but I don't doubt they've got a subset who are willing to take things even further. If she managed to make a good case for it being better for freak kids to be raised by fellow freaks—and notice she only took the ones too young to talk, so they probably won't even remember their original parents after a while—I don't see how she'd have much trouble convincing some of the fringies to help."

"Damn." He began pacing again, unable to stay still. "Well—I've already got word to my agency. Can you reach out to your trusted Freakshow friends and see if any of them might have an insight?"

"Yeah, but I'll have to be careful. I never would have suspected *any* of them of something this crazy. I'll keep you posted, though. Thanks, Doc. This might be what breaks this case open. And maybe we can be a little more confident the kids are still alive. That's a good thing, right?"

"It is. But I'll feel a lot better when they're safely back with their parents."

Stone heard back from Renata Huxley early the following morning.

"That's quite a speculation you've got there," she told him.

"Do you think I'm right?"

"I don't know. But it sounds plausible. I've alerted various law-enforcement agencies all over the country, in case she's taken the kids out of state. I don't have any evidence she has so the FBI isn't officially involved yet, but I think it's coming. A lot of high-profile people are getting very interested in this case."

"I'm not sure that's good or bad for the children, but I'll have to hope they know what they're doing. There isn't much else I can do to find them at this point, but I'll keep trying. Perhaps my contacts will come up with something else. I don't think she can hide forever. Especially if she's mentally unbalanced. She'll make a mistake at some point, or one of her accomplices will, if she's working with any."

"Yeah. I agree. But I hope that mistake doesn't put the kids in danger. Thanks, Stone. You might not think you've done much, but your information's going to move us a lot farther forward than we were before."

Knowing Huxley's people were back on the case eased a little of Stone's stress, but not as much as he'd hoped.

Usually when he felt like this, a long run would do a good job of taking the edge off it. He preferred to run at night, but it was a cold, crisp morning and he didn't think he'd get back to sleep anyway, so he fed Raider and headed out.

To his surprise, the run *did* calm his clamoring thoughts. He settled into a steady pace and did his best to turn his brain off, and by the time he checked his watch again his long strides had covered nearly nine miles in close to an hour. He was tired, but it was a good tired, the kind where it would feel lovely when he got home and stepped into a hot, steamy shower.

The route he'd taken was a big loop that started at the Encantada house, wound around through the town and then through Stanford and back. He had just started toward home when his phone buzzed.

Again? Normally, he didn't get this many phone calls in a week. Most of his friends preferred texts, which he could respond to at his convenience. Nonetheless, he slowed his pace and pulled it from his pocket.

Another unknown number—but this one was based in the UK. A shiver went down his neck. Something about Brathwaite?

"Hello?" For now, he kept running, but had reduced his pace to barely more than a slow jog.

"Hello. Is this Alastair Stone?" It was a woman—all his calls seemed to be women lately—and her accent placed her somewhere in the northern part of England.

"It is. Who's this?"

"I don't want to say. I could be in a lot of danger for calling you."

Stone stopped. "Danger? What are you calling about?"

"I've…heard you're looking for someone."

He could almost picture her face changing from concern to resolve. His shiver intensified, moving from his neck down his back. "I…am. Do you know where this person is?"

"I…" She hesitated. "I think I might."

"Can you tell me where? Do you know where he is now?"

Another hesitation. "He? You're not looking for a woman?"

Stone mentally kicked himself. Of course anyone who didn't know Brathwaite's history would see him as female, now that he occupied Miriam Padgett's body. "Er…yes. Of course I am. I'm sorry. I'm actually looking for more than one person connected with two completely different situations, and the other one is a man. But do you know where she is?" He hoped she wouldn't get suspicious and hang up. Despite her resolve, her voice still shook a little. She was nervous.

"Not right now. But I've seen her more than once."

"Where?"

"Listen, Dr. Stone—I won't lie to you. I'm scared. If she finds out I told you…"

"I promise, I won't tell her."

"I don't think you will. But she might have ways of finding out. I won't tell you over the phone. I need to meet with you in person."

Stone frowned. He'd already been fooled twice, and Brathwaite knew he was looking for him now. "I'm not comfortable with that. This woman is good at setting ambushes."

"Look," she said, her voice shaking even more. "I know you're scared too. But it's got to be in person. You name the place— somewhere public, in England, in the middle of the day. But it's got to be this way. I can't—"

His phone made the *boop* sound indicating another call coming in. "Hold on, please," he told the caller, and pulled the phone around so he could see the screen.

The number this time was familiar: Amber.

"Dr. Stone?" The voice was louder now, so he could hear it even with the phone away from his ear.

Reluctantly, he let Amber's call go to voicemail. He didn't like it, but he didn't want to lose this woman. Not if there was any chance she was legitimate and knew where Brathwaite was.

"Okay," he said. "I'll meet you. But it *will* need to be somewhere public, and I won't give you the exact location until it's much closer to the time."

"You *are* scared."

"Bloody right I am. I've been fooled too many times. If that's a problem—"

"No, no, it's not. I get it. I—"

The phone made the familiar buzz in his hand, signaling a new text. "One second," he said quickly, and looked at it.

Several seconds passed as he stared at the words on the screen.

"Dr. Stone? Are you still there?"

He didn't answer.

"Dr. Stone? Please, are you there?"

With a numb hand, he brought the phone back to his ear. "Yes. I'm still here. But I'll have to get back to you. Something…urgent has come up. Can I reach you at this number?"

"Yes, but only for a couple of hours. This is a burner phone."

"Okay. I'll…call you back shortly. I promise I want to talk to you, but I'm sorry, but I've got to deal with this emergency first."

He hit the button to break the connection, then stood there by the side of the road and continued staring at the text from Amber, holding the phone with a shaking hand.

Please call back ASAP. Someone's taken Jaden.

CHAPTER TWENTY-FIVE

THERE WAS NO LEY LINE near Jason and Amber's Santa Cruz home, and no quick way to get there. He called Amber back as he drove, splitting his concentration between the conversation and the disregarding spell he had going on the car so he could drive faster.

She answered on the first ring. "Alastair! Thank God." She sounded frantic, nothing like her usual calm, measured tones.

"Amber. Please—try to calm down." *Right,* said his little mental voice. *Like there's any chance she'll do that.* "I'm on my way to you now. Tell me what's happened. Where's Jason?"

"Still in L.A. He's trying to catch the first flight back, but it'll be at least three hours before he can get here."

"Okay. Tell me what's happened." He was glad he'd driven this route many times, because at this point he was essentially doing it on autopilot. At least there wasn't much traffic.

She took several deep, gulping breaths. "I was only gone for about half an hour. I drove down to the store to pick up a few things, and left the kids with Sarah."

"Sarah—that's your nanny?"

"Yeah. She doesn't live too far from here, so she helps out when I'm away or busy."

Stone's mind was already spinning out questions. "What about Alice? Is she gone too?"

"No. She's fine. She was safe in her room playing when I got back." She dropped her voice lower. "The police are here doing their examination, and they'll want to talk to me again soon. But Alastair—I'm sure it had to be somebody with supernatural abilities."

"So am I," Stone said grimly. "With the wards you have around your house, no one else should have been able to get in."

"See, that's the thing—I don't think they *got* in. I think they lured Sarah out with Jaden, or got them when they were playing in the backyard."

"What makes you think so? Is Sarah all right? Did they hurt her?"

"No." She lowered her voice again. "I'll be honest—the urge to rip her limb from limb was the first thing I felt when she told me Jaden was gone. But she's not involved. I'm certain of it. Somebody got to her."

Stone didn't doubt her words. As a quarter-bear shifter, her sense of smell was stronger than a bloodhound's. She could detect lies and subtle shifts in mood as well as he could with aura reading. "What do you mean, 'got to her'? Did they incapacitate her?"

"When I got back, she seemed out of it. She doesn't remember what happened. One minute she was pushing Jaden on the swings, and the next minute he was gone. When she looked at her watch, ten minutes had passed but she didn't remember them."

"Bloody hell." There were any number of ways that could have happened, but almost all of them were supernaturally related. An alchemist could have dosed her with some kind of mist, a mage could have obfuscated her memory, or a Changeling could have used the same kind of mind-muddling power they'd used on him a few months ago in San Francisco. Unfortunately, mundanes were far more vulnerable than mages and other supernatural beings to having their minds tampered with.

A chill ran down his back. Could this somehow be related to Brathwaite? Or to Charlotte? Jaden was a Changeling, albeit not an unattractive one, but he was also the son of one of Stone's dearest friends. That made either possibility likely. *Don't jump to conclusions. Jason and Amber deal with a lot of dangerous people. This could be related to their work.* "Was Alice out in the yard too? Would Sarah have left her in the house?" He took the Highway 17 onramp too fast, and augmented the disregarding spell. He couldn't afford to get pulled over now.

"She must have been. Sarah wouldn't have left her by herself in the house."

"But she was in the house when you got back? Where was Sarah?"

"She was inside too. Like I said, she seemed out of it. If I hadn't known better, I'd say she was on drugs or something. But she wasn't." An edge of desperation began to creep into her voice again.

"Okay. I know this is terrifying, Amber, but we've got to keep our heads. We'll find Jaden. They can't hide him from us. I assume you already did what tracking you could?"

"Yeah." The desperate edge disappeared, replaced by a cold resolve. "There were two of them. If I smell them again, I'll know it. If they've hurt Jaden—if they've even made him *cry*—I'm going to rip their heads off."

"Let's—leave the head-ripping for now. First we've got to find Jaden. How far did they get before you lost them?"

"Not far. They had a car waiting. I can probably follow the traces for a while, but tracking people in cars is a lot harder. This was definitely coordinated, Alastair. They were watching the house, waiting for me to leave. If only I'd sent Sarah to the store—"

"Now, come on. You know as well as I do that isn't going to help. We'll put our heads together on this. I'll call Verity and the two of us will do a combined tracking spell. Jaden's related to her and my range is long enough that they probably won't get out of it. How long has he been missing?"

"About an hour. I had to deal with the cops before I called you. They had a bunch of questions for me. They want to know if anybody got in touch with me with a ransom demand, but so far nothing." She sounded annoyed, as if answering the mundane police officers' questions was a waste of time if it delayed calling in magical help.

"Okay. I'll be there in less than thirty minutes. Did you already call Verity?"

"Yeah. She's on her way, but she has to come from San Francisco. I—oh, hang on, the cops are coming out. They want to talk to me again. Please get here as soon as you can, Alastair."

"I will. Already breaking several speed limits and a couple laws of physics. Keep it together, Amber."

"Yeah. I'm trying."

The trip to Jason and Amber's home from Encantada normally took a little less than an hour with no traffic. Stone made it in thirty-five minutes. As he turned the black BMW onto the winding gravel driveway toward the house, a uniformed policewoman raised a hand indicating for him to halt. Beyond her, a police car blocked the way.

"I'm sorry, sir," she said. "You can't come up here right now. This is an active crime scene."

"I'm a friend of the people who live here," Stone said. "Amber called me."

"Alastair!" Amber strode up, ducking around the police car. She held Alice by the hand. "It's okay," she told the officer. "He's a friend, and I did call him."

"Okay. But he can't come up to the house. Nobody's allowed up there while the CSIs are processing the scene."

"We can talk here." Stone indicated for Amber to follow him past the BMW, where they could talk without the policewoman hearing. To ensure that, he quickly cast his 'cone of silence' spell.

"Hi, Unca Alicer," Alice said. She looked happy to see him, but also confused.

"Hello, Alice."

"Let the grown-ups talk now, baby," Amber said. "Okay?"

"Okay, Mommy." She crouched and began examining rocks from the gravel driveway.

"Good girl."

Stone noticed how firm Amber's grip on Alice's hand was. He doubted she would allow the little girl out of her sight for the foreseeable future. "How are you holding up?" he asked softly.

"My son's missing and I don't know who took him or where he is. You tell me."

"We'll find him." He forced himself to sound more confident than he felt. "Have you got a tether object for him?"

"They wouldn't let me inside the house." Her jaw tightened. "But if you need me to, I'll—"

"No. Don't arouse their suspicions for nothing. I've got other ways to do this." He pulled a white handkerchief from his coat pocket. He always carried one, but not for its intended purpose. They were dead useful for all sorts of magic-related activities. "Give me some of your blood. We can use that. Might even be better, unless you want me to destroy one of Jaden's favorite objects. Children that young can be more difficult to track with a spell, since they don't have as much time to develop emotional attachments to many objects."

She glanced at Alice, who was now twittering away at a stick she'd picked up. "Blood?" Her meaning was obvious: *I don't want my child to see me bleeding.*

Stone didn't want the policewoman to see it either. He gave her the handkerchief. "Block it with your body. I'll use an illusion to make sure no one else sees." He nodded significantly down at Alice.

Amber turned away from the cop. She took out a pocketknife and made a small slice in her hand, letting the blood flow until it covered the middle of the handkerchief. Stone kept the illusion up until her natural regenerative abilities closed the wound, and stowed the cloth back in his pocket. Then he pulled out his phone and called Verity.

She answered immediately. "Did Amber call you?" She sounded almost as stressed as Amber had.

"I'm here at their place. Are you on your way?"

"Yeah, but I'm still a ways out. I used the dedicated portal from the San Francisco shop to the Sunnyvale one and borrowed one of our employees' cars, but I'm still at least half an hour away."

"Okay," he said. "I can't wait another thirty minutes to start. If they're on the move with him, that might be enough time for them to get out of range." He turned back to Amber. "Is there a place around here I can do a ritual? Away from your house, for obvious reasons."

She thought about it, then nodded and pointed toward the road. "Yeah. Our neighbors down the road a mile or so are away for the weekend. If you can get into their garage, you can use that. It should be empty."

"Okay. Good. Verity, did you hear that?"

"Yeah. You get started, and I'll meet you there."

He ended the call and gripped Amber's arm. "We'll sort this out, Amber. We'll get him back. I'll do everything in my power to help make that happen."

"So will I," she said grimly. "And if I find them first, there won't be enough left of them to bury."

Stone didn't doubt it—which was why he was determined to find them first.

By the time Verity arrived, Stone had already located the garage, popped the lock on the side door, and was setting up the ritual circle on the concrete floor.

"Thank God you made it here so fast," she said, immediately heading to the open black leather bag that held his ritual supplies.

"Have you been up to see Amber yet?"

"Not yet. I figured it was more important to get this done. Jason texted me again—he's still stuck in L.A. His plane doesn't leave for another two hours, and he's pretty frantic."

Stone pictured Jason seething in an LAX security line, trying to get the plane there faster by sheer force of will, but there was nothing he could do about that. The ritual was under his control, which meant it had to be his sole focus. With luck, they could track Jaden and locate the boy in time for him to call the woman in the UK back about Brathwaite.

With Verity's help, the two of them completed the circle quickly. "Do you remember how to do the combined ritual?" Stone asked her.

"Yeah. I've practiced with Ian. We've both come a long way since you were away."

"Brilliant. Let's get started, then, before the kidnappers take him out of our range."

It was a lot harder to maintain objectivity with a ritual when looking for someone you personally cared about, and this was no exception. Still, Stone and Verity were both seasoned mages, so they both used every mental technique they could manage to remain calm and perform all the steps correctly. Stone reminded himself that this wasn't necessarily a one-chance thing; he had no way to be sure the kidnappers would take Jaden out of his range, since even if they knew he was a mage, they probably didn't know how far he could search.

He and Verity stepped grimly into the center of the circle and clasped hands over the small brazier containing the blood sample. "Focus on your connection to Jaden," he murmured.

"I know." She spoke softly, with no hint of "don't tell me how to do my job." The only important thing now was to find the baby and get him back to his parents as soon as possible.

The ritual progressed as they expected, which relieved Stone. If a mage—particularly one of Brathwaite's or his associates' caliber—was involved, they could hide Jaden from tracking rituals. Even one as powerful as Stone's and Verity's would be unlikely to find him. But as they completed the ritual and the familiar tendril snaked up through the garage roof, Stone got no hint of anyone trying to interfere.

He also got no hint that Jaden was dead. He shot a quick glance at Verity, who'd bowed her head in relief. The boy was alive. That much, they were both sure of. It was a start.

The tendril wound up and out, searching, pointing first in one direction and then in another. Normally, with a clean ritual and no interference, the trace would cast around for a few seconds and then head directly for the target. That didn't happen in this case, which told Stone that *something* wasn't normal. He pulled in more Calanarian power, meshing it with Verity's sensitivity and continuing to watch the tendril.

Finally, after what seemed like far too long, it seemed to get its bearings. It shot off to the east. For a moment, it seemed to be heading in a specific direction, but then it got confused again and began casting around.

"What's wrong?" Verity whispered. "It doesn't feel like a mage…"

"No. Something's interfering, but not enough to stop us. Shh…focus."

The tendril continued heading east, undulating back and forth like a snake. After another five minutes, it thrashed around and winked out. The ritual collapsed, and the handkerchief in the brazier went up with a tiny *whoosh*.

Verity dropped to her knees, panting. "What did that mean? I've never seen a result like that."

Stone pulled up the map of California he'd prepared, trying to find the location before it faded. "He's alive," he rasped. It had been a long time since a tracking ritual had tired him that much. He felt as if he'd had to wrestle the tendril the whole way to keep it from going off track. "And I think we've got a general area."

She leaned in to peer over his shoulder at the map. "How general?"

With a pen, he circled an area near highway 152, between Watsonville and Gilroy.

Verity let her breath out. "That's a pretty big area. Several square miles. And we don't even know what vehicle the kidnappers were driving. How are we going to—"

Stone's phone buzzed.

"Oh, bloody hell," he murmured. He'd forgotten about the woman from the UK who'd called earlier. Was she calling back?

"What?"

He didn't answer, though. The number on the display wasn't the UK one. It was another blocked one. What *now?* "Hold on. I've got to get this." He hit the button to answer. "Yes, hello?"

"Hello, Dr. Stone. This is Charlotte."

CHAPTER TWENTY-SIX

STONE TENSED, feeling like someone had just punched him in the stomach. He glanced at Verity, who was looking at him questioningly, and addressed the caller. "What do you want?"

"I want to talk to you. Now."

"You are talking to me. But I haven't got much time. I—"

"You've got time, Dr. Stone. Especially if what you're doing is looking for that little boy."

Rage washed through him, but he forced himself to keep control. "You've got him."

Verity's eyes widened. She opened her mouth to say something, but Stone held up a hand.

"I don't have him personally," Charlotte said. "But my associates do. He was a little hard to find, way out there in the sticks where your friend lives, but we have our ways. Don't worry, though—I promise he won't be harmed—not unless you won't talk to me."

"So talk, then." Stone indicated for Verity to begin cleaning up the ritual materials as he stalked around the garage. "I'm listening."

"Not on the phone. I want to talk in person."

"About what?"

"I'll tell you when you get here."

"Where is *here*?"

"Los Angeles, near Hollywood. I know you've got a way to get here, if you're not already here."

"I'm not in that area now. It will take me some time to get there. I've got to find a flight—"

She laughed. "Don't treat me like an idiot, Dr. Stone. I know what you are, and I know you have a lot faster ways to get down here. I'll give you an hour, and then I'll call you again with the location of the meet. Believe me, I don't like to say this, but if I see any police or if you don't show, your friends will never see their boy again."

"Wait!" Stone snapped. "I—"

"One hour, Dr. Stone. Tick-tock."

The line went dead.

"Alastair?"

Stone lowered the phone in his numb hand and didn't answer.

"Who was that? Was it about Jaden?"

"It was Charlotte. The Changeling we've been looking for. She says her people have Jaden."

"Oh, my God. Where?" She'd already half-finished gathering the ritual materials, but now she stopped and stalked over to him. "What does she want? What did she say?"

Stone fought to control his thoughts as her words battered him. "She's in Los Angeles. She wants to meet with me. She's given me an hour to get there."

"Did she say why? Anything about what she wants?"

"No. She said she'll tell me when I get there."

"I want to go along."

"You can't, Verity. You can't get there fast enough. Even if you leave here now, it will take you almost that long just to get back to the Sunnyvale portal. And I thought Bron's people didn't have a private one in that area."

She glared at him, but he could tell she knew he was right. She let out a loud growl and clenched her fists. "They don't. Nick's people do, but I'm not sure I can get them to let me use it—not fast enough, anyway. Damn it, I want to *help.*"

His thoughts were still churning. The beginnings of a plan were forming in his head, and he spoke before he worked through it. "Listen," he said urgently. "I've got other news—and a possible idea. You might be able to help with something else while I deal with this."

"An idea? Help with what?"

He looked around, as if expecting someone to break in on them. "I've got to talk fast—there isn't much time, since I've still got to get to a ley line before I can go. Just before I got the news about Jaden, I got a call from a woman in the UK who claims she knows where Brathwaite is."

"*What?*" Her glare got more intense. "Where?"

"She wouldn't tell me on the phone. She wants to meet in person." He glanced at his watch—less than an hour remained of the time limit she'd given him before she tossed the burner phone. "I told her I didn't like that idea because Brathwaite's burned us twice before, but she says she wants to meet in a public place. I think she's scared of him, and I'm almost positive she knows something. This might be our best hope of finding him, Verity."

"Yes, but Jaden—"

"That's what I'm saying. You can't help with Jaden—except to call Amber and give her the information we found. It's up to her whether she wants to alert the police or go search the area herself. With her tracking skills, she's got a good shot at it. But you *can* help with this."

"How?"

He pulled his phone out again. "I'll call her back and set up a meet. I'll tell her I can't meet her in person but I'll send you—and Ian, if you can reach him and he wants to go. You meet with her—for gods' sake be careful, though, and don't let her convince you to go anywhere that isn't surrounded by people—and find out where Brathwaite is. Once I've got the Jaden situation sorted, I'll come over there and we can find him together."

Verity was staring at him like he'd gone mad—but as he finished, her expression slowly changed to dubious agreement. "That's a lot of ifs, you know."

"I do. And I hate this. But I'm the only one who can get to Charlotte, and finding Jaden is more important than risking letting Brathwaite get away. This way, we might have a shot at both of them." He gently gripped her wrists. "Will you do it? Assuming my UK contact is willing to meet with you instead of me, anyway."

She held his gaze for several seconds, then reluctantly nodded. "Yeah. I'll do it. Amber isn't going to like it, though. If she goes after the kidnappers herself, she'll want me to go with her."

"I know. I get it. I wish there were another way." He sighed, trying to quell his growing frustration. "But if we don't find Brathwaite—if *I* don't find him—before my time period is up, I'm terrified of what might happen. Not to me—if it were just me, I'd let this go and take a chance on trying again later—but to those I care about. Believe me, this person makes Brathwaite look like small potatoes, vengeance-wise. I won't let that happen, Verity. Please. Promise you'll do this."

She bowed her head. "I wish you'd give me more information. But then, I *always* wish you'd give me more information. I trust you, though. I'll do it."

"Brilliant. Thank you, Verity." He shoved the map into her hand. "Take this, and get in touch with Amber. Call Gina, too—she might have some Changeling associates who can help them track. I'll call my contact, and then I've got to get going."

He walked to the other side of the garage and tapped the burner number, hoping desperately that the mysterious woman hadn't gotten spooked and tossed the phone early.

But no, she answered on the first ring. "Hello?" It was definitely the same voice, and it sounded shaky and urgent.

"It's me. I'm sorry I took so long to get back to you, but we had an emergency here."

"Are you coming?"

He took a deep breath and hoped for the best. "No. I can't come myself. But I'm going to send someone in my place."

"No! I won't—"

"Please, don't hang up! Listen—if you're familiar with me at all, you know who these people are. My former apprentice Verity and my son Ian. They can speak in my stead, and you can tell them what you were going to tell me. I trust them implicitly."

There was a long pause. "I don't know…I don't like it. Why can't you come yourself?"

Stone considered. He couldn't risk letting her get away from him—but could he trust her with the truth? He glanced at Verity, then said, "The baby son of a good friend has been kidnapped, and I'm the only one who can find him in time."

She gasped. "Oh, my God. That's terrible." Then more hesitantly, she added, "Do you think it could be related to—"

"No. It's not related to the person we're talking about. I'm certain of it. Please, I'm begging you—let me send my apprentice and my son. I give you my word you can trust them. I want you to meet in a public place—as crowded as possible. You're worried for your safety, and I'm worried about theirs. We'll keep this safe."

Another long pause. Finally, she said with obvious reluctance, "Okay. I'll meet with them. I don't like it, but I will. You need to know about this, and if this is the only way—"

He let his shoulders slump in relief. "Thank you. When this is all over, I'll make it worth your while, I promise."

"That's not necessary. This is something I need to do. Give me your apprentice's phone number, and I'll call her when I get a new burner."

"Here—I'll let you talk to her in person. You two can set up a codeword so you'll know it's really her." He handed the phone to Verity and mouthed, "*talk to her.*"

While Verity and the woman made their plans, Stone finished gathering the last of the spent ritual materials into a plastic bag he carried in his leather one. By the time Verity gave him back his phone, he had the garage looking like no one had been there.

"Are you set?" he asked her. "Plans made?"

"Yeah. We're meeting in a couple hours in London. I'll text Ian and see if he's available." She sighed. "I still don't like this."

"I don't either. Believe me, if there were any other way to do this, I'd take it. Go on, now—call Gina and get the information about Jaden to Amber. I've got to go."

She pulled him into a hard hug. "Be careful, Alastair. For yourself *and* for Jaden."

"I will. And you, too. I want Brathwaite, but not at the cost of you or Ian getting hurt."

"I want him too," she said, a hard edge creeping into her tone. "I'd be willing to get hurt to take him down, if that's what it takes."

Stone hurried out of the garage to where he'd parked the BMW down the street. Before he pulled away and headed back to Los Gatos and the nearest ley line, he made another quick call.

CHAPTER TWENTY-SEVEN

CHARLOTTE CALLED STONE when exactly one hour had passed since she'd hung up. He was sitting in a booth at the Green Room, trying to quell his agitation about both Jaden and what was happening in England with Verity. He had the phone sitting on the table in front of him, and answered before the first ring faded.

"I'm here," he said without greeting. "At the Green Room. Where do you want to meet?"

"Good, I was hoping you'd go there. I'm not far away. But I'm telling you again—if I see any sign of police, none of you will ever see the boy again. Please don't make me do that. I don't want to."

Stone noticed it again: she'd said "none of you will ever see him again," not "we'll kill him." Never once had she threatened to hurt Jaden. "I know you don't want to, Charlotte," he said gently. "Believe me, I want to resolve this safely as much as you do. Where should I meet you?"

"There's an old warehouse a couple miles from you." She gave him the address. "It's closed, and the windows are all boarded up, but you can get in through the door in the back. I'll leave it propped open for you."

"Have you got Jaden?"

"Not with me. Like I said, we have to talk first. Depending on how that goes, I'll call my people and have him returned to where you can pick him up."

"Charlotte, if you've hurt him—"

"He's fine. I promise." Her voice shook a little. "Nobody wants to hurt kids, Dr. Stone, least of all me. Please don't make me do anything I don't want to do."

"Okay. We'll play it your way for now. Give me a few minutes to get there."

"I'll be waiting." The line went dead.

As Stone got up and paid his check, an uncharacteristic wave of indecision struck him. What if he was making the wrong call? This wasn't some abstract case this time—it was the infant son of one of his closest friends. If he mishandled this and something happened to Jaden, Jason and Amber would never forgive him for it.

He'd never forgive *himself* for it.

He shook his head. No time to think about that now. He'd made his decision, and he needed to follow it through. It was too late to do anything else.

On his way to his rented car, he made another phone call.

The warehouse was right where Charlotte said it would be, set back from the street by a weed-choked parking lot surrounded by a chain-link fence. The two-story building had obviously been abandoned for a long time, judging from the graffiti sprayed all around its lower floor and the plywood covering the holes where windows used to be. There were no cars in the front lot, but when Stone drove around the back he spotted a pair of clapped-out trucks near the loading dock. Both were weathered and rusty, with cracked, flat tires and broken windshields. Obviously, neither had moved for a long time.

He drove past and parked his rental car two blocks away, using a disregarding spell to make it blend in with the rest of the area. He used another on himself as he strode back toward his destination. It was early afternoon on an overcast day, but none of the cars driving by seemed to notice or care about his presence.

He waited for the street to clear, then used an invisibility spell while he levitated over the fence and quickly covered the distance to the rear door. As Charlotte had promised, it had been propped open: a broken mannequin arm held it slightly ajar.

Inside, he found himself in a large, empty expanse. A dusty skylight far overhead provided faint illumination over the center, but the walls of the cavernous space were wreathed in shadows. He looked around, spotting a series of skeletal metal shelving units, some against the walls, some toppled over onto the floor. More broken mannequin parts, clothing racks, dress forms, boxes, and swatches of ripped fabric littered the floor. This place had obviously been used at some point by someone in the fashion industry. Perhaps Charlotte had chosen it because she'd been familiar with it at some point.

He didn't see any sign of the woman, though, with normal or magical sight. "Charlotte?" he called, raising his invisible magical shield. "I'm here to talk, and I'm alone. If you're here, please come out."

For a few seconds, nothing happened. Then a figure stepped out from behind one of the larger boxes on the other side of the space. It didn't approach any closer.

Stone was still using magical sight, and he forced himself not to wince when he got a look at her. The people who had described Charlotte's Changeling form hadn't been pulling punches: she was ugly. Catastrophically ugly. Her basic shape was that of a humanoid toad with shiny skin and bulging eyes, covered in bumps and wrinkles. But as the faint light from the skylight revealed, it was worse than that. Her features seemed not to be arranged properly, as if a child had tried to build a toad out of spare parts without a clear idea of what one was supposed to look like.

Charlotte seemed to pick up on his reaction anyway. "Yeah, I'm pretty grotesque, aren't I?" Her tone was conversational, with just a hint of an edge. "You can go ahead and say it. I'm a freak."

"I would never say that, Charlotte."

"But you're thinking it. I can tell. I know you're a mage, so you can see."

"You're right—I *can* see your true form. But I see a lot of things." He shifted back to mundane sight, and her squat, stocky figure immediately resolved into something taller and thinner. He couldn't see her human features from this far away, but he recognized her confident stance from the videos he'd watched.

"What do you see?" Her voice dripped with contempt.

He took a few steps forward, but stopped when she tensed. "Don't worry—I'm not coming after you. I'd be a fool to do that."

"You're right, you would. I've still got your friend's boy, and I control whether they ever see him again."

Stone nodded, as if thinking. "Yes. You do. You asked me what I see—that's the first thing. You don't want to hurt Jaden."

"Of course I don't. I told you that already."

"Then why take him at all?" He began pacing the area, still without getting any closer to Charlotte. "I think my friends and I have figured out what you're up to, Charlotte."

She snorted. "Yeah, right. You'll never figure it out."

"I think we did. Do you want to hear our guess? If we're wrong, you can have a good laugh about it."

"Whatever. I'm not staying here forever, though, so we need to get on with why I had you come here. I don't trust you not to bring in the cops."

"That's fine. And I promise you, I haven't brought in any cops." He stopped pacing and faced her. "I've learned quite a lot about you and what you've been through. How you had trouble coping with your Change, but eventually realized that you still had value, no matter what you looked like. Your friends from Freakshow convinced you of that, didn't they?"

"What if they did?" she snapped. "And you're right—I *do* have value. If the rest of the world can't stand looking at me, that's their loss, not mine." She spread her arms wide. "*This* is the real me, not that pretty, superficial shell."

"That's a healthy attitude," Stone said. "I applaud you for that, and for overcoming your issues. That's something to be proud of."

"Don't be patronizing, Stone."

"I'm not. I'm serious. But…" He changed his tone to something softer, quieter, so she had to strain to hear. "You can't keep doing this, Charlotte. It's not right."

"Doing what?"

"Kidnapping unattractive Changeling children and…what? Placing them with other Changelings?"

He'd shifted back to magical sight to watch her reaction, and was rewarded with a bright red flash. He'd hit the bullseye, just as he knew he would.

"That's none of your business!" She took a few steps forward. "But you're right about one thing—that's exactly what I wanted to talk to you about. I guess it'll be easier if I don't have to explain it to you."

"Please do explain it," Stone said. "I know *what* you and your associates are doing, but I'm not sure I know *why.*"

"Why?" Her voice rose. "Why? It should be obvious! Those kids are freaks. Ugly. Every time they look in the mirror, they're going to see something hideous—something that doesn't look like their parents and siblings and friends. And their families don't even *know* what they're going through, because they can't see it and the kids are too young to tell them. Not that the parents would believe them anyway." She visibly attempted to pull herself together. "Changeling kids should be with other Changelings, Dr. Stone. Especially freaks. They need to grow up with other freaks, so they can learn they're as normal as everyone else. They need to learn as early as possible that they don't have to be ashamed of what they look like."

"So you've taken it as your crusade to 'rescue' as many of these kids as you can. No matter what effect it has on them. Like little Montrel LaRue. He was the first, wasn't he?"

Again, she looked startled. "How did you—?"

"How did I know that? Because I saw the video of a party you attended. He was there, with his parents. What's his form, Charlotte? Obviously I couldn't tell that from the video."

She bowed her head. "He looks like a…sort of a warthog, with tusks and a big snout and wrinkly skin. When I saw him there, held in the arms of his beautiful parents, something just…snapped." Her voice caught, and she sniffed. "I couldn't stand the thought of that sweet little boy growing up, looking at himself compared to his parents, and thinking he's disgusting. Can you imagine what that would do to a little kid's self-esteem, Dr. Stone? I don't have to imagine, because I *lived* it. And I was a full-grown adult when it happened."

"So you consider that justification for taking them away from their real parents, who love them?"

Her snort this time was full of derision. "Yeah, right. Love them. Do you think Montrel LaRue's social-climbing parents would still love him if they knew their perfect little angel really looked like a warthog? I know their type, because I *was* their type. Appearance—beauty—was everything to me. I honestly couldn't understand why ugly people even wanted to live, can you believe that?"

"Is that for you to decide, though?" Stone asked softly. "Charlotte, you've got to give those children back to their parents. Where are you even keeping them? Wherever you've got them, do the people looking after them even know the proper way to take care of them?"

"Of course they do!" she snapped. "They're all fine, healthy, and safe. They're being looked after by loving Changelings—freaks like them. It's better for them, Dr. Stone. And there's no way we're going to send them back to live in Hell again. That's why I called you here: because that's my ransom demand for your friend's boy. Stop this investigation. Stop trying to find the freak kids. If you agree to that—not just you, but your friends, too—I'll arrange for the boy to be returned safe and sound."

"And if we don't agree?" Stone asked softly. "What then? Are you going to kill Jaden? You're not, are you? Because I believe you when you said you don't want to hurt children. *Any* children."

She swiped her hand across her forehead, clearly agitated. "No. You're right. We won't hurt him, any more than we'd hurt any of the others. We'll find some Changelings to look after him, too."

Stone shook his head. "Bad choice, Charlotte. Honestly. You don't know much about Jaden's parents, do you?"

"I know his dad is one of your best friends. Would you want to be responsible for his kid disappearing?"

"He is. But Jaden's mother is, too…and she's not strictly human. I won't tell you what she is, but I *will* tell you that she will move heaven and earth to find her child, and she won't quit until she does. Plus, Jaden's parents have access to some fairly powerful people. I'm only one of them—and I'm not even the most dangerous. They *will* find you. Do you know what Jaden's mother said to me when she told me he was missing?"

Charlotte didn't reply.

"She said, and I quote: 'If they've hurt Jaden—if they've even made him *cry*—I'm going to rip their heads off'. That isn't hyperbole, Charlotte, I promise. She *will* do it. She will find every last person involved with this and she will kill them—and I suspect her relatives will join her." He resumed pacing. "That's the truth, and there isn't anything I can do to stop it. Honestly, I wouldn't try. So you might want to rethink this plan of yours."

Her aura showed her growing agitation. "That's not what I *want*. It was never what I wanted. We don't want your friend's kid. We just want to be left alone so we can let the freak kids have a life where they won't feel like they're horrible! Don't you *get* that?"

"I get it, Char," said another soft, gentle voice from the doorway. "But there's got to be another way."

Charlotte jerked her head up, her aura exploding with shock. "*Holly*?"

Stone didn't move, except to make an inviting gesture for Charlotte's sister to approach him.

Charlotte glared at him. "*You! You* brought her here." Her hand moved toward her pocket.

"Don't do it, Charlotte," Stone said. "Don't call anyone yet. Please. Yes, I asked Holly to come here. I thought she might have a better chance of getting through to you than I would."

"Why?" She snorted, redirecting her glare to her sister. "How could *she* possibly understand? *Look* at her!"

"Yes, Char, look at me." Holly spoke in the same calm, loving voice as before, undeterred by her sister's ire. "Really *look*, though. If you do, you won't see what I look like. You'll see that I love you—that I've always loved you—no matter what *you* look like. Do you think that even *matters* to me?"

Stone took a step to the side and watched the conversation. Charlotte was still looking angry, but she hadn't pulled out her phone. It was a start.

"I don't care what you look like, Charlotte," Holly was saying. "You have to believe that. You're my sister, and you've always been beautiful to me."

Charlotte made a sound that was half-snort, half-sniffle.

"It's true. I know you don't believe me, but look at me and tell me I'm lying. I love you, Charlotte. None of us have any control over what we look like, but we *do* have control of what kind of people we are. And I know you don't want to hurt those kids—not physically *or* emotionally. Please—let them go back to their parents. You know it's the right thing to do."

Charlotte hesitated. The anger still showed on her face and in her aura, but now it was mixed with something else. Her hands shook.

In Stone's pocket, his phone buzzed for an incoming text. Moving with care so as not to upset Charlotte, he pulled it free. He needn't have made the effort; the toad Changeling's attention was focused fully on her sister.

He glanced down at the screen. The text was from Amber, and included only a single line:

Got him. He's safe.

Stone let his shoulders slump in relief. That changed everything, and gave him more options—but he still needed to be careful. Several more children were still out there somewhere. For now, he decided to let Holly take the lead.

Charlotte was visibly shaking now. "You don't *get* it, Holly. You can't. I know I was a terrible sister. I treated you like crap when I got the looks and you didn't. After I Changed, I thought God was punishing me for being so vain—and then when *you* Changed, I was sure of it. It wasn't until after I met some Freakshow people that I came to realize that's not true."

"Of course it isn't true," Holly murmured. "You're a good person, Char. I never stopped loving you."

"Even when I was so horrible to you?" Tears ran down her cheeks. "I was more horrible when I was pretty than I am now."

"I don't think you're horrible. I never cared what I looked like. You know that. Believe me, if I could trade with you, I would—but I don't think you want that anymore, do you?"

Charlotte bowed her head. "I…no. I don't." She gave a wet little chuckle. "I guess I kind of have the best of both worlds now, don't I? I'm still me as a human, even though I can't see it anymore…but my true self reminds me that looks don't matter as much as what's inside."

"Yeah…" Holly was crying now, too. Before Stone could stop her, she dashed across the warehouse and flung her arms around her sister.

Charlotte jerked, startled, but then returned the hug and both of them were sobbing.

"I'm so sorry, Holly…"

"It's okay. I love you…"

Stone didn't want to interrupt the family reunion, but his stress was growing again with each moment he was away from the Brathwaite situation. He cleared his throat and approached.

"Ladies…I'm sorry, but there's still the matter of the children."

They broke their embrace and looked at him. Charlotte bowed her head again. "I still don't think it's right. They need their own kind to help them through what they'll need to deal with."

Stone thought fast. "What if…" he ventured slowly, "the Changelings told the children's parents what was going on? I know someone who's got a lot of contacts in the community, and I'm sure you do, too. Maybe they can arrange for the children to be exposed to other Changelings—possibly even Changeling counselors. That way, they can remain with their parents where they belong, but still get some help. Do you think that would be a reasonable compromise?"

Holly's eyes widened. "Char? That sounds like a good idea, doesn't it? I'll help if I can—if you think I'll do any good."

Charlotte was clearly on the fence, afraid to give up on what she felt was the right thing to do. "I don't know…"

"I'll help too," Stone said. "We'll make this happen."

She swallowed. "I'm…going to jail, aren't I?"

"I don't know." He wouldn't lie to her. "It's possible. But this isn't a normal mundane case, and it won't be handled by the mundane courts. There's an agency that deals with things like this. As long as those children were treated well and have suffered no ill effects…perhaps some accommodations can be made. I honestly can't say, though. It isn't up to me."

Charlotte and Holly exchanged glances. Finally, Charlotte's shoulders drooped. "It's okay," she said. "I screwed up. I deserve to pay for it. It never even occurred to me that we might be messing those kids up by taking them from their real parents. I was so focused on what they'd think when they saw what they looked like…"

"I understand." Stone didn't, not completely—he'd never understood that kind of zealotry on anything but an academic level—but he could work with it. "Listen—I just got a text from my friend, and they've found Jaden, safe and sound." He realized he should probably ask Amber how many of the kidnappers she'd killed, but that probably wasn't the best thing to bring up now. He pulled out his phone. "I'm going to call my friend at the agency, and you're going to call *your* friends who are holding the children and tell them to hand them over. Okay?"

Charlotte nodded miserably. "Yeah. I will. I'm so sorry for all of this. I just want it to be over."

Holly hugged her again. "We'll get through it together, Char. That much, I *do* promise."

Stone arranged for Agent Huxley to call Charlotte back on her phone and make the arrangements to hand over the children, then moved off to the other side of the warehouse to make his own calls.

The first was to Jason. "Did you hear?"

"Oh, my God, Al. Yeah. Amber got hold of me. Jaden's okay." He sounded frazzled, exhausted, and relieved.

"Are you still in Los Angeles?"

"Yeah, about to board my plane. Where are you?"

"I'm here too. The other children will be returned to their parents as well. It's over, Jason."

"Thank God. And thank *you*. That's another one we owe you."

"I can't take all the credit for this one. It was a group effort. Perhaps we can all go out and celebrate soon."

"Are you coming home? And what's going on with V? Amber said you two did a tracking ritual to find Jaden, but V couldn't go with her to get him. She said she had something else urgent going on. What could be more important than this?"

Stone paused. "Er. It's a long story, and it was my fault. We'll talk about it later. But all's well that ends well for now."

"Al…"

"Please, Jason. I haven't got time to talk about it now. I need to leave."

"Leave? You mean to head home?"

"No. I don't know when I'll be back."

"This has to do with where V went, doesn't it?" Suspicion seeped into Jason's tone. "You sent her somewhere."

"It does, and I did. I'm sorry, Jason, but I can't discuss it now." He glanced over to where Holly and Charlotte were still talking. "Oh—before I go. You talked to Amber, right?"

"Yeah, of course. She called me the second she found Jaden."

"Did she…hurt anybody?"

"No." He paused. "It's freaky, Al. She said when she found Jaden, the people with him were taking good care of him. They'd changed his diaper, given him a bath, and he had toys and stuff. They even had a puppy for him to play with. She said she didn't get any malice at all from them. You want to tell me what's going on?"

"Talk to Gina. Tell her I said our theory about Charlotte wanting to help the kids was right. She can talk to her Changeling friends and work out the rest. I've really got to go now."

He had an almost tangible sense of the clock ticking on the Brathwaite case. Perhaps if he could get to England fast enough, he could join the meeting with the mysterious woman.

"Al—"

"Talk later, Jason." He broke the connection before his friend could say anything else. He'd make his apologies later, but for now he had other things on his mind.

He was about to say his goodbyes to Holly and Charlotte when his phone buzzed with an incoming text. He shot it an annoyed glance—was Jason still trying to get Verity's location out of him?

But the text wasn't from Jason, and it wasn't from Verity.

It was from Ian, and Stone's blood chilled as he read it.

Dad, text me back as soon as you get this. Verity's disappeared.

CHAPTER TWENTY-EIGHT

STONE CALLED IAN the instant he got to his rental car after taking his hasty leave of Charlotte and Holly. At this point, he hoped they would do the right thing, but it was no longer his concern.

"What do you mean, Verity's disappeared?" he demanded as soon as Ian answered.

"She's gone, Dad. I have no idea where she is." He sounded even more frazzled than Jason had.

A horn blared. Stone punched the gas, barely avoiding getting broadsided by a delivery truck. Only then did he realize he'd run a red light. He took several deep breaths, forcing himself to calm down and watch the road. The ley line was only a couple of miles away. "Okay. Okay. Where are you now? Did you go to the meeting?"

"I'm in London. Yes, we went to the meeting. Verity texted me and I met her here."

"Where was the meeting held?"

"Dad—please—can you just get here? It's easier to give you the details in person."

"Are you looking for her? Are you doing a ritual?"

"I did one, but I didn't find her. She's alive, but somebody's concealing her. I'm trying to get hold of Gabriel to do a better one."

Stone thought fast. He wanted all the details *now,* but Ian was right—it was better to do this in person. "Okay. I'll be there in a few minutes."

"Where are you now?"

"Los Angeles."

"Los Angeles? But there's no—oh. Right. That secret ley-line thing of yours."

"Yes. I'm driving now, and the ley line is only a mile or so away. I'll be there before you know it. Keep trying to reach Gabriel. And I'll want the whole story of what happened."

He abandoned the rental car when he reached the ley line, leaving the keys inside. He literally didn't care what happened to it—if someone stole it or trashed it, he'd buy the agency a new one. He dashed behind a building and two minutes later he appeared in the sitting room of the London house.

Ian was already there, pacing around. Stress sluiced off him like water.

"What happened?" Stone demanded.

Ian jerked and spun around. "You're here. Thank the gods."

"What *happened?*" he snapped again. "Ian, how did you lose Verity? Sit down and tell me everything. And has Gabriel responded yet?"

"Not yet. Sometimes he takes a while." Ian threw himself onto a sofa, leaned forward with his elbows on his knees, and plowed his hands through his hair. He took several deep breaths and began his story.

"V contacted me and told me you guys had a line on somebody who claims to know where Brathwaite is. She said you couldn't go because of something about Jason and Amber's son getting kidnapped—" He glanced up. "What's that about, by the way? Is Jaden okay?"

"He's fine," Stone said impatiently. "Keep going."

"Yeah. Okay. Anyway, she asked if I wanted to go, and of course I said yes. She said the woman wanted to meet somewhere public, and you wanted us to as well so we didn't get ambushed again. We decided on Market Halls Victoria—open late and lots of people. We figured it would be pretty hard to get any zombies in there. So we headed over, honestly halfway expecting the woman wouldn't show."

"But she did?"

"Yeah. She was there, right where she said she was. We did a little recon first—you know, checked her out from cover to make sure she wasn't playing us. But we were pretty sure she wasn't. She looked nervous, like she was as scared as we were. She kept looking around like she expected somebody to jump her."

"So you went to talk to her?"

"Yeah. We introduced ourselves, but she didn't. She said she didn't want anybody to know who she was. We both looked at her aura and didn't see anything weird. I mean, yeah, she was nervous, but so were we. We kept looking around trying to spot anybody paying attention to us, but nobody was. Everything looked completely normal."

"So, what did you talk about? Did she tell you where Brathwaite is?" Stone realized he was peppering Ian with questions like bullets, but he didn't care. Verity was gone, and he needed all the information he could get if they were to find her.

"No. She didn't get a chance. That was where we made our mistake." Ian's expression twisted. "It was my fault, Dad. I let her out of my sight. The woman said she had to use the bathroom before we talked—said she was so nervous and had drunk too many cups of coffee while she waited for us to get there. Naturally, we didn't want to let her go alone, since we were afraid she was going off to alert somebody. So Verity said she'd go with her."

Stone was beginning to see where this was going. "What did you do?"

"What *could* I do? I couldn't exactly go in the ladies' room with them. So I followed them and waited outside, figuring I'd hear if V yelled. The bathroom wasn't that far from our table."

"And—?"

"Ten minutes passed, and they didn't come back out. I know women take longer sometimes, especially if there's a line, so I didn't think anything of it. I texted V to ask if everything was all right. And she didn't answer."

A chill settled over Stone's body. "Then what did you do?"

"What I probably should have done all along, but I felt creepy about it if nothing was wrong. I used an illusion to disguise myself as a woman and went in to look at her." He looked at Stone, his eyes haunted. "Dad—she was gone. So was the other woman. They'd completely disappeared."

"Oh, bloody hell…" Stone murmured. "Did you check every-where? Were there any other exits from the bathroom?"

"No, just the one. I checked all the stalls, scanned the whole area with magical sight, and even popped the lock on the janitor's supply closet in case they were hiding in there. But she was gone." He bowed his head and let out a ragged sigh. "Somehow, they must have gotten past me—but Dad, I never took my eyes off the door. I promise I didn't."

Stone believed him. Ian had always been a bit irresponsible be-fore, but in the years since he had taken his three-year hiatus, his son had developed a maturity that had never been there in the past. If he said he'd been watching, he'd been watching.

"Okay," he said. "You said you did a ritual?"

"Yeah. I used the circle here at the house, so it was easy to set it up and only took a few minutes. Like I said, she's alive, but she's either being concealed or she's out of my range. Maybe both. I don't know, Dad." He yanked his phone from his pocket and glared at it. "Why doesn't Gabriel get back to me? He's a lot stronger than I am." He swiped his hand across his face. "You should look, Dad. You're stronger than me, too. Maybe you can get more."

Stone wanted to do just that, but Gabriel would be a better choice if he got back to them soon. Ian didn't know just how *much* stronger and more experienced his teacher was than either of the two of them. "Let's give Gabriel a little more time to respond." He paced, forcing himself to think logically. Going to pieces wouldn't help any of them. A thought popped into his head, and he whirled back around. "This woman! What did she look like? Can you describe her?"

Ian jerked his head up. "I can do better than that! Remember I said V and I did some recon?" He thrust his phone out. "I took some photos. They're not great, but the zoom on my phone camera's pretty good." He cued them up and offered it to Stone.

Ian was right—the photos weren't great. They'd been taken from some distance away, and the place was crowded so he hadn't gotten a straight-on shot of the woman. He zoomed in as much as he could and peered at her.

The woman wore a dark-green sweater under a gray, medium-weight coat. She had dark, curly hair and a narrow face. She wasn't looking directly at the viewer, but even in the grainy zoom Stone could tell she was nervous.

She also looked vaguely familiar, but as hard as he tried, he couldn't dredge up where he'd seen her before.

He gave Ian back his phone. "Send me those photos. And did she say *anything* at all that might help us before she got up to leave?"

Ian shook his head. "No. I've been going over the conversation in my head ever since it happened, and there was nothing. All she said was that she'd been sitting there for a while and she'd had two or three cups of coffee." He tapped his phone for a moment. "There. You should have them now."

Stone verified the photos had arrived, then began pacing again. "If Gabriel doesn't get back to you in the next five minutes, let's try another ritual. Verity said she'd been practicing the dual tracking spell with you—do you remember how to do it?"

"Yeah. We can—" He stopped, jerked his phone from his pocket, and glared at it. Then he let out a loud *whoosh*. "Finally!"

"Is that Gabriel?"

"Yeah." He was already texting furiously. "I'm asking him to come here." After waiting a few more seconds, he nodded. "He says he's on his way."

The time ticked away with agonizing slowness, but it was less than ten minutes before Gabriel strode into the room. He looked as well put together as always, dressed in designer jeans, a black silk shirt, and leather boots. His gaze locked onto Stone and Ian as he entered the room. "Verity is missing?"

"Yes," Stone said. "And we're fairly sure Brathwaite is involved. Tell him what you told me, Ian."

Ian repeated the story of their meeting at Market Halls Victoria, and Stone watched the young dragon's expression as he listened. Gabriel revealed nothing, but merely nodded at the appropriate times. His eyes never left Ian until he finished.

"You have no idea who this woman is?" he asked.

"No," Ian said. "I'm sure I've never seen her before in my life." He offered his phone. "I took some photos—maybe you recognize her?"

Gabriel looked at them and shook his head. "She isn't familiar to me. It's possible she was using an illusionary disguise, though."

"I don't think so. Verity and I both looked her over fairly well before we headed to the table. And you know how good I am at seeing through illusions."

"True."

"I can't help thinking I've seen her before," Stone said. "But I can't put my finger on where. It's difficult to tell from those photos."

Ian frowned. "You know, now that I think of it, it's possible Verity might have had the same thought."

"She recognized her?" Stone demanded.

"I don't know. I mean, there was definitely no flash of recognition. But I did notice when we got closer, she looked like she had something on her mind. I didn't get a chance to ask her before the two of them went off to the bathroom."

"Damn." Stone paced again. "And it won't do us any good to check the bathroom at this point. That place is bloody crowded, which means dozens of people will have passed through there since you left. Unless something horrific happened in there, they'll have obliterated the traces by now."

"I don't think anything horrific happened," Ian said firmly. "I checked pretty thoroughly with both magical and mundane sight, and didn't get any sense of that."

Stone nodded. "I'll take you word for that, since I know how good your sensitivity is." He turned to Gabriel. "We need your help. Ian tried doing a tracking ritual—he says he knows she's not dead, but she's either under protection or out of his range. Will you help us find her?"

Gabriel didn't answer for a moment. He appeared to be turning something over in his mind. Finally, he inclined his head. "I'll help you with the ritual. But that's all I can do."

Stone glared at him. "What do you mean, that's all you can do?"

"I'll do my best to help you find her. But I can't help you retrieve her."

Ian's glare was even stronger than Stone's. "You can't? Why not?"

"I have my reasons, Ian. I can't explain them to you, but I promise I do."

"More secrets." Ian's tone was harsh and bitter. "Gabriel, what the hell? After everything we've been through together, you're still keeping secrets from me?"

"Gabriel," Stone said, trying to keep his tone even, "this is *Verity* we're talking about. Our best guess at this point is that Brathwaite somehow managed to get hold of her. And you know as well as I do what *that* means. What he could do to her if we don't find her fast."

"I know." Gabriel's tone was as even as Stone's. "So that's why we should get to finding her, isn't it?"

Ian and Stone exchanged glances, and Stone could see his own anger mirrored in his son's eyes. "Fine," he snapped. "Let's find her. Then we can discuss our next steps."

They adjourned to the downstairs circle, and Gabriel immediately began clearing away the debris from Ian's failed one.

"Do you have a tether object?" he asked Stone. "I can do it without one, but we should maximize our chances of success if possible."

"I do," Ian said. "Hang on." He dashed back upstairs and returned with an elegant leather jacket. "She wore this at the meet, and left it at the table when she went with the woman."

"Good." Gabriel took the jacket and set it aside. "Where do you keep the ritual materials, Alastair? It would be better if we had some blood from her or a close relative, but I can work with this."

Stone showed him to the cubbies on the far side of the room, which he kept well stocked. "I wish we could get some blood, but I haven't got any of Verity's, and I believe Jason is currently on a plane from Los Angeles to the Bay Area. We haven't got time to wait." A sudden thought struck him. "Hold on—I might have an idea! Finish constructing the circle and I'll let you know."

He strode off to the other side of the room and pulled out his phone. It was late in London, but eight hours earlier in California, so he might get lucky.

The phone rang a few times before the caller picked up. "Hello?"

"Hezzie? It's Alastair Stone."

"Oh. Hi." She didn't sound enthusiastic to hear from him. "If you're looking for Verity, she's not here."

"I know. That's why I'm calling you."

"What's that supposed to mean?"

"She's gone missing, and we're trying to find her."

"Missing?" Now she sounded more concerned. "What do you mean?"

"Long story. We've got it under control, but we need to do a ritual. I was wondering if there was any chance you might have some of her blood on hand. I figured with all the alchemical rituals you two do, it was worth a shot to ask."

"I do. You want it to use in the ritual?"

Stone didn't pump his fist, but he felt like it. "That would be a big help, yes. Can I come pick it up? Are you at the shop?"

"I'm at the San Francisco shop, but I can use the dedicated portal to go to Sunnyvale."

He almost told her not to bother, but he didn't need someone *else* knowing he could pop around without portals. "Yes, please, if you could do that it would be brilliant."

"Do you want me to help?"

Her offer warmed Stone's heart. He knew how much Hezzie didn't like being around him or any man, but she was still willing to put that aside to help her friend. "No, thank you," he said gently. "We've got it under control. But the blood might make all the difference. I'll come to the Sunnyvale shop now. Thank you, Hezzie."

"Yeah. Please let me know how it goes, okay?"

"I will—or Verity will let you know herself. Because we're going to find her."

He hurried back over to the circle, where Gabriel and Ian were hard at work customizing it for the new ritual. "I've got to go for a few minutes," he told them. "I can get us some of Verity's blood, from Hezzie."

Ian brightened. "Oh—right. Didn't think of that. This shouldn't take us too long, so please hurry." Despite his expression, his stress was obvious. He clearly felt responsible for Verity's disappearance, and wouldn't be satisfied until she'd been safely located and returned.

Stone used the London house's private portal, since it was nearby and didn't take any longer once he took the time to visualize the pattern into account. He reappeared at the Sunnyvale portal and dashed up the stairs to the hidden hallway where it was concealed.

Hezzie pushed open the door leading to Sybil's Apothecary. "Come on in," she said. "I've got the blood in the warded fridge in the back. We were going to use it for a new concoction we're working on."

Stone checked her out with magical sight as he followed her inside. She was never one to display strong emotion, but her aura didn't lie: she was worried. He didn't blame her. As far as he knew, she and Verity weren't romantically involved (Verity had once told him Hezzie was straight, despite her outward demeanor), but she obviously cared deeply about her friend.

Hezzie disappeared into a back room and returned with a capped and sealed vial of blood. "This was taken a few days ago, and it's got a preservation spell on it."

"Thank you."

When he reached for it, though, she pulled it back. "Are you sure I can't help? What's happened to her? How did she go missing?"

Stone understood. If the situation were reversed, he'd be asking the same questions. "You can't help," he said. "Trust me—we've got some serious power devoted to this. We *will* find her. As for how she went missing—that's a story I can't tell right now."

"It's that thing she was working on for you, isn't it? She told me before she left with Ian, but she wouldn't say what it was." She looked at him with narrowed eyes, as if trying to work out how responsible he might be for Verity's disappearance.

"It…is." His stress was rising again; he didn't have time to stay here and give Hezzie a long explanation. But he owed her something. "She *was* working on something for me, but I promise you, Hezzie, it's not just for me. She wanted to do this. It was very important to her, and she would have been very angry with me if I'd tried to leave her out. Please believe me about that. This was her choice."

She looked hard at him for several seconds, then nodded. She offered him the vial with a sigh. "Yeah. I know what's she's like, and I do believe you." She swallowed. "But you find her. And get her back here safe. We've got things to do next week, and tell her she's not getting out of them."

He smiled faintly. "We will find her, and I'll pass your message along. I've got to go now, though."

She nodded again and turned away. "Good luck."

He left without responding, his mind already seething with images of what Brathwaite and his people might be doing to Verity. He refused to let himself think about Sharra.

Ian and Gabriel almost had the circle finished when he returned.

"I'm impressed," he said, standing back to watch them put the final touches on the far edge. "You two work well together."

"Always have," Ian said, but Stone didn't miss a faint hint of bitterness in his voice.

"Did you get the blood?" If Gabriel noticed Ian's tone, he didn't acknowledge it.

Stone pulled out the vial. "Got it right here. It's a few days old, but it's got a preservation spell on it."

"That's fine. We're just about ready to get started here." He levitated the vial across into the center of the circle, broke the seal, and poured the blood into the brazier. "We'll do the modified group ritual, but let me take lead. I've got some…" He shot a quick, significant glance first at Ian, then at Stone "…improvements."

Of course he did. He'd told Stone before that dragon tracking rituals were different from human ones, and Stone had seen it in action when he and Gabriel had performed one to locate Ian. He hoped this one would have better results, since as far as he knew, no dragons were involved. A dragon wouldn't work with a necromancer.

Brathwaite's still a strong mage, though, his unhelpful mental voice put in. *If he's hiding her—*

He brushed the thought aside. Now was the time to concentrate, not to let his thoughts get fragmented. Verity was counting on them.

"I just tried to text Verity again, and call her," Ian said. "No answer. I didn't expect one, but I'd feel pretty stupid if we went through all this effort and it turns out there's a logical explanation for where she is."

Stone didn't answer; he didn't need to. They both knew if there was any way for Verity to get through to them, she'd have used it.

They took their places at three points around the inside of the circle, and clasped hands in silence. Stone didn't miss the faint shake in Ian's hand. He wasn't angry at his son for losing Verity, since it sounded as if there wasn't anything he could have done about it. For now, they all needed to be focused on finding her.

He forced himself to remain calm as Gabriel began the ritual. Verity hadn't been missing for long. If Brathwaite had any plans for her, he'd need time to prepare them.

But he could have taken her anywhere, his unhelpful interior voice said. *If he took her through a portal, she could be on the other side of the world by now. Even Gabriel's range isn't limitless.*

Involuntarily, he tightened his grip on Ian's hand. His son shot him a questioning glance, but he shook his head. He needed to clear these unhelpful thoughts and concentrate.

But his inner voice wasn't in the mood to be shut up. *She could be dead already. Remember Sharra? He kept her on ice for a while before he did his ritual on her.*

Again he gripped Ian's hand harder.

"*Dad?*" Ian mouthed, concerned.

He shook his head once more, more violently this time. *Stop it. You're acting like an apprentice. Get control of yourself!*

He took several deep, centering breaths and forced himself to be present in the moment, with the ritual his only concern. All those other intrusive thoughts wouldn't get him closer to finding her, and would in fact make it more difficult.

Gabriel was murmuring in a language Stone didn't recognize. He cast a surreptitious glance at Ian, who didn't look like he did either. But he was holding up his end of the ritual, directing his attention at the blood in the brazier. It had begun to swirl, sending up wispy tendrils of red smoke.

Still, Gabriel continued his soft chant. It seemed to go on forever, lulling Stone into a semi-trance. He could feel the young dragon reaching out to him for more power, and gave it without question. He would do whatever it took to get Verity back, no matter the cost to him.

The blood continued to swirl, and the smoky tendrils continued to waft around. This wasn't the same as the ritual Stone was used to, but more similar to the one he and Gabriel had done to look for Ian after Aldwyn had taken him. It shouldn't be that difficult, right? If no dragons were involved and she was still on this dimension, Gabriel should be able to find her with no trouble, right? He realized he'd never asked Gabriel, or Kolinsky, or any of the other dragons if their tracking spells had any limitations.

Even dragons have limits, right? They're not omnipotent or omniscient. You've seen that for yourself. It was his interior voice again, and this time he couldn't silence it.

The ritual was winding down. Gabriel watched the smoke, his jaw tightening and his smooth brow furrowing. It looked as if he were trying to corral it and direct it, but it was resisting him. Finally, he let his breath out and his shoulders slumped. The smoke collapsed back into the brazier. The blood didn't disappear, but it was dry now, almost like it had been scorched.

"Did you find her?" Stone and Ian asked in unison.

"Not…exactly." Gabriel's handsome face appeared uncharacteristically tired and discouraged.

"What do you mean, not exactly?" Stone demanded. "Did you find her or not?"

"I know she's still alive."

"*I* know she's still alive," Ian protested. "You must have gotten more than that."

Gabriel refused to be baited. "I did. I don't think she's far away—probably somewhere in the UK, Ireland, or the western European continent."

"That's a bloody big area," Stone snapped. "That's the best you can do?"

He bowed his head. "I'm sorry. Something odd is going on. I believe she's under strong protection, which as you know gets harder to pierce the farther out the target is."

Stone glared at him. "I don't believe this! This is *Verity* we're talking about, and Brathwaite might be turning her into a bloody *zombie* as we speak! Come on, Gabriel! You've got power I can't even touch! You're a bloody *dragon!* You—"

He stopped, as two pairs of eyes suddenly focused on him with hawklike intensity. He replayed his words, and something in the pit of his stomach clenched.

Oh, no…

CHAPTER TWENTY-NINE

"**W**HAT DID YOU SAY, DAD?"

Ian's voice was calm and deliberate on the surface, but Stone didn't miss the faint tremor in it even without looking at his aura.

"I—"

"Did you just call Gabriel…a *dragon?*" He turned his gaze on Gabriel.

Stone, for his part, was looking at Gabriel, searching the young man's face for any sign of an emotion. He held his breath, bracing for what might be coming. He didn't, however, raise his shield. If the dragon wanted to retaliate against him for revealing the secret, he deserved it.

The terrifying thing was that Gabriel's smooth face *didn't* show any emotion. None whatsoever. He was still watching Stone, but he could have been watching boats floating by on a lazy river.

"I'm…sorry, Gabriel," Stone said softly. "I didn't—"

"It's all right," he said in the same tone. "I suppose it was inevitable that he would find out at some point. I must admit this is a particularly inconvenient time, though."

"Then…it's true?" Ian asked numbly, shifting his gaze back and forth between the two of them. "You're a—"

"A dragon. Yes," Gabriel said.

"And…you *knew?*" This was directed at Stone.

"I did. But I wasn't supposed to tell anyone."

Ian turned back to Gabriel. "That's…the secret you've been keeping from me all this time."

The young dragon inclined his head. "Yes."

"You're…a real dragon. A giant, fire-breathing *lizard?*"

"I don't breathe fire." The faintest hint of amusement touched Gabriel's tone now. "And no, I'm not a lizard. Not here on Earth, anyway."

"Not—here on…" Ian's face had gone pale, and he looked like someone had punched him in the gut. He put a hand to his head, shifting his attention back and forth again. "You two knew this…and you didn't tell me."

"Ian—" Stone began.

Gabriel held up a hand. "It's all right, Alastair. He has valid concerns, and I need to address them. But not now. We need to find Verity. That's our number-one priority right now."

He was right, of course, but Ian seemed to be having a hard time accepting it. Finally, he took a few deep breaths of his own and nodded, still looking shellshocked. "But…you said you couldn't find her."

"I said I couldn't find her *here*," he corrected. "If the range is an issue, we can repeat the ritual at other locations until we track her down."

"But that could take hours," Stone protested. "Brathwaite could have done anything to her by then. We don't have that kind of time."

Gabriel sighed. "I don't know what to tell you, Alastair. The only other thing I can do is try contacting some of the others—"

Ian's head snapped up. "Others? You mean, other…dragons?"

"—but I don't think that will be the most productive use of our time," he finished, still addressing Stone with a significant glance.

Stone let out a ragged sigh. This whole situation was spiraling out of control, and Verity was still missing. "You're probably right. They won't want to get involved either."

"Wait," Ian said, louder. "Don't ignore me. There are other dragons, and…you *know* them, Dad?"

Clearly, there was no getting around at least some of this. He gripped Ian's shoulders and looked deep into his eyes. "Ian… Yes. There are others, and I do know some of them. This is a very long story, and you deserve to know the truth. But not now. Not while Verity is still out there and Brathwaite might have her. Can you focus on the problem at hand right now?"

"I promise, Ian," Gabriel added, "we'll tell you. We'll answer your questions. But your father is right—we need to find Verity first."

Stone felt sorry for Ian. It was clear from watching him that he was going through a profound mental struggle. He obviously didn't *want* to let this go and wait for more information later. But he just as obviously cared for Verity.

"Okay," he said at last, sounding tired. "Okay, I'll put this aside for now. But I'm holding you to that promise. Both of you."

Gabriel inclined his head solemnly. "Don't worry, Ian. As your father can assure you, dragons don't break their word. You'll have your answers." He turned away, looking at the remains of the circle, and when he turned back, his expression was brisk and business-like. "Our next step should be to travel somewhere near another portal and try again. My suggestion would be Berlin, since Brathwaite has been known to operate in Germany. We—" He stopped, looking at Stone. "Alastair? What is it?"

Stone had been only half-listening to Gabriel. He'd been think-ing about how he was going to tell Jason his sister was missing on a mission *he'd* sent her on. Jason would be justifiably angry—but he'd also want to help. How could he tell his friend that this wasn't the sort of thing mundane detective work and technology could—

"Oh, bloody hell…" he murmured, hardly daring to hope.

They both spun on him. "What is it?" Ian demanded.

He yanked his phone out of his pocket. Back when they'd been hunting for Daphne Weldon in Minnesota, he and Verity had been separated. To help them keep track of each other, Verity had suggested enabling a feature on their phones to allow them to track each other's locations in real time. It had been more than three years since they'd done that, and he'd recently replaced his phone with a newer model. But had he possibly—

"Dad?"

He continued ignoring them, tapping the icon for the tracking app.

No contacts showed in the list.

"Damn it…" he murmured, feeling suddenly almost physically ill. It had been a good idea, but either he'd cancelled the tracking at some point or switching to a new phone had cleared it.

"What are you doing?" Gabriel and Ian were both watching him now, confused.

He held up the phone. "We were tracking each other's locations a while back. I thought it might still be in effect." He locked his gaze on Ian. "You weren't tracking her, were you?"

But once again his hopes fell as Ian shook his head. "No. Didn't even think of it, to be honest, but I doubt she'd have gone for it. Most people don't like to be tracked. Sorry, Dad. I—" He stabbed a finger up. "Wait!"

"What?"

"Jason!"

"What about him?"

"He's her brother! Maybe they'd track each other, especially if she works with him at the agency!"

"But he's on a—" But was he? He glanced at his watch. The flight from Los Angeles to San Jose wasn't that long. Jason might have landed by now.

Gabriel watched them with interest as Stone tried to call Jason. "I should go," he said. "I still won't be able to help you beyond finding her, but I can get started looking in Berlin. I'll call you if I find anything."

"Why can't you help?" Ian asked. "Is this related to you being a…dragon?" He still hesitated before using the word, as if he didn't believe it was true.

"Yes. I'll call you, Ian. We need to be efficient about this." Before Ian could respond, he swept out of the room.

Stone, meanwhile, was listening to the phone ring. "Please don't go to voicemail…" he murmured. "Please don't go to voicemail…"

"Hello? Al?" Jason sounded breathless. "We just landed, and I'm headed for the parking lot. Is something wrong? Jaden—"

"Jaden's fine, as far as I know," Stone cut him off. "Listen, Jason—this is important. Do you and Verity track each other on your phones?"

"Uh—yeah, I think we still have that active. Why?"

"Because I've got to find her fast. Can you tell me where she is?"

"Why?" He sounded suspicious. "What's wrong, Al? I can tell from your voice that this isn't just casual."

Damn Jason and his perceptiveness! "Er—yes. Something's wrong, but I haven't got time to explain it right now. She's gone missing, and I need to find her. Can you check?"

"Missing? What are you talking about?"

"We think someone took her, Jason. We're wasting time."

"Someone…took her? Is this related to what happened to Jaden?"

"No. Definitely not." A sudden thought struck him with near-physical pain. "Oh, gods, if they have her, they might have shut off her phone."

"Al, you are *gonna* explain this to me. But if the phone's still near where she is, it doesn't matter that they shut it off."

Hope rose again, but he barely dared to acknowledge it. "It doesn't?"

"No. It's a security measure. If a phone gets shut off, it doesn't broadcast its real-time location anymore, but it *does* send out the last place it was before it was shut off."

Stone held his breath. "So if they didn't take it away from her right away, and didn't realize that was true—"

"Yeah. A lot of people don't know that. Hang on—it's cycling. Al—do we need to call the police?"

"No. This isn't something the mundane police have a chance of helping with. Anything?"

"Hang on…Huh. That's weird. Why would she be there?"

"Where?" he demanded. "Where is she?"

"The phone's pinging somewhere in northern England. Not too far from the Scottish border. Place called Windermere. Do you know where that is, Al? Who would take her there?"

Stone's hand froze on the phone as an image popped up with a dot showing the last known location of Verity's phone.

"Al?" Jason's voice grew more insistent.

"*Dad?*" Ian mouthed, eyes widening. "*What is it?*"

"No…" Stone whispered. "It can't be…He can't be working with…"

"Al, damn it, *talk* to me!" Jason yelled. "What's going on? Why is V in northern England?"

"I've…got to go, Jason." Stone spoke robotically, ignoring his friend's agitation. "You can't help with this. I'll…be in touch." He tapped the button to break the connection before Jason could respond and lowered the phone.

"Dad?" Ian demanded. "What's going on? You went pale as a ghost. What's in Windermere?"

He raised his head, realizing how haunted he must look. "Your great-grandmother."

CHAPTER THIRTY

IAN DIDN'T EVEN TRY TO HIDE his shocked astonishment this time. "My—"

"Your great-grandmother. Yes." Stone's tone was still numb, his brain only half focusing on what Ian was saying. Could it be possible? Could Brathwaite be working with Nessa Lennox and her druids?

That didn't make sense, though. It had to be a coincidence. Nessa might have been an evil old witch whose priorities were severely twisted, but she was still a druid, and druids revered Nature. She wouldn't be any more likely to work with a necromancer than Kolinsky and the rest of the dragons.

Was it possible Brathwaite had set up a base in the area without knowing about Nessa? She and her group *were* reclusive and secretive, and Windermere was a magically potent location.

Or was it possible that Verity's disappearance didn't have anything to do with Brathwaite at all? That didn't make sense either, since the woman who'd called them had said she knew where he was. She'd also almost certainly been an accomplice in Verity's disappearance.

"Dad?" Ian grabbed his shoulders hard and spun him around. "What is going *on?* You need to tell me. What's this about my great-grandmother? I thought we didn't have any relatives on your side."

"Yes, well…I wasn't entirely forthcoming about that, I'm afraid. I—" He stopped as another sudden thought popped into his head. He yanked his phone back out and pulled up the camera app, staring hard at the photos Ian had sent him from the meeting with the mysterious woman.

"Dad?"

"Just a moment," he said impatiently, waving Ian off as he zoomed in on the woman's face. "That's it…" he whispered.

"That's *what?*" Ian sounded like he was on his last ounce of patience. "Dad, if you don't tell me something *right now—*"

Still ignoring Ian's words, Stone stabbed a finger down on the phone screen. "I know who she is now! I know why she looked familiar!"

"Why?"

"Because I've seen her before, several years ago." He took a few deep breaths to get himself under control, but it didn't work very well. "We haven't got much time to spend on this, Ian. Not until we've got Verity back. Will you settle for an abbreviated version now, if I promise to tell you the whole story later?"

"Do I have a choice?"

"Not really, unfortunately. I'm sorry this all had to come to a head for you now—believe me, I understand how you're feeling. I've had similar shocking revelations over the years, and it's never easy. But will you do that for me now?" He stared hard into his son's eyes, silently pleading for him to understand.

Ian let out a long, ragged sigh. "Yeah. Of course. Verity's our top priority. But please—tell me *something.*"

Stone turned away and began pacing, trying to corral his spinning thoughts into something that would make enough sense to tell Ian quickly. It wasn't easy. "Okay. Okay. First thing is, you've got a great-grandmother. Her name is Nessa Lennox, and she runs a coven of mad druids up in Windermere."

"Mad…druids?"

He shook his head quickly. "Okay—maybe not all of them are mad. Let's just call them druids for now. Nessa's definitely mad, but the jury's still out on most of the rest of them."

"How…do you know this? How did you find out?"

"That's a story we haven't got time for right now. But the woman in the photo—" He held up the phone "—is one of Nessa's druids. She was a lot younger when I saw her. Verity and I were attending a dinner with them, and she was one of the acolytes doing the serving. But it's definitely her. She's older, obviously, and she's changed her hair, but the eyes are the same."

Ian was looking confused and frustrated. "So…wait a minute. Are you saying that somebody from my great-grandmother's druid group…kidnapped Verity? Why would she do that? And what's it got to do with Brathwaite?"

Stone went over the phone conversation he'd had with the woman. She'd sounded scared then, and he would have bet a lot of money that she wasn't faking it. "Nessa grabbed Verity before, for…her own purposes. They didn't work out, and I thought I'd rather violently discouraged her from messing with me or anybody I care about ever again. I haven't heard a peep out of her in almost seven years."

"So you think she's grabbed Verity again? And you still haven't told me why you think this Nessa woman is connected with Brathwaite. You said she's a druid. Druids hate necromancers, don't they?"

"They do, yes. So do dragons, by the way."

"Is Nessa a dragon too?"

"I doubt it. She's just a mad old woman with a lot of power and a lot of delusions. But you make a good point—Druids *do* hate necromancers. But the woman I spoke with—the one you met with—told me she knew where Brathwaite is." In the background, his mind was turning over all the facts as he knew them, but something wasn't fitting. A *lot* of things weren't fitting. But that wasn't important now. The important thing was getting Verity back.

He jammed the phone back in his pocket. "Listen, Ian—I've got to go. I need to get to Verity before Nessa does something we're all going to regret."

Ian glared. "Hold on. You are *not* going without me, Dad. You can't just…drop all this on me and then *leave* me here."

Stone's frustration was bubbling up fast and hard. "Ian, I haven't got a *choice.* There aren't any portals up there that I have access to, and we haven't got time to drive. It would take more than five hours to get there from here, and we haven't got that kind of time. *Verity* doesn't have that kind of time."

"You can't go on your own. You said yourself that Nessa is powerful, and she's got this druid group on her side. That's not even taking Brathwaite into account. If he's there too, there's no way you're going to take them all out on your own. Hell, it sounds like the two of us will have trouble."

He made a good point. "Ian—I don't *want* to leave you behind. Please, believe me. Your power would be a big help. But I don't have any way to—"

He stopped.

"Dad? You're doing it again. What's going on?"

It was a reckless idea—but given the events of the last few minutes, it had a better chance of working than it had before. "Just a minute." He spun away, pulled his phone out again, and texted Gabriel. *I need your help. We've found where she is.*

The reply came back quickly. *How did you find her?*

Technology. Please—come back. You've got to help us.

The dots cycled. *I told you, I can't do that.*

Stone growled, fingers flying as he tapped out the words. *I know you can't help us deal with the situation directly. But Ian knows about you now, and I need him. He can't travel there on his own in time. I can't take him. You can.*

Another long pause, this time with no dots.

Gabriel—come on. This is Verity. Please. I'm begging you.

"Dad, who are you texting?" Ian grabbed his arm.

He tore it away. "Just wait, Ian, please." His heart pounded harder as he continued staring at the screen like it was the most important thing in the world. At this moment, it was.

At last, the reply came back. *All right. That much I can do. I'm sorry, Alastair. I wish I could help you more.*

Yes, so do I. But I understand your constraints, even though I don't agree with them. Come soon, please. We need to go.

He turned back to Ian. "You're about to add another shock to your stack, so be prepared."

"What are you—"

Gabriel strode into the room, looking serious.

Ian gaped. "Gabriel? You're back already?"

"He's your ride, Ian."

"What are you talking about? He—" But then the beginnings of light dawned. "Wait. This…has something to do with how you use ley lines to travel, doesn't it?"

Stone flashed Gabriel a manic, mirthless grin. "I told you he was sharp."

Ian ignored him, shifting his gaze back and forth between his father and his teacher. "Does that mean…*you're* a dragon too, Dad?"

"No. Gods, no. Not exactly, anyway."

"Not…*exactly?*"

Stone waved him off. "That's for later. I'm not a dragon—I promise. But the ley-line travel technique is a draconic one, and I've learned it."

His eyes widened as he turned to Gabriel. "You're going to teach it to me?"

"We'll talk," the young dragon said. "Not now, though. We haven't got time. But I'm going to take you where you need to go."

Ian looked confused again. "But…if you can do it too, Dad, why can't you just—"

Gabriel answered before Stone could. "Because he's *not* a dragon, and only dragons can safely carry certain sentient passengers over the ley lines."

"*Certain* sentient…" Ian was clearly trying hard to keep this all straight and keep his brain from exploding from all the new inputs. "So that's why you can take Raider to San Francisco, but you can't take any humans, Dad?"

"Got it in one. There's more to it than that, but it will suffice for now." The last thing Stone wanted right now was to confuse Ian even more with the concept of scions.

Ian took a deep breath, let it out slowly, and glared at them. "Okay. This is all seriously blowing my mind, but I'm trying to prioritize. Verity first—but after that, you both are going to have a lot of explaining to do. And I'm not going to take no for an answer. Got it?"

"Absolutely," Stone said instantly.

Gabriel nodded. "I probably can't tell you *everything* you want to know—even Alastair doesn't know everything about draconic society—but I think I can answer enough of your questions to satisfy you. Fair enough?"

Ian hesitated, but finally nodded. "Yeah. I guess. But I'm done being kept in the dark. No more secrets, Dad. About dragons *or* about family."

"I promise," Stone said. "Now, let's go."

"Where are we going?" Gabriel asked. "You haven't told me yet. I take it Jason came through with something?"

Stone's phone buzzed. He took a quick glance at it, saw it was Jason again, and put it away. He felt bad about ghosting his friend, especially since it was his sister in trouble, but there was literally nothing he could do to help with this situation. He didn't even have anyone in the area who could bring him through the portal.

Instead, Stone addressed Gabriel. "Yes. Technology for the win, as my students used to say. We're going to Windermere." He pulled up the image Jason had sent him of the location dot and showed it to the dragon. "This is where we're going—or at least close to there." With the tip of a pen, he drew an invisible circle around the area encompassing what he remembered of Nessa Lennox's compound. "Don't pop us too close to that area—though I doubt you can. It's probably warded."

Gabriel narrowed his eyes. "What is this place? It sounds like you know it."

Stone wasn't sure whether to be relieved or disappointed that the dragon wasn't already familiar with it. "It's…the home base of someone I know. Someone powerful."

"Someone who's working with Brathwaite?"

"We don't know yet, but we suspect so."

"We should go," Ian said. "Much as I want to hear all this, we need to find Verity."

"You're right." Stone pulled up his mobile ley-line map of the area, consulted it, then returned to Jason's image and pointed to a spot a mile to the south of the complex. "Can you take Ian there? I'll meet you, and we can go from there."

"I can, yes."

Ian was looking at him again. "I still don't understand why you can't just come with us—help us. Verity's your friend too."

Gabriel appeared uncomfortable. "It's…complicated, Ian."

"Is this more dragon stuff?"

"Yes. I promise you, if I could do it without causing serious problems, I would. But there are some things I can't do—not even for you. I'm sorry."

Ian held his gaze, then nodded. "Okay. I trust you. Let's go, then. We'll talk about it later."

Stone watched them as Gabriel led Ian to the other side of the ritual room. A moment later, the two of them both disappeared.

He stared at the spot where they'd been, wondering if he'd just sent his son to his death. As he visualized the pattern in his mind for their destination, some corner of his mind continued chewing over what possible reason Nessa Lennox or any of her other druids might have for working with a depraved necromancer like Brathwaite.

The room faded around him without a clear answer. Ultimately, though, he supposed he didn't need to know—or care. He had only two priorities now: retrieve Verity safely, and kill Brathwaite.

Everything else could wait.

CHAPTER THIRTY-ONE

IT WAS DARK where Stone reappeared. Before his vision even cleared, he got the smell of clean, damp air and trees. As the world solidified around him, he discovered he was standing in a clearing surrounded by tall oaks and maples, with an overcast, moonless sky above him. Twenty feet to his right, a narrow, graveled road snaked around a corner and disappeared.

"Ian?" He tried to call quietly, not wanting to alert any perimeter guards Nessa Lennox might have on patrol. *She doesn't know you're coming,* he reminded himself. *She might know you're on your way, but she doesn't know about ley-line travel. You have time.* "Ian?" he repeated, turning in place.

"Dad?" The voice came from behind him.

He spun around to see his son emerging from the trees on the far side of the clearing. He looked confused and a little disoriented.

Stone hurried to him. "Are you all right?"

"That was…weird."

"Yes. You'll get used to it. Where's Gabriel?"

"Gone already. He didn't seem like he was happy about it. What's going on? Why can't he help?"

"It's a long story, as I said." He lowered his voice to a whisper. "Short answer is that dragons have had a pact for thousands of years that they don't interfere directly in human affairs. They're fairly sticky about it, because if one of them gets caught doing it, it could unravel their whole truce."

"Truce? So they don't like each other?"

"Some of them don't. And none of them trust each other." Stone looked around as his vision became accustomed to the dimness. "We don't have time for this now, Ian. Please stop asking about the dragons. We need to find Verity."

He nodded, jaw tightening. "Yeah. Where are we? Do you know where she is from here?"

"I need to look around. I'm not sure exactly how far we are from their compound. But we need to be careful. They're powerful witches, and they don't like visitors. We'll need to be very sneaky, especially when we get closer."

"Sneaky I'm good at."

Stone headed out of the clearing and stopped at the edge of the road, switching to magical sight. "I don't think they have the whole complex warded—that would be difficult even for them—but I'm sure they've got magical alarms set up to warn them when people enter, and if I remember correctly, they also employ illusions to keep the mundanes from getting curious. Let's look around near the road. If we spot the alarms, we can disable them. Don't stray too far away, though."

Ian nodded and jogged to the other side of the road, where he stopped and began turning slowly in place, obviously using magical sight.

Stone did the same thing on his side, inching forward.

"I think I found something," Ian called softly after a few minutes.

"Where?" Stone hurried to where he'd heard the voice, and found Ian staring straight ahead, eyes narrowed.

"Over there." He pointed. "Use magical sight. It's hard to see, but there's a little green glow that's brighter than the trees."

Stone followed Ian's line of sight, magical sight at full strength. At first he didn't see it, but then the faint glow appeared two feet from the ground. "Bloody hell, you're right. That *is* hard to see. Come on—let's check it out, but don't walk past it."

As they drew closer, Stone risked a faint light spell to get a better look.

Ian leaned in. "I'm impressed. I don't know much about druidic magic, but that's a nice little setup."

It was. Someone had wrapped a thin strand of braided vines around the narrow trunk of a tree, and attached what looked like a primitive construction of sticks to it. To an untrained eye, it would merely look like part of the tree; even most magical viewers would probably miss it if they weren't looking directly at it. But once Ian pointed it out, Stone saw it was obviously some sort of passive alarm or alert.

"What do you want to do with it?" Ian bent closer. "If you destroy it, will it alert them?"

"Hold on. Let me take a closer look. You look too." Stone crouched next to it, only a few inches away, and switched to the deeper form of magical sight he used for stronger rituals. After a few moments of examination, he spotted a faint green tendril extending upward from it, twisting around the tree until it disappeared into the branches high above. "Do you see that?"

"Yeah. I don't think we should break it, though."

"Nor do I. But perhaps we can redirect it. If it's directional, we can point it somewhere else. It won't stop it from going off, but it might give us enough time to get past and away before it sets off the alarm."

"Tricky magic," Ian said dubiously.

Stone smiled. "You're up to the task, I think—especially now that you know who your teacher really is."

Ian held his gaze for a few seconds, then nodded. "Okay. Let's do it."

It *was* tricky magic, but between the two of them they managed to unwind the green tendril from the tree and carefully reposition it so it was pointing back toward the road where they'd come in. Stone's heart beat fast and his hands shook with tension—sometimes the smallest magic was the hardest to manage, and nature magic wasn't his forte—but before long he let his breath out in relief. "I think that's done it. Good job. You really *have* improved in the three years I've been gone."

"Thanks." Ian sounded proud. "I'm a fully trained mage now—Gabriel said so."

"And he'd know. Okay, let's get moving. Once we get past this spot, we're going to need to risk a levitation spell. I'm not sure which way the complex is from here, except that it's somewhere ahead. Why don't you do that? Your concealment has always been better than mine. Be careful, though."

"Yeah." They slipped forward, both of them tense and stressed until they'd safely passed the barrier beyond the redirected alarm. Then Ian shimmered to invisibility with a soft, "Back soon."

He returned in five minutes, appearing in front of Stone, who hadn't moved. He pointed to the northeast. "The complex is that way, about half a mile. You didn't tell me how big it is, but there's a spread-out cluster of buildings and paths up that way, near a small lake. I assume that's the place?"

"Yes. We need to take care. It's been a while since I've been here, and they might have added to it since then. Before, they had a lot of underground passages and chambers, so they could pop up anywhere." He wondered if they'd repaired their main ritual chamber since he'd trashed it last time he and Verity were here. That had already been seven years. It certainly didn't seem like that long.

They set off through the forest toward the complex. They walked in silence for a while, with no sound except their soft breathing, the rustle of the trees in the faint wind, and the far-off calls of birds and small animals. But then Ian spoke softly in the dimness. "Dad?"

"Yes?"

"You said this Nessa person is my great-grandmother. How long have you known that?"

"Around seven years."

"That's it? How did you find out? And please don't tell me it's a long story."

"I won't…but it *is* a story I don't want to go into now. It's a painful one."

"Related to our family, though?"

"Very much so."

Ian remained silent for a while, then said, "You said before, back when we were dealing with the stuff under the house, that none of our family farther back than my grandfather were good people. Is this related to that?"

"Surprisingly, not much. That bit was all related to the family on your grandfather's side."

"So…there's no connection between this Nessa woman and you-know-who." He glanced around nervously, as if expecting Brathwaite to pop out and attack them.

"Not that I'm aware of. I didn't even know Nessa knew anything about him. His existence hasn't exactly been common knowledge since he returned."

Ian spoke slowly, like he was thinking it through. "Is it possible he could be taking advantage of Nessa somehow? Could she be his prisoner? Is that maybe why the woman connected with her asked for help?"

Stone hadn't considered that, and he supposed he couldn't blame his son for trying to find some way to absolve his great-grandmother of potential wrongdoing. "I guess anything's possible, but I doubt it. Nessa's smart, and she's powerful—probably at least as powerful as he is—and she's got a lot of loyal people around her. I don't think it would be easy for him to get the drop on her. I think it's much more likely that Nessa sent the woman. Remember, she initially wanted to talk to me."

"So, you think she wanted to grab you?"

"It's happened before."

"Wait, what?" Ian stopped, turning to stare at him. "She grabbed you before? When? Why?"

"I'll tell you later. But she had Verity at the time, too, so I know she knows her. That's why I'm so concerned."

"You think she wants to kill Verity?"

"I haven't got a clue *what* she wants to do. She didn't want to last time, but she didn't have her nasty little collaborator whispering in her ear last time. That's why we need to get there before they do it." He realized he had picked up Ian's habit of not referring to Brathwaite by name, almost as if speaking his name would summon him to them. It was absurd, but there was no use taking chances.

They both subsided into silence, picking their way through the underbrush and fallen leaves, and trying not to make too much noise.

"You know," Ian said softly, "I can't help resenting the fact that you've kept all this stuff from me."

Stone bowed his head. "You've got every right to, and I don't blame you. Not the bit about Gabriel—that wasn't mine to tell. But you deserved to know about your family."

"Why didn't you tell me?"

"I don't know. I've always been rubbish at this sort of thing, and I guess I figured Nessa was out of my life and it would be best if she remained out of yours as well."

"She never tried to contact you again, after all these years?"

"Not once. I'm not surprised—I told her if she ever did, we'd have…well, more than words." He sighed. "She's toxic, Ian. She's deluded and she tried to do something horrific that resulted in not only my father's death, but my old master's. I hope you can see that I wasn't in any hurry to dredge her up again. I just wanted to forget about her."

"Wait." Ian stopped. "Nessa killed my grandfather? And William Desmond?"

"Not…exactly. She didn't kill them, *per se*, but her activities were indirectly responsible for their deaths. And…there's more to it. Please don't ask me to tell you now, but I give you my word I will tell you everything once we get through this and get Verity back." He pictured the severe, eerily familiar face of Acantha Lennox, the twin sister he'd ashed to save Verity. How would Ian react to *that* revelation? He'd have to tell him, though. No more secrets. He was tired of secrets.

"Okay." His son's voice was soft in the dimness. "I get it, I guess. But like I said before, I'm going to hold you to that promise."

"You won't need to. If we all survive this, I *want* to tell you. You deserve to know everything." He slowed his pace. "We'd better be quiet now, though—I think we're getting close, and I don't—"

"Stop!" a female voice ordered from somewhere in the trees. "Don't move. You're surrounded."

CHAPTER THIRTY-TWO

STONE SPUN, RAISING HIS SHIELD. The voice had come from nearby, but he didn't see any sign of a human presence other than himself and Ian. Even shifting to magical sight didn't reveal them.

"Dad?" Ian's voice sounded strained behind him.

"Be ready," he murmured. "If we need to attack, hit hard and don't hold back."

Before he could do anything else, though, a figure stepped out of the trees in front of him. It was obviously a woman, clad in a dark-green cloak with a hood obscuring her face.

Stone raised a hand, gathering magical energy.

"Stop," the woman called. "We mean you no harm, Dr. Stone."

Ian moved up next to Stone, and glanced sharply at him.

"Keep your shield up," he whispered. "Let's hear them out." Louder, he called, "If you're planning to capture us, you might find that more difficult than you anticipated."

"We're not planning to capture you." The woman approached, but stopped a few feet away. "But there *are* several more of us hidden in the woods, so please don't use any offensive magic."

"Okay," Stone said. "So you're not planning to capture us. What *are* you planning to do?"

"We need to talk. Will you come with us?"

He snorted. "Do you think we're fools?"

"No. But we *do* think both you and your friend Verity are in danger. We can help, if you'll trust us. Something's going on here—something wrong."

Stone looked at Ian again, who shrugged. He shifted to magical sight once more and examined the woman's aura. It was jade green, a similar color to Verity's, and although it contained the obvious faint red flashes of nervous concern, he didn't spot any malevolent intent. "Where do you want to take us? We don't have a lot of time."

"We know. That's why we need to hurry—and we must go someplace where there's no chance we'll be overheard. Please—follow me, and remain quiet until I tell you it's safe to speak."

Stone wasn't sure about this, and he could tell Ian wasn't either. Nessa Lennox was devious—last time he'd come here, her druids had dosed his drink with a knockout drug—and he wouldn't put it past her to try another sneaky tactic. But on the other hand, this woman's aura seemed sincere. He was sure Ian was checking too, and Ian's auric sensitivity was even stronger than Verity's. If he wasn't raising warning bells, Stone was willing to trust her for the time being.

"Okay," he said at last. "But if I sense any funny business from any of you, you'll find out why that's a bad idea."

"No funny business, I promise." The woman looked around quickly. She seemed stressed, as if being out in the open made her nervous. "Come, please."

Stone and Ian followed her as she turned and disappeared back into the forest. Stone still didn't see any sign of the other women, and had no idea how many of them there were. It was possible the rest of them were mere illusions and their guide was alone, but he didn't think so. The Windermere druids knew these woods intimately, and probably had all sorts of tricks for concealing their presence while within them.

They were heading vaguely to the east, rather than north toward the center of the complex. Stone grew increasingly more concerned as he strode along behind the small, fast-moving woman. Were they leading him and Ian away from whatever was happening to Verity? He decided he would give them five more minutes, then stop and demand they take him where he wanted to go.

He didn't need to do that, though, because the woman only walked through the forest for a couple more minutes before stopping at a narrow, concealed path.

"Here," she said, pointing. "There's a clearing at the end of this path, and my associates and I have temporarily warded it so no one can overhear us. We can speak more clearly there."

Stone and Ian followed her down the path, which was barely wide enough for them to pass without brushing their shoulders against branches on both sides. It twisted a couple of times, turning first to the left, then to the right and down toward a large rock that obscured the area beyond.

The woman stepped around the rock, and Stone and Ian quickly followed before she could get away from them.

She didn't try, though. Instead, she stopped and indicated the area in front of her. "Welcome, both of you."

The clearing wasn't large—mostly circular and about twenty feet in diameter. Thick trees and underbrush surrounded it, and someone had carefully cleared the leaves and debris from the ground inside. A gray, stone object that resembled a glowing birdbath pulsed softly in the center. It didn't take special sight to tell it was strongly magical.

Stone took all this in quickly, but he was more interested in the six other hooded women who stood along the far side of the outer perimeter, all of them watching him and Ian. "What is this?" he demanded. It didn't look like a ritual, since nothing was drawn or carved on the ground around the pulsing object.

"Please," said another of the women. "Don't be concerned. The object in the center is designed to prevent eavesdropping, and to conceal our location from anyone who might happen by. It is necessary."

"Okay. Fine. Start talking. Who are you? Obviously you're connected with Nessa's little group, and obviously you know who I am. Not sure if you know why I'm here."

"You're here to get your friend back," the woman who'd led them here said. "You don't remember me, do you, Dr. Stone?" She threw back her hood to reveal a pale face framed with dark auburn hair. Her eyes, intense and dark, also looked a little amused.

Stone stared at her. He knew she looked familiar, though for a second he couldn't place where he'd seen her before. Then it clicked. "You're the woman who took us through the portal the first time we came here."

"Good memory! Yes, my name is Lila." She glanced at Ian. "I haven't met you, though."

"This is Ian," Stone said before his son could speak up. He didn't see any value in giving these women more information than they needed—at least not until he was sure of their motives. "If you know about my power, know that he's got nearly as much."

"That's good," Lila said grimly. "We're going to need it."

That wasn't what Stone had expected to hear. "What? Why? Where's Verity?"

"I'm right here," said a voice. The woman on the end pushed her hood back and stepped forward.

"Verity!" Stone and Ian yelled her name at the same time, neither making any effort to hide their relief. Ian strode forward, but Stone put out a hand to stop him.

"Wait! How can we be certain it's truly Verity? You people are masters of illusion."

Ian stopped, narrowed his eyes, and peered at Verity for several seconds. "It's really her. No illusion."

"Yeah, it's really me." Verity had been smiling, but now she looked as grim as the others. "Thanks for coming to rescue me, but as you can see, we've already got that covered."

Stone likewise made no effort to hide his confusion. "I think you lot had better start talking."

"No kidding," Ian said. He glared at Verity. "Did you ditch me?" He pointed at the other women. "Is one of you the woman we met with?"

"No," Lila said, bowing her head. "Verity didn't ditch you, and the woman you met with isn't among us here. That was Meara, and she's in trouble. We couldn't get to her before they took her."

"Took her? *Who* took her?" Stone shot a glare around the whole group. "Somebody start talking. Now."

"Yes," Lila said. "We don't have a lot of time, but we'll tell you as much as we can." She began pacing around the clearing as the other hooded women backed off. "As I'm sure you know, all of us here except Verity are part of the same group you encountered several years ago. Some of these women are newer members, so they weren't here…before."

Stone almost said something, but didn't.

"After…the events back then, our lives returned mostly to our usual pursuits—magical study, helping the magical and mundane communities in the area, alchemy. We didn't bother anyone else and they didn't bother us. Madame Nessa went into seclusion for a while, but eventually she emerged and took her place as our leader once more."

"Brilliant," Stone muttered. Part of him still regretted he hadn't killed the old witch when he'd had the chance.

"I know you don't approve of some of our pursuits, Dr. Stone, and I don't blame you for that. But I give you my word that our activities since then have been benign. Until recently."

Her tension increased, and she snatched more glances around as if expecting an ambushing force to pour in. "Over the past few months, Madame Nessa has begun acting…odd. She traveled more than usual, and when she was here, she sequestered herself away with a few senior members of our group. Some of us began to believe she was working on a new project—one she didn't want the rest of the membership to know about."

"What a surprise." Stone couldn't help it. His mouth acted before his brain could stop it. "She is barking mad, after all."

Lila didn't react to his sarcastic words. In fact, she bowed her head. "She wasn't—not before. Even…what happened with you and Verity before had its reasons."

"Let's not go there," Stone growled.

"Of course not. But what I'm leading up to is that several of us—especially some of the younger and newer members—began to think Madame Nessa might have developed…some sort of obsession. But none of us could get close enough to her to figure out what it was. Until a few weeks ago."

"What happened then?" Ian asked. He was switching his gaze between Stone, Lila, and Verity.

Verity remained silent and still. She'd obviously already heard this story.

"One of our number happened to overhear her speaking to someone in her private chamber. Another woman, but one she didn't recognize. What she overheard shocked her." She turned haunted eyes on Stone. "She was discussing necromancy, Dr. Stone."

"That doesn't surprise me either. That's what your associate—the one who contacted us—told me. That she knew we were looking for someone, and that she might know where this person is."

Lila nodded. "I don't understand all of it. The person Madame Nessa met with—the necromancer—was a woman. We didn't get her name, but we're certain that was what they were talking about."

"But wait," Stone said. "You people are druids. I'm not that familiar with your magical style, but I *do* know you abhor even the *concept* of necromancy. The thought that some of you might be considering *practicing* it—"

"Grief can do terrible things, Alastair," Verity said softly.

He jerked his head up. "Grief? Grief over who? Did someone else die? I didn't think that old bat *had* anyone close to her anymore."

Lila didn't take offense at his words. "To understand that, you have to understand some of the magic we've been working on here. It's something the senior members of our group have spent a great deal of time focusing on, and they've managed to perfect part of it—to an extent, at least."

"What are you talking about?" Stone was still feeling the pressure to act. Having Verity here lessened it somewhat, but if Brathwaite was also here, he still had a job to do. He didn't want to lose the necromancer again.

"I'm talking about a magical technique designed to capture a person's echo and store it in a form of stasis." Lila's voice shook a little as she said it.

"*What?*" Stone glared at her. "That's impossible."

Lila didn't look at him. "The technique is experimental, and our study of it was limited because, believe it or not, we *do* try to be ethical in our methods. We weren't willing to kill anyone to test it. The research suggested it would be much more likely to work properly on someone with a high magical potential. So we put it in place and prepared to use it if an opportunity should ever present itself. Once, several years ago, they tried it on one of our older members—a volunteer suffering from an incurable and terminal disease—but it failed. Madame Nessa began to lose hope that it would ever work at all, but still she and her inner circle continued experimenting."

Stone glanced at Verity. *She* wasn't looking at him either. A faint knot began to form in his stomach.

"And then, a year later, another opportunity arose," Lila continued. "Although Madame Nessa and the others weren't thinking about it at the time. They had…other things on their minds."

The knot in Stone's stomach began to burn. A faint, horrifying thought was forming, but he refused to accept it. He had to be wrong.

He had to be.

Even his mad grandmother wouldn't go *there*.

Lila took a deep, shuddering breath. "It wasn't until several days later that Madame Nessa remembered what she and the others had set up. They thought it must have been destroyed, along with the chamber, when…" She waved vaguely, but didn't finish the sentence.

"Oh, bloody hell…" Stone murmured. "Are you saying what I think you're saying? Verity?"

Verity nodded miserably. "That's what they told me."

"Wait," Ian protested. "What the hell is going on? Does everybody here know what's happening except me?"

Stone sympathized with him. He'd felt the same way a few years ago when some of these revelations had been dropped on him. When he spoke, it was in a lifeless monotone. "I think we do, Ian. If I'm understanding these people correctly, anyway. It's another part of our sordid family history I never told you, because I never thought it would be relevant. But it's beginning to appear that it might be again."

"Family history?" Lila asked, shifting her gaze to Ian.

"Ian is my son," Stone said in the same dead tone. "And Ian—I think what they're trying to say without saying it is that my mad old grandmother somehow managed to collect the echo—the *soul*—of the twin sister I ashed to save Verity's life."

Ian's eyes got huge, and his mouth dropped open, but Stone barely noticed because the other piece had just fallen into place. He took a staggering step back and nearly fell before he managed to right himself.

"No…" he whispered. "That's why she's contacted Brathwaite, isn't it? Because she *had* Acantha's soul, but she couldn't *do* anything with it." He turned a burning gaze on Lila. "She's working with him to try to return Acantha's echo to a human body, isn't she?"

Lila didn't answer, but Verity did. "Yes. And that's where Meara is now. That's why they grabbed us, Alastair. Meara was on the level—she was trying to warn us. She'd heard from one of Nana's network that you were looking for Brathwaite. But somebody from Nessa's circle found out about it and followed her. When they saw the two of us head to the bathroom together, they took their chance. They used an alchemical mixture to scramble our minds, and an illusion to get us away from there before Ian caught on."

Stone's brain felt like it had been put through a blender. "But— you—"

"They were originally only going to take Meara," Verity said gently. "They felt she was a traitor, so that made it all right to steal her body. But when they found the two of us together, they figured they'd bring us both—you know, give Acantha a choice." Her expression hardened. "Apparently, she picked Meara. I don't know, I was unconscious at the time. But when I woke up, my guard helped me get away. She told me Brathwaite had ordered me held prisoner."

Stone's stomach knot clenched harder. He almost didn't want to consider the thought of what the necromancer had planned.

Verity nodded as if he'd answered. "She didn't say why—I don't think she knew. But I'm sure that was what he wanted—once the ritual to return Acantha's echo was done, he wanted to take me and…do what he did to Sharra." Her voice caught, both with grief and with rage.

"No…" Stone whispered.

Lila spoke then. "I don't know what you're talking about specifically, but we—many of us—refused to be part of this any longer. We don't know if Madame Nessa has gone mad with grief and is grasping at any straw that might return her granddaughter to her, or if this Brathwaite person has somehow wormed her way—" She tilted her head. "Wait. You called Brathwaite 'him.' But the person Madame Nessa is working with is a woman."

"Long story," Stone said numbly. "Brathwaite has a lot of experience transplanting echoes into other bodies. He's really a male master necromancer who died almost two hundred years ago, but his echo managed to stick around, tied to his body in a sarcophagus. When the sarcophagus was opened a few years ago, his echo escaped. He searched for a distant descendant to inhabit, but the only one he could find was a woman named Miriam Padgett."

Lila stared at him in shock. "This is worse than we ever imagined."

"Yes." With effort, he gathered himself. He still had a job to do—two of them, now, since he had no intention of allowing his grandmother to transplant his twin sister's echo into another body. "I think that's enough to be getting on with, but now we've got to go. I'm going to kill Brathwaite, with or without your assistance,"

"Not if I get him first," Verity growled. She turned to Lila. "Thank you for getting me out of there. But he's right—we need to do this. Brathwaite did something horrible to one of my best friends, and I've been waiting a long time to make him pay for it. Will you help us?"

Lila looked at the other women, most of whom were still hooded. All of them inclined their heads. "Yes," she said. "We'll help. Meara is our friend and sister, too. We don't know what this Brathwaite person has done to Madame Nessa—or worse yet, if she's doing this of her own accord—but even allowing a necromancer access to our lands goes against everything we believe in.

We've got to move fast, though. They've already started the ritual, and I don't know how far along they are."

"Why now?" Stone asked. "It seems a bit coincidental that they're doing this right when we've shown up, doesn't it?"

Lila shook her head soberly. "Brathwaite had wanted to start sooner, but Nessa hesitated. We think she'd convinced one of her inner circle to volunteer for the good of the cause, but she didn't want to use someone that old—or one of her close friends—to house her granddaughter's echo."

"So she waited until Meara quote-unquote 'betrayed' her," Ian said. He looked as grim as Stone had ever seen him.

"And when Verity presented herself," Stone added, "she decided the time was right."

"Exactly," Lila said.

"Okay—then you're right. We've got to move." He glared at the women. "I want you all to understand something, though, before we go: I am *going* to kill Brathwaite. I won't allow him to leave this place alive. Is everyone clear with that? If you try to interfere, it won't go well for you."

Lila held his glare, but her face remained calm. "We don't care what you do with Brathwaite, Dr. Stone. He is a necromancer, which is abhorrent to every one of us. The world is better off without him." She took a deep breath. "But I ask something in exchange for our help, because I promise you—you'll never make it to the chamber where the ritual is being held without either being killed, captured, or misdirected to the point where you'll have no hope of finding it."

Stone was afraid he knew where this was going. "What?"

"Please—don't kill Madame Nessa."

His eyes widened. "You…*want* this noxious old woman alive?"

"Believe it nor not, she's not noxious. Normally, she's kind and intelligent and intense, and without a doubt the most powerful and knowledgeable practitioner among us. She has done a lot of good.

You saw her at her worst—as you are now. As Verity mentioned before, grief can drive even the strongest and most honorable person to…unwise choices. Don't get me wrong—I don't agree with what she's doing. None of us do. But we will deal with her in our own way."

Stone could hardly believe what the woman was saying. After what Nessa Lennox had done to him—after she'd indirectly caused the deaths of his father and his master, not to mention orchestrating a mad plan to increase his magical potential before he was born so he could be used as a sacrifice to summon some great elder god—he couldn't imagine anyone thinking of her as "kind" or "honorable."

But he also knew Lila was right. The druids of Windermere were a powerful lot even without Nessa, and their complex was designed to confuse and deter any unwelcome visitors from locating their secrets. Without the women's help, even if they managed to burn down everything between here and the center of the complex, they wouldn't be able to do it before Brathwaite slipped away.

"Fine," he said, and it came out as a grudging rasp. "As long as she leaves me alone, I'll leave her alone. If she tries to kill me or Ian or Verity, though, all bets are off."

"Of course. I don't think she will. She definitely bears no ill will against Verity, and if I'm correct, she isn't even aware of Ian. You…might be another story, though."

"Because I killed Acantha."

"Yes. Her grief has done nothing but grow and fester over the years, and she does consider you responsible. So I can't honestly say what she will do if she sees you."

"We'll just have to find out, won't we?" Stone drew a deep breath. "Let's go. Are you certain the ritual has already begun?"

"No, but I strongly suspect it has. Madame Nessa has been working with Brathwaite for a while, so most of the preparations have been in place for some time. Only the specific alterations for Meara were needed."

"Come on, then." Stone was impatient to leave. His highest priority was finding Brathwaite before he got wind they were on to him or that Verity had been released from captivity and did a runner, but if he could stop the ritual before it completed, that would be a bonus.

You're not even sure it will work, he reminded himself. But that, too, was irrelevant right now. He started for the edge of the clearing.

Lila raised her hands. "Wait, please. We need to prepare."

"We haven't got time for—"

"This won't take long." She indicated for one of the women to come forward.

The woman crouched near another large rock and rose carrying a bundle of dark-green fabric, which she brought over.

Lila took it from her, separating it into two long, hooded cloaks, which she handed to Stone and Ian. "Put these on. They're enchanted to adjust to fit you."

Stone eyed his dubiously, running his hands over its soft, light fabric. "If you're trying to use these to disguise us as two of your group, I think our height is going to cause a problem."

"This is only the first component of the disguise. I am sure both of you are skilled in illusions, right?"

"Of course."

"Good. You'll use illusion to appear as women, so if anyone stops us and wants to see our faces, you won't betray yourself. Three of our number will remain behind, and you'll assume their appearances."

"What about the wards? You said they were tuned to prevent unauthorized intruders."

"Yes." She indicated the women again, and two of them removed the pins that held their cloaks closed. "You'll wear these—

they're enchanted to allow passage through the wards all around the complex. There are too many of us to alter the wards themselves to accept us all without some way to separate the authorized from the unauthorized."

Stone shifted to magical sight and examined the object. It was a small triangular brooch with rounded corners. It depicted a wide-trunked tree in gold with bare, reaching branches over a green background, with a darker green gem at the point where the trunk spread out into the branches. The whole thing radiated strong magic.

"Nice trick." He made a mental note to reverse-engineer the concept so he could build something similar for Jason and his family to use. "This will get us through the wards?"

"Through everything but the entrance to the main ritual chamber. That, you'll be on your own for. But I think between the three of you your power is sufficient, given what happened last time you were in there." Her faint smile was wry, but also sad.

"Let them try to keep us out." He donned the cloak, pulled it around him and fastened it with the brooch. "This is all very *Lord of the Rings,* isn't it?"

"Trust me," Lila said, her smile fading. "We might have a lot of trees, but this place is no Lothlórien."

CHAPTER THIRTY-THREE

STONE HAD FORGOTTEN how large the Windermere complex was. He dropped back with Ian and Verity as Lila and two of the other hooded druids led them along a series of narrow, winding paths in a generally northwestern direction. Overhead, the tree branches grew so densely that they almost obscured the dark, overcast sky.

"So they just…let you out?" he whispered to Verity. "They took you prisoner, but then didn't hold you?"

"Yes." Her face wasn't visible inside the large hood, but her voice sounded troubled. "That's what they told me. Like I said before, I was unconscious for most of the time. They must have brought me through a portal—I'm sure they have a private one in London somewhere."

"I still can't believe they sneaked you past me," Ian said, disgusted. "They played me."

"They didn't, though." Now Verity spoke more gently. "Don't feel bad about it, Ian. Remember, Meara was on the level. She didn't have any ulterior motives. All she wanted to do was warn us—originally warn Alastair—about Brathwaite. So there wouldn't have been anything for you to pick up on. The only reason she was nervous was because she was afraid someone might be watching us."

"And they were." He still didn't sound happy. "I just let you two go off alone. I should have followed you."

"Into the bathroom?" Verity chuckled. "That's a little creepy, Ian."

"I could have waited outside, not sat around on my ass for ten minutes expecting you to come back."

"Maybe, but even *that* might have been creepy. The people who took us were well coordinated. They had us out of there before you even realized anything was wrong. Seriously, Ian, don't feel bad about it. It's all good now."

"Let's get back to why they let you out," Stone said. "What happened when you were here?"

She increased her pace a little to move up next to him. "When I woke up, I was in a cell, being guarded by a couple of women. They'd used their anti-magic concoction on me—"

"Wait, what?" Ian demanded. "Anti-magic concoction?"

"It's a very specialized alchemical mixture. They need the blood of the recipient to make it work, so it's not just a generic thing." She glanced at Stone. "Anyway, since we were here last, they developed an antidote to it—or else they're admitting to it now. When my guards changed, Lila was one of the new ones. She and her people sneaked me out and gave me the antidote, and left two more of their people at the cell—one disguised as me, and the other one acting as a guard."

"Bloody hell…" Stone murmured. "This is a fairly wide-reaching conspiracy, then."

"A lot of us are worried about Madame Nessa," Lila said. "And very unhappy about the use of necromancy on our sacred lands. But it's still a small subset of the group, and that's part of why we need to hurry. If our people at the cell are caught, it won't go well for them."

"Not to mention they'll know I've escaped," Verity added. She walked in silence for a few seconds, then shuddered. "I'm trying not to think about what might have happened if Lila and her people hadn't gotten me out of there."

"Yes. If Nessa agreed to *that,* then there's no way I can ever see her as 'kind.'" He raised his voice a little so Lila and the others could hear.

"I know," Lila said. "I'm trying to get my mind around it too, based on my experiences with Madame Nessa. I'm honestly not sure she's in her right mind at the moment, though whether that's temporary or permanent isn't for me to say."

"Well, if I've got anything to say about it," Stone said, "she's not getting her granddaughter back. Not if it means stealing someone's body to stuff her echo into. It's bad enough she's trying to do it at all, but…no. That's unacceptable."

"I just hope we get there in time," Ian said. "This is taking forever."

"We have to go carefully." Lila didn't sound any happier about it than he did. "We've already passed several checkpoints that would have alerted the wrong people if you weren't with us and wearing those amulets. If we try moving too fast, we could lose everything."

Stone had been watching her while she spoke, and saw no sign of a lie or misdirection. He exchanged glances with Ian and Verity, both of whom shook their heads. They hadn't either. As far as all of them knew, Lila and her band of dissidents were on the level. He hoped they were right, since they were staking their lives on their certainty.

They walked for a few more minutes, then Lila stopped and held up a hand. "We're getting close now," she whispered. "Stay quiet."

An unpleasant crawling sensation scuttled up Stone's back as the memories returned. This was the part of the complex that had been included in the tour Nessa's people had given him and Verity when Verity was considering studying with the druids. Not far ahead would be the hidden entrance to the underground chamber where everything had gone down all those years ago—when Nessa and her druids had attempted to force him and Verity to conceive a child for them to use as a sacrifice in their desperate ritual.

He glanced at Verity. It was hard to tell what she was feeling since the cloak and hood covered most of her body, but when he switched to magical sight he didn't miss the uneasy red flashes in her jade-green aura. He was certain she had the same things on her mind as he did.

He increased his speed to catch up with Lila, who was moving slowly. "How many of them do we expect to find in there?" he whispered to her. "Do you have any idea what we're facing?"

"Not really, unfortunately. My best guess is that about a third of our number are still supporting Madame Nessa, which means there could be as many as twenty in there—not including anyone Brathwaite brought with her…uh…him. That would be a tight fit, though, and Madame Nessa has to have some of her people on guard." She pointed. "Here's the way into the chamber."

Stone wouldn't have noticed it if she hadn't indicated it. Tree limbs and bushes grew over it in such a way that it was almost impossible to see, and he suspected there might be some illusion involved as well. When they moved past the greenery, the space opened onto a narrow entrance carved into the hillside, completely hidden from the path.

What he did notice, though, was that Lila hesitated at the entrance. "Is there a problem?"

She didn't reply for a moment. When she finally spoke, her tone was heavy. "I'll be honest with you, Dr. Stone—I don't want to go in there. I don't want to take my people in there."

That didn't surprise him; in fact, he'd almost expected it. "You don't want to risk hurting your own people," he said gently.

She nodded reluctantly. "I don't want you to think we're deserting you, or that we've somehow led you into a trap. But…"

"It's okay," Verity said, coming up alongside her and closing a hand over her shoulder. "We understand, Lila. Believe me, I'm grateful for everything you and the others have done. I think we can handle this from here."

Lila looked relieved. "We're not combat-trained anyway, so we won't be much help. The good news is, most of those likely to be inside aren't, either. We're scholars, healers, and alchemists, not fighters." She gazed hard into Stone's eyes. "Please, Dr. Stone—don't kill anyone if you don't have to. Except Brathwaite, of course. Most of them really are good people who only want to do the right thing. Their only crime is that they're too loyal to Madame Nessa."

Stone couldn't promise that, so he settled for a noncommittal noise.

"We'll do our best," Verity said.

Ian remained silent and watchful, turning to look back the way they'd come, then forward toward the passage opening.

"We'll watch the ways in," Lila said. "We'll make sure nobody else comes in. There are two other hidden entrances, so I'll send my people to guard them as well. At least you'll only need to deal with the people already inside."

"Thank you." Stone's heart was beating faster now, partly in fear and partly in anticipation. Brathwaite was in there, within his grasp. He wasn't going to escape this time. He—

A low rumble, like a minor earthquake, rippled through the ground beneath their feet. From somewhere deep within the passageway, a faint light flashed as if a lightning bolt had gone off inside.

"What was that?" Ian demanded. He raised his hands, flowering magical energy around them.

"Oh no…" Lila swallowed hard. "I think we might be too late."

"Too late?" Stone grabbed her shoulders. "Too late for what?"

"For the ritual. I think they've completed it."

Stone exchanged horrified glances with Verity and Ian. "You mean they've already—"

"Completed the transfer." Lila nodded. "Assuming it even worked correctly, of course. There's no guarantee it did."

"We've got to go, then." Stone's heart was pounding now. If the ritual was complete, that meant Brathwaite would send someone for Verity—or he'd escape through one of the other exits. Regardless of what they were doing in there, he wasn't going to let that happen. "Anything else we need to know, Lila?"

"No." Lila looked miserable. "The amulets will get you through the wards. It's not far down the passageway—just down the steps and past the curve. Good luck."

Stone didn't wait to reply. His single-minded focus was now on getting down that passageway as quickly as possible, before anyone figured out they were there. If he and the others could hit Brathwaite fast and hard, they could take him out before he even saw them coming.

"Focus on Brathwaite," he hissed over his shoulder as he moved. "Everything you've got. Do *not* hold back, and don't let him escape. He dies today."

"Damn right he does." Verity's tone was every bit as implacable as his.

The path led them down via series of rough-carved stone steps. As they reached the bend in the passageway, they heard more sounds coming from the chamber beyond: a combination of a low hum, a faint rumble, and a toneless chant. Green light pulsed in a slow rhythm. Stone crept around the corner, feeling a nearly imperceptible buzz—the last ward, which their tree amulets allowed them to pass harmlessly through.

He stopped, holding up a hand for Verity and Ian to stop behind him.

The chamber was familiar—it was the same one where Nessa and her druids had staged the previous ritual. Obviously, they'd repaired it in the seven years since he and Verity had been here last. It made sense—he hadn't brought the whole place down, and they undoubtedly had earth witches who could manipulate living rock among their number.

The area was roughly circular, fifty feet in diameter, rising so high the ceiling was lost in dimness. As before, some kind of phosphorescent moss covered the walls, along with climbing vines. Sigils and symbols were carved into the spaces between them, creating an interlocking design. Glowing sconces placed at intervals provided more illumination.

All this was as Stone remembered—but the circle in the center was not. Before, it had been a beautiful thing, incorporating more of the green vines and creating a space consecrated to life, to creation, to beginnings.

Now, though, everything about the structure in the middle of the room made him uneasy. The vines were still there, but now they were gray and dead, writhing like snakes to create the perimeter of the circle. The candles on poles around its edge flickered with eerie colors, and the intricate symbols on the floor seemed to crawl of their own accord.

In the center of the circle were two carved wooden pedestals. The first, human-sized, held the robed body of Meara, the woman who'd met Verity and Ian in London. Her eyes were closed; she appeared either sleeping or unconscious. Or possibly dead.

The second pedestal was smaller, and held a glass globe on a stand. The globe measured a foot in diameter, and appeared gray and clouded. The top was shattered. It looked to Stone like a spent ritual component—or the milky eye of a long-dead corpse.

The only other things he spotted, before his gaze settled on the triumphant, scarlet-robed form of James Brathwaite/Miriam Padgett standing in the circle on the other side of the platforms, were Nessa Lennox seated in a thronelike wooden chair near the rear wall, the series of cloaked and hooded figures ringing the room—and three more hulking forms, gray and silent, each one standing near one of the room's three entrances.

Rage filled Stone. He had no idea if the ritual had succeeded, and he didn't care. He had eyes only for Brathwaite. "Go!" he rasped, already pulling in Calanarian power. He slipped around the figure guarding their entrance, pointed his hands, and released the power.

Brathwaite actually showed surprise—for a couple of seconds. Then his thin lips split into a wide smile as the energy reached him and dissipated harmlessly off an invisible shield surrounding him. He did stagger back two steps, but caught himself quickly and regained his footing.

"Ah," he purred. "Dr. Stone is here, and he's brought some friends. Good. The more the merrier."

Stone didn't stop. Behind him, Verity and Ian didn't either. Their attacks—three powerful beams aimed at the center of Brathwaite's body—hit him and once again bounced off.

"What is going on?" Ian demanded. "How is he—"

But Stone had caught on. "It's not just him," he said through his teeth. "It's all of them. This is their home ground. They're protecting him." He risked a quick glance at his grandmother, who still sat serenely on her throne. "Why would you *do* this, Nessa? Why would you welcome a *necromancer* into your sanctum? I know you're mad, but this is—" He couldn't even think of a strong enough way to finish the sentence.

"This is none of your business, Alastair." She still sounded calm, but her anger was clearly growing. "You have no place here. You murdered my dear Acantha, and now she will be returned to me. If you interfere, I will kill all of you."

Verity and Ian were still aiming attacks at Brathwaite, but now his three undead creatures were taking action. The one nearest them raised its massive fists and slammed them down on to Ian's shield, staggering the young man with psychic feedback.

A flicker of movement caught Stone's eye. He risked another look, this time at the center of the circle. Meara had stirred. As he continued to watch, she rose to a sitting position and her eyes flickered open.

Stone had never met Meara before, but that didn't matter. He would have staked his entire fortune that the consciousness looking out from her eyes was no longer hers.

The cold, mocking gaze and the small, triumphant smile belonged to someone else entirely.

Acantha Lennox—his twin sister.

The one he'd ashed all those years ago.

Against all possible odds, Brathwaite's ritual had succeeded in returning her echo to a physical body.

Nessa let out a high, keening shriek of triumph. "Protect her!" she screamed. "Get her out of here and protect her at all costs!"

Instantly, three of the cloaked figures broke from their positions along the walls and hurried into the circle to hustle the woman off the platform.

Stone ignored them. Acantha wasn't his concern right now—not until Brathwaite was safely dead.

"No!" Brathwaite boomed. "No one leaves here until Stone and the others are captured!"

"Ignore her!" Nessa yelled, just as loudly. "Get Acantha away!"

The good news was, Nessa's people were clearly more loyal to her than they were to Brathwaite. Two more of them hurried toward the circle, shifting their focus to protecting the newly-transplanted Acantha, which took some of the potency from Brathwaite's shield.

The bad news was that one of his other undead creatures had planted itself in front of the far-side exit, blocking the women's path, while the other creature joined the third to attack Stone, Verity, and Ian.

Stone could see right away that these were no garden-variety zombies. Large and broad-shouldered, they all stood half a head taller than Stone and nearly twice as wide. Their fists, the size of canned hams, battered against his shield, sending bright lances of pain into his head with each one. He didn't know how many of them he could take, but he didn't think it was many.

"Get some height!" he yelled to Verity and Ian. "They hit hard, but they can't fly!" He ducked to the side, narrowly escaping another pummeling blow from the nearest zombie, and launched himself into the air. Ignoring the pain in his head, he continued channeling pure Calanarian energy at Brathwaite.

Nessa Lennox was no longer paying any attention to them. She had risen from her throne, leaning heavily on her walking stick but now facing the far door. "Get her out!" she screamed. She waved her free hand and some of the vines along the walls began to move, reaching out to wrap their thick tendrils around the zombie and try to pull it away from the opening. Acantha's escorts formed ranks around her, trying to find a way past the blockage without attacking directly.

"Help me, you fool!" Brathwaite was screaming. "Your people let the bitch get away! She is *mine*! All three of them are mine! That was our deal!"

"I made no such deal!" Nessa boomed. "You were only to take the woman!"

Brathwaite's face was twisted into rage now. "I will take them all, and you won't stop me. You have your granddaughter, as promised. Defy me and I'll have my servants kill her as well!"

As if to punctuate his words, the zombie ripped the vines loose as if they were barely an impediment, and lunged toward the women protecting Acantha. It grabbed hold of the closest woman's arm, pulling her in close before anyone could stop it and clasping its arms around her chest. Everyone present heard the loud *crack* as her ribcage broke, and her piercing, agonized scream. The zombie threw her body aside as if she were trash.

By now, Verity and Ian were both in the air too. They both looked shaken from the zombies' attacks, but they were still focusing their attacks on Brathwaite as well. His shield had weakened without support from all the women, but the zombies, apparently smarter than the ones they'd dealt with before, now began snatching up the metal poles holding the candles and flinging them like javelins at the floating mages.

Stone snatched another look at Nessa, and what he saw shocked him. Her eyes burned with every bit of the rage in Brathwaite's—but now it wasn't directed at Stone and his allies.

She was looking straight at Brathwaite.

Behind him, Ian screamed.

Stone spun in the air and his breath caught in his throat. One of the zombies' javelins had pierced his son's shield, powering through and embedding itself in Ian's side. Ian's scream cut off abruptly and he fell, saved a hard fall only by Verity's quick-thinking telekinetic assist.

This wasn't good. Ian wasn't unconscious—in fact, he was still doing his best to use concussion magic to send the nearest zombie flying—but he wasn't at his full strength. Verity was still aloft, sending punishing power from both hands at the zombies, but she couldn't last forever either. None of them could. Brathwaite had definitely improved his undead servants over the last three years, and these were even better than the ones they'd fought recently. Probably his personal guard.

Panting, Stone used a concussion blast to barely divert another javelin from hitting him. It slammed into the wall hard enough to drive its point several inches in. The zombies' strength was astonishing.

He jerked his head around again, taking in the room. Ian was still down. Verity was faltering. The women still hadn't succeeded in getting the newly-born Acantha past the third zombie and out of the room despite Nessa's onslaught of magic.

And Brathwaite was moving toward the fallen Ian. He had a new spell up now—in addition to his weakened shield, he'd now created four illusionary copies of himself. Stone quickly switched to magical sight, but it didn't help. So much magic was flying around inside the room that between the powerful aura of the chamber itself, Brathwaite's necromantic "enhancements" to it, and the magic surrounding the people in the room, he couldn't pick out which one was really the necromancer—if any of them at all were.

Stone chanced another glance at Nessa. She was fully focused on the far door now, but he thought he saw something in her face that hadn't been there.

Indecision.

Regret.

He acted without thinking, booming his voice out into the chamber from his position high above the action. "Nessa! Ian is your great-grandson! Do you want to let this vile monster kill your own blood?"

The old woman jerked her head up. Her gaze burned into Stone, and the indecision changed first to shock, then to rage. She spun, barely seeming to need her walking stick, and pointed her hand at the flock of Brathwaites that had surrounded the fallen Ian.

Instantly, one of them began to glow, limned all the way around with crackling, bright-green energy. It had bent, reaching its hands toward Ian's neck, only inches away.

Stone knew this was likely the last chance he was going to get before the slippery necromancer figured out what was happening and either got his bearings or found a way to escape. "*VERITY!*" he screamed. "*Now!*"

The two of them must have been of one mind. She spun around at his voice, using magic to grab another of the metal candleholders from the center of the circle. Stone yanked out the one the zombie had flung at him earlier.

Together, they gathered every ounce of magical energy left in their bodies and, like a precision drill team, rocketed the two poles toward Brathwaite.

Stone's powered through the remains of the necromancer's shield and pierced his head, going in through the back and out the front, stopping scant inches from Ian's weakened shield.

Verity's pierced the center of his back and likewise continued through.

Brathwaite shrieked in agony, flinging himself backward, but the pair of spears stopped him from going over. He slipped, flailed, and then fell, crashing on his side to the ground, blood pouring from his twin mortal wounds.

Stone, panting, dropped back to the ground, preparing to turn Brathwaite over and verify that he was dead. Before he could do it, another voice cried, "*Destroy the echo!*"

Nessa.

Stone didn't hesitate. He snapped to magical sight in time to see a faintly-glowing puff of arcane energy emerging from Brathwaite's twitching body. Roaring with rage, he gathered the last of his power and surrounded the puff, engulfing it. The prison shrank smaller and smaller until, with a psychic scream of pure hatred, the puff winked out.

Stone dropped to his knees, panting and spent. If Nessa's people wanted to take him out now, he'd have no defense.

But they didn't. At Brathwaite's death, the zombies, deprived of the force providing their orders, simply stopped moving.

The women trying to hustle Meara/Acantha out of the room likewise stopped, still surrounding her but turning uncertainly back toward where Nessa stood as if awaiting orders.

Verity staggered over to Stone and helped him up, and the two of them hurried to Ian.

"I'm—okay—" he muttered through gritted teeth, trying to rise.

"Enough of that," Stone ordered. The spear had pierced his son's side, but his powerful shield had stopped most of its momentum so it hadn't gone in very far. "Verity—can you—"

"We'll help too," said a firm voice from the far side of the room. Lila and several of her people entered from all three sides, ignoring Nessa and hurrying over to cluster around Ian. "We've got this," she told Verity gently. "He'll be fine. This is what we're good at."

That left Stone and Verity to stand and face Nessa.

With dignity, she lowered herself back into her wooden throne. Two of her women immediately flanked her, taking up protective positions on either side.

"My great-grandson," she intoned, looking at where the other women were working on healing Ian.

"Yes," Stone said. "As reluctant as I am to say this, I've got to thank you. Your spell quite likely made the difference that let us succeed. But I have to ask you why. You certainly don't care about my line, do you?"

"I do not," she admitted. "But I do care about Acantha—and I do care about keeping my word. That vile person—" She waved a contemptuous hand toward the remains of Brathwaite "—broke her word to me. She promised to return my granddaughter to me, at the cost of providing one of my people in exchange."

"You were going to give him one of your own people?" Verity demanded, her voice shaking with rage. "Like you sacrificed Meara to get Acantha back?"

"Meara betrayed us," Nessa said dismissively. "She sealed her own fate."

"And what about *me*? You were going to hand me over to him in place of one of your other women." Verity took a step forward, and immediately the two guardians did too. "Do you even *know* what he had planned for me?"

Nessa didn't reply.

"You *don't,* do you?" Verity's eyes widened with astonishment, but then the rage was back. "You were so blinded by the chance to get Acantha back that you didn't even consider what you were selling out to. Do you know what he did to my friend?"

"You call her 'he.' Why?"

"Oh, I don't know," Stone said, his voice dripping with sarcasm. "Maybe because you couldn't be arsed to figure out that he was nothing but a two-hundred-year-old echo squatting in a body he stole? You're slipping, Nessa. I'll bet you didn't even *check,* did you? *That* is what you trusted to bring you back your granddaughter."

"And he did it," said another voice from the other side. Meara—Acantha now—stepped forward, aiming a challenging, shrewd glare at Stone. "He did it, *brother.* You killed me, and he brought me back. So who do you *think* Grandmother should trust?"

Oddly, though, Nessa was looking less certain.

Verity went in for the kill. "I'll tell you what he planned to do with me. Because he did it before, to a dear friend of mine. That's why I had to help Alastair kill him. He kills mages and turns him into those…*things.*" She pointed at one of the motionless zombies. "Only they *know* what they are…and what they were. *That's* what he would have done to me—and Ian, and Alastair—if you'd let him have us."

Nessa's eyes were hard, but she swallowed uncomfortably and her hand shook on the knob of her walking stick.

Acantha started to say something else, but Nessa raised her hand.

"Enough," she said. "This is over now. My Acantha is returned to me. Unless you plan to try to murder me—or her—in cold blood, which I warn you might be more difficult than you suspect, especially since you are all exhausted, I suggest you leave here now. And take *that* with you," she added, pointing at Brathwaite's body.

Stone didn't want to do it. His every instinct was urging him to take his best shot at killing both his grandmother and his newly-resurrected twin sister. But he knew Nessa was right. He was exhausted, and so was Verity. Ian would be weak from blood loss even after the druids healed him. Even though *he* would almost certainly emerge from a fight alive, he couldn't be so sure about his companions. Plus, now that Brathwaite was dead, he had no idea which side Lila and her dissidents would come down upon.

"Fine," he rasped. A thought occurred to him as he glanced at Acantha. Even though he'd never seen Meara before, he was still convinced those who had known her in life would barely recognize her anymore. "But before I go—is he truly dead? There's no chance your diabolical ritual, or device, or whatever, has captured his echo?"

Nessa actually shuddered. "No chance. I know you have good reason not to trust my word, but in this case you can be safe in doing so. Even if it had managed to capture his echo before you destroyed it, I would not have allowed it to remain viable. I have done what I had to, to return my granddaughter to me. But there will be no more."

Stone held her gaze for a few more seconds. He did believe her, though, much as he didn't want to. He nodded once. "Okay. But this isn't over. Stay away from me and the people I care about, and I'll do the same. Otherwise…"

Nessa's smile was both knowing and mocking at the same time. "Go ahead and posture, grandson, to make yourself look strong. I expect it of men. Now go. I believe you know the way to our portal. You needn't bother to return the brooches—we will be recalibrating our wards as soon as you have left our domain."

Stone hated this. He didn't want to leave her like this, but sometimes even the powerful had to make choices they didn't like. He bent and pulled Ian up, draping his son's arm over his shoulder. "Come on. I'm sick of this place. And I've got somewhere I need to be."

Verity removed her cloak and tossed it over Brathwaite's broken body. Then she grimly used a levitation spell to lift it, still pierced by the two candle-stands, and float it along next to her as they exited the chamber.

Stone looked back over his shoulder once before they left. Nessa still sat on her thronelike chair, watching them with a steady, ice-chip gaze. Next to her, Acantha had taken the place of one of the two guardians. She met Stone's eyes for a brief moment, and gave him a sly, knowing smile.

Stone pointedly turned his back on her. "Let's get the hell out of here."

CHAPTER THIRTY-FOUR

STONE HAD ASKED AUBREY AND SELBY to avoid the Surrey house until further notice. Loyal Aubrey wouldn't have batted an eye at the magically-preserved corpse laid out on a tarp on the great-room floor, but he wouldn't expect Susan or Selby to be quite so understanding.

It was late on the day after they'd returned from Windermere. Verity and Ian had returned home—Lila's druids had been as good as their word, healing Ian so well that the makeshift javelin hadn't even left a scar, and as soon as they returned to the portal room in the Encantada house's basement, he'd taken his leave.

"I've got a lot to talk about with Gabriel, if you don't need me anymore," he'd told Stone, his expression half-grim, half-anticipatory.

"No, no, go on." Stone wished he could have been part of that conversation, to hear what Gabriel would tell his son, but he had more pressing matters to attend to.

"I'm coming back, though, because I've got a lot to talk about with *you*, too. And you'd better not hold anything back this time."

"Don't worry. You deserve to know everything about our family history—on both sides. Don't feel that you have to hurry, though—the story isn't going anywhere, and I guarantee I won't forget any of it."

Verity was a little harder to convince. She stared down at Brathwaite's twisted, cooling body, her face harder than Stone had ever seen it. They'd removed the javelins and used magic to burn any traces of blood from them, but otherwise they'd done nothing to the body. His left eye was missing where one javelin had obliterated it, and a massive dried bloodstain from the other one passing through his chest barely showed against the red of his robe.

"Hard to believe he's finally dead," she said, pacing around it. "I was starting to think we'd never get him."

"Well, we got him." Now that it was over, Stone felt nothing but exhaustion. He'd deliberately avoided calling Jason because he didn't want to go into everything that had happened, but Verity had texted him to let him know all was well and she was safe. When Stone had checked his own texts, he'd found several from Gina, assuring him that all of the kidnapped Changeling children had been recovered safe and well—so safe and well, in fact, that she said the authorities were baffled by the motives behind the kidnappings.

Charlotte's disappeared, though, she'd sent in her last text. *I'm guessing FS is probably shielding her. Dunno where that will end up, but I think she's over what made her do it.*

Stone answered with only a thumbs-up emoji and *Thanks. Talk later.* He expected he'd be hearing from Ren Huxley soon too, but right now the Changeling case was farthest from his mind.

Now, he looked at Brathwaite's body and back at Verity. "I'm afraid I'm going to have to go now," he said gently. "I've…got things I need to do, and you can't be part of them."

"You need to hand him over to whoever wanted you to kill him," she replied in the same tone.

"Yes."

She came over and hugged him quickly, then let go. "You do what you need to do. You know when you get back you'll need to deal with Jason, right?"

"I'm aware…and not looking forward to it."

"I'll see what I can do to soften him up. You *are* responsible for getting Jaden back, so that should count for something."

"Here's hoping."

She watched as he levitated Brathwaite's body and took it with him through the portal. When he looked over his shoulder, she was still watching.

Now, he stood in the great room, looking out the window into the fairy-lit back garden. He'd half-expected Aldwyn to contact him, to somehow be aware through his preternatural dragon methods that the deed had been done.

But he didn't contact Stone, and Stone thought he knew why.

This was his job, and it was up to him to call it done.

He paced back to the middle of the vast room and stood next to the body. "Aldwyn!" he called into the dimness. "I've got something for you!"

"Well done, Alastair," came a voice from above him.

He spun around to see a familiar, shadowy figure descending the staircase. "So you've decided to come here now instead of dragging me to you. Thanks for that—I'm a bit tired of traveling lately."

Aldwyn said nothing else as he completed his descent. He was dressed as always in a fine suit, this one of dark blue, with an open-collared white shirt. He looked relaxed and settled as his gaze shifted from Stone to the body on the floor.

"I must admit to being impressed," he said. "You have completed your assignment with several days remaining in your allotted time."

"Yes, well, I guess I'm just efficient like that." Stone wasn't in the mood for verbal sparring, and refused to be drawn into it. "I hope you plan to take him off my hands—he doesn't go with the décor, and the preservation spell is only going to keep him from stinking for so long."

"Indeed I do." Aldwyn approached the body and circled it with slow, deliberate steps, as if entering every feature into his memory. He stopped at the head. "Do you have anything else you would like to share with me?"

"Like what? He's dead. That was the job, right?"

"It was indeed. But I thought perhaps you might wish to tell me about…the circumstances."

"Not really. To be honest, all I want to do is take a hot shower and sleep for two or three days. Stress plays hell with the sleep cycle. So if you could just gather up your little package and—"

He stopped. He'd been staring down at Brathwaite's body, but when he replayed Aldwyn's words, something about the dragon's tone struck him as odd. He raised his head and fixed his gaze on the other man.

"You knew," he said in a dead tone.

"Knew what?" Aldwyn never showed much emotion on his face, but now he projected a faint aspect of mocking amusement.

"You knew what Brathwaite was up to. You know about Nessa Lennox, and what she had planned."

Aldwyn didn't reply.

Stone drew a slow, deep breath. "You *knew.* That's why you gave me the job at this particular time, and that's why you gave me this particular timetable." His memory wasn't as picture-perfect as Eddie Monkton's, but he'd always been good at remembering conversations when they were important. Now, his mind went back to the last words Aldwyn had spoken to him at their previous meeting.

A word to the wise, from someone who shares your blood, and perhaps does not bear you the ill will you might suspect: this assignment is one you yourself will wish to complete, and quickly. My timeframe is not arbitrary, nor is it punitive. Things are in motion that it would be in your best interests not to allow to come to fruition.

He sharpened his gaze. "You...*wanted* me to get to Brathwaite before he brought Acantha back."

The dragon shook his head. "I did not care either way. I merely wanted him dead."

"But you knew *I* would care." He couldn't believe this could possibly be true. "Aldwyn...were you, in your convoluted way, actually trying to...*help* me?"

Once again, the dragon didn't reply. "If I were, it appears I was not successful. But no matter." He nodded down at the body. "Brathwaite is dead, and thus I declare your second task to be successfully completed. I will be in touch with you at some future date regarding the third and final one. Until then—" He made a languid gesture, and Brathwaite's tarp-wrapped body rose from the floor.

"Wait!" Stone had almost let him go, but then a thought popped into his head.

"Yes?" Brathwaite's body hung serenely in the air next to Aldwyn, who looked mildly annoyed now.

"You know I didn't manage to keep Nessa and Brathwaite from returning Acantha's echo to a physical body."

"Did I not say that?"

"Yes, but—" Stone struggled to make the words line up in his head before speaking them. "Acantha. She's back. She's my twin sister. Does that...make her a scion too?" Another chilling thought struck him. "Is Nessa a dragon? Or a scion herself?"

Aldwyn studied him with his cool, appraising gaze, and for a moment Stone thought he wouldn't answer. "Nessa Lennox is neither a dragon nor a scion. I will leave it to you to discover what else she might be."

That was a strange statement, but Stone let it go for now. He knew the dragon would leave any moment, and he had another question he was far more interested in the answer to. "But...Acantha is of my blood. She's part of the line. Does that make her a scion?"

Once again, the dragon didn't answer for a long time. Finally, he shook his head. "No."

"Why not?"

Aldwyn narrowed his eyes. "I must go, Alastair. I will not remain here all night satisfying your curiosity."

"It's not just curiosity. It's important. I wanted to know if I'll have to worry about you—or some other dragon—manipulating her, too. So why isn't she a scion?"

The dragon relaxed his shoulders ever so slightly. "First and most importantly, because she is a woman. In our family, scions follow the male line."

That made sense, Stone supposed. "And there's another reason?"

"Yes. Because she died."

Stone blinked. "What? She didn't, though. Nessa's people managed to keep her echo on ice until they could work out how to stuff it into another body."

"Indeed. But for purposes of determining scion lineage, both the body and the echo—the soul, as it were—are equally important." He raised his hand, and Brathwaite's body rose higher. "That is all I will tell you now, Alastair. Your questions begin to try my patience. I will leave you to deal with the situations you have created, until I require your services again. Good evening."

"Wait!" Stone called, stepping forward.

But this time, it was not to be. Aldwyn faded from view, along with the body, leaving nothing behind.

Stone stood in the middle of the room and let his shoulders slump. "Bye, then," he murmured.

He remained where he was for nearly five minutes, then trudged toward the massive sofa in front of the dead fireplace and slumped down on it.

He would need to go home soon, back to Encantada. He'd need to talk to Gina about the Changeling case, and endure Jason's anger over leaving him out of the whole Brathwaite thing—especially after Verity had gone missing.

And more importantly, he'd have to figure out what—if anything—he was going to do about Nessa Lennox, and Acantha.

They might leave him alone. Nessa had what she wanted, after all, and she'd never seemed terribly vengeful as long as he stayed out of her way.

Acantha was another story, though—and one he didn't think had reached anything close to its conclusion yet.

And what about Aldwyn? *Had* the dragon actually been trying to help him? That opened entirely new vistas of confusion. Dragons had always been inexplicable, but his ancestor might turn out to be the most inexplicable of all.

He didn't have to deal with any of that now, though. He settled back on the sofa and stared into the empty fireplace. All of that could be for another day.

Right now, all he wanted to do was rest.

He'd earned it.

**Alastair Stone Will Return in
Alastair Stone Chronicles
Book Thirty**

Look for it in Summer 2022

WE LOVE REVIEWS!

If you enjoyed this book, please consider leaving a review at Amazon, Goodreads, or your favorite book retailer. Reviews mean a lot to independent authors, and help us stay visible so we can keep bringing you more stories. Thanks!

If you'd like to get more information about upcoming Stone Chronicles books, contests, and other goodies, you can join the Alastair Stone mailing list at **alastairstonechronicles.com**. You'll get two free e-novellas, *Turn to Stone* and *Shadows and Stone!*

WHO IS THIS R. L. KING, ANYWAY?

R. L. King lives the kind of exotic, jet-set life most authors only dream of. Splitting her time between rescuing orphaned ocelots, tracking down the world's most baffling cheese-related paranormal mysteries, and playing high-stakes pinochle with albino squirrels, it's a wonder she finds any time to write at all.

Or, you know, she lives in San Jose with her inordinately patient spouse, three demanding cats, and a crested gecko. Which, as far as she's concerned, is way better.

Except for the ocelots. That part would have been cool.

You can find her at *rlkingwriting.com*, and on Facebook at www.facebook.com/AlastairStoneChronicles.

Printed in Great Britain
by Amazon

80006351R00215